David M. Schroeder

The Surfman

A Novel

Paperback ISBN: 978-1-300-50912-7

Hardcover ISBN: 978-1-300-50913-4

for Thora

Acknowledgements

Your help is all around you, what your eyes take in, your ears hear. It is every word you've read and place you have visited. All of it is behind what you write and much of it makes its way, inevitably, onto the page. But nothing is better than the word 'no', the statement 'I don't understand this', or questions like 'why did you have this character say that?' That's the best help of all and for their honesty and insight I offer great thanks to Sarah Scherer, Rachael Lutcher, and Jen Glass. They freely gave the hardest thing to give, their time.

Preface

There are an estimated three million ships on the floor of the world's oceans and thousands of them rest along the east coast of the United States. They were lost in storms, sunk by pirates or warships, or were wrecked in collisions with others. Fires, too, took their toll. Before navigation aids were available, ship captains often followed the shoreline in their north-south passages, a practice known as "coasting". Because of this many ships were caught on shoals where the sand held them and the wind and waves would break them apart. Few people lived along the coast at this time and ships sank and disappeared in sight of land, but there was no one there to see or offer aid. A few volunteer groups were formed, but for most parts of the country there was little hope for ships taken by the elements or for sailors who could not swim. There was so much loss of life that several 19th century publications, in their articles and political cartoons, called for the government to act, and as a result, in 1878 the U. S. Lifesaving Service was formed. The men of this federal agency patrolled the beaches and watched for ships in trouble, warning them away from shore, or rowing out to them to ferry passengers and crew to safety, and in some cases shooting a line to them to send a life car or breeches buoy to transport them to land. Stations were located five to seven miles apart and the men who worked there were called surfmen. They had to speak French, master semaphore signaling, be fit, and pass a physical test of strength. Most stations were isolated, and there were no roads or other means of transportation. The men trained six days a week, dragging a thousand pound, twenty-seven foot long surfboat over the sand and into the water, and in one drill, practiced capsizing it and climbing back in. It was a hard, harsh life, but these men took their responsibilities seriously. Their motto: You had to go out. You don't have to come back.

I have been fortunate in my research to spend time at a restored surfboat station in Sussex County, Delaware, touring the station, observing demonstrations, and viewing documents and logs which describe actual rescues. The museum staff there is dedicated to portraying life in the service as it really was. As a member of the USLSS Heritage Association I have visited other stations and observed that excellent organization's efforts to educate members and to help preserve stations around the country, many of which are on an endangered list. A novel tells a story. It is my intent to tell a story that might not have happened, but could have. It is written against the background of the times and shows the way of life of the surfmen. It is historical, not history, general, not specific, and if it follows a wide path to its destination, I have tried to stay to the middle of that path.

More than 178,000 people were served by the surfmen. In 1915 the lifesaving service became the U. S. Coast Guard.

PRINCIPAL CHARACTERS

Delaware Coast

The surfmen:
Ezra Stock, Station Keeper
Will Vickers, Station Keeper
Jack Light
Preacher Gunn
George Kimball
Matthew Hastings
Edward Chase
Jonas Hope
Ben Wolcott
Calvin Massey
Thomas Steele

Boston, Massachusetts:

Elizabeth Harrison, Heiress
Guillaume LeFrank, Ship Captain
Guy Salete, LeFrank's Man
Hillaire Chien, Thief
Jane Barr, Actress
Sean Barry, Priest

Newport News, Virginia:

Daniel Armistead, Constable
Billy, His Deputy
Joan Markley, Tavern Girl
James Kensel, Cemetery Keeper
Peterson, Stone Carver
Clint O'Neill, Trader

Others:

Strell, Ship Captain
Strell's Man
Lamp, An Orphan
David Marshall, Ship Captain
Ellen Brahe, Ship Passenger
Martha Rampele, Ship Passenger
Cora Trussel, Ship Passenger

Table of Contents

CHAPTER 1

The Beach

Delaware Coast, October 1

The surfman stood in the tower atop the lifesaving station and looked out over the Atlantic. There was little to see. Most of the men were asleep in the room below and the surfman could hear nothing but the endless pounding of the waves. A pillar of light struck the sand below him as Jack Light and William Sutter opened the door and stepped out of the building. He watched them until the door closed and they disappeared into the night, Jack walking south and William to the north.

Jack didn't expect to see anything on this walk. Any ship captain who knew the treachery of the fall weather along the Atlantic coast would either already have put into a port, or be off to the east, away from the coast. They all knew what wind from the northeast could do. As he looked out at the ocean he judged the visibility to be fifty yards or less and what he could make out was a churning confusion of waves roaring toward him over the sand bars and holes. They were hard to see, but making themselves heard. No ships or sailors to rescue tonight, he thought. Patrols between stations could take four hours and Jack knew it would be quiet, nothing but a little weather and the sand to keep him company. Tomorrow they were supposed to take the boat out. Jack thought about it as he walked along. It would be cold and wet. He was not one to dwell on the negative, however, and privation and harsh conditions were part of his way of life. Better to drill now, capsize the surfboat and practice climbing back in, than be slow to do it in the middle of a rescue.

He moved closer to the water's edge where the beach was a little flatter and the sand was firm. A form caught his eye. Was that a child, alone on the beach in the cold of the night? The thought flashed through him, stunning him. It was at his feet before he saw it and he stumbled over the body in the blackness, lost his footing, and fell onto the sand. Jack Light pushed himself up and reached for his lantern. Before he could see what had made him trip he had to brush away the wet sand, first from his hands and then from his face. In the dim glow from his lamp he saw before him not a child, but a baby seal that the waves had abandoned on the strand. He held the light over the body, spit away some of the grit that had gotten onto his lips, and looked closely. The surfman was wary. He knew how vicious and aggressive seals could be, despite their appearance of wide-eyed innocence. It was a young pup, maybe a harbor seal, that was migrating along the coast, or simply lost, when it got sick or injured and died. His breath slowed. He guessed it had not been dead long since it was whole and in fair condition. The crabs and their friends had not had a chance to begin their work. Now it would be the birds and the small animals from the dunes and surrounding marshlands that would bring to a finish what the relentless forces of life had begun. He stood up and pushed at the seal with the toe of his boot, just to be sure.

Dead. It was always this way when the weather came from the northeast and the surfmen knew they had to watch for debris on their walks along the shore. The beaches, known as "pathless deserts in the night," changed constantly, and the men often carried a staff to steady them on their patrols. The philosopher said one could not step into the same river twice. His student corrected him and said you couldn't step into the same river once. Sometimes walking on the beach was like walking on water. The beach was itself a fluid, a river next to the sea with its own tides and currents, never the same. And at night the beach, like everything else, was different.

Jack shook the persistent sand from his oilskin coat and pulled it tight about him. Although it was not bitter cold, November loomed ahead, reaching back into this black October night, and he could feel its chill. The taste of salt was on his lips. He licked them and wiped them with the back of his hand. Jack was not far into a five mile patrol along the Delaware seacoast. Surfmen, the men of the US Lifesaving Service, watched America's coastal waters and stood ready to help when ships and mariners were in danger. They kept watch from towers built into the roofs of their stations along the shore, and looked to the sea during regular foot patrols between stations that were located every five to seven miles along the coast. When he was about halfway to the next station Jack would meet another surfman walking north. To prove they had met they would exchange patrol checks and upon their return give them to their station keepers, a guarantee that they had done their duty. The USLSS was part of the Revenue Cutter Service, the federal force charged with enforcing smuggling, piracy, and slavery laws.

He turned south and hummed the song he had been singing when he fell. Most of the tunes he knew he learned from his mates in the service, and most of them were songs of the sea—work songs, love songs, and songs of adventure. He liked to make up lyrics for them and he would often compose nonsense verses about what was happening around him as he sang. "What do you do with a drunken sailor, early in the morning?" He sang the first line and then paused to think. The usual refrains, and there were many of them, sought to teach this intemperate sailor a lesson by doing things like "shave his belly with a rusty razor," or "put him in the longboat until he's sober, early in the morning." A favorite verse was, "put him in bed with the captain's daughter." Jack improvised. "What do you do with a falling surfman…give him the sun or a pair of glasses, let him walk with a couple of lasses, make him wait until night passes, early in the morning." He laughed at himself and sang it again, loud so he could hear his own voice over the raucous wind, and a little off key.

He thought there was something in the water. Jack stopped and strained his eyes into the night. He watched, holding still, now feeling the cold more than before, unwilling to leave without making sure there was nothing there. The ocean changed its sound. Jack heard it echo along the beach, pounding out its power for the land and those on it to hear and heed. Be warned, it said. The pounding struggled with the wind, grappling in the air for his attention. The wind whistled, the waves crashed, and the water hissed at him. Something was missing, something was wrong with the night, but he couldn't find anything among the waves. He turned and made his way south again, more slowly now, looking back, but seeing only the vagueness of the waves. His mind assembled the faint light, thunderous sound, sharp smell, and misty spray into an ocean for him, one he knew and one that had fooled him before.

Jack's father, a surfman before him, had taught him to enjoy every day and to see the fun in life. "Use your mind, laugh, and the world will be a sight for you to see." His father knew that if emotion ruled your life, life was a tragedy, but if you lived within your boundless intellect, life was a comedy. His father was gone, but the words stayed with him. They came to mind often. Jack thought it was amazing that the ideas usually came right at the time when they were needed. His life was even and uneventful; he didn't face hardships or have to make great decisions, but he was on his own and his father's memory was his companion. His father was a curious man, but realistic in his approach to life and he often said, "Do your duty and you'll be doing right." It was true. Jack's duty was to watch the water. Help others. That's what he was doing. As best he could.

He walked on more quickly now, peering ahead, less intent on his footing than watching for the other surfman. He couldn't see much, but he knew they had to be getting close to each other. He wondered how, without landmarks, without a way to measure the motion of time, he knew he was about at the midpoint between stations. Things inside you telling you things. When he saw the first glimmer of light from the approaching man's lantern, he tried to guess who it was. Over the years he had come to know most of the men from the stations to the north and south of his barracks. They came and went, some unable to stand the work, others longing to return to the sea, or go back to their families and farms, or were killed in action. But most of them stayed, despite the pay and conditions. Some men were cut out to be servicemen. Organizations laid out a grid for the lives of their members—they knew where to be, what to do, when to do it, and what uniform to wear when they stood on this square or that.

He liked to guess from their walk, or how they held their lamps, which one he was about to meet. In daylight long bushy beards or droopy mustaches were easy to spot. At night, however, the men wore dark uniforms, so in that they all looked much the same, but despite the darkness he could see that the light was held high and steady. It was Matthew Hastings he was sure. He was a very tall man who characteristically held the light aloft and walked straight and true, like a soldier or a king. Every service man in the state was older than Jack, but they were the closest in age of any of the men, Jack twenty, Matthew only a few years older.

Jack called to him but his words were lost in the swirl of the gale winds. Hastings was probably calling out also. He wondered why the light came to his eyes before the sounds came to his ears. Matthew Hastings swung his light from side to side, a signal to Jack that he had seen him. He answered in kind. They moved toward each other, eyes to the light, both feeling good that they had done half their duty for the night. They drew up next to each other, nodded, and held out the brass station checks that would prove they had met. Each one bore the district, station, and surfman numbers that identified its source. Jack took the one Matthew offered, his fingers feeling the familiar shield shape, and slipped it into a pouch at his belt. Most of the men had several years of service to their credit and the station keepers did not doubt them. But the service had its procedures. The captains and lieutenants from the Cutter Service conducted inspections at the stations and no keeper wanted to lose his post or his pay for want of good records and logs. There were as yet no time clocks on the beach and this system was one that was foolproof.

"Matthew."

"Jack."

"Any news or letters?" asked Matthew.

"The captain has a few new magazines, but he's not finished with them yet. Tomorrow night or the next there will be a *Saturday Evening Post* to send down. Anything for us?"

"Just this one book, we're returning it," said Matthew.

"What is it?"

"I don't know. He wrapped it up, so I didn't see it." Jack slipped the packet into his coat. Maps, mail, anything on paper, were always protected from water by careful wrapping.

They faced the east and silently watched what they could barely see. It was a moonless night and thick clouds, black as soot, hid the stars. The spray stretched along the beach like a bank of fog. After a while Hastings turned from the sea and asked if there was news about the men from Jack's station, how they were doing, if the captain was drilling them hard.

Like most members of a service, Jack and Matthew spent a great deal of their time waiting. They studied, practiced, and drilled— keeping strong, being ready. The studies involved the weather, the sea and tides, first aid, service regulations, and semaphore signaling. They had to know how to speak French since they were often likely to come into contact with the crews of French or Canadian ships. The learning was done at a slow pace, but it was continuous. Cleaning or training was a six-day-a-week routine. Hardest of all were the drills. Every station had a surfboat to be used to go out to a ship or a man in trouble. They had a sheer design with lapstrake sides to help them plow through the waves. Their boats were twenty-seven feet long, weighed a thousand pounds, and had to be rolled out through large doors at the end of the station house, dragged across the sand, and heaved into the surf. They were used when ships foundered, and that usually meant that the weather was bad. In an emergency the surfmen manned these boats and strained at their long oars, pulling themselves away from the safety of land and into the watery part of the world when it was at its most dangerous. Part of the training involved deliberately capsizing the boats and then righting them.

These words the surfmen knew were true: "You have to go out, but you don't have to come back."

Jack remembered again that tomorrow they were supposed to take the boat out. Their training was regularly put to the test. This stretch of beach was one of the most dangerous in America and collisions and wrecks were commonplace. Shipboard fires took their toll. Whalers, cargo ships, fishermen, military craft, and virtually every other kind or size of vessel afloat, wood or steel, sail or steam, traveled along the coast. It was a highway for the eastern part of the country since at this time there were few roads, fewer rail lines. This ocean road was old and primitive and always under construction: tide and wind and wave and current and fate were at work on this road. It changed constantly and many ships ran aground on newly formed sandbars and became caught in the tides. These shoals were just as dangerous as the rocks that lurked under the surface in other parts of the eastern seaboard. Small, inert, mindless, these same grains of sand that gave way underfoot or fled like ghosts through parted fingers, once pressed together by tons of seawater, became immovable ridges. Ships held in their grip were often beaten to death by the weather and the men on them lost. The earth and sea held them and the air and sky hit them. Air and water, with which the ship had been so intimate, became relatives and friends stoning a sinner to death. Many thousands of ships rested on the Atlantic's coastal shoals and thousands more lay in the dark depths of her mile-deep canyons and trenches. Even those men who jumped ship and made it to shore often perished, for the edges of the country were still naked. Few lived along the bare sands of the coasts and there was little to shelter the forlorn survivors. It was safer to chart a course a hundred miles away from shore and follow the north-south routes where the water was deeper, but many ship's captains, operating both within and outside the law, took their chances and tried the faster way to their destinations. They risked much with this practice called "coasting," but many of them did it, as any chart of wrecks would plainly tell. Miles are things that go under you. The miles along this coast often passed close to the keel.

The keeper of Jack's station, Ezra Stock, was a good man to work for, as long as you worked hard and did what he told you. All keepers were political appointees and some of them were fully unqualified for what they had to do. Ezra was an exception, his years on the sea and working as a surfman combining in the best possible mix of experience for the job. The rank of surfman was the lowest in the USLSS and over the years Stock had trained many of these men and most of them were better for it. The crews were always changing since men often quit the service or moved to other stations in order to be able to be promoted. Like all of the men in the service, Stock did not ever want to lose one of his men or fail to bring the people in peril safely to shore.

Jack looked at his friend Matthew. "You know Ezra Stock. He doesn't let any barnacles grow on us."

Hastings, taciturn, seemed to have forgotten his question, and just nodded. Huffs of sand blew stinging into their faces. They winced and whisked at their eyes with their fingertips. After a minute Jack shrugged his storm suit up around his shoulders and looked back to the north. He was ready to go. "On the way down I tripped over a seal pup. Fell flat on my hands and knees. Didn't even see it."

"Yeah," said Matthew, "it's like the holes in hell opened up tonight and let out the dark. Be careful going back. There's no telling what else is waiting out there for us." This was more words than Hastings normally said at any one time. It made Jack smile.

"Good night, Matthew."

"Night, Jack."

Jack walked north, into the wind. It was harder going and he had to blink his eyes repeatedly to squeeze the tears away and keep his vision clear. Every now and then he walked a short stretch with his head down. He stopped frequently to search among the waves. Following storms like the one that had just passed, there was often a whole litany of flotsam and jetsam that found its way to land—logs, chunks of pilings, ballast, parts of ships, things that were thrown away by men or had been stolen away by the sea. The sea was an architect and a builder, always changing things around. It was also a destroyer and sometimes a thief. He was glad that the rain and extreme winds, the worst of the storm, had moved away. For a few days they'd feel the tail of the weather, mostly just strong wind gusts and rough water. It was at these times that ships could be forced toward the lee shore and into the danger waiting there. Despite the secretive clouds overhead and the unfriendly ocean keeping him company on his right, Jack felt his mood lighten as he thought of getting back to his quarters. The warm stove and hot tea would be welcome tonight. Matthew's mood and words were gloomy, and Jack didn't like keeping company with black thoughts. He walked on, somewhat distracted, but he couldn't keep the dark thoughts away entirely. Something was looming in the hidden part of the world. A few times he stopped, thinking he'd heard a ship's bell crying faintly to him over the water.

He kept singing and trying not to think about tomorrow and taking the boat out.

CHAPTER 2

Angel Flight

The feet of terrified men pounded on the boards above the ceiling of her cabin. Elizabeth Harrison had not been asleep. She couldn't sleep and only when exhaustion claimed her had she lost her vision and drifted off into small, brief, welcome deaths. She moved off of the narrow rack that served as her bed and wrapped the coarse wool blanket about her. It was all they had given her. She had no shoes, no clothes, only the stark white nightgown she had been wearing when they took her. A low hideous moan rose up from below her. The keel of the *Hathor* seemed to cry out in pain as the ship dragged across the hard sand and jerked to a halt. The fear she had been living became even more concentrated. She steadied herself as the floor beneath her stopped making sense and pitched away from her in unnatural ways. With careful steps she made her way to the bulkhead and looked out through the hatch window to try to see what was going on. Salt pebbled the glass and water leaped up to splash against it and obscure her view. Her cabin prison was near the stern on the starboard side of the boat and as the deck tilted down with the passing of another swell she could see breakers; they were close to shore. She gripped the window latch to keep from falling. The backs of the breakers tumbled away from her like arms beckoning her to come along with them. She could hear the ship's bell ringing, not with the lazy random song played on it by the rolling and swelling of the surface of the sea, but with an urgency meant to alert all hands that they were in trouble. A horrible fear and a strange calm pierced her heart at that moment.

It was not like the time, not that many days ago, when this had all started. On that night she had been gripped by shock and had not been able to comprehend what was happening to her. All she felt then had been panic and denial. She had had a quiet meal with her beloved Nana, the governess who had raised her, and had read for a while before going to bed. In the middle of that night the door to her bedroom crashed open and three men walked in. In the forefront was LeFrank, the man who had been her guardian since her father's death. He held an oil lamp close to her face and told her to put on the red-lined black cloak he held in his other hand. She screamed for them to leave.

She remembered every minute of what happened.

"You're coming with us, right now," LeFrank told her.

"Get out, all of you." She climbed from the bed, backed away, and crossed her arms in front of her.

Behind LeFrank were Chien and Salete, the surly low types who worked for him. They were rarely seen at her house and when they were there she usually avoided them.

LeFrank pushed the long dark cloak toward her and growled, "Around you, now."

She backed against the wall and wiped the tears from her eyes. Her hands were shaking uncontrollably.

LeFrank called to Salete. He walked back to the doorway of her room, held up his knife, and smiled at Elizabeth. She shivered and drew her head back, her arms and hands moving to conceal herself from him. It was only when he raised his eyes that she realized what he was telling her. He was nodding in the direction of Nana's room. His knife flashed a glint point at her from the fire in LeFrank's hand. If she didn't obey, Salete's face said, he would go upstairs and kill her. When he saw that she understood he smiled at her. His knife disappeared into his coat. She thought his look was the most horrible thing she had ever seen. She looked back in bewilderment at LeFrank.

"LeFrank, what is this all about? Are you insane?"

He stared at her for a moment, then turned and jammed the cloak into Chien's hands.

"Bring her. We'll move the carriage to the side door," LeFrank said as he and Salete left the room.

LeFrank stopped in the doorway, and pierced her with his eyes, "This is your doing, remember that! Your choosing."

Choosing? she thought. Choosing? What on earth is he talking about?

She could hear LeFrank's boots as they carried him down the main stairs of the house. She whispered a prayer of thanks to herself thinking that at least Nana was safe and wondered if she had heard her screaming. Chien moved toward her. He threw the long coat onto the bed. From his pocket he drew a small pistol and he aimed it at Elizabeth's heart. He was breathing heavily now and he began to reach for her. He pressed the muzzle of the gun against the base of her throat. She was too stunned to move at first, but she held her hands over her breasts and then fought him as he started touching her. Around her neck was a simple necklace with amber-colored glass beads on a slim golden chain. Nana had given it to her and told her it was from her mother. Elizabeth didn't remember her mother but treasured this one thing of hers. Now this keepsake cut into her neck as he put his wrist across her throat and pressed her to the wall and reached down with his other hand and pulled her gown up so that he could get at her body. The gun fell to the floor, its sound heavy and solid. She cried as his rough hands and broken nails trailed up the flesh of her thigh. She couldn't speak and twisted her head away from Chien as he tried to kiss her.

The blood pounded in his chest and he was panting with an intensity he had never known in his life. He coaxed her, "Come on...come on...I've been watching you...a long time...a child...a girl...waiting...for now..." He was so intent that he did not know what had hit him when Salete slammed his fist into the side of his head. Chien crashed to the floor, dragging Elizabeth with him. She pulled away from him and tried to pull her gown down over her knees. It was tangled around her thighs and ripped at the neck. Salete kicked Chien in the ribs and told him to leave. Chien crawled across the floor, one hand at his side, picked up his gun, and looked from it to Salete. Salete just stared at him. Chien cursed him and put the gun into his coat pocket.

"I will have her," he yelled, his eyes burning as he skulked away from Salete. He looked back at Elizabeth as he left the room. "I will," he told her. His face was flushed and sweat dripped along his cheeks and into his beard. He bent and coughed in pain. She stared at him, feeling as if she could no longer breathe, choking and sobbing, feeling like she was dying. Salete reached down, grabbed her arm, and lifted her up off of the floor. She tried to pull away from him, but he was far too strong. He picked up the cloak and held it out to her. She put it around herself like a shroud, terrified of what it meant might happen to her once she was taken away, but thankful to have it as a shield to cover herself. Her hands fumbled at the heavy gold clasp that held it closed at the neck. It reached to the loops at either side.

On her it smelled faintly of perfume, and shadows. A short time later it would be taken from her, leaving her all but naked. Salete looked into her eyes and promised her, "Chien won't hurt you." A slight smile came to his face and then was lost as it disappeared back into him.

Elizabeth looked into his eyes, understanding in that moment that while Chien was a miserable creature, the worst of humanity, Salete was like something from beneath them all, something that was not human, something unnamable. She didn't think she had ever before felt hatred in her life, but now she knew what it meant to want to be away from something and to know that it had been destroyed. The something was alive and she wanted to see it killed. It was her original sin.

Salete turned and told her to come with him. He walked from the room with an arrogance that told her he knew she would do what he said. There was a photograph of LeFrank on the chest by her door. Photography had become very popular and LeFrank was fascinated with his own image. He had had numerous tintype portraits done, sitting or standing, posed pompously, and had given one to Nana and one to Elizabeth, acting as if he was sure they would be as pleased with them as he was. She was reluctant to even have it, but she had been raised to be a lady, educated to be genteel, and felt it would be impolite to refuse it or to put it out of sight. She had never liked being around LeFrank, but when she was ten years old he told her that he had been named by her father as her legal guardian, and that was something she could not control. All Elizabeth could think of as she left the room was that she had to let Nana know what had happened. In a desperate act she grabbed the picture and turned it upside down, hoping Nana would see it and know that LeFrank was involved in her disappearance. As she withdrew her hand she pushed her gloves and handkerchief onto the floor. It was all she could do in her haste and without Salete hearing her and she hoped the message would be seen and understood. Nana was very smart and would suspect what had happened, but Elizabeth wondered what she could do to help her. Nothing about this was congruent with their understanding of things.

Outside in the chill, the world had lost its detail. There was nothing to see but the absence of light. Before she was pulled into the carriage she glanced back toward her house. It was the only place she had ever lived and now, as it faded away from her, it stood dark and empty looking. She wondered if she would ever see it again.

They had taken her aboard the ship *Hathor*, a sailing ship that LeFrank had bought from an Egyptian merchant who had sailed around the old world and had come to realize how much he could profit from living in the new one. *Hathor* thought she was better than any ship on the sea.

Elizabeth's abduction had been timed. They had to steal her away on a moonless night, unseen, the last piece of cargo to be loaded just in time to sail with the tide. The wind, too, had been an accomplice, powering the ship relentlessly into the dark Atlantic. Since then she had not seen or talked to anyone except Salete; he brought her meals she could barely eat and fierce stares that made her think of taking her own life. At first she tried to ask him what they were going to do with her. His only statement was that Nana was dead, that he had killed her before they came into her room, and that no one would ever know what had happened to either of them. She feared that these words were true, but she held the shred of hope that they were not. The words put her into a despair that lasted for days. Neither of them spoke after that. She didn't know how long she had been held by these brutal men, had lost track of days, had no real frame of reference since to her every day was the same. There was nothing in the cabin, and only a monotony of the sea outside her window. Sharp storms slowed their progress and rough water slashed at the ship's hull. At times the rolling of the ship made her nauseous. A few times she had seen a faraway slice of the land, but she didn't have any way of telling how far they had traveled.

She had heard whispers, vague stories of the crimes committed against women, slavery and forced prostitution, but always thought they were untrue, or at least things that happened in worlds far removed from hers. Servants said things, she had heard a hushed drawing-room rumor, but she could hardly believe these things possible. On the third day at sea she had opened the closet in the cabin to find a horrible, grisly truth. Things were far worse than she had imagined. There was nothing in the closet, but scratched into the paint on the inside of the door were the pleas of numerous young women, names, dates, cries for help. When LeFrank took them, how Chien and Salete and the other crewmen lined up to rape them. You yearn for yourself, but Elizabeth also felt great sorrow for each of them. She read their brief stories over and over and memorized the names so that if she ever got away she could try to help them.

Anna Ulter.

Carina Hauser.

Lena Gray.

Margery Lane.

Victoria Seltman.

Lilly Rimmer.

There were thirty names in all. None of them were familiar to Elizabeth. But they were all now the same person. They were her.

She had no idea what was going to happen to her but feared it would be death, or worse, some dreadful existence she could not escape. None of the men had assaulted her. Thus far. A ridge of sand created with indifference by a swirling random ocean had captured the proud ship *Hathor*, and in so doing had given her a choice and a chance to be free. She made up her mind.

An intense fear and a strange calm came from making the decision. The fear and calm warred within her but it was the terror that strengthened her. Still, her hands shook and she could not slow her breathing. She wrapped the blanket around her, not thinking that it would be no help in the cold water, not thinking that if anything it would make it harder for her to swim. She didn't really know how to swim, but she had seen young boys dive into the Boston Harbor on hot summer days and knew that they moved their arms and kicked their feet. She remembered going to the beach as a young girl and wading and floating in the cool water. Usually the men and women used the beach separately, so she hadn't seen the men swim, only the women, wrapped in their swimming costumes, and they didn't really venture far from shore, but would only stand where the water lapped their thighs and splash about, their skirts puffing in and out like they were grey jellyfish. She hoped the waves would befriend her and push her to the safety of land. She remembered reading that dolphins were called the sailor's friends because if they came upon someone in the water they would help them by nudging them to shore. The men of the whale ships in New Bedford and Nantucket told tales of it happening. She wondered if it was true, or just something people say, wishing it were. There were so many odd tales about that it was difficult to know what was true and what was not. Maybe a dolphin would help her tonight. But it didn't matter any longer. Nothing did. This would be her only chance. The ship was stopped and it was close to shore and they would have a hard time finding her in the water. Whatever happened she was sure it would be better than the fate that awaited her at the end of this voyage. She had to get away from LeFrank and whatever madness had overtaken him.

She looked around the cabin. There was nothing she could take but the names of the women, and she clutched them in her heart. Nothing that could help her. She turned the latch to open the window and pulled it toward her. It squealed on its hinges as it went past her and the noise was a harsh alarm that scared her and made her look at the door. She pulled herself up, ducked her head through, and put one leg, then the other, over the ledge. Her legs and feet rubbed against the wet hull of the ship. The boards were rough and the hard lumps of paint and pitch scratched deep cuts into her calves. She felt the sting of the cold salt water running into the cuts. The cold water felt like fire. Half in and half out of hell. She looked out, thinking she saw a faint light on the shore. When she turned for a final look back into the cabin the water dropped and the ship plunged downward and the window swung toward her. The glass shattered in her face, stunning her, and she lost her grip and began to fall from the portal. As the ocean rose and threw the *Hathor* back up toward the black sky she was tossed into the air and then dropped into the cold Atlantic.

Jack was almost sure he could hear a bell ringing. He held the light high on the end of the pike he had been using as a walking stick. The fog made it hard for him to see anything.

An angel fell from the sky.

It was a brief apparition. He squinted and used his hand to shield his eyes from the wind that howled as if it did not like white spirits flying through the night. There was a flare he could use to signal the ship and call the men from the station, but he didn't want to make a false alarm so he waited, scanning in a regular pattern as he had been trained to do. He thought he saw a light, but then it was gone. What had he seen? Was it just a fountain of foam from the crashing of the waves? He kept looking at that point in the water where he first saw something, moving his search to the left and right of it, and from there to the shore. If something were in the water, the surf would move it toward him. The bell stopped ringing.

Salete ran down the steep narrow stairs, his hands and elbows gliding down the handrails, and raced to the stern. He pulled the bolt back from the iron staple that held it and opened the door. Damn. She was gone. LeFrank would take his whip to him if she escaped. He looked through the window frame but saw only the uproar of the surf. Water had splashed through the open portal onto the deck at his feet and he lost his hold as the ship lurched again. He grabbed the window frame to steady himself and drove a splinter of glass deep into his hand. He cursed again. Blood dripped from his hand and he was transfixed as he saw it run across the dark wood of the deck and mingle with her blood on the broken glass. Threads of their blood wrapped themselves together and around each other, a double helix in the salt water. The prow of the ship was still on the bar and it scraped and bumped as the water rose and fell with the incoming tide. The *Hathor* cried out again below him. The stern was still free and the waves rolled the ship from side to side. Salete gripped his hand to stop the flow of blood and yelled for LeFrank as he hurried up to the main deck.

"Where is she?" LeFrank called to him as he appeared at the hatch.

"Gone. She jumped out her window."

"God damn you to hell, Salete. If you don't find her, you'll pay..."

LeFrank and Salete separated and moved toward opposite ends of the ship. They leaned over the side and ran back and forth looking among the waves. There were twenty men aboard the *Hathor*, all of whom lived outside the law, all of whom were loyal to their master as long as he gave them what they needed: protection, the chance to rape and steal, their share, and sometimes a beating. They all knew what to do. They climbed the rigging to try to take in some sail, all the while turning frequently to look toward shore. It would do to be the one who spotted the girl. Their lives would be hell if she were lost. They knew that for sure. They didn't know what he was doing with her, but his curses and his bearing told them to look to themselves and do what they were supposed to do. His whip would fly if they didn't. One of the men aloft shouted that he thought he could see a light on the shore. All hands strained their eyes to find it.

Jack thought he heard the bell again and what he thought were the shouts of men over the roar of the waves. Without taking his eyes from the direction of the sounds he reached into his coat and pulled out a flare. He pointed it east into the sky. He wanted the light behind the ship, between him and his lifesaving station to the north. That way it would be seen by the surfman watching in the tower of the station, and it would illuminate the water between him and the ship. The pyrotechnic device reached into the blackness. Everyone on the ship instinctively looked up. Jack looked down. He knew to shield his eyes so as to not lose his night vision. When he raised his head he saw his fallen angel. The blanket she had had around her had been lost and the whiteness around her mixed with the violent froth of the surf. The waves tossed her form toward him. He was afraid that whoever this was would surely be dead. The cold of the sea would probably have been enough to stop any heart beating in this unforgiving night. He pulled off his storm suit and hat and the wool coat beneath it and struggled into the surf. It knocked him down and he had to fight his way to get to the person before him. The water was so cold it almost took his breath away. It burned. He saw arms flailing and reaching and he went farther out than he should have. He knew this was foolhardy, but couldn't abandon this poor soul now. A wave broke over his head and for a moment he lost sight of her. Then she was in front of him and he saw that it was a woman. He grabbed her, strained with all his might to lift her above the water and slog through the surf onto the beach. The ocean which had helped free her, borne her along and had pushed her toward land, seemed, at the last minute, to change its mind and be unwilling to give her up. Jack's feet sank into the soft sand at the water's edge and he staggered his way to where his lantern and coat lay and they fell down side by side. He had spent his life with men, hard and muscular and rough. His hands were now around her waist and he noticed how soft and smooth and tender she was. His fingertips pushed into her flesh and he felt her ribs and the tops of her hip bones. She coughed and cried and told Jack that he had to save her. He answered over and over that she was safe and he reached for his coat and covered them both with it, pulling it over them like a blanket. It was of little help since they were soaked, but it cut off the wind. It provided a small strange thrilling feeling in both of them as they seemed to be safe inside, hiding from the world. Together.

The flare dropped into the water. All was darkness again, yet he saw her clearly, as if her innocence had penetrated the dark. Jack pulled the lantern under the coat with them and looked at the woman. She stared back.

"You have to help me."

"I will. I'll get help. Our barracks is less than a mile from here. Let me get my breath and I'll run for help. We'll have you warm and dry soon." Jack smiled at her and tried to reassure her, "I'll even fix you tea."

She grabbed him, her freezing hands on either side of his head and put her face so close to his that their lips were almost touching. "Listen to me. When he comes for me he'll kill me. You have to save me from this."

"You're safe. No one will hurt you. I'll make sure our captain protects you, I promise."

She pressed her hands against him, her nails digging into his scalp. She was frantic. "No! He'll turn me over to them and I'll never escape them again. It's up to you. You saved me once, and I am begging you, you have to save me again." She started crying and begged him over and over, "Please...please...please..."

There was with her an intensity Jack had never seen in his life. The strange night, the confusion of what this woman was telling him, and more than anything her presence so close to him were more than he could understand. But he knew she felt a real fear. Somehow she was in danger. Whatever it was made her prefer diving into the cold night to staying on that ship. She hadn't fallen overboard, she was escaping. All of this was overpowering. He pulled himself back, feeling panic in his heart and mind, not knowing what to do or say. Then he saw the blood running down her face. He reached his hand to her forehead and gently pulled her straggly hair back. She watched him, held still for him. There was a cut on her forehead, long and deep. The salt and cold had probably stopped the bleeding while she was in the water, but it had started weeping blood now. His hands shook as he used his thumbs to push softly against the sides of the slit, but his first aid training took over and he held them together, trying to slow the bleeding. They both stared at each other. Eyes told eyes. They were both shivering. Jack withdrew his hands from her face and she lowered her hands, her cold fingertips tracing lines along his face and neck. She reached one hand inside her gown and touched her necklace and the other she placed against his chest. Her touch made it almost impossible for him to breathe. His chin quivered and his teeth clicked until he ground them together and hissed the sharp air in through them.

He looked down at her gown, soaked and plastered against her body. She was thin, her face pale and her lips blue and quivering. Her eyes could not have been darker. Her breath told him that she had eaten poorly. He reached down along his waist and brought out his knife. "Let me have your sleeve," he said and moved his hand toward her. She pulled back and curled her knees up between them and began sobbing, "No, don't..."

Jack didn't understand. "I have to have a bandage for your head. I don't have any cloth I can use. I need something, just a small piece from your sleeve. It's ruined now anyway, with the water and the blood and the sand. What is this on you, pieces of glass?" He looked at her, a question in his eyes. She kept crying, but held out her arm and let him take a band of cloth from the sleeve. His knife was sharp and his touch was gentle. Her sleeve melted away from the edge. Still, she shook violently. She picked at her hair, found more glass. She rasped a thank you to him as he placed a small pad of cloth on the wound and tied a band around her head. This small simple act calmed her. Her eyes stayed closed for a moment. Small clear beads of tears spilled from their corners.

When he was finished she looked closely at him and held him with her composure. She wiped her nose, she sobbed, and her lips trembled. Her shoulders rose as she took a deep breath. "I'm begging you. Hide me. Just for a short time so I can get away from here. If you don't do it, I'll suffer a horrible death. You know I'm telling you the truth."

"What..."

"There isn't time. I swear to you that if you don't help, they'll kill me."

"I'm not supposed to..."

"I'm begging you!"

Jack had always been told to do his duty. His father told him that if you did what was right, you weren't doing what was wrong. Now his duty and what seemed right were two different things. Was one more important than the other? Could doing what he had been taught, what he had sworn to do as a member of the service, be more right than what he felt at this moment about this woman. She had given herself over to him, only to him. She trusted him and Jack now understood that trust was a kind of slavery. Moreover, in some way it seemed that if he didn't act on her wishes, he'd become responsible for her death. It was a bizarre gift, this gift of self, one which took away his freedom and cut him adrift from the life he had lived up to this moment. Yet wanting to be bound this way seemed to have something within it that he had always wanted, though he couldn't imagine how this could be so. She had thrown him into the storm even as he had pulled her out of it. Second by second he was pulled by the currents of her will and her emotion until the shoreline of his world could no longer be seen.

He threw back the coat and jumped to his feet. He looked quickly back up the beach and again out into the black east. "Listen." He held out his coat. "Put my coat on. It's dry. It'll help you some. I'll wear my rain gear and they won't be able to tell. The men," he said to her as he thought to himself. He looked toward the station, expecting to see the others. "Go west—away from the water. You'll be walking through dunes, bayberry, pine trees. When you come to a path go to the right. It's got crushed shells so walk beside it so you don't cut your feet. Stay with the path until you see a white building. It's up on blocks, for the tides. Don't go inside, crawl under it and bury yourself in the sand the best you can. Make sure my coat doesn't show. I'll come as soon as I can. I don't know when that will be, but I will come. If anyone finds you, it will ruin my life, don't forget, so stay until I come." He pulled her up and put his coat around her, "Do exactly what I said!"

She nodded, squeezed his hands in hers in thanks and staggered into the cover of the dunes. He was hypnotized as he watched her disappear. Her hands were cold and strong. His felt hot and they burned in the wind.

He'd been worried about taking the boat out. Worried about tomorrow. Would the sea still be so rough? Would they wind up in the water? It was a necessary part of their training, and he liked to swim, but he never liked to go under water in the fall. That's what he had been worrying about. It was one of the things he and his father often laughed about—something usually came along in life that was worse than the thing that you were dreading. And then that thing was itself bested by the next one. The thought occurred to him that he was probably safe for a while; there could hardly be anything waiting in his line of troubles worse than what he had gotten himself into now.

Jack could hear the bell again and he put on his rain gear and started running to the station. Soon he saw other surfmen coming to meet him. He stopped to catch his breath as they approached. He was bent double, gasping as he told them that there was a ship aground a mile or so down the beach.

"What happened?" they asked. "How did you get wet?"

Jack hated to lie to them. It was something he had never done before.

"I thought I saw something in the water and tried to reach it, but it was nothing." Ben Wolcott, a local man who had been a surfman for a long time, just nodded. He had seen a lot in his years. Including things that were not what they seemed. Jonas Hope, another of the older surfmen, made one of his non-word noises. Hope didn't seem to see the need for, and therefore rarely used, consonants, only vowel sounds. Yet you always knew what he thought. So maybe he was right and all other English speakers were wrong, a notion occasionally bandied about in mock serious discussions in the boat room.

Jack looked around and his eyes met with the plain unyielding stare of George Kimball. Jack looked away. George had been his father's closest friend, and like Ezra, had helped to raise him. Jack felt sick at his stomach. His father had called Kimball a saint. He didn't curse or do anything that was proud or selfish or hurtful. No member of the service worked harder than George Kimball. Jack had never known anyone like him. Yet for all of what could be regarded as his perfection, it had always seemed to young Jack as if a piece of him was missing, like a limb severed and cast away. The men of the station had only lately learned what had happened in his youth and how it had changed his life irrevocably. Time had been slow in knitting up the sleeve.

Ezra Stock was the last to reach the men. The older man lumbered up, panting hard. Jack repeated his story. "What do we need to do, Jack?" Jack felt terrible. These men relied on one another. He'd spent almost every day of his life among the men of the service. And yet he felt that he shouldn't tell them what had happened. They could take the girl away from him and return her to the ship and the people who terrified her. Saying it was not their affair. Worse, Stock always treated him as an equal. He showed a respect for Jack, asking him in front of the men, all older than Jack, how they should proceed. Now his lies would sever that tie. "I can barely see her light, Captain, when the fog moves, but she's aground. The sound of the bell stays in one place. We won't be able to signal them until there's more light, but we ought to have the gun ready in case we have to get someone to shore."

"We won't take the boat out in this," Stock said as he looked up at the sky. There was no moon and heavy storm clouds hung low, covering the stars. It was if some distant gravity had taken all of the light away. Held it back. Jack suddenly realized this would be a good chance to get back to the station when no one was there. "Maybe you should go down and look for a bit, check if anyone can see better than I could. My eyes were burning from the wind and the water. You might be able to see better."

Stock considered this for a moment and then told the men to follow him. As they moved off Jack ran toward the station. He was scared. The feeling was unpleasant, a burning in his stomach, and he felt his heart race in his chest. What need had brought this devious part of him so easily to the surface? It was distressing to him to know it had always been inside of him, waiting to be used. This lying, instinctive as breathing, was surely within him. How near the surface it seemed to be, and how well he used it. What else made up Jack Light? Was he the same as the worst of men everywhere? No different? Now there was no choice—he had to get this woman, or girl, whatever she was, whoever she was, away from the coast. There was no other place she could go now. They were in a remote part of the state, with few roads and even fewer people. Before there were lifesaving stations, those who made it from shipwreck to shore alive often died of starvation or exposure along the sparsely populated east coast of the new country. From the station Jack traveled to his own house by boat. It wasn't on an island, but water lay between his work and his home and the most direct route was over a shallow inland bay. He would have to take her there. He would have to row there in an open boat without anyone seeing. All this if she made it through the night alive, and if she was not discovered.

When he entered the building he saw that there was tea on the potbelly stove, just off to the side, keeping itself hot. He savored the warmth of the small kitchen and pulled his heavy coat off so as to dry himself and his clothes. Like all USLSS stations, this one was Spartan: wood floors, hard furniture, and plain things were all they had or needed. There was little budget money for much else. Downstairs there was just the kitchen, pantry, and a small sitting area on one end, and the boathouse and office on the other. Upstairs there were two rooms, a private room for the keeper and a large dormitory for the men. Their beds lined the stark wood walls. The only interruption to the line of the dormitory was a small set of steps that led up to a cupola from which the man on duty could look to the four points of the compass. Looking for trouble.

He didn't know how much time he had so he grabbed a mason jar and filled it with tea, swallowed a few mouthfuls to warm himself, sliced some bread and packed it in a towel, and raced up the steps to see if he could find something to use to warm the girl huddled outside in the cold. Jack had some of his own clothes with him so he opened his footlocker and pulled out the warmest pants and shirt he had, added a pair of socks, and returned to the kitchen. He looked out the door to see if anyone had come back. The station was empty. At least he thought it was since he had not accounted for everyone when they met at the surf. Maybe he was not that cunning after all, he thought. He figured that this was the best chance he'd get and he picked up the food and clothes and slipped out.

She didn't move when he called to her. To avoid frightening her he reached down and patted his hand on the sand under the building, trying to get her attention. This outbuilding was used for housing the families of the men and was, like most of the structures in the compound, set up on blocks to protect it from high water. He thought maybe she couldn't find the group of buildings that made up the station. Maybe she was lost. If she was dead, what would he do?

He called again, "Lady, Miss, it's me." No answer. "It's the one who gave you his coat…the surfman, the one you said had to save you…"

Jack jumped as she rose up out of the sand directly in front of him. Then he laughed. She looked at him, bewildered, shocked, and confused, wondering why he was laughing. She was coated with sand, as if basted and floured and ready for frying, like the fish Jack caught in the bay by his house. He handed her the tea. She gulped it down, swallowing sand, nodded her thanks, and took the bread he held out to her. She ate it and drank the rest of the tea, watching him, then coughing, then again nodding her head in thanks as she ate. After each sip and bite she spit daintily, feeling the sand on her tongue. Jack realized she didn't know how to spit. She was embarrassed and tried to brush the sand off of herself.

"Put these clothes on. You'll have to take off that wet gown if you want to get warm. I need to get my coat back to hang it out in the shed. They'll wonder if they don't see it hanging with my gear. I'm going to take you to my cabin, west of here. It's the only thing I can do…there's nowhere else to go, do you understand?"

Elizabeth stared at him and nodded. "Where are the men from the ship? Are they here? They'll come for me, I know they will." She searched the compound with her eyes, craned her neck toward the roar and rush of the surf. "We've got to go now, before they come."

"Look, when it's light we'll signal them that we haven't found anyone and they'll probably be able to free the ship when the tide comes in. They'll probably just sail on."

He looked directly at her, "What's this all about anyway, why would anyone want to hurt you, you're..." he didn't know how to say what he was thinking and his voice trailed off.

It wasn't her words, it was the terror in her eyes that made Jack realize that he was going to have to do what she wanted. The names scratched on the door swam before her. She started panting and shaking again, turning her head to look around, straining to see the beach.

He sighed, "Okay, here's what we have to do. Get up and change your clothes." Jack helped her get away from the building and then turned his back so she could change. He began to shake when he saw her white gown fall to the sand beside him. He could hear her complain to herself about how big his clothes were and mutter about tying knots in them so they would stay on. She told him it was alright to turn around. She had gone this night in his eyes from pure white, to water clear, to the color of sand, to the dark gray and navy blue of his everyday clothes. She sat down and pulled on his socks. She let him help her up and stood close to him. She looked from side to side and then back at him, her head tilted up to his face. He was a head taller.

"Can we go now? Please, right now!"

"No, not until tomorrow. I can't just leave. They'd know something was going on. I've got to go back to the routine. Listen to me. When it starts to get light, make your way to the west. It's that way. Stay low. Bend over when you walk. Keep under the trees. You've got to be away from here when the sun comes up or they'll see you from the tower atop the station. They mostly look east, out to the ocean, but they can see for a long way inland too. Try to go straight west and walk until you come to the shore of the bay. It's a couple of miles at most. When you get there, go to the right and follow the shore until you see a small boat up on the beach. That's my boat, has a blue bottom on it. But keep going. Past it. Find some tall reeds where it's dry and get down in them and wait for me. Don't leave or both of us will get lost. Just wait, okay?"

He could see that she was terrified, but thought that somehow she had the strength to do what he said.

"Should I wait here until then?"

He pointed to the outlines of the dunes behind him. "Better walk that way for now, get a few dunes between you and the barracks. Try to keep out of the wind."

For the second time that night she placed her hands on him, squeezing his arm, and looked at his face closely. "I won't forget what you are doing." Without another word or a look back she picked up her gown and wrapping her arms around herself, walked with straight true steps, brave steps, off into the gloom of the night.

Jack looked around and then ran back to the station. When he got to the door he came face to face with the preacher. He wasn't really a preacher, but that's what everyone called him. Old Gunn, or Preacher Gunn was all Jack had ever heard him called. He didn't know his real first name. He was the oldest surfman at their station and he knew a great deal about the service and about the world. He read the Bible constantly and spent a lot of time preaching to the men. "That's enough, Preacher," Ezra would say from time to time when Old Gunn went on too long or too strong about living right and sin and salvation. Jack didn't mind listening to him. You could learn from anyone, his father had taught him. But if pressed, Jack wouldn't have been able to name a single sin he had committed. He had never really had the chance. Not until tonight. In Jack's small world there was nothing to take, or even covet. He never thought to kill or hurt anyone or be selfish or cruel. Was this wrong? Is it what is in your heart or is it what other men say God wants, that cuts the sin or soothes the grace onto your soul? Jack wondered how he could be judged when he had to decide about something that was beyond his experience or imagining. Now he had a secret. There was no one to tell. And everyone on earth but one person to keep it from. Every person on earth. He wondered how many men were with him on the planet.

Gunn had come back from the beach to take up his post as a lookout in the tower of the station building. Ezra knew the cold could wear down an older man and gave him a break from hard duty whenever he could. Gunn was a big help to him. Experienced men made their leaders' jobs easier.

"What are you doing out here, Jack?"

Jack found it even harder to lie to the preacher. "I had to shake the sand off of my gear and take a few minutes in the privy. My stomach doesn't feel good...probably just the cold."

Preacher Gunn stared at him and Jack was sure he could tell he was lying.

He tried to get away from his gaze and moved to go inside. The preacher just stood there, fixing Jack with his eyes, blocking his way. "Is that all it is?"

Jack looked away and answered, "I'll be okay, let me get to the fire." They went in together. Jack began to pull his clothes off and spread the things on the chairs by the stove. He only then realized he was still carrying the package Matthew Hastings had given him. It seemed like a long time ago. It was jammed into his belt line. He opened it up and laid it on the table. The words on the cover said "Twice Told Tales" and it was wet on the edges but would be readable when it dried out. The preacher glanced at the title and gave it a snort and a frown.

After a few minutes by the stove in the kitchen Jack climbed the steep, narrow steps up to the bunkroom and got a towel and a change of clothes. He worked the towel hard and rough on his body. The salt water left him feeling itchy, adding to his overall discomfort. He lay down on his bed and pulled the blanket around him to try to warm up completely. Old Gunn came up after him and went to the center of the room to take up his post at the tower. He stepped up onto the platform and put his face close to the glass. For a few minutes both men were silent.

"Could you see the ship?" Jack asked.

"We found it. There was a break in the mist. She's stuck out there alright. Probably come up off the bar with the tide in a few hours.

He thought about what would happen tomorrow. His stomach began to hurt and he was shivering again. He felt anguish for himself and for the poor girl outside in the cold and darkness. Jack had never known the hollow feeling of stress and fear, at least not this kind of fear. It was a new fear and he didn't know how to fight it. You were afraid sometimes in the surfboat, but the other men were with you. You weren't alone. Even when his father died in a service accident and he was alone in the world, he didn't feel anything like this. Alone. It was a horrifying word. But of course, he realized, he wasn't alone. Now he was with her. Jack's blanket was rough and narrow and he pulled it around himself and tried to sleep. From time to time the preacher turned from his window and looked down at Jack, and prayed for him.

CHAPTER 3

The Marbury Theater

Boston

They entered noisily during the overture. It would be another full house. Some of the actors were still in their dressing rooms, applying make-up, getting into costume and into character. The nervous ones fretted over their scripts and their lines. Some limbered up their voices, others their limbs. Not all of those involved were the most experienced or professional. It was one of the things Jane Barr didn't like about these shows. She saw herself as an actress equal to Sarah Bernhardt, who was now the rage in New York and abroad. Given the chance she was sure she could do anything the other, famous actresses did. But she was stuck, for now she assured herself, with near amateurs, doing these lighter bits for the general audiences of the Boston theater crowd. It was good, but it was not Europe or New York, and the newspaper accounts of the scandalous life of Lillie Langtry described the world she longed to inhabit. For now she had to contend with those less talented than she, furious stage managers, overly dramatic conductors, the musicians who were sometimes a little off and the constant stream of young girls who passed through the business. These girls danced a little and sang a little and acted a little, and they failed and disappeared a lot. Many of them were good; few of them had the beauty and voice and presence she had. The ones she introduced to LeFrank were either very good or very bad. What he did with them, where they went when they left she didn't think about; all she knew was it meant she didn't have to work with the ones whose miscues might throw her off, or the ones whose talents might begin to approach hers. No matter what, she loved it. Tonight when the curtain went up all the eyes would look for her. They wanted to see her beauty and hear her voice and be taken in by the emotion of the scenes she would make alive.

As the time drew nearer and the main hall of the Marbury Theater brimmed full, the noise rose even more. Jane was excited as she looked through one of the many peepholes that had been punched into the wall along the proscenium. She searched the rail along the first balcony looking for LeFrank. He was supposed to come tonight and take her out after the show. She liked being with him. He was well off and there was a danger to him that she loved. Others spent their whole lives looking for peace and safety, hoping for security and the chance to live without risk. Jane was the opposite. Living, like acting, was only worthwhile if your pulse raced and you always feared you would fail or suffer or be hurt. LeFrank fit her. He swept her into the world of things that could not be said. When he took her to stay with him in his cabin aboard the *Hathor* their nights were filled with hellish dares and embraces of the edge of things. It was he who had paid the theater owners a large sum to induce them to put her at the head of the playbill, but she had done her part. Her talent was considerable and he did intend to see her become a star. He wanted to own a star.

"Jane."

She didn't turn.

"Jane, it's five minutes."

Jane scanned the boxes again and again. Where the hell was he? He had promised and he had never before broken a promise to her. Her assistant touched her lightly on the shoulder and she turned to her and nodded her understanding. Jane Barr was half mad, half fearful. But she was not going to let that stop her from making a great performance this night. There would be time to settle things with LeFrank later.

She let the young girl touch her face and hair and primp her costume. She crossed the stage and moved through the twitching group of cast members to get to her mark. Jane could do what all great actors had to do. She put things into other compartments in her mind and became unaware of their existence. She could focus, recall, impersonate, create, obliterate. The energy of the moments before curtain surged through her like thunder in her ears and veins. She was now someone else, someone who didn't even know LeFrank. If he had been there that night, he would have seen the best performance Jane Barr had ever given.

But LeFrank had been on his ship, smelling the weather, looking at the tide and the wind, getting ready to put to sea with his beautiful women—his ship *Hathor* and his ward Elizabeth—the one faithful and the other as good as dead.

CHAPTER 4

A Visit from the Devil

The Delaware Coast, October 2

The morning brought broken clouds, lighter winds, and warmth from the sun. Ezra roused his men and told them to haul out the surfboat. Semaphore exchanges with the ship spelled the message that some members of the ship's crew insisted on coming ashore. The *Hathor*'s lifeboats were not as seaworthy as the surfboat so Ezra Stock agreed to come to them and transport them to shore. Once they had eaten a little food and were suited up, the surfmen began the laborious task of getting the boat to the water. With their boots, and heavy coats, and cork-filled life vests strapped around them, their work was even harder.

There were lifesaving stations all along the eastern seaboard, up the Mississippi river, around the Great Lakes, and even along the Alaskan coast. While some were similar in style and layout, the service had no standard table of organization and equipment. They were all a little different, one from another. Some stations had mules to pull the boats, but this one didn't. They did have a boardwalk and a system of using a modified wagon to help handle the boat, so most of what they needed was muscle and skill, the skill developed from the many hours of practice. The crew moved the boat down to the water.

The Atlantic was cold and rough and hungry. Jack took his place in the middle of the boat and rowed hard as they fought the surf near the shore. Once beyond it, their work was easier and with long coordinated pulls they soon began to gain speed and momentum. The surfmen were all big men, their strength verified with an annual physical, and they achieved leverage from the long travel of their oars.

Morning noises are unique on the water and the gulls and terns squawked and called and dipped into the ocean at the stern of the

Hathor. Jack allowed himself a few brief glances over his shoulder at the large craft. She looked like she was totally black, blocking the sun that rose behind her. It was a beautiful shape, this silhouette, sharp, exotic. The ship was supposed to be a merchantman, but looked like a warship, strong yet sleek. This was a time of transition when steam powered ships were seen more frequently and economic factors influenced ship design. Ships with simple sail arrangements sailed out with smaller crews. Steamships were limited in range by the amount of fuel they could carry. The longer sailing ships could carry much more sail and were called clippers because of their speed. But unlike the motor powered craft they were at the mercy of the wind. *Hathor* had her own beauty, and dark appeal. There was no ship like her in the Americas.

If he felt bad and physically exhausted from the night before, in his mind this morning Jack felt even worse. He felt despondent and afraid of the men from this ship, whatever it was about them that had so frightened the woman he had pulled from the ocean less than twelve hours ago. He had never feared any man before and now he was stunned to think that he was terrified of people he had never even seen. How could your life change in just hours, just minutes? Something not your fault. Something you could not help. When you were doing what you were supposed to be doing.

Worse, he was now suspicious of the other surfmen and imagined a motive for any comment any of them made about the previous night. The other men were only curious, it never entering their heads that good, young Jack Light had done or would ever do anything wrong. Asked, they would have said he was the ideal son, young man, surfman. They just found it odd that Ezra was going to bring someone ashore for no good reason they could think of. It only meant work, and danger, for them. Jack thought about the girl, wondered if she was safe. Again he was afraid she'd be found, maybe be found dead. Wearing his clothes. Near his boat. In the same thought was the possibility of seeing her again, helping her again. He longed for the chance to do something for her, to have her thank him. That was what he wanted, but without the danger or the tightness in the pit of his stomach.

"Jack!"

He looked up. They were drawing alongside the ship.

"Jack, ship oars." Ezra stared at him, a question and concern on his face.

Jack saw that the men had all pulled their oars into the boat and he quickly brought his up with theirs. They held them straight up, like infantrymen at attention and rifles ready. Water ran down the shafts. George Kimball looked back at Jack. He knew something was wrong. They were in shadow and the air felt cold as the two craft bobbed and bumped together. Jack looked back at Ezra, but the captain was busy watching for the line the *Hathor*'s crew was lowering to them. Once there were ropes fore and aft holding the surfboat in place, Stock climbed a rope ladder up the ship's side and over the rail to the main deck. A few hands reached for him and helped him over the rail and then he disappeared. For the first time any of them could remember as they craned their necks to see, they all looked up, but no one looked down at them. After a few shrugs and grunts the men hunched down on the benches and settled in, half asleep, to wait until it was time to row ashore. Servicemen got rest when they could.

In minutes their rest was over as Stock surprised them by calling down to them, telling them to stand ready to cast off. They wondered at the lack of shipboard hospitality. He scrambled over the side and down the wide rope grid followed by three men. There were no introductions made and the visitors took seats at the stern and stared grimly ahead. The lines were loosened and drawn back up over the gunwales of the *Hathor* and the surfboat pushed away. The three men didn't move or change expression the whole way in. The rowers faced the stern and the passengers faced forward and all was silent except for the language of the eyes and the talking of the ocean. The surfmen watched them suspiciously and were watched in return. Stock and all his men knew something was wrong and it crossed all of their minds that these were surely men who had something to hide, probably a hold full of contraband. Not a soul appeared on the deck of the waiting ship.

Jack studied the three men. He was careful not to stare. It was plain who was who. The leader was dark, fierce, and handsome. He was tall and had brown hair and eyes, his features sharp and regular, everything where and how it should be. The clothes he wore were not those of a ship's master. They were those of a rich man. He was unhappy and angry and his expression did not change as he stared at the surfmen, measuring them, one by one. With him were two underlings. One was small and withdrawn, his face mostly hidden by a low cap and a beard. He looked furtively toward shore as they rode in, his head turning from side to side as he squinted to see the beach.

When he looked to the south Jack could see that he had bad bruises around his temple and eye on the right side of his head. He looked as if he had recently lost a fight. The third man, who Jack would later learn was Salete, sat straight, but looked relaxed and unconcerned, as if bored by what happened around him. His hand was bandaged and he kept it tucked into the front of his coat. Salete, however, took the chance to study the faces of the surfmen. He did this wherever he went, looking for deserters, people he had beaten on the orders of his captain, threats to LeFrank. Salete had enemies, and he was wary when exposed. He was slender and nondescript, not unpleasant looking, and there was in him a look of grace, like that which would reside in one of Lucifer's messenger angels.

At the beach LeFrank and his men immediately climbed from the boat, and ignoring Ezra's questioning look, left the surfmen and walked up the slope of sand to have a better look at the lay of the land. LeFrank spoke briefly to them and they split up and walked in opposite directions along the water's edge. He looked back at the boat and stood there staring until Ezra walked up to him.

"Show me your station," LeFrank said to Ezra.

Stock didn't answer. He didn't like this man or his tone, but he would be hospitable and bear the man's impertinence until he could get him and his crew safely away. The truth was that seafaring men were often different, but you could be eccentric, yet still courteous. A poor man could be clean, one in pain could be kind. Anyone who had what this dark fellow had, Stock thought, could use a little of the manners he surely knew, to oil the workings of normal discourse. He walked up the boardwalk and LeFrank followed. Jack and the rest of the crew dragged the boat up far enough so that the waves wouldn't steal her away. The tide was coming in. Jack hoped it would soon free the *Hathor* and carry these men away from him and the young woman. When he thought of her and looked at them it was no wonder she wanted to get away from them. She seemed as fragile as they seemed strong. But she was at least as determined to escape them as they were to find her. Jack had no doubt they were ashore for one reason, to search for her. LeFrank looked intently at the exterior of the building and the outbuildings around it. He asked the keeper about the number of men on duty, where they were the previous night, and if they had reported anything.

"Just that they heard the bell and saw your lights. They were faint, but we saw them, could tell when the ship pitched side to side.

Now what is this all about? You said there was a problem. On your ship you said you would tell me when we came ashore. What is it?"

"We lost a passenger. A young woman. She apparently fell overboard."

The weight of this hit the older man. This was what his life was supposed to be about, saving lives, helping those who wound up in the water.

His normally quiet voice barked out at LeFrank. "Why didn't you tell us? We could have been looking for her. I'll send our men back out." Stock turned, but LeFrank's words stopped him.

"My people will look along the shore. We didn't want to say until we searched the ship."

Stock did not understand. "Was she lost on your ship?"

Again LeFrank paused before speaking. He did not look directly at Stock, "She may...have been hiding."

"From what!"

"She was a very nervous person and would have been afraid of the storm. Or when we ran onto the bar. Enough to go down into one of the holds. We were afraid she'd gotten trapped there. Some of the cargo shifted when we came aground. Our men worked through the night to lash some of the casks and crates and secure them. When that was done and we knew she wasn't on board...we signaled to you to come here." LeFrank made up the story the night before and embellished it enough to give it a ring of truth.

"One of the men thought he saw something in the water, but it was nothing."

LeFrank's head turned abruptly and his eyes burned, "Who was it, what did he see?"

"Jack Light, a young man, one of my best men, but there was no one there."

LeFrank looked around him. "Bring him here."

Stock didn't like the tone or the manner of this command, but he did want to get this over with. He pulled on his graying beard and looked toward the beach where Jack and some of the crew were using large rags to get water down the scuppers and out of the surfboat. He waved to the men and pointed to Jack, indicating that he wanted him to join them. Jack walked up the boardwalk to the back of the building.

Ezra looked at him, "Jack, this is Captain LeFrank, master of the *Hathor*. He's looking for a young woman from their ship. They think she fell overboard during the night." Jack tried to keep still and keep his eyes from giving him away. "You said you saw something in the water. What was it?"

His mind raced. "It was nothing…just a baby seal…dead in the water."

LeFrank stared at him. Jack tried to keep his eyes and face and voice normal. His fatigue was real, penetrating every part of him and that helped him.

"I pulled it in from the surf. Then I saw what it was. It was too dark to tell until I got the lantern on it." Jack pointed down the beach. He was blinded for a moment by the morning sun, but when the flash cleared from his eyes he could see Salete walking along, looking from side to side, pausing at times to look up into the dunes. As he held out his arm he saw the blood on the sleeve of his coat. LeFrank saw it as well. Their eyes met. He had seen Elizabeth's blood on the deck in her cabin when Salete had taken him below decks and showed him how she had gotten off the ship.

"Where did that blood come from?"

Jack could feel the strength of will that LeFrank had brought to bear on him. This man was like a force, pressing into him. His response was a pure one. There was no duty, no doing what was right. He was now driven by instinct. He would do anything to protect the woman. He would give his life for a stranger, someone whose name he did not even know. He was not surprised at himself for this felt natural to him, good, despite the risk, regardless of the danger. Every rescue had risk, but this was different…this was protection, care, a promise made, and strangely there was something in it for him as well as for her. He was afraid of LeFrank, but he would challenge him if he had to. "Who is this woman you're looking for?"

It was clear that this angered the powerful man before him and his face hardened. "That does not concern you."

Jack shrugged.

LeFrank persisted. "The blood?"

"Like I said, it was from the seal."

LeFrank let his gaze and his contempt stay on the younger man. Jack turned away to return to the crew. As he crossed the distance to the boat, Salete drew abreast of him. Salete ignored him and began speaking to the Captain. LeFrank interrupted him and ordered him to speak in French. "En Français." Jack caught parts of their conversation. He heard LeFrank say "la femme," not "epouse" or "fille." This meant that she probably was not LeFrank's wife of daughter. He felt relief at that. The wind took away most of what Salete said, but Jack's head snapped up when he thought he heard Salete say "la putain." Jack made himself look busy, joining the men as they filled their time pulling out lines and inspecting them.

"Sur le plage, un phoque mort?"

"Oui." Salete looked to the south to see if the seal was visible, but it was too far away.

"Et le sang?"

"Non, il n'y a pas de sang."

At the pause in their discussion the two men walked a few paces, taking them out of earshot, but Jack was worried again. The sly-looking one told his captain that he had seen the seal, but that it was not injured and that there was no blood on it. He did not have to look up to tell that LeFrank's eyes were on him again.

The woman had been telling him the truth. These men were not concerned for her—they were furious with her. It was a barely concealed rage they harbored. She had escaped from them and Jack knew she was right, she must never go back to them. He wondered what she was to them and why she wouldn't tell him. He felt hunger and thirst and exhaustion and wanted to go to his bunk to sleep, but knew he had to stand by to see what would happen. Ezra Stock waited stoically at the door of the house and the men finished their work and stared sullenly at the unwelcome visitors. They leaned against the boat and waited. They watched as the third man joined them. He hunched over and shook his head at the questions asked him. Jack was relieved that this dirty odd little man had nothing to report. Again he wondered if the woman had survived the hours since he had sent her off shivering into the wilderness west of the station.

LeFrank spoke to them, "Maintenant…allez…a l'ouest…." Jack could not hear it all but could only stand there dreading what might happen as the two men split up and moved inland, wandering into the dunes looking for the lost woman. LeFrank strode purposely back to the door to the station and looked at the keeper. Stock led him inside and together the two toured the facility alone.

Outside, the men stood silently until the preacher said, "It's like seeing the devil himself when you see someone like that captain. Remember what I say, men, we've had a visit from the devil. I know it. I can tell, I've met him before, in the Bible. A few times on this land as well. And I heard him say something about a whore. That's probably who's on that ship. He takes whores to the men on the islands and the slave ships, sells them, most likely. That's why he didn't let the captain visit with him. I'll be glad to see him gone, and the lot of them. I'll tell the captain to report them to the Cutter ships. Let them board her one day, see what's what." No one argued with Old Gunn. Jack had a chill go through him. What if this woman was as bad as the men who were looking for her? He couldn't believe that, but he had no idea what this could be about. Could she be using him? No, he thought, that was not possible. She was an innocent. He knew it in his heart. Tired as he was, his mind would not let him rest. He kept looking toward the dunes. They waited. George Kimball stood transfixed the whole time, off to himself, as if he were alone upon the earth. They all knew something was wrong.

CHAPTER 5

The Forest

Jack's Cabin

An hour after they had walked to the west looking for Elizabeth, Chien and Salete returned. Jack hoped that she had done what he asked and had stayed hidden. They rejoined LeFrank, talked briefly to him, and then they all walked down to the boat. Chien kept his hands in his pockets. In his right hand he held a glass bead, rolling it between his thumb and index finger. He had found it, and a line of others, each a blaze along the trail that led to the bay. He liked the way it felt and how it reminded him of her. It slid along his fingertips as it had the silken skin of her neck. "Leaving me a trail, so I could find her," he said to himself. "And I'm the only one who knows."

Stock decided to leave Jack and the preacher behind. They watched the men launch the surfboat. "We're all thankful for seeing the backs of them." Like the others, he had seen that the three men had all carried guns with them, barely concealed in their coats. Jack thought then about how to get away. He wanted to leave at once, but held himself back, assuming correctly that he couldn't go to the girl without knowing that the black ship had gone on its way. She would insist on knowing. He went up to his bunk and curled up under the covers.

Jack's arm slid over the edge of the bunk and he awoke suddenly. He sat up quickly, felt lightheaded and held still for a moment to let the unsettling feeling pass. He looked out of the observation window and what he did see gave him a feeling of relief. The surfmen were headed back to shore and the *Hathor* was plunging into the waves toward the east. The wind blew across her beam and LeFrank had his crew aloft crowding on the canvas. He seemed cruel even to his ship. Soon every sheet was full, straining out, and the wooden ship opened the sea like a steel plow ripping its way through soft earth.

When the men got to the water's edge Jack went out to help them. It was another hour before the gear was cleaned and put to dry and the boat had been returned to the house. Before doing what he had decided he must do, he went to talk to the captain.

"Captain. I need some leave. I don't feel good and it's been a while since I've been back to my cabin. Can you spare me for a couple of days?" Jack wondered what he would say if the older man refused. This was his second father and he knew that to Ezra Stock, who had never married, he was like a son. More so since Tom Light had died, in effect willing Jack into his care. For Jack, work was life and he seldom took leave, so he was sure his absence would not be a problem.

Ezra looked intently at the young man. Here, he thought, was the kind of person anyone would want as a son. Smart. Open. Intelligent with wonder. Jack was tall and strong. Ezra thought he even looked strong in his face. It was clear and despite the strength that it showed, still somewhat fine. His hair was light and short. He kept clean shaven. His dark brown, wide-set eyes smiled, but Ezra noticed that they were different today, they look strained, and for Jack, a new look, worried.

"Can I help, Jack?"

"Thanks, Ezra, but no. I'll be alright, I just need a few days."

His captain nodded to him, gave him a small smile, and went to his room. In his years of teaching and guiding young men, Ezra Stock knew that there were times when one had to let them go. Jack wasn't going to tell him what was wrong and he wasn't going to be any good to the other surfmen until it was over with. Whatever it was. No leader of men liked to deal with brooding and discontent. Like all of the other men, Ezra too needed a rest. The long night and the experience of those strange men had tired him. Except for the lookout rotation and the beach patrols, he gave the men a break from their regular duties for the day. Most of them slept, but some read or did some sewing or carving or cleaning their equipment. For now they didn't talk about the men of the *Hathor*. They wanted to forget them. Jack was left alone.

He walked outside and went down to the water's edge. The ocean was still a hard grey, but it was not as rough and the wind had shifted from the northeast and now came more from the west. Some of the gusts made his pants rattle around his knees. He watched as the *Hathor* continued on her way. As it moved further off it looked as if it was descending into the underworld. When the curvature of the earth made the tip of its mainmast drop into the water he turned and walked up the boardwalk used for the surfboat and passed the south side of the barracks. The large doors to the boat room were open and he looked in at the surfboat. A triangle of light painted the floor and part of the back wall. Late morning. Pale fall yellow. Tobacco smoke, reluctant, took its time drifting out of the building. Its smell was rich and familiar. Jack liked it when there was just enough to smell. He nodded to a few of the men who sat relaxing in the straight wooden chairs inside. They had them rocked back so that only the two rear legs were on the floor, finding places of rest in the numberless scars and dents left by the weight of those who had lived the same lives as theirs. They leaned against the wall and dozed or talked idly. They acknowledged him with a slight tilt of the head or a small wave of the hand, but thought no more of him as he continued on his way.

In minutes he was away from the compound and out of sight of the outbuildings. He checked to make sure that the lookout could no longer see him and then quickened his pace. Beyond the ranks of dunes was a stand of trees and brush and he was comforted to smell the loblolly pine and see the bayberry bushes and walk on the thick pad of pine needles. Here the sand didn't give way as much and the footing was easier. He crossed the north-south road, more a wide path and a discontinuous one at that, which led to Henlopen and Lewes. Some late migrant birds flitted among the branches of the trees and the fall warblers were letting each other know where they were. Jack's house, a cabin really, was in the thin low woods of the Delaware coast and his spirits lifted as he moved toward it through this narrow stretch of trees. His home had seemed empty in the years since his father died and most of the time he slept at the lifesaving station. But it was still home, his real home, and tonight it would become a refuge for the woman waiting nearby, waiting for him to take her there. As he got closer to the place he had left his boat, his heart began to race with that confused feeling that he had had the night before on the beach. He at once liked it and didn't like it. He smiled to himself. Now I'm afraid of a woman, he said to himself, someone else I don't know. He stopped at the edge of the woods and scanned the bay shore for his boat. It was off to his right. It rested safely up on the sand where he had left it. The thoughts raced through his mind. She's pitiful and weak, he said to himself, but she's still strong, I can tell. He blew out a long breath, stepped past a loose line of groundsel trees with their tiny paintbrush blooms swaying in the breeze and moved into the open. He began to sing, mostly to himself but also to alert her. If she were sleeping, he wanted to wake her gently. He did not want her to be afraid. If anyone else was nearby, he would rather them hear him singing than calling out for her.

It was an old ballad, sweet, with a simple melody, and it just came to him on its own. It was one of the ones the men all knew and sometimes sang together. Jack never knew why. The men knew. Most of them sang it and others like it, and thought to themselves of someone they knew, someone from before.

Jack had told her to walk beyond the boat and hide. If she'd made it to this place and done what he told her, she should be just ahead, along the shore. The beach was flat and firm. Embedded in it were myriad shells, and the sword and shield remains of horseshoe crabs were scattered along the gently curving way. It was about fifty yards to the closest concentration of marsh plants. He scanned the beach, looking for her footprints. He sang a little louder and walked casually along the beach. The frequent checks he had made during his walk from the station made him confident that no one had followed him. There could still be someone hunting or fishing in the area, but he knew from living there all his life that that was unlikely. There were much better places to go for food and very few people lived in, or traveled through, this part of the county.

Before he got to the tangle of cordgrass spikes, now sure they were alone, he called out, "It's me, from the lifesaving station…the surfman. You can come out, it's just me." He was aware of the lap of the waves in the bay. Little swishes, followed by a long pause, followed by a gentle slap. Cries of distant birds faded away. Otherwise there was silence. He repeated his call to her. "Miss, I'm alone. They've left…the ship, it's gone."

Then he saw her. She looked funny in his clothes, stepping through the edge of the tall dry marsh grass and into the sunlight. She held his pants up with one hand and pushed her hair back with the other. She had her gown wrapped around her shoulders like a shawl. It was wet and torn. Jack just stood there and smiled.

"What was that you were singing?"

Jack was surprised by the question and shook his head slightly as if he didn't know if he had heard her correctly.

"I'm sorry, ma'am?"

"You were singing about the sun, the moon, and the stars. It's a song I don't know. Well, I know the melody from some of my music books." She paused, looked away from him, swallowed hard, and made her lips stop quivering before she went on, "But I have not heard those words before."

This was not what Jack expected to be talking about. "I don't know, Miss, it's just a song the older men sing sometimes. I just like the sound of it. I never thought about the words really. It's...I like the way I feel when they sing it, I guess."

She wondered why he was singing a song he didn't understand and he wondered why, with what had happened to her, she was talking about a song.

"We should get away from here. Away from the open." Jack looked up and down the line of sand. "There is no place of lodging anywhere around here. Come to my cabin and you can rest and eat and we can decide what to do next."

She didn't move. She tilted her head and asked, "Why did you have me hide away from your boat? There are woods close by and those bushes with the waxy berries. Better places. Those reeds stick you." It was almost as if she were accusing him of something.

"Well, Miss, it's what the birds do. And the bushes are bayberry."

She thought of the smell of bayberry candles burning in her home.

Elizabeth raised her eyebrows. Jack was taken by the look of her eyes and it was a moment before he realized she was waiting for more of an explanation. He also realized his mouth was open and he was staring. He looked away. His father had taught him it was impolite to stare at someone. The reminder of his father stirred him to action. His father got things done. He had better get things done—take charge of this woman, protect her, and get her on her way. He started to walk back toward his boat. She moved beside him, staying between him and the water. "The birds...well some birds...when they leave their nests for food or maybe just to stretch out and get a look at things, they don't fly right back. They fly to a place near their nests and stop to look around to see if they were followed. When they see that it's safe, then they go back. That way they don't lead any predators to their eggs or their young." He glanced to his side to look at her and she nodded. She seemed to understand. They came to his boat. Jack checked it to be sure it was okay and heaved it down to the water. The keel drew a straight line in the hard white sand. It rocked slowly when it began to float and then settled down as if it now felt more comfortable than it had on land. The sun was overhead and the wind had become just a breeze. Jack took her hand and supported her as she stepped into the small craft. It was long and narrow with three thwarts to sit on and it had two old oars at home in their oarlocks and a pole to push if needed. Stowed in the bow were a rope and an anchor. Jack rarely employed them since this boat was mostly used for him to cross the bay to go to the station. When he fished he just drifted; this was the best way to get the flukes he loved to catch and cook for sweet, fried-fish dinners. He made sure she was settled in the stern and he moved to the center seat to take up the oars. Their weights balanced and the boat sat nicely in the bay, rocking just a little. She placed her hands on the sides of the boat and frowned as her eyes raked the horizon.

Compared to the work on a surfboat, moving this little skiff was easy. The water was shallow and most of the way he could have walked and used the painter to pull the boat behind him, something he often did when the air and water were warmer. He used the oar to move them off the sand and into the bay and began rowing with long, regular strokes. It felt good. It felt good to be taking this woman, who now sat a few feet away from him and stared at him intently, to be taking her with him to his home. Until now it had not occurred to him what he would do with her once they got there. He would build a fire and get her food…he had food…and let her get cleaned and rested. The rain barrels would be full from the storm and he could boil water for her to bathe. That would be alright. He could do all of that.

After a few minutes her head nodded and she slipped into an exhausted state of sleep. Jack suspected she had not had much rest hiding in the reeds. Her face was crusted with the dried blood from her head and the bandage was russet, dirty, and askew. He could see that she was still losing a little blood. Her dark hair hung past her shoulders and her hands were muddy from the marsh. The thin gown was now blood stained and torn and hung limply around her neck. But to Jack she was without a spot. While she was becoming physically more substantial to him, it was still the idea of the situation she was in that had the most powerful effect on him. The uncertainty of all of this was overwhelming. Innocents made self-aware by another like themselves, they slid over the water.

He had been taught that feelings may be allowed to catch up with you, but they must never be allowed to overtake you. It had never before been hard advice to heed. But it could not have been these feelings his father had been describing, Jack was sure, when he proffered this advice. Not with a lady like this involved. Everything now was new. He was rowing slowly, making precise, deliberate strokes, trying to go as fast as he could but still not awaken her. The oars clunked louder than usual in their locks. There was some water in the bottom of the boat, and Elizabeth's feet were wet, but it didn't seem to bother her. The sun felt good and he pulled the oars over and over, bent and pulled, bent and pulled, until he neared the western shore of the bay. The oars rubbed against the gunwales and the oarlocks groaned a little in their holes.

When they reached his landing spot she awakened and sat upright. The scrape of the hull on the sand alarmed her. She looked inland and her eyes peered into the woods. She seemed a little in awe of it; it was much thicker that the irregular patches of trees and shrubs she had passed through the night before. Farther from the water the trees were bigger and the forest darker. Jack saw her look of worry. He felt he knew what she was thinking. "We're close to my place. It's not a fancy house like I guess you're used to, but it's safe. You can warm up and get clean and I'll get you something to eat." He wondered to himself how he came up with that idea, that she lived in a fancy house, but it just seemed to him that she did. Just from the look of her.

Her eyes wide, she watched the forest as he helped her out of the boat. She looked around as he dragged his boat up from the water. She wondered if there was more danger for her here. She was not afraid of the young man who was helping her. He wouldn't hurt her. She just wasn't sure he would be able to help her get home. But he'd been good to her so far. Her escape was now a reality. She realized that she had never really believed she would get away from LeFrank and Salete. But now it struck her. She had. And now she knew that what she must do was to return home and find out if Nana was alive. Salete said he had killed her. Pray God he was lying just to hurt me, she thought. She had to go home. If she tried to get word to anyone, there was a danger LeFrank would learn of it. He had to think she was dead.

"Miss?"

She turned to him and nodded toward the woods. He led her into the dark, cool shelter of the long needled loblolly pines. After a short walk, Jack stopped. He was still and looked around. Like that bird going to the nest, Elizabeth thought to herself.

The cabin was very old. Jack's father had bought it from one of the descendants of an early settler. The Nanticoke and the Lanni-Lenape Indians who first lived in this area had probably seen this cabin. It was built in a clearing not far from the water and the various people who had lived there over the years had made improvements to the surroundings more than they had to the interior. Hickories and hollies and oaks and birch and cherry trees had been kept at bay. There were paths and benches, and storage sheds for tools and equipment, and to keep the firewood dry. But it was sturdy and clean and weather tight.

Jack opened the door and led her inside. She stopped inside the doorway and peered into the one big room that was where this man lived. It was a far cry from the beautiful house she owned in Boston. Jack's parlors were outdoors. The bay was one of his rooms, she realized, the ocean another; those rooms, she mused, were infinitely larger than the largest rooms in her house, and far more grand. She had two kitchens, a pantry, a larder, a formal dining room, and sitting rooms for tea. Rooms for sewing and for music. Two floors of bedrooms upstairs, a garret for the servants. As he opened the shutters and the light shone upon him, she looked at him and could tell from his face that he was proud of his home. It was as good a place as he had ever known. In fact, it was one of the few buildings Jack had ever been in. He had spent some time in the modest homes of his father's friends, made a few trips to some small churches and stores in the area, and even went to a one-room school for a few years, but in essence he lived outside the walls of what was man made.

It was quiet inside.

Remembering their manners they spoke simultaneously, their words went on top of each other. "Thank you for bringing me to your home." "Make yourself at home." He laughed. Embarrassed, she turned away and walked around the room and looked more closely at what lay therein. Slowly she began to see that this was where he lived, and this told how he lived, and this was who he was. There were guns and fishing gear and clothing for the outdoors and for cold weather. Things were out in the open, cooking things, tools, a few pieces of basic furniture, and surprisingly, a shelf full of books. Most of what he owned was hanging on the walls on pegs or resting on shelves.

His world was horizontal. Hers was vertical.

Everything here was horizon, long lines of beach or stands of trees, all left to right. The bays were flat. His property was spread out. This room, his only room, was large, but the house had only one floor and a small loft reached by ladder and used for storage. Outside was the same.

There was no precedent for him as to what to do. It was obvious that she needed to be fed and to get clean and be able to rest. It was now well after noon and she had been under a great strain for a long time. He did what he thought was needed most. His Service training came to mind: food, water, shelter, warmth, rest, quiet. He had her sit on a bench at his table and got her some hard biscuit and water and dried fish to eat. He brought a blanket from the bed and put it over her shoulders. She nodded her thanks and wrapped it around her. She ate slowly, chewing hard on the tough, salty meat and sipping the water after putting each piece of biscuit into her mouth, to soften it. She licked her fingers. He started a fire and soon the cabin was warm and the slight stale smell of the air inside was replaced with the perfume of burning wood. Jack mixed the woods for a good burn and some of the pine logs lent a delicious flavor to the sauce of the atmosphere. The fire popped and sang a comforting song. The fireplace had iron pots hung from swinging hooks and bread ovens and warming nooks built into the stone, and Jack put a kettle over the flames to boil water for tea. He offered her sugar and she sweetened it and held it up to her lips, kissing it as she sipped, like it was something dear. The warmth helped her. He pulled a long galvanized tub away from the wall and got some cloths for her to use as towels. He began to fill the tub with boiling water from the large pot that hung from a cast iron hook in the fireplace. She watched him, but said nothing. It took some time but he slowly filled the tub, and when it was ready, he put his hand in the water to test the temperature. Swishing his hand on the surface, he judged it to be good and nodded, wiping his hands on his britches. Then, from the corner of the room, he dragged a large chest from the shadows. Three latches held its lid tightly against the sides.

"This was my mother's," he said. "Dad kept her things. He didn't know anyone to give them to. I guess he was saving them for you."

Jack smiled and she looked at him, trying to decide if he was just saying this or if he really believed it. Jack didn't think about it one way or another; it just came out of his mouth. He lifted the lid and poked around inside, holding up several garments as if to try to figure out what they were. "I hope some of these things will be okay, I mean that...fit you and all." He didn't know what to say since he knew nothing about women's clothes. "Get a bath and see if you can wear something for now and anything else in there that you can use. Sew them to fit you better. I'll go out and tend to some things around the place...just call me when you are through. Don't worry, I'll be close by. The water is real hot, ma'am, so pour some of the cold in until you get it right. There's a pitcher of cold water there and some soap."

Elizabeth nodded and said thanks. She waited until he had gone then burst into tears and cried bitterly as she undressed and eased herself into the water. Her grief was now from her thoughts of Nana. The young man was worried for her because of LeFrank. He didn't know about Nana. He had no idea of the life she had had and how she had been ripped from it. She had held that back, not even crying through the long night she had spent out in this wilderness, terrified, alone. Her tears ran down her face and breasts into the water that surrounded her. The names of the women who had not escaped burned her eyes. Lydia Child, Carina Hauser, Anna Ulter... She sobbed through the list she had memorized until her exhaustion stopped her. When she had let some of it out of her, she began to wash. Her hair was a tangle and she had to rub hard to get the mud and blood off of her hands and feet. The water and harsh soap stung the cuts and her forehead began to bleed again. She dabbed it repeatedly with the cloth but every time it came away from her face a bright red. She was aware of how thin she had become and how weak she felt. When she stood up she looked down at herself and saw the welts and scratches that hurt from the strong soap and from her rubbing them. Her skin was raw and chafed everywhere. A thousand cuts.

She wondered idly what the surfman thought when he looked at her. How she must look. How she smelled after so many days without being able to clean herself. Who could tell. He might as well be from a foreign country. Even with the kindness and care he had shown so far, she was scared—not of him but of being here, and no one knowing. It was this forest, and being so far from anything, and the sadness that mixed with the fear.

The water was so dirty she couldn't see her feet. She stepped from the bath and dried herself with the large cloth he had left for her and wrapped herself in it and walked to the window. She looked out cautiously and saw the young man at the far side of the clearing. He was removing stores from one of the outbuildings, moving side to side to be sure he kept his back to the cabin. Gallantry here was unexpected. It was hard to know what to think of him.

She found some underclothes and a white blouse and a long brown skirt that were a little large for her, but she pinned them in a few places with the large safety pins he had left out. She felt good to be dressed after so many days of confinement in nothing but a nightgown. She shivered when she thought of how those men had degraded her. They were base creatures, locking her in a room with a chamber pot, a little pitcher of water that smelled of the barrel that had caught it from the rain, her body theirs to see. She thought no bath would ever wash away the marks their eyes had left on her body. The simple act of dressing had restored her somewhat. She wondered again about the surfman. He had offered to sew clothes for her, she who had done elaborate needlepoint and had made many things for herself and Nana and others.

She went to the door and called out that she was finished. Jack crossed the clearing quickly and came to the door at once. He smiled when he saw her, saying, "You look nice." He felt a little foolish at blurting that out, but thought he could see that in some flicker of her expression she appreciated it. He knew from his dad that if you had something good to say, as long as it was true, it was okay to say it. And it was true. She really did look nice.

Her footprints on the floor told him she had been watching him from the window. He realized he had to get her something for her feet. Jack stood close to her and looked intently at her face. "You need to sleep now. But first we have to see to that cut on your head. I'll have to stitch it up."

"Stitch it?"

"It won't heal like this and you'll keep losing blood." He looked directly at her. She held his gaze for a moment and then nodded. She knew he was right. He wanted to ask about the cut, how it had come to be there, but sensed that she'd tell him if she wanted to. Get her stitched up, and on her way, he thought, and I can get back to my job.

He took a case from a drawer in the chest near the bed. She watched as he held the needle and thread and made his preparations. He had her sit on one of the benches by the table and face the light from the window. He cleaned the needle with alcohol and rubbed a light wax on the thread. He stood over her and took her hands in his and placed them so that she was lightly pressing the sides of the cut together with the tips of her index fingers. He leaned in close to her and with exquisite gentleness slowly pierced her, pushing in and pulling out the thread with care, drawing the places together. Her eyes never left his. The cut ran from the middle of her eyebrow up to the hairline. Traces of bruising and a slight swelling were painted faintly up its sides. When he was finished with the needle and thread he carefully took her hands and moved them down from her face. With a clean cloth he dabbed alcohol onto the stitches. Her body shuddered and her breath quivered into her, but she held her head still until he was finished. He stepped back. "Good. That stopped the bleeding."

Jack carried the sewing kit back to the chest and put it away. He was standing by the bed. He drew back the counterpane and looked expectantly at her. Without any hesitation she went to the bed, raised herself over the side frame, and lay down on her side. She pulled her skirt down to rest over her legs and crossed her arms in front of her. He covered her and then moved slowly back out of her line of sight. He waited. In one minute she was dead to the world.

CHAPTER 6

Strell

Newport News, Virginia

Strell watched the man pacing the deck of the ship *Luluwa*. He stood in the shadows by the wall of the chandler's office with his hat pulled low on his face and his coat collar up around him. Strell was a patient man, unlike O'Neill, who Strell called the "little weascl." O'Neill trudged along the rail of his ship, eyes darting left to right and back again as he searched the narrow sector of sea lane that gave him a view of the horizon. He was looking for the *Hathor* and her cargo. The ship was late. Three days had passed since the ship and her crew had felt the terror of the sand grabbing at her from the bottom of the sea. It should have made the trip from Boston to Newport News by now, and be anchored across the harbor, in view of his ship *Luluwa*. He muttered and cursed and even though he knew how hard trips along the coast could be for a sailing ship, he still could not hold back the flood of worries that rose around him. What if a Revenue Cutter patrol had gotten LeFrank? The weather here had not been that stormy, but what about up north? When it blew bad, sailing ships like the *Hathor* had no say in where they went. Delays, sometimes long ones, were not uncommon. For that matter she could be lost, gone to the bottom with a cargo of O'Neill's hopes. Or had LeFrank made another deal, cutting O'Neill out? The little man was furious, and scared. No matter what, he had to get the cargo from that ship, and he couldn't put from his mind the thought of what might happen to him if he failed.

He pulled the chain that led to the watch pocket of his vest and let the watch emerge from its niche, the line of gold links running through his fingers like a serpent as he raised his arm. He flipped the timepiece open. O'Neill squinted at the dial and then at the entrance to the harbor, as if thinking that checking the time would make the *Hathor* appear. The ship was now far past due, even counting for the weather. She was a fast ship with a daring and skilled master and there was always wind fuel in the North Atlantic at this time of year. He could hear the wind now as it made the pennants topping nearby ships flutter and snap, and see the wind making the masts of the smaller ships rock, crazed metronomes marking the tempo of the choppy water.

He wondered if he could put off his buyer for a few more days. Thoughts of that man passed over him and chilled him. Something made him look behind him. Strell stepped out into the open and O'Neill cursed silently as his mouth went dry and his heart began to pound in his chest. Strell was never supposed to come to the ship unless O'Neill had put a signal flag aloft telling him it was time to make a trade. Strell went straight up the gangplank; O'Neill took a step back and failed to muster a smile. O'Neill felt the cold as Strell gripped him with his hard gray eyes.

"Ah, Strell…I was just thinking about you. Glad you came to see me. I, uh, fear there is some delay we don't know about. No trouble, I'm sure. I'll get word from the ship any time now." O'Neill looked hopefully up at Strell but saw no understanding or forgiveness in his face. This was the coldest man O'Neill had ever met. Worse than LeFrank. O'Neill almost smiled to himself at the thought of those two meeting. Like two mad dogs, he thought. Both sons of bitches. But their money was good; both of them paid, good money and fast, cash on the barrel head. Strell had made purchases from O'Neill before, arms and whiskey and counterfeit money, and the girls, yes Strell liked the girls. But he had never been more fierce about anything than he was about this shipment. He wanted the guns, but he seemed obsessed with the girl. O'Neill had given Strell the picture LeFrank had sent him and, well, the girl was a beauty alright, some rich Boston blue blood, but whatever it was about her that Strell liked, it burned in him so you could see it. Just from him standing there. The other girls he had gotten in the past were mostly island girls and even some children, boys and girls. Nobodies. He had never sold girls from LeFrank to this buyer. Maybe he liked girls from up north, O'Neill thought. O'Neill had to admit that LeFrank had sent him some beauties, actresses he said they were, but he had moved most of them out west or to the Gulf coast. None of them were as elegant as this one, though, dressed in finery and posing like royalty, in a house unlike any O'Neill had ever been in. You could see the signs of wealth that surrounded the girl as she stood for the photographer. He looked away from Strell, back to the open water, hoping to see the ship, thinking if she was lost it might mean his life. He became aware that he still clutched the watch in his hand. It was early afternoon but it had never registered with him what hour it was. He still held it out in front of him, the case open. He snapped the cover shut and turned. Strell was gone. O'Neill muttered under his breath, "Goddam him, he's just disappeared, like the devil crawling back down his hole into hell."

Strell glanced over his shoulder as he walked down the dock and saw O'Neill standing there, holding his watch out like a fool. He slipped down the alley behind a shipping office and folded himself through the small door of the waiting horse-drawn carriage. He met the eyes of the other man inside and shook his head. They sat in the dark cab for a minute and Strell said, "We wait." The other man used the butt of his pistol to hammer the wall of the cab in front of him and the driver let the reins shake and the tip of the buggy whip snap just above the haunches of the two horses before him. Their heads jerked back as they took off for the quarters they had rented at the western edge of the city. Strell peered through a slit in the tightly drawn curtains of the carriage.

His man knew what he was thinking. Strell was dedicated, on a mission. When he had to wait for his plans to work out he invariably occupied much of his time thinking not about the future, but about the past. His planning was so meticulous and thorough that in his mind it was the future that was set and the past that could be changed. The days ahead would be as he had arranged them to be; what he regretted about the days already lived, he sought to view differently, to change, if only in his mind. As it often did, one thing stood out—an incident he had wrestled with many times during the intervening years, but could not fully acknowledge or manage to reconcile to the conception he had of himself. His man was correct in his surmise: Strell was thinking about the past, reconstructing it, trying it out in the different light of the present, like an adversary that one fought repeatedly, but never bested. Strell was thinking about something that had happened a long time ago. He and his man had served together on a large merchantman out of Boston called the *Christian Frederick*, led by the kindly seeming Captain Arnold and several decent officers, but manned by a crew of some of the worst men on the Atlantic. Common seamen were at best an unreliable and surly lot. When it was time for a ship owner to sign on a crew, the pickings were never good, but this group was uncommonly bad.

It was a time charged with the passion that sets fire to history. The states warred with each other over slavery, and love and hatred ruled the country. Uncertainty within and among nations boiled on the surface of things. Strell and his friend were young men out to make something of their lives, oblivious to any trials but their own. Removed as they were from news of the world, they could concentrate on the matter at hand—learning a trade.

Morning light and the ship's bell brought all of the men on board running to the foremast of the *Christian Frederick*. Leaning against it, as though asleep, was the old seaman who had stood the last watch of the night and the last one of his life. When the first mate ordered one of the men to rouse him, the man shook his shoulder but quickly jumped back from the dead cold of his body. He looked at his hand and rubbed it as if trying to scale ice off of it. At the sailor's touch the dead man slumped over onto his side and the men recoiled from the smell and the foul wetness of his breeches and the dark crescent mark left on the deck. More of the black stain dribbled grotesquely from him and was pulled away from his body by the pitch of the ship. Men stepped back from its death smell. Frozen like statues, Strell and his man watched as a sailor named Brock, a heavyset man weighed down with muscle and superstition, grabbed a fire bucket and sloshed it violently onto the deck. What followed was not what he had intended. The water hit the stinking puddle and splashed it up in all directions so that it soiled the bare feet, clothes, arms, and even faces of a dozen of the men who formed an arc around the corpse.

A scream came from a man nearby as he felt the wetness on his face, in his eyes and mouth. He had seen the diseases of the world firsthand on other voyages, and fear was in his eyes. He retched violently. All of them knew of smallpox, yellow fever, malaria, the wasting sicknesses. The affected man too grabbed a bucket, and poured the cold green seawater over himself, spitting and coughing and rubbing at his eyes. The man was called Mugs, for he drank and fought and whored in taverns the whole time he was in any port. Mugs swung the empty bucket with all his power and crashed the heavy oak container squarely across Brock's wide, flat face. Both men screamed and cursed about gods and mothers and the devil. Blood and anger poured forth and at once a number of the men began to fight, some taking sides, others just striking out at whoever was standing before them. Strell and his man and several others were pushed back by some of the officers and craned their necks to watch as the yelling and punching and pushing continued. Brock staggered to his feet and pulled a long knife from his waistband, and soon there were more weapons drawn and the fight had reached a point where blood and death were certain. Old scores were settled under the cover of this incident and four men lay dying underfoot before the captain had retrieved his pistols from his cabin and fired one of them just over the heads of the men. A streak of smoke from the shot scarred the air. As one they stopped and turned their faces towards him. Though known as a soft-spoken and just man, Arnold had not survived in his long and successful career by being weak. So out of the ordinary was his demeanor that not one of the assembly made a single noise. This was a shock, but other aspects of his character would expose themselves in the days to follow. From his place on the quarterdeck he stared them down. He held two pistols out in front of him, aimed into the center of the melee. In his sash were two more. From this range he could not miss. Any one shot could pass through one of the tightly bunched men and kill a second one. His voice was not loud, his words cold, "If any one of you moves against another, you will die. If you do not drop your weapons now, you will all hang. Today."

Following a slow beat of understanding, knives, cudgels, belaying pins, and even a sword rattled down onto the boards. The officers and a couple of crewmen quickly moved among the combatants and picked them up. Strell and a number of others stayed where they were and watched the drama unfold. One man at a time, the officers marched the bloody crewmen up to the captain and stood them in a line before him. As they waited, breathing convulsively and heads hung low, the captain consulted in whispers with his officers. A wave came aboard the ship and spread the black fluid farther across the planks with its spray where the old seaman lay stiff and forgotten.

When they had agreed among themselves as to the eight men who bore the blame, they separated five of the men from three others and tied them to the rail, on deck where they were exposed to the weather and could be seen at all times. Mugs and Brock were bound close to each other, face to face. It was decided that these five men must be put ashore somewhere since they would without doubt cause more trouble in the future and could even resort to mutiny. There were islands to the south suitable to the purpose and the captain plotted the way and ordered the helmsman to set a course heading to take them there. The other three, followers all, were, unfortunately, needed to sail the ship.

Strell and his man learned much from this incident, including the fact that they now had extra duties since the prisoners not only did no work, but had to be guarded and fed. They were nonetheless excited by this very unexpected happening. Both of them had heard that troublemakers were often left to make do for themselves on deserted shores. Sometimes they were picked up by passing ships, but more often they starved or were killed by natives. This was to have been a routine trip when the two friends could learn about sailing and ships and begin their careers. Its effect on them both was so strong that Strell and his man spoke about it from time to time during the ensuing years and Strell pondered it often. He asked himself how he would have done something versus how it had been done. Could that captain have handled the men in a different way? Flogged them? Hanged two of them, but saved the others? And what of his treatment of the deceased? He had immediately pitched the men overboard. Strell thought at the time that he too was afraid of the sickness, but later discerned that the Captain simply wanted to remove any reminder of danger to his men. His ship was quarantined, isolated by the sea itself, so get on with business, that was Strell's take on the captain's actions and orders. Shipboard routine reestablished, the men went back to their duties, glad of the work for once and believing the worst was behind them. A greater shock awaited the two young men, one that made them who they were.

Two days later, the ship moving slowly down the coast, the lookout called below to tell of a sailing ship on the horizon. It was on a westerly bearing and as it came into better view was calculated by the captain to pass close to them. The officers held out their glasses and peered cautiously across the waves. Every other vessel on the ocean was a potential threat, especially to a cargo ship like the *Christian Frederick*, heavily laden and poorly armed. The captain did not relish freeing the men he had secured to the rail, but might need to do so, and might need to give them weapons if it came to a fight. Small light chasers, positioned at bow and stern, were the only canons on board and they would be useless against a warship. Or a pirate. From what they could see, the approaching ship was large enough to carry thirty to forty heavy guns.

A consortium of businessmen owned the *Christian Frederick*, men who, when they learned of it, would already harbor displeasure over the disease and death of the old sea dog and the resulting shipboard brawl, not to mention the death of four others in the fight and the resulting marooning of five men. Any of these incidents could affect future trade and profits. Grudges settled and retaliation made were costly. A man might survive punishment, escape from the island, and one day seek revenge on the ship's owners. His family might take legal action and insurers and financiers abandon the owners, marooning their ships in their own home ports where they would die—the same punishment given to the miscreants. No one wanted to send their goods off to their customers aboard a cursed ship or do business with a poorly run company.

The eyes of the crew strained across the space, all looking for one thing—a black flag. The man in the cross trees called out again, relief in his voice, "British! She flies a Union Jack." Though still wary, the captain instructed his mate to pull in sail and prepare to greet the approaching ship. He knew that they could never outrun or outfight it in any case. Plodding away from the wind, the ship slowed and turned east. The other craft was seen to be altering her course to come about. Strell and his friend climbed the rigging to watch and hear what would transpire.

When the ships were alongside of each other, Captain Arnold immediately had a longboat lowered and went to visit his fellow captain who stood waiting at the waist of the large ship. The men bowed slightly toward each other, talked privately for a moment, and then went below decks. The crews stared at each other and waited. It registered in Strell's mind how few men there were on so large a boat as this. The ones who were there were ordered roughly about by a tall dark man whose eyes and manner were bold and sure. He carried a whip. "Guillaume!" The dark man looked back, stroked the coils of the whip, and answered, "Aye, captain." Arnold, holding a large pouch with both hands, at once climbed down to his boat, came back to his ship, and thereupon spoke decisively to his officers. With speed and determination they untied the five prisoners and had them ferried over the waves to their new home. With care both helmsmen began to maneuver the vessels away from one another, but within clear view and earshot Strell and everyone else on the *Christian*

Frederick witnessed an unearthly event. Lines of coal-black men, fastened to each other by cruel neck and ankle chains, were led onto the deck for their weekly look at the world by the man called Guillaume. His whip snapped with uncanny accuracy as he nipped cuts across the shoulders and backs of any man lagging along. The watchers gaped and strained out across the gunwales to see as another line followed, this one a long bracelet of young, mostly naked women. Strell gripped his man on the arm and they climbed a few feet higher up the shrouds and leaned out to see. Guillaume's eyes gleamed as he peered at the bent and cowering girls and casually, gripping the thick shaft of his whip in his hand, laid dark welts over the bellies or breasts of some of them for no reason at all. More horrible to the men of the *Christian Frederick*, however, was the sight of their former shipmates being added to the line of men, lengthening it by five stripped, white, quivering bodies. Hammers rang with finality as pins were driven into their collars and leg irons. Strell saw too that a dozen or more men, all armed with rifles and swords, had emerged from their hiding spots on the deck of the ship. Apparently they had been at the ready in case threat or opportunity changed the interaction between the ships. As they moved off and the harrowing screamed pleas of the newly enslaved faded from their hearing, the men of the *Christian Frederick* looked back at the poop deck. A mate called Ford stood there alone, staring grimly ahead, the other officers and Captain Arnold having retired to his cabin.

No one dared say a word about the incident. Nor did a single man of them fail to jump at any order, but only executed it smartly and without comment. Only when the ship stopped to unload its cargo in the Caribbean and shore leave was granted did the men dare to gather and talk. Strell and his friend followed along, sat at a rough table in a dank inn, and listened to the opinions of the older hands. Most of what was expressed was inspired by fear, drink, baseless theory. "This is one a' them ships as is cursed." "We're to be sold as well, mind." "We'll all be hanged as slavers." "I say it's the plague— what got the old man an' killed him. We'll be next, an nothin' we can do but pray, mates." They stewed in their juices until they were joined by the junior officer of the ship, a man not much older than Strell. It was Ford, and they saw immediately that he was drunk and disgruntled. Two sly crewmen eyed each other and welcomed the man, offered to buy him another mug of ale and had him sit among them. Before long they had learned what had happened that day. The ship flew a British flag but was really owned by a French privateer who showed, depending on his longitude, the colors that were to his advantage. He carried a sea chest full of various flags for just that purpose. Across her stern was a board incised proudly with her name, *Vainqueur*. Britain ruled the Atlantic and stood neutral in the American war over slavery, even though it was the official position of the Crown that slavery was wrong and ought not to be tolerated. *Vainqueur* was a captured and converted old English warship, her name changed, packed with slaves from the coast of Africa and bound for the West Indies. Ford had overheard enough from the other officers to piece together most of what had transpired. The two captains had explained their positions, found mutually agreeable terms, and struck a deal. Arnold got rid of the troublemakers, received a heavy sack of gold coins for his trouble, and the captain of the slave ship upped his inventory with strong, healthy men who would be prized by some of the islands' landowners. Both men were more than satisfied with the trade. Upon his return to the ship, Captain Arnold settled some of the gold on his officers, purchasing their loyalty and most importantly, their silence. Ford, held in low regard by Arnold, was left out of the bargain.

Strell did not dwell on the remembered faces of the five men, nor on the echoes of their panicked screams, but rather mulled over and over again the acts of his captain. Without any consideration for them, Arnold had condemned the men to a brutal life and a certain death. Set off in a small boat or left on an unknown shore at least they had some chance of life and survival. Slaves did not; they had pitiful lives and mercifully early, unmourned deaths. What had Arnold felt at those moments when the idea of selling the men was conceived in his mind? Did he ever regret what he had done? How did the slavers reconcile these gross acts in their souls? He kept seeing the dark man, Guillaume, with the whip, caring for men no more than if they were dogs. Tracing a sign of the cross on her form, Strell's eyes moved over the *Christian Frederick*, from the tip of her mainmast to her waterline, and from bow to stern as she stood dockside back in her home port. Relief washed over him after he had disembarked and he watched curiously for a minute thinking he saw the ship strain at her mooring lines as though anxious to get back to sea.

More valuable than the newly gained knowledge of sailing and his small lay from the profits of the voyage was his understanding of what could be accomplished by cunning and imagination. View the world through Captain Arnold's eyes and everything was clearer.

Their carriage rattled along as they neared their lodgings. Surely Arnold and the slaver never felt what Strell did, his man thought, when he purchased slaves from O'Neill. They would never have felt what Strell would feel when he had the rich woman from Boston in his hands. Many thoughts tortured Strell, but of one thing his man was sure. On this brief carriage ride the past had been relived, but had not changed.

CHAPTER 7

Awakening

When her eyes opened Elizabeth didn't know where she was. Then she sat up in bed and saw the young man, the surfman, rolled up in a blanket and sleeping on the floor in front of the fire. It made her sad to think what she had done to this young man. He had no idea what was happening to him. She, herself, was just beginning to understand what it was all about. LeFrank had never been forthcoming about his business—her business, really, since she owned most of it—but had always just said that what was involved was men's work and men's affairs, and that she would be told everything when she reached her majority. Women had no standing. They couldn't vote or do much of anything except be a wife or mistress or work for others. Many unmarried women became prostitutes; many worked at menial jobs for pitiful wages, their stomachs never filled, their bodies cold, and their hopes fading day by day. No need to worry or question things, LeFrank said, the business flourished with him looking out for it and for her.

She had never thought about it, and being powerless anyway, had instead chosen to concentrate on the other part of her life, with Nana and her schooling. Life for her had been music and literature and art, learning about everything in the world but never venturing out into it. It was what she and Nana preferred. They were self-sufficient, happy in their own world, a world of their making. Nana refused to let her become selfish, however, and they gave to the poor and attended church, and made clothes and fixed meals for the needy. There were maids and cooks and gardeners and housemen to help, but they did a lot of the chores around the house themselves. Nana wanted her to know everything, and know how to do everything she would need to be the head of a grand house. Now, at twenty, she had a classical education of great depth and breadth, but no worldly experience. She was adequate as an artist and played the piano and sang for enjoyment. She had spent ten years with concern for little else; knowledge, curiosity, diligence in her efforts to learn and memorize and understand, these—and helping others—were her work and her play. Nana was mother and teacher, best friend and protector. It never occurred to her that those days would ever end. She had not lived long enough to possess anything other than a subconscious idea of a mindless immortality.

But now there was a new reality. Guillaume LeFrank was a criminal. It made her feel sick to let her mind drift toward thoughts of what specific things he had done. She kept thinking about the list of names scratched desperately into the wood of the *Hathor*. She was at a loss as to what she could do about it. He probably had paid off the local politicians and constables. She stared hard into the dying fire as she remembered the judges and councilmen who had been brought to dinner at her house. His guests. People who had most likely taken his money and looked the other way. There might be no authority she could rely upon to help her fight him. She had to go back to her home, but didn't know what she would do when she got there.

She looked back at the young man who slept the sleep of surrender, there by the fire. He had no idea about this, but now she did. Things fell into place in her mind. There were memories of comments made by members of the household staff, Nana, a few of their guests. She tried to bring to mind times when she overheard Nana and LeFrank arguing about her, but couldn't remember them exactly. Like breadcrumbs dropped along a path in the forest, these recollections led her to a better understanding of what LeFrank was and what she was up against.

The young man rose. "Miss?" The look of concern on his face faded slowly as he saw that she was sitting quietly on the edge of the bed. He looked around the room to see if everything was alright and without the betrayal of self-consciousness reached over his head with the backs of his hands together and stretched himself from the tips of his fingers to the tips of his toes. Elizabeth thought he looked like a diver who was upside down. She thought of a painting of a man she had seen, pulled to a long length by the artist's brush, with his fingertips resting on the surface of the water, about to pass from one world into another at the end of his dive.

He crossed the room and stopped by the bed and put his hand into his pants pocket and then held it, his fist closed, out toward her. She didn't move her head, but only lowered her eyes from his face to his hand. When he opened it Elizabeth saw a collection of amber glass

beads and a length of gold chain. Her hands flew up and she placed her
fingertips along her collarbone. She shook her head from side to side
and began to cry. She didn't cover her face and she just said the words
"no, no" over and over. After a long time, she stopped and reached out
and took the remains of her necklace from him.

He spoke softly, "I found it in the tub when I emptied it. You
were sound asleep. It must have been inside my clothes, the ones you
were wearing. Probably fell out when you undressed." He was a little
embarrassed to be talking about this and changed the subject. "Tell
me about the necklace." The softness of his voice helped to calm her
and make her feel like it was okay to let this part of herself out for
him. She knew in the back of her mind she was going to keep most
of her story a secret. The less he knew about her, the better. It would
be unfair to him to involve him further. If she stopped now and went
no further into this, the surfman could go back to his life. He could
forget about her. She didn't know what he had done or said, but
feared he would lose his job because of her, or be disciplined in some
way. She had to get away from him as soon as possible. At least then
he wouldn't be at risk from LeFrank.

"It was my mother's. It is the only thing of hers, a personal
thing, that I own. There was no value to the necklace, only that it was
hers. She wore it on her neck and it reached to her heart and it makes
me think of all the things she did wearing it."

"I can fix it for you. I guess some of the beads are lost. I looked
around outside and in the clothes. Tomorrow I'll look in the boat."
He tried to sound hopeful. He wanted this woman to be happy. It
was inexplicable how much that meant to him. He would do anything
to see her smile. Or hear her laugh.

She just nodded and toyed with the beads in the palm of her
hand. She rolled one of them between her thumb and forefinger.

Jack decided she should rest more and get used to him and his
place. He knew she was afraid to be out in the wilderness, alone with
him. "Come outside and let me show you what's here and then we'll
get an evening meal and a good night's rest." He leaned in closer to
her and she watched warily, suddenly alarmed by the look on his face.
She said, "What is it?"

"The cut. It looks better. It stopped bleeding."

She touched her forehead, drawing the tip of her middle finger
down along the bumps of the stitches. When it reached her eyebrow she
stopped and then used her hand to smooth the brow, grooming herself

unconsciously. She had forgotten about the cut, the bleeding, how he stitched it up. There was a soft, pleasurable soreness she felt when she touched it. She looked around. There was no mirror in sight and she felt silly asking for one so she only said, "Good...thank you."

He handed her a bulky coat from a peg on the wall by the door. It lapped fully across the front and had inside and outside buttons and loops to keep it closed. She took the belt he offered and cinched it around her waist and tied it in a loose knot. The sleeves were long and it was very snug and warm. His mother's boots were made to fit with the addition of two pairs of socks. She ran her fingers into her hair, combing it out to cover her ears and neck and drew her hands up into the sleeves. She closed her eyes for a minute and thought how terrible she must look to him. Thin. Scarred. A horrible tangle of hair.

Jack led her outside.

There were stars overhead. You could leave the earth behind just by staring at them. The smell of the fire hung in the clearing, different from the way it was in the cabin, and Jack nodded his head toward the woods for her to follow. She was frightened of the woods, the night, the loneliness of this world. She had never seen such absolute darkness. She walked close on his heels, terrified of losing sight of him. They kept on walking until they came to a small clearing. "Watch," he said.

She went to him and they leaned shoulder to shoulder against a large tree, looking at open land and the slow river that divided the area. She knew to be quiet. Soon she was aware of things moving out beyond the grasses that lined the edge of the water. She looked at Jack and he would indicate with his eyes, or the mere incline of his head, or his smile, where to look. Deer. A raccoon. Some unknown shapes and splashes in the water. They were not alone after all. She was scared, but his smile made it easy for her to relax somewhat. His teeth were very white against his tanned skin and looked whiter for the intense darkness. Her interest in knowing about everything allowed her to forget for a while the situation she was in, and she whispered questions to Jack about the noises or about the shapes of a few birds passing overhead. The water was tidal and the smell of the marsh was strong. The city had its smells to be sure, but not like this. She found it pleasing in an odd way. She felt like she was touching elements. After a while Jack straightened up and whispered for her to follow him. They walked out from under the tree and he stopped and looked up at the sky. There was no moon and their vision had adjusted completely to the starlight. She had never seen the heavens like this.

"Someone spilled paint up there."

Jack nodded, "Mmmm." They stood side by side for a long time, watching, out on the edge of the planet. She was more at ease on the walk back to the cabin and some of the noises off in the woods she found more interesting than startling.

Inside, Jack restored the fire and lit a lantern. Its glow didn't reach far into the corners of the cabin. They were confined to a small area, the light keeping them close together.

"I want to help with the dinner," Elizabeth said.

"Good. Let me get the game."

"Game?"

"Well, rabbit. I snared a marsh hare while you were asleep. I didn't go far. I wouldn't leave you alone. I could see the cabin and hear you if you called." He rushed the words.

"Oh, yes...I mean...I was surprised that you could get something to eat that easily. I'll dress the rabbit." She went to the table and waited for him. "What do you have here?" She looked around the cabin. "Let me fix the dinner."

Jack was pleased she was recovering and at the same time a little worried he wouldn't have the ingredients she would want. He surely wouldn't have what she was used to. "I have biscuit, peas, rice, uh...vinegar, salt, sugar, coffee, tea, pepper, beans and lentils." He went to a cupboard and looked in, then peered down into a bin by the fireplace. "There's some oil, and corn and dried fish. Salted. Cornmeal. A can of lard. Venison. Onions, potatoes, flour. Some canned goods. And, oh yeah, some cheese." He looked up, his eyes questioning her. She picked up a knife and waited.

Except for a few times when she asked him for water or a pan or a utensil, or if he had some ingredient or other—none of which were in his kitchen—she worked confidently at preparing a meal for them. He admired the deft way she moved and handled the tasks. It took a while for the lentils to cook but Jack didn't mind. She concentrated on her work and he rested his chin on his hand and leaned on the table and watched her. At the edges were vague thoughts of his mother and father.

He couldn't remember a meal he enjoyed more. She was very pleased when he told her so. Although she didn't smile, he could tell. When they had cleaned the table and dishes it was late and they were both very tired. He turned his back to her and she slipped on one of his mother's nightshirts and climbed into the bed. She closed her eyes and listened to his movements. When he dimmed the lantern she pushed herself up on one elbow and looked at where he lay by the fire. His back to her, his body was a silhouette against the flames.

"I can't let you sleep on the floor with just those few blankets."

Jack rolled over and looked up at her. "I'll be fine, Miss, don't worry."

"No, it would be rude of me, and I was not raised to put someone out of their own house and bed."

"You should rest. You fixed that supper and did all of that for me…I'll sleep fine here."

"I insist." She stared at him. Jack sat up. He had no experience with dilemmas. You did what you were told. Things pretty much were or they weren't. He was not going to put this lady on the floor while he slept on the bed and yet he could see that she was unyielding. It would be a relief to have her on her way and get back to the station.

They watched each other. After a minute Jack got up. Elizabeth waited while he put his boots on and wrapped a coat over his nightshirt and fired up the lantern and went outside. When he came back inside he was carrying a long, thick board and a handsaw and hammer and nails. He held the board up to the side of the bed to measure it and scored the wood with the point of a nail. He knelt on the board on one of the benches at the table and with long powerful strokes cut off one end. The sharp saw sang. They both liked the sound it made.

"Did you ever hear of bed boarding? Or bundling they call it?" Jack pitched the scrap of wood onto the fire. She shook her head.

"It's what people did on the frontier, the early settlers. One family would visit another and their children, or young people courting, would share a bed. They didn't have extras. Move over and pull the covers over and I'll show you." She moved to one side and he placed the board on edge in the middle of the bed and nailed it in place at the foot and head of the bed. The hammer cracked and the bed shook as he pounded the spikes in. It was a bit of rough carpentry, but it worked. For a minute she just stared at him and he was afraid his idea was going to make her mad at him. He thought how stupid he had been, that she would never let him get into bed with her. Then she understood, "Clever."

They were both a little embarrassed at the whole procedure, but once they were settled and were sharing the covers they were both happy. She felt safe and warm; he was working to calm himself. Being so close to her was intoxicating. He didn't think he was going to be able to sleep. As he drifted off he thought about the dinner she had fixed for them. He realized he had been leaning on the table just the way his father had done, watching his mother.

CHAPTER 8

Fugue

"Nana Nana Nana nnnnnnnn." He was in an instant fully awake. He sat up in the bed and looked over at the huddled form on the other side of the bed board. Elizabeth had rolled herself into a tight ball, knees to chin, arms squeezing calves as if she was trying to break them. He didn't know what to do. It was coming light outside, yet she was in a deep sleep, mumbling strange sounds, and shaking and crying. He feared she was having some kind of fit, and didn't know what to do about it. Surfmen learned various forms of first aid, most of it rudimentary, and already obvious to anyone with common sense. On any frontier, people knew how to do for themselves. He jumped from the bed and went around to her side, thinking only that all he could do would be to see that she didn't hurt herself. He was unsure about waking her, thinking it might be better if she got out of the fit or nightmare or whatever it was on her own.

She surprised him by a sudden uncoiling of her body, stretching it out into a long rigid form, like a forest sapling that could be snapped over one's knee. Worse, she began to scream, making deep, fearful sounds that seemed larger than her body could support. Between these unintelligible calls, her chest heaved and her hands clawed at her face. "Nana…no, no…unh, unh, women…unh…" Jack thought he heard her saying names, then, as he leaned toward her, was sure of it: "Victoria, Lilly, Margery, Anna." It sounded as if her throat must be bleeding. There were other names he could not catch, marched out from her lips in a sing-song that reminded him of his short time in school when as a group the children in the class chanted out long, repetitious rhymes to learn their lists of sums. Her speech paced faster and faster and turned to gibberish.

Jack watched all of this and wanted to stop her from grabbing at her face. He thought she might hurt her eyes or bite her tongue, but was partially relieved to see her relax a little and was reassured when he saw that she was breathing alright. Against any reason or expectation, she was suddenly awake.

"Get away from me!" Her eyes flashed at him and she slashed out at him with both hands. He was out of reach, but leaned back instinctively, shocked by the violence of her screams as she warned him off over and over. He held his hands out defensively, trying to calm her, "Miss, it's me, the surfman. You're safe. It's okay, shh, shh, you're okay, okay…I'm here. There is no one to hurt you. I'm here." He talked softly, fruitlessly, against her yelling. Then, as if he weren't even there, she fell back into the bed and cried for herself and her fear and her despair.

Abruptly, she turned away from him, faced the middle of the bed, and pressed her forehead against the board. He moved to the foot of the bed and could see that her stitches were being pulled apart. She clutched the coverlet, slid it over herself, and retreated into the curled position in which he had first found her. Jack didn't move, lest he rouse her again. He waited for the heaving of the bedclothes to subside, and could tell when its slowing tempo showed him that she was sleeping. Maybe not peacefully, but sleeping. Up until this time she had been wary, intense, worried, yet always courteous to him in a strange, formal way. Was she a madwoman? Escaped from some legal custody? An asylum? Had he interfered with her handling? No, he couldn't believe that was the case. Yet what could account for this bizarre behavior?

"Do what you have to do, son." Tom Light often said that to young Jack right here in this room. He thought about the dictum now and tiptoed away, gathered his clothes and moved close by the warm ashes lingering in the fireplace to put them on. He forced himself to relax his clenched fists and his hunched shoulders and he wiped the sweat from his face with the sleeve of his nightshirt. He wanted to dress, set the fire, get more wood, see about some food, have something to drink. Each step along the way he stopped, waited to be sure she was in the same position, and then continued. Soon he was moving about the room in a nearly normal way, doing the usual things, only more cautiously and with deliberation. None of what he did seemed to affect her. He wanted to hunt, to have some good food for them, but dared not leave her. She might hurt herself, run off and be lost, forget who he was and what had happened.

She barely moved the rest of the day. Toward evening Jack worried about her waking during the night, since she had been asleep for so long a time. It would be best, he reasoned, if he stayed away from the bed, and when he had eaten and read a book by the fire for a short while, he blew out the candles and wrapped himself in a blanket and lay on the floor by the hearth. He had barred the door as usual, and placed one of the benches in front of it for good measure. He didn't think she would be able to move it without waking him.

Dimness replaced the total black of the forest night. It wasn't there and then it was. Jack opened his eyes and could see that Elizabeth was sitting on the edge of the bed, her back to him, her head downcast. She was as still as death. He got up and said softly, "Hello, Miss, it's Jack. The surfman. Here. By the fire." She got up from the bed and went to the door. He decided to move the bench, open it for her, and wait. She walked outside, barefooted, and went to the outhouse. He closed the door and watched from the window. It was near freezing outside and some white patches of frost crusted the fallen leaves. He opened the door at her approach and closed it behind her. She paid no attention to him and sat at the table. Jack poured water from a pitcher into a mug and set it and some bread and cheese in front of her. He got busy with the fire. He saw that she didn't blink her eyes or show any emotion or expression. She ate and drank a little and returned to her place in bed. The cold came off of her bedclothes. He could see the leaf litter stuck to her damp feet, but thought better of mentioning it to her. She obviously didn't feel it. Muddy footprints marked her path back to the other side of the room. With the board in place, her back to him, and the covers stretched almost over her head, she was hidden from him. He decided that there were things he must do, so he went ahead with them.

Elizabeth could tell that she was alone in the cabin. She turned in the bed, dizzy and lightheaded, let her eyes open enough to see the light in the room and settled herself again. Throughout the day Elizabeth slept and emerged into a hazy wakefulness, over and over. She dreamed about her home, saw parts of some of the rooms, servants walking in and out at the edge of her dream vision, heard sentences which never reached their ends. She saw her table laid out with her beautiful dishes, bearing meat and vegetables, waiting for her...Nana and LeFrank said the same things again and again. "Of course the young man is interested in her. They all want..." "No," LeFrank boomed back, "It is for me to say..."

"But it's time…"

"No, it is for me…"

"The young men…"

"No men around her!"

"She's beautiful…the young men…"

"I will tell you what…"

"You won't stop young Parsons. He asked me if he could court her. Asked me for her hand. He is in love with her and thinks he only needs to spend time with her to convince her of his worthiness. He…"

"No! I hired you, Miss Whitehall, to protect her and educate her, not sell her off to some society pretender. She won't do anything but what I demand of her. Unless I allow it. Understand? You'll do what I tell you or suffer the consequences."

Some of it was dreamed, some remembered. All of it was real.

The piano. She was practicing in the next room. When she paused to turn a page in the music she could hear their harsh whispers. Snatches of debate, arguments over her. Heard things said while she looked over the notes. Someone had written those notes, blots on a score, running up and down little lines on paper. Those lines were like fences that contained you, or rails to keep you on track. They told you the direction you must take, where to start and stop and pause. Quickly, louder, lower, in harmony with another, they said. The composer, dead for decades, was still able to make Elizabeth do what he wanted her to do. Place your fingers there, hold that note, play softly, feel the passion of the music, fill yourself with it, fill the world with it. Build, build, hold, tempt, faster, endure, endure, release, crescendo, fall away in a dream.

Then harsh words. Nana was angry. Elizabeth had never seen her angry, not with her, but she could hear it, feel it. Telling LeFrank. What? Nana and LeFrank, like the composer, telling her what she had to do. What was it? Something… Then everything was gone.

She woke again. There was someone in the room. The surfman. He went in and out. She fell back into sleep and into the river of dreams. Nana was standing up to LeFrank. Defying him. Telling him that Elizabeth no longer needed him. He was merely Elizabeth's employee. The company was hers, not his. He should no longer come to the house. Leave her alone. More of it came to Elizabeth: Nana telling the man Elizabeth would do as she pleased now. She had no use for a guardian. There were some men her age who called upon her, their purpose obvious. There was young Parsons. He should no longer come to the house...

All of it was clearer to Elizabeth now, even in the remote time and place where she lay, than it had that day when she heard the words. Jack became aware of her change of attitude. She all but ignored him, but he could see the resignation in her manner. She was like a child's cloth doll, torn, missing the stuff that once held it up, slack in its look and spirit. The day wore on and Jack ventured a little farther from the cabin from time to time, looking for food, and watching to be sure they were alone.

When it was dark, she called to him, "Here, sleep here. I'm sorry. Sorry. For all of this. I didn't mean to do this to you. I'm sorry, sorry." She didn't look at him, curled on the stones. He heard her crying. It seemed she was crying for him, and not for herself. He sat up on the hearth and saw that she had pulled the covers away from his side of the board. He was relieved that she had emerged from the lost and hidden world that had held her for the last two days. Her ravings had told him nothing; they were bits of sound that named people unknown to him, cries of pain inconsolable, fitful sleep and horrible dreams that tortured him as they did her. He was almost as grateful, he admitted to himself, for the chance to sleep in a warm bed as he was that she was again at least aware of what was happening. Jack settled himself in the bed and tried to reassure her, "You're safe. I'm here to be sure you're okay." She made a small sound. He wasn't sure what she said. Then she was asleep and he soon joined her.

CHAPTER 9

Love Songs

He had slept, and slept well. It was the fatigue and the stress inside him, the cold cabin around him, and the warm feather bed over him, he thought, that were responsible. He slowly inched his way up into position so that he could look over the board and see her. It was all he could do not to reach over and touch his fingertips to her face. Dark hair flowed away from her. She was clear and fair and her wide-set eyes rested under long lashes. It was impossible not to imagine kissing her. Oh God, he thought as he slowly let out the breath he had been holding. She breathed a slow and regular rhythm; she was off in a land of peace. Finally. She had had a harrowing few days—escaping from the ship, spending a cold night outside alone, coming here with him, raving inside herself for the last two days. He hoped this peaceful state would last. It was making him nervous doing what he was doing. He could not take his eyes off of her, but he didn't want her to catch him looking. It seemed wrong, but only slightly, like something you could justify. How could anything he thought about or did with this beautiful girl be a sin. She had become the object of a craving that until a few days ago he did not know even existed. No, everything about her was good. It occurred to him that he had been nothing but nervous the entire time he had known her. It also occurred to him that he had the muscles of his face and neck and shoulders flexed into one big unified grimace. It was painful. He laughed at himself as he relaxed and he thought how foolishly he was acting. Some of the lines from the songs he knew danced into and out of his mind. So that's what that line meant, he thought as he remembered bits from the love songs and the ballads about courtship that the men sang in the long days and nights of living as surfmen. I guess it does feel that way.

"What is it?"

He was surprised to realize that she was awake and staring into his eyes.

"Is everything okay?"

He smiled at her and nodded his head. "I was just looking to see if you were still asleep."

The small lie passed unnoticed. She stretched and moved up so that she was even with him. They both moved their bodies and pulled at their nightclothes and shifted the covers until they were comfortable. She grabbed at her hair, fluffing it up, and rubbed her eyes and yawned. She pulled the covers up to her chin. They turned their faces toward each other. She settled and he did as well. Both of them smiled. Hers was embarrassed and she looked away and combed her hair with her fingers.

When they were both staring straight ahead, toward the front of the cabin, she became serious, "These past days...I'm sorry...it was more than I could..." she cried softly. "It was too much for me..."

"Here, now, there's nothing to cry about. You've cried enough. I think it must have been what you needed. Before. These past days."

She dried her eyes. They were quiet for a while.

"It's so quiet here."

"Is it noisy where you come from?"

"Yes...the city. There is always something, someone, making noise. A whole range of noises, in fact." He was tempted to tell her she could stay, but wanted to hold her in the mood she was in. It was one he had not seen. "I think the words come from the same idea. City and civilization, that is. There is a root word meaning those in cities are civil. Being civil must involve making noise."

"Then I guess those of us who live outside of cities are uncivilized?," he said with mock seriousness.

She was pensive. "It's all backward, isn't it? Here it's quiet and people are nice. There it's noisy and there's a policeman on every block. I think civilization is being confused with wealth or commerce or culture. Something like that."

"So I'm nice but lacking in culture, is that it?"

Her face relaxed into a faint smile. "I wasn't talking about you."

"Oh, it's all the other people you know hereabouts. They're the ones you mean?"

She lifted her head to look at him with amusement bright on her face, raised her eyebrows as high as they could go, and nodded her head. He saw her scar wrinkle up, but the stitches held. She had not expected repartee from the surfman. They settled back, quiet for a moment. He thought about Old Gunn, what he would say if he saw them, in bed together, more or less, talking about culture before the sun even rose fully to its place in the sky. But all of this was foolishness and soon he knew she'd be gone and he'd return to duty. Still, Jack wanted to know about her. He decided to talk about himself to see if he could draw her out, her memories reciprocal to his. He thought back to the beginning, to the few earliest things he could remember.

"When I was little I cried a lot. Some babies are fussy, or so my father always said. He raised me, my father did, after my mother died. She was healthy and strong, but got the influenza, and it was too much for her. But we were happy. She sang with me and we played games and I helped her with the chores." Jack paused for a minute and then went on, "It was a shame…she died just when I really could help her, not just pretend, like when I was growing up. I never remember crying when I was small, but I cried when she died. I was just seven years old. I remember crying then. But I was always happy, except when she passed away. My father made sure of that. From that time on I was with the surfmen almost all of the time. Another man had a place that was his Harvard College and his Yale. Mine was the barracks and the boat and the ocean and the bay."

She nodded in thought. It was hard to picture living here, alone. She longed for her own home.

"I didn't know my mother. Too young to remember her. I don't even know how she died, only that she was sick. My father was older and always away on business. So my world…my civilized world," she added with a small pretty laugh, "was inside myself. I was raised by a nanny, a governess she was called, who became my mother just by devoting herself to me. She gave her life to me and lived for my happiness." Elizabeth cocked her head away to the side and then turned again to look at Jack. "She's gone now too. I know that."

Jack didn't want her to be sad or talk about the unhappy parts of her life. He steered the way back to the conversation they had been having. But he wondered about what she had said. What had happened to her governess? "Did you ever run and climb trees and fish and play tag?"

"No, my running was all through the pages of my books, and up and down the musical scales, and across the scenes drawn and painted by artists. It was all there inside of me. Besides, there were no children for me to play with. But Nana, my Nana, she challenged me with hard games of words or mathematics. She made me learn languages and read the philosophers and know the histories. Science was the hardest, but in a way I liked it the best. She talked about the time when it was possible for a man to know everything there was to know. She meant the principal theories and general doctrines, you see, not all of the individual facts. I think she wanted that for me. I worked around our home, but none of it was as practical as your education here."

They each thought to themselves, wishing they knew what the other knew. They learned that they both spoke French. He tried out his French on her and Elizabeth came to realize that the man in bed beside her was not just a poor, uneducated laborer. Indeed, she was taken with his easy wit and unconscious confidence.

"Your French is far better than mine," she said.

"Ah, but yours is more civilized!"

"Sans doute."

They stayed in bed, comfortable, talking and enjoying each other's company. When they got up, they knew they would have to face their lives again, each deal with the situations that their crossed paths had brought to them. So they just settled in and told each other what they remembered about growing up. She had a faint accent to her voice and he couldn't pinpoint where she had lived, but guessed that it was New England. When the time came to rise, Jack left the bed and said he would go outside to get some wood while she got up and dressed. He told her to call him when she was ready. When he got to the door she said, "Elizabeth."

"What?" He turned to look back at her.

"My name. It's Elizabeth."

Jack's face lit up with a huge smile. "I'm Jack Light." When he closed the door he said her name to himself several times as he walked to the edge of the clearing and began to load his carrier with firewood. He wasn't paying attention and he put so much wood in the canvas sling he could barely lift it. He laughed at himself and lightened his load. It felt good to have the fresh air on his face and draw the sharp cold into his chest. As he worked he remembered LeFrank and his men. They had called her a whore. He could not conceive of any other woman in the world being as refined and perfect as Elizabeth. How she come to be involved with them?

CHAPTER 10

The Raven

Jack worked outside, taking his time so that Elizabeth could do whatever she needed to do in privacy. His mind wandered and he thought back to the day, a little over a year ago, when he and all of the other surfmen had learned a profound secret, and seen a broken man restored and made well. Why had this memory come to him now, he wondered? Jack believed that the soul was the part of you that supplied your next thought. It was where you faced things and made decisions. His soul must want him to think on this. He pictured the day. It had been a quiet period. Mild weather was being kind to the surfmen. The days were easier and there was less work to do. Time relaxed on its way by.

The Atlantic was never at peace for long, however, always ready for the seduction of the wind and pulling allure of the moon to arouse her. Even then, the grounding of the ship was only partly from the windy weather and the restless water and the mischief of gravity. The best sailors, including the blue-water mariners who had tasted the air over all of the earth's seas, even those men ran aground at some time or other. They knew the thing to do was get a pole to the bottom, see if they were on rock or sand or mud or a wreck, and get off as quickly as possible.

It was a clipper ship that carried the grim story of David Marshall to the surfmen on the Delaware shore. She was a great beautiful ship, proudly running south when her tacking brought her too close to the edge and she grazed the long side of a ridge of sand just south of the station house. Even the most cautious and expert seaman could fall into the traps set for them by the sea. Speed was a temptress. The captain of the ship had run this route many times before and reckoned he had her far enough off shore to move freely with good wind and a right sea. Ezra was called to the lookout tower and he peered through the glass in the mid-morning light. The ship was called the *Mercury*. He could see her name on the stern. From her topmast a long blue streamer adorned her and below it her American flag stretched itself out in the sun and wind. She was a wooden ship with some square rigging and a sharp prow, made to fly through the sea like she was more of the air than the water, 185 feet long and needing a crew of thirty-eight to make her behave. Her crewmen could surely see the station clearly, but made no signal. Ezra decided to send a boat out to her. It was good, he thought as he climbed down the narrow dark stairway of the station house, to go out when you were sure you would come back.

When they pulled alongside the *Mercury* the men in the surfboat were amazed. They had never seen a ship like this one. It was beautiful. It looked new and it was decorated with intricate carvings of people and classic scenes and motifs and they could read the verses and maxims inscribed along the trim, the indentations that formed the letters filled with gold paint. Fleecy sheep rested in the wood as swift horses ran by and doves flew overhead, all brought out of the planks of her sides. Many of the ships that plied the waters along the coast were old and worn, creaky and loose, with tattered canvas, rotting hulls, and ragged crews. Many looked to be on their last voyage. There were many magnificent ships as well, but this was not what they were accustomed to. The surfmen looked about and then at each other, smiling and shaking their heads in wonder.

Above them a voice called out, "Hail to the surfmen…come aboard, every man of you." His voice was a boom. It smiled. The men looked to Ezra. None of them wanted to miss this. He shrugged and raised his eyebrows and shook his head up and down and the men tied the surfboat fast and scrambled up the rope ladders that *Mercury*'s crewmen had lowered down the side of the ship.

What they saw from their vantage point at the waterline of the vessel was forgotten when they got on deck and had their footing. Around them was a ship that was more like a piece of fine furniture than a working craft. The wood of the cabins and doors and hatches and railings had been rendered as works of art. Gentle curves and soft turnings ran to powerful brass plates and supports. Everything was clean and shining. The bright work was electric. Ezra and his men looked around them. The men wore a kind of uniform, not military, just plain shirts and britches. Each man stood at ease, acting as if he were the captain. It was clear, however, who that man was.

He was the oldest and, like many a man of power, he had presence. He was smiling too and he walked among the surfmen and shook their hands and welcomed them. "Welcome to the *Mercury*. Tell me your names, please, so we can record them in the log of visitors to our ship." Ezra Stock was speechless. The stationmaster thought to himself that when you thought you had seen everything, then came a comeuppance.

"I'm Ezra Stock," he finally managed. Then Ezra named the rest of the men, calling out and pointing to each of them as he did. Jonas Hope and Jack Light and Ben Wolcott and Old Gunn and George Kimball and Edward Chase. When he was finished, the men noticed that the captain of the *Mercury* was staring at George Kimball. Kimball's face was red and his fists were clenched. His lips were pressed tight. He didn't look at the captain. He stared at the deck.

Suddenly the captain called out, "My name is David Marshall." With that he walked directly across the deck and knelt down on one knee before George Kimball and said to him, "I beg your forgiveness. I would give my life to you now, on this spot, if you demand it." All motion stopped. Both crews stared in wonder. Kimball raised his eyes away from the spot on the deck where they had burned and looked for a long time at the man. He nodded his head and reached out and helped David Marshall to his feet. They embraced each other and then stepped back and stared into each other's eyes. Very old tears moved slowly down their faces. They just looked at each other and nodded and wept and wept.

Their last time together had been a harsh, horrible day of pain and blood and death. On that day perished their friendship, their trust, their careers, and an innocent young man like them. George Kimball and David Marshall were raised on adjoining farms just west of the city of Baltimore. Lilting hills of corn and tobacco and low rows of summer crops surrounded them. Their families helped each other at harvest when the fields were full and the late summer winds formed swells and breakers on the wheat tops. The boys walked together to the same school, sharing their learning, as well as their living. Any time they got to go to the city they begged their parents to let them go to the port to see the ships. They drew ships, modeled them, dreamed them, and finally, went together to enlist in the Navy to serve on them. As young ensigns they were assigned to the warship *Raven*. The captain of the *Raven* was a stupid and hate-filled man named Baldwin. He equated cruelty to discipline and was a man with no friends, only acquaintances. Baldwin's men feared him and despised him. They performed with precision, no man wanting to risk his notice.

The *Raven* was making its way south in the Atlantic under orders to patrol the waters around Cuba, and stopped to take on water and fruit on the north Florida coast. When the men were back safely aboard, Baldwin gave the order for the ship's crew to move offshore a short way and fire their cannons toward the land as a training exercise. Hitting various trees and rocks and other features on the beach would be a test of their marksmanship. The captain's order was repeated by the first mate and the word moved down the line. *Raven* had two gun decks. Ensigns Marshall and Kimball were assigned to be gun commanders of two adjoining batteries of cannon starboard and aft on the first deck. The two friends stood side by side in a thick cloud of acrid smoke barking orders to the crewmen—the loaders and rammers and sponge men—and changing the loads and the inclination of the guns in order to correct their aim and send the heavy round balls crashing into the wall of trees that stretched before them. *Raven* was like an old ship of the line and her sixty guns did not swing left and right, only up and down. It was breezy and overcast. The *Raven* was moving very slowly as the helmsman and the men aloft worked in unison to hold her steady and parallel to the shoreline for the firing. She shuddered as the explosions thundered from her sides and the big guns rolled back from the ports with each shot. The gunners were finding their marks and the trees and rocks ashore were shattered under the assault. Giant smoke rings rode the wind.

In the midst of the exercise Marshall looked to his left where Kimball's men were reloading his closest gun. Knowing that one of his crews was ready, he screamed over the noise of the shooting, "Fire!" The report was an enormous boom and he didn't hear George Kimball call to him, "No!" As the cannonball whistled out of the muzzle the recoil sent the gun rolling back on its carriage. What Kimball had seen was a ship's boy, a powder monkey, bending over to set down a bucket of water. He was bent over and slightly behind Marshall, and Marshall had not seen him. The back of the gun hit him with such force that his ribcage was crushed and his neck broken in an instant. He dropped to the deck, dead. Hopelessly dead. As battery commander Marshall was responsible to watch everything to do with each shot and be sure all was clear. Marshall couldn't move. He stared at the small fair boy, probably not fourteen years old, lying broken on the deck. This lad's job was to bring round balls and powder, canisters and water to the gun crews. Marshall's mind told him over and over that he had killed someone. He had murdered by neglect. Some great force had cursed him and he feared he would suffer damnation for something he didn't do. He never intended this. Down the side of the ship the guns roared and rolled back on their chassis, ready to be swabbed, loaded, pulled forward and fired again. He didn't hear the other canons thundering or smell the burning powder or hear the yelling of his shipmates. The body of the thin young man whose spirit had only just left him was warmer than Marshall's. George Kimball immediately ran along the line telling the men at each battery to cease fire. The silence brought the officers and the captain of the ship below to the gun deck. He found Kimball at the center of the group of men that surrounded the dead boy. He was kneeling down holding the young man in his arms.

"Who gave the command to stop the firing?"

Kimball did. "I did, Captain."

Baldwin flew into a rage. "You'll pay for this. No man disobeys my orders."

Kimball stood, looked to David Marshall, his friend, for help. Marshall, who had caused the boy's death, was ashen, and his eyes landed on nothingness, his ray of vision stopped in a void between him and everything else. His eyes would not meet Kimball's.

"But sir," Kimball began. "The lad is dead, I…"

In a fury Baldwin raised his fist and shook it inches from Kimball's face, "What is that to me? You dare to override my order, to question me. You'll be lucky if I don't hang you."

Kimball looked about, but none of the other officers or men would meet his eyes. They had shrunken into themselves. They seemed as insubstantial as the wisps of smoke drifting from muzzles of the guns that now too stood silent and looked away. Murder weapons with nothing to say. Had they tried, the men could have heard the pounding of the rage and blood in the captain's chest. The swollen veins along his neck twitched and pulsed in dark anticipation. Baldwin turned to his first mate and told him to secure the gun deck and bring the prisoner, as he now referred to Kimball, to stand at the aft mainmast. The men, these men who thought themselves to be brave warriors, followed, terrified. When they were on deck the captain mounted the quarterdeck and looked down on them. They were huddled in a semi-circle. The men were close and deathly quiet, but Baldwin screamed at them.

"If there is a battle and a man falls, he is to be left where he is until his body can be disposed of. You are useful to me when you are alive. When you are dead you are just refuse we must throw overboard. Sure we'll wrap you up pretty and play a tune and read some words, but all you are is dead. Like an empty barrel or a spiked cannon. That's all that boy is now. I don't even know his name, nor do I care to, except to place it in my ship's log. And then all he is is a blot on you. He is your failure. And failure is to be reckoned with.

"Do you know what the men of the Roman legions did to those who failed? If a man was found sleeping on watch, or stealing, or ignoring an order? He was stoned to death by the men of his cohort. His blood brothers. He was given what he deserved. That is what I am going to do right now. Because none of you bastards, you cowards, are strong enough to do it. Your mothers wombs were polluted with you!" His voice was a shriek.

Jack felt a shiver, just like he had the day when this story was told. He looked at the cabin, but there was no sign of Elizabeth. He wondered what she was doing. His mind went back to the day when they had boarded the *Mercury*. He remembered every word of the story Kimball and Marshall had told that day and, as he waited for Elizabeth to call to him, it played itself out in detail.

George Kimball looked around for David Marshall, but couldn't see him.

Just then the captain called out his name. "Ensign Marshall."

Marshall stepped forward from behind the mainmast and walked up to the front of the group. No one moved. Kimball looked at his friend, hoping the captain would ask about the incident and discover what had happened, and that the truth of the matter would help him and Marshall out of this.

"Marshall, you and the prisoner are friends. So I am going to give you a chance to show what kind of man you are. I am going to let you be the one to flog him." The men on the deck all stood still, their eyes darting at Marshall and then quickly away. They were rigid, afraid to move. They all knew this was wrong; it had been an accident. They were now going to be forced to witness a perverted act.

Marshall stood silent and numb. This was impossible. He knew that if he did anything or said anything Baldwin would have him beaten also, maybe worse. The contingent of infantrymen aboard the ship stepped forward and with a nod from their lieutenant they did their duty. Kimball was stripped to the waist and bound wrist to wrist with his arms around the mast. One of the marines beat a dirge on his drum. The whip was pressed into Marshall's hand. The captain called for twenty lashes and warned that they be good ones. Marshall stepped up to his friend and Kimball stretched back as far as he could so that he could twist his head around and look at him. Kimball pleaded with him with his eyes, but there was no reaction from his friend. The ship drifted and the sheets flapped and faint shadows made patches of dark and light on the deck. Marshall drew back and brought the leather through the air to land with a sickening crack across the exposed flesh. Blood ran freely at once. The drum pounded with the running blood. Once started, he seemed in a hurry to get it over with and he stroked again and again as the men counted and Kimball cried out and each time there was a new welt and more blood and flecks of his friend's body splashed back and spotted his face and went in his mouth and stained him and then it was twenty and Kimball's bowels let loose and he hung unconscious—some thought dead—from the base of the giant wooden mast. Marshall looked up at the captain. He smiled and nodded his head to Marshall and then turned and spoke to the first mate to set a new course. Baldwin made his way down the hatchway to his cabin. He poured himself some brandy and trembled slightly as he slowed his breathing and looked astern. A white churn drifted aft. He had to hold the glass with two hands to bring the fluid to his mouth. The men were relieved to be able to divert their attention to the ship's business. Eager to be aloft, they monkeyed along the footropes and let the sails out. They had descended into hell and now climbed toward the heavens, getting as far away from the ship as they could. They would whisper about this later. Every one of them thought in his heart of mutiny, or desertion, or at least of getting out of the service as soon as possible. But they knew that the voyage they were on would be one of years, terrible years marooned on a ship run by a madman.

The ship's surgeon was summoned and he ordered two cabin boys to throw buckets of seawater onto George Kimball to wash him and wake him and they stripped him of his britches and sloshed the filthy, runny shit off of his legs. It mixed with his blood and sweat and ran down the scuppers to become part of the sea. Kimball cried silently. No one could bear to see the look on his face. It folded in on itself to hold the sadness.

Sorrow is the greatest pain.

In the doctor's area below decks Kimball was treated more gently. It was not the first time the doctor had treated a poor soul who had been scourged to the edge of death by this captain, although it was rare for an officer to receive such treatment. The doctor mopped the blood and held presses on him until the bleeding gradually stopped and then salved and bound his torso. He gave him laudanum to hide the pain from his mind. For two days the *Raven* labored southward and Kimball languished in his rack. He heard the pipe play when the dead boy was dropped into the water. The weather was lousy. No one came to see him. A cabin boy brought him the food the common seamen ate, no more of the better fare from the wardroom. Even the doctor, though gentle and attentive to him, wouldn't speak to him. He had become a pariah and he knew there was for him no future aboard this ship.

About halfway down the length of Florida, the ship anchored for the night, Kimball stole away from the floating hell. He stowed his clothes, some cork floats, a few bottles of medicine, and the tincture of laudanum in a sea bag and slipped over the side and slowly, painfully, paddled his way toward the shore. In an act of mercy, the doctor, having looked in and seen his patient missing, and knowing what had probably happened, did not report it until dawn. Even then he reported it to the first mate, asking innocently if he had taken Kimball and returned the ensign to duty. He did not mention the missing ditty bag or the stolen medicines. Following a vain search of the ship, the captain happily made an entry in his log, calling Kimball a deserter. This placed a death penalty over him and tarred his name.

David Marshall buried himself in an endless sadness. He had killed a young boy—his shout, his order had done it. Except for what was required of him in the performance of his duties, he never said a word to any man for the remainder of the time he was under the command of the monster aboard that cursed ship. Except for one time, at the end. None of them would, in turn, ever look at him. He was even able to keep from the officers and men the strange thing that had happened to him. He had lost feeling in his right hand. It was as if his heart could not bear to support the instrument that he had used to beat his friend. To kill him. They wanted to be together and be on a ship and be upon the sea. Now neither would have any of that. Worse, Marshall felt sure that his friend was dead, lost at sea and gone down into the deep in a hopeless effort to escape. Marshall was certain Kimball could never have made it to shore, not after the beating he had given him.

When Kimball awoke he was tangled in the brush at the edge of the beach where he had crawled, exhausted, sometime during the night. His back throbbed and he was all but overcome with hunger and thirst. He crawled back to a spot where he could look out to sea and also north and south along the beach. He feared the captain would have search parties looking for him, and he knew that if he were caught, he would die kicking at the end of a rope before the day was out. He held still and watched and watched, but the ocean was empty. Finally he fell asleep and lay motionless for another hour. The sun burned him awake. The mosquitoes had feasted on his face and ears and arms and one of his eyes was swollen shut.

In the days that followed he found water and then fruit and then was able to move further inland. He could put on a shirt and move with less pain, but even in the heat his soul was cold and damp. He used the drug to help him to gain sleep, meting it out every night until the bottle was empty. When he came upon a group of farms he was able to sneak into the fields at night and get vegetables. He stole eggs from hen houses and ate them raw. Solitude and loneliness slowly drained him of life and he cried at night, mostly for the loss of the friend he had loved. He never cursed Marshall for a coward; he only mourned his loss. David would never have hurt anyone—the boy had been where he should not have been. But Kimball knew that they both had been raised to not make excuses, to take what was coming to them. That was what made Kimball's bitter disappointment so profound. David should have told the captain what happened. Then, if he had been treated unfairly, he could have decided what to do. Both men would have given their lives in the performance of their duties, but neither would have willingly submitted to inhuman treatment. Marshall should have come to him, then come with him, away from the ship. He wondered at the fate of the men who stayed aboard the *Raven*. Before the voyage was out, Kimball wagered, all of the men on that ship would envy him.

He had watched several of the farmers in the area and there was one who he thought he could approach. It must have been the look of him, and the way he worked hard every day that made Kimball choose this man. At midday, with the strong Florida sun overhead, when the man had stopped work and moved off into the shade for lunch and a short rest, Kimball walked out of the cover of the palm trees and scrub and came up to him. Kimball looked like a beast. The farmer, whose name was Morgan, did not seemed alarmed, and stared at him curiously.

"Can I talk to you?"

The farmer shrugged, nodded slightly.

"My name is George Kimball. I'm out here alone, with all I have in this bag. I've been stealing food from your crops, and from others, to keep alive. To be honest...there was some trouble, but it's over now. I never hurt anyone or anything and until now I never stole anything in my life." George looked around them. "If you can use a hand, I'd like to work for you. Just for a place to stay and for some food. To pay you back, and then some. It's...well, just say I was raised on a farm...you wouldn't have to show me anything, and I can fix anything and handle stock, and..."

He stopped talking when he saw that the farmer was handing him some bread and moving along the log so Kimball could have room to sit. Morgan was a religious man and Kimball's confession had struck him. Earnest truth is easy to see and know and the farmer was sure that was what he was hearing. This was a chance for Morgan to do good for his fellow man. And he did need help. Few people lived in the area. It was a frontier for the time being, waiting for the railroad barons to connect it to the rest of America. This Robinson Crusoe was the first of the many men Morgan would eventually employ. Kimball ate the bread first and then prayed his thanks. Kimball did nothing else in those years but pitch himself into helping this farmer and his family—every day a day of atonement.

Ezra and his men sat on *Mercury*'s deck, perched on rails and barrelheads and gangway steps, and listened as Marshall and Kimball told this story. They took turns, and despite the hundred eyes fastened onto them, the two men confessed this long, intimate, and wandering tale to each other as if they were alone. They held nothing back, telling each other what they thought at the time, confessing, explaining. Marshall's crew was as astonished as Stock's. Both groups had always known that these two men were in some way extraordinary, but the story they were telling them was one none could have imagined. Some of those listening were remembering things about these friends, things they had seen and heard over the years and nodded to themselves in their minds, that they now knew or understood what they had witnessed, what was heard, what was meant. The ship creaked its interest and the waves slipped by slowly and quietly, as if listening.

David Marshall walked around the deck of his ship and spoke of the days that followed Kimball's disappearance. He was speaking more to his crew now than before since they knew nothing of this event and little of his experience in the Navy. Some of his men had brought a cask of ale out and brought a cup to Kimball first, then served Stock and the other surfmen, and then the others of the ship's crew helped themselves. Kimball leaned against the mainmast and listened to his old lost friend speak. As Marshall told his parts of the tale, little shocks of pins and needles twitched in his right hand. Something he had not felt in years. "I read a quote in a book that said, 'The Navy is the asylum for the perverse, the home of the unfortunate. Here the sons of adversity meet the children of calamity, and here the children of calamity meet the offspring of sin.' I don't want any of you to think that. But for the mean spirit of one man, George and I might have lived our lives as Naval officers, happy with the service and the sea we had always loved. We're both in a service now, and we are both united with the sea. And in answer to my many prayers, we have met again." As Marshall said this last, Kimball nodded in agreement. Marshall began to cry again and had to wipe his eyes and stop before he could say more.

"We were bound by our oaths to the service and subject to its law. In the Caribbean we fought some small battles with pirates, chasing and catching some, losing others. Two years went by. Things were unbearable on the ship, as there were more and more beatings and punishments. I served in silence through it all and was left alone by the captain and the other officers. The only words I spoke were orders for the men and they obeyed, but never looked me in the eye. They couldn't stand to look at someone who had brought death and shame into his soul, as I had. Once, in a storm, I stood on the foredeck and let wind and waves thrash me and hoped for God to wash me overboard and kill me. Other times I prayed to God to let me go on and do someone some good in my life. And then there came the time when I was past care. We came upon a slave ship carrying poor, wretched people only recently stolen from the islands. Her name was *Afreet*. She was drifting in a queer way, and as we came along the side of her we saw that it was the slaves themselves trying to sail her. It was a plague ship and the captain and crew were all dead or dying and the slaves had torn the ship to bits to free themselves. Some had pieces of plank hanging from their shackles where they had ripped the boards of the hold apart in order to escape. But they couldn't sail the ship and there was little water or food aboard."

Marshall stopped to drink from his cup and continued, "Baldwin was terrified. He thought of the disease, whatever it was, and what it had done to the crew of the ship."

All of the men on *Mercury* stared at Marshall as he told the story of what happened that day. Baldwin cowered behind the ship's rail. "Move off! Helmsman, to starboard!" The men jumped at his order and as *Afreet* foundered *Raven* turned slowly away. The men and women thus abandoned wailed and pulled at their hair and ragged clothes and stretched their arms toward the retreating ship. Their cries were as horrible as anything you could hear. They turned to their medicine man. They believed his obeah shield had killed many of the slave masters while, like a pagan passover, it had protected most of them from the sickness. Now they doubted his magic. At the first sight of the American flag flying from *Raven*'s lines, the people had rejoiced, knowing they would be saved, set free, maybe even returned to their homes. After all, the story of the recent Civil War was known to them and slavery was supposed to have ended.

When *Raven* was clear, the captain ordered the ship to move upwind and come about to a course parallel to *Afreet*. He stood on the poop deck and screeched his order to the men watching him, "Sink her. Now. Strike her at the waterline and blast her to hell."

"No!"

Marshall's voice thundered across the deck as if in its years of rest it had gained a supernatural power. The two men stared at one another, their gazes locked. Baldwin's eyes and face were red, the pink hot red of unlimited hatred and rage. Marshall was calm. This was the end for him, and one way or another, he had freed himself. The men knew it. The captain too.

"God damn you, Marshall, you will hang this day. No man can command me. On this ship I have the divine right to rule over you. You are sworn to obey." He looked to the small troop of soldiers who served on the ship and ordered their lieutenant to seize Marshall and bind him hand and foot. Marshall did not move a muscle. Nor did the lieutenant. Their immobility held the rest of the men fast. Baldwin screamed and stamped and threatened, and when he could go on no longer and was wheezing and shaking speechless at the rail, Marshall spoke. "We are going to help these people. If you don't agree, I will put you aboard that ship and leave you with them. Then you can help them sail it. Alone."

Baldwin stared with dead eyes at nothing and lowered his head. The men of the ship all turned and looked at Marshall. They gave him silent thanks. Now they had to trust him to make this decision, one he had made for all of them, free them, not condemn them to death. No one noticed the captain skulk down to his cabin. Marshall was still an ensign. He turned his head to the three men aboard who held a higher rank. As one they saluted him, making him the leader of the band of men who were all, now, mutineers. Every man aboard the ship, except for Baldwin, had, without a word or even the slightest movement, become a criminal, and sentenced themselves to death.

Under Marshall's command, the men brought the *Raven* near to the crippled ship. He shouted orders to the few slaves who seemed able to understand what needed to be done and they pulled in all the sail so that they came to rest on a smooth rolling Atlantic. Marshall stood at the front of the longboat that worked over to *Afreet* and was the first man aboard her. His ship's doctor followed. When they had taken stock of the conditions they found there, they put the dead to rest below the waves and fed the living and gave them water. *Raven*'s carpenter came aboard with his tools. They freed the captives from their chains and put them in hammocks to rest. The ones who were able gathered around Marshall and kissed his hands and in various languages thanked him. He knew their words as if they had spoken in tongues.

Marshall looked around at the band of sailors and surfmen.

"You wonder what became of the men of *Raven*. I sailed her back to the big island and some of our crew stayed aboard *Afreet* and helped her follow and make land there. Her passengers were freed and the few slavers who were still alive did not stay that way for long, once they were taken by the governor's men. We filled our stores and turned north, sailing home. Along the way I went to the captain's quarters and told him what to write in the ship's log. Without a word he obeyed. Many pages were torn out and I kept them. Everything on those sheets testified against him in his own hand. I made sure no word of trouble with the crew remained in the book. The other officers corrected their personal logs as well and they all gave me signed statements about what had happened in case we ever needed to defend ourselves. Baldwin knew he could never command the crew again and he stayed below. Though none of us ever said it aloud, he knew and we knew that he could not condemn us when we came to port. One of us would have killed him; every one of us would gladly have done it to save the others. His word would never have stood. I heard he resigned after that and no one knows or cares what happened to him.

Marshall hung his head, but spoke in a loud voice, "My greatest sin, one that dwells like a devil in my soul now, is that I cannot in my heart find a way to forgive him. I have killed a lad I didn't know and abandoned a man I loved like a brother, and I carry a mark of Cain as the worst coward that ever walked on boards over the sea. Those sins cannot be undone and can never be forgiven, for I am unable and refuse to forgive myself. But I could forgive Baldwin, and am not yet man enough to do so. I am still a coward."

Jack thought about the words Marshall and Kimball had said that day. He wondered if they had felt what he was feeling now, for he too had broken a trust, and he too could not see a way to undo what he had done. He looked again at his cabin and admitted to himself that he didn't want this to end; he wanted Elizabeth to stay.

For some days after that, *Mercury*, freed from the bar, rode at anchor by the station. Kimball and Marshall spent many hours alone together on board and walking along the shore. George recounted his steps, told how he had moved from Florida slowly north, working here and there until he came to the Delaware coast and settled. He found contentment, something most men never realize, and then, from this new peace, he learned to travel across the great distances in the universe within himself. He learned he could have another life, be a different person to those he came to know. The Lifesaving Service gave him everything he needed, sustaining him while he served its purpose. The acts and words of the men were an unraveling of the human code. He learned from living and working with them what bits and pieces he was made of. How they fit together and warred with or assuaged each other. Morgan still wrote to him with regularity, always offering him land and a partnership in his large collection of farms. Kimball had at his own insistence lived in the barn for the first year he spent working there, in a kind of self-imposed penance. It was not the guilt for stealing from Morgan and the other farmers he felt, but the uneasy pain of the soul that lives deep inside one who feels he has failed. Morgan could tell that the man who had come to him from out of the wilderness was, at heart, a good person, lost for the time being, but a man who would find his way. Several years later Morgan gave him his house and moved his wife and family to a new larger one more central to the operation Kimball was building for him. In that time Morgan became very wealthy and he tried repeatedly to give half of his gains to Kimball, but was refused. Morgan gave Kimball's share to his church. It was enough for the parishioners to build a splendid new place of worship. Kimball never knew it, but his name was written on a cornerstone and on a carved wooden plaque with gold paint mounted at eye level in the middle of the sanctuary.

During these years, Marshall, having resigned his commission, also returned to the land. He too had a new energy and worked ceaselessly at the business of farming in an effort to put time between himself and his memories of life at sea. Eventually he was given a large sum of money from his family holdings and he decided to try to relive his dream of commanding a ship. His ardor convinced several investors to risk the large amounts of capital needed to launch such a venture. He built *Mercury* and found men willing to sail her for the life and the adventure and a larger than usual share of the profits from her trade. Sometimes she carried passengers, but mostly she delivered goods to port cities in the Americas. She helped the US Revenue Cutter Service with rescues and reported suspected smugglers and pirates. Her commercial success was great.

Marshall had changed the *Raven*'s log to show that his friend George Kimball had served bravely and had died while saving others. He was officially noted as lost at sea. Irony in the truth. The story he told the Kimball family gave them a kind of peace. George explained that he had never contacted his family, fearing that they would have been shamed by his desertion. They might have rejected him or, knowing he was alive, tried to help him. He felt no good could have come from this knowledge in any case and he wanted to protect them. He did not want to be apprehended and executed. He had tried himself in his mind, in his own court of law, and knew that he did not deserve death. The silent tribunal over which he presided was flawless. As judge, prosecutor, witness, defender, and accused, he knew all of the truth with certainty, something that never happens in life when there is more than one man involved.

The two friends talked about each member of the two families and Kimball was overcome with joy and sadness as he heard the stories of lives known long ago and, for him, stopped without resolution. He had new family members and had lost ones dear to him—children he had not greeted and old friends gone and not mourned. He could not decide whether to reunite with them and told David he would wait until later to think what he should do. "I have a new family now. They are as dear to me as anyone could be. I cannot say."

Jack stared without seeing, thinking of the day *Mercury* sailed. All of the surfmen and sailors had enjoyed visiting each other. The visit had become a celebration. It was a thing few people in the world would ever experience. They could not grasp what Marshall had done and lived through, and in their minds George Kimball had become even more than he already was, a man to revere. Afterward he talked about David Marshall as his sainted friend. Many times in the quiet evenings at the station, Kimball, at the urging of the men, told them other pieces of his story.

Then Jack remembered where he was. Was he like Marshall, a betrayer of principles, untrue to those who had brought him up? Or had he been brave and his "bravery" merely cowardice? Had this girl made him into someone who would be an outcast as Kimball had been? He looked back at his house. The sun came off the glass and reflected in his eyes. He couldn't see anything.

CHAPTER 11

Lamp

Newport News

Waves of light came to him, but in his worry and fright O'Neill did not register what he was seeing. *Hathor* was now in plain sight, and yet he didn't recognize her.

"Ship!"

The cry came from a lad named Lamp, a layabout who seemed to live nowhere but always managed to keep alive, apparently by doing odd jobs and begging and using his nimble fingers along the docks. Things left for the taking were quickly taken in the harsh world called the waterfront. All of the characters within earshot of his cry, around the docks and on the various ships in port, turned their eyes to the east. Some of the lookers were merely curious; others, not interested in a visit from a Cutter Service ship, were apprehensive. O'Neill struggled up the rigging of the *Luluwa* and squinted into the eastern sky. It was a large ship, no question. He came back on deck and pulled a glass from its sleeve. Resting his elbows on the rail to steady himself, he held the long brass scope to his eye, extended it, and twisted the image of the vessel into view. Big. Black. Its masts rigged strangely. Pushing the world out of its way and coming straight in, having to tack only slightly to keep on course. *Hathor!* Now everything would go as planned. Get this damned woman from LeFrank and into Strell's hands or bed. Let him do whatever he wanted with her. Thinking of Strell made him look back toward the city, trying to reassure himself that Strell wasn't lurking nearby. Maybe LeFrank had some others on board to make things sweeter. More money for him and more girls to make Strell happy. Get the "cargo" on shore for him to inspect. Get the gold from Strell and give LeFrank his share. Then he would see if there was anything he could sell to LeFrank to carry back on the return trip. His storehouses were full of questionable goods, boxed up and ready to go. Profit at every turn was what he wanted. It was his delicate handling of these two men, bringing them together while keeping them apart, and especially his brains and cunning, he said to himself, that let him survive the danger and profit mightily from it. He congratulated himself and allowed himself a smug smile.

In every business since commerce began in the long-ago reaches of the world, there were good times and there were bad times. Times were harder now that the Cutter Service was putting pressure on his trade. The thought lurked in his mind that maybe some of the privateers were gone because the Cutter Agents had gotten them. In fact, the ones who bought the slaves from him were almost all gone. As were many of the runners that brought them to him. God damned northerners. He had enough to keep things going, a pretty good book of trade, but you always had to have new suppliers and new customers. Success was never final, and cash flow was the name of his game. This was a deal he needed and two customers he needed to satisfy. Buy from one and sell to the other.

It was late in the day when the ship anchored. The Newport News Harbor was crowded with ships and *Hathor* swung at the edge of the channel used to access the harbor. O'Neill had a crewman run up a signal flag to show the *Hathor* that it was all clear and waited for LeFrank's men to launch a longboat to bring him over to the *Luluwa*. As they approached, O'Neill recognized the two rats LeFrank traveled with, Salete and Chien. He greeted LeFrank but ignored those two and left them on deck to wait. When O'Neill turned his back, Chien crossed the deck, went down the gangplank, and slipped into the regular traffic of carts and vendors and seamen who moved about their business along the docks. The workday was drawing to a close and he moved unnoticed. Without a word the two ship's captains descended into the stern and sat down for the dinner that awaited them in O'Neill's quarters. His servant put wine before them and filled their glasses and with a glance from O'Neill, left the cabin.

"Do you have the 'special shipment' ready?"

"Most of it."

O'Neill looked up sharply, "What do you mean?"

"She's gone, Clint."

O'Neill stared. He was not used to being called by his first name. Usually he was the only one who used it, when talking to himself, whether berating or praising. And he was afraid of what he had heard LeFrank say.

"What?"

"She jumped from the ship. We ran aground in the wind off of Delaware. While we were trying to get off the bar she tried to get to the shore. Probably chewed up by the fish by now."

"You mean you didn't find her?"

"It's why we were late. Looking for her. We went up and down the beach. No body. She's dead alright. Elizabeth Harrison, that cold bitch. Cost me plenty, the minx did." O'Neill noticed that LeFrank had an odd look in his eyes, a faraway look, like a man awake yet drifting in a dream world.

O'Neill wondered if LeFrank was up to something, had cut him out of the deal. "What the hell am I going to tell my man?" He leaned across the table pointing his fork as he spoke. "He'd as soon kill me as look at me."

LeFrank stared at the fork aimed at his face and then looked into O'Neill's eyes. "Raise your voice at me and point anything at me again, Clint, and when he looks for you he won't find you."

He lowered his hand and swallowed hard. Now he was in a spot. Between these two monsters. But why worry about LeFrank—Strell would kill him first.

"I don't know what you are going to do about him. And I sure as hell don't care. For me you're going to get the contents of my hold onto shore and into your warehouse, and give me my money. I can send you another whore for this man of yours the next time. My plan is the same, it's just modified some to fit these new circumstances. Not my fault if you don't have yourself a way out."

O'Neill buried his face in his hands.

LeFrank thought about Jane Barr, some of the others from the theater troupe he had been watching recently. He needed one with dark hair, the right age…

He thought about Jane Barr herself.

Suddenly suspicious, LeFrank said, "Wait. I've sent you lots of girls. What is it about this one?"

O'Neill kept his hands over his face and shook his head wearily. "I don't know. I've gotten him others before—never one of your girls—but from some of my other contacts, just barmaids and old cows and island girls he takes to the clubs on the Louisiana coast, I think. Sells 'em to the owners, maybe. He never says. I know where your girls went, but not any of his. But this one's different. When I gave him the picture you sent me, with her all dressed up fancy and rich, he got strange, he looked like he was hungry, and he just hissed at me and said, 'Get her for me.' Christ, it was like he was gonna' eat her or something."

O'Neill thought for a moment. "Maybe he wanted this one for himself, you know, to keep around. Like bedding a rich one would count for something...hah...give me one of your actresses...I don't want some 'lady' who thinks she's better than me. I'd like to have more of them theater girls."

LeFrank sat back in his chair, held up his goblet, and looked at the light from the lantern piercing the deep, red, bloody body of the wine. Turned just right, the glass reflected his twisted image and he smoothed his collar and smiled at himself.

"Was she the only one?"

"What?" LeFrank said.

"Are there any others on board?"

"No, no other women. Not this time."

LeFrank thought of some of the others, the ones he had sold. Mary Lytton, Lydia Child...that fiery one, Nora Godey. He remembered the ones who were so easy. They never even suspected what was happening to them. They were the amusements he loved. Toys. O'Neill chewed his lip nervously. Both men were silent. Neither man ate.

Outside the cabin, Lamp squatted down on the pier and pretended to whittle a scrap of wood with his jackknife. The sudden interruption in the conversation he had been listening to made him stay very still. Lamp had grown up in a state of constant fear, and he was always ready to flee for his life. He looked around to check on his possible exit routes. The talk inside the cabin resumed, louder this time.

"I can get you out of this. But it'll cost you."

O'Neill leaned forward, his forearms on the table, his fists tight.

"You have to keep him on the line a while longer. Like playing a fish. Give him this shipment a lot cheaper. Give it to him for half if you have to." He stared down the protest that spluttered from O'Neill's red face. "And that comes out of yours, not out of mine."

LeFrank leaned back in his chair and though about Elizabeth. He had arranged to become her guardian when she was ten and he was twenty-eight. LeFrank had insinuated himself into her father's company, running the ships, making the old man a lot of money. He eventually got a small share of the business. When Martin Harrison died ten years ago, LeFrank found himself the minority partner of a young girl, fair to see, and full of promise, and very rich. There is nothing easier than bribing a Boston politician and he saw to it that he became her guardian. He had laughed at the time that he had even used her money to do it. Martin Harrison's will was changed, papers were filed, judges were told what to do, and the girl and access to some of the money were entrusted to him. But he didn't have title to the ships or possession of the majority of the company stock. Once she was his ward he fired the entire household staff and hired Anne Whitehall, who became her beloved Nana, to tutor her and be her companion. She was a prudish, self-educated woman with thin lips, high-collared dresses, and hair forever concealed in a tight bun. Sexless. The perfect harpy to keep the girl safe. For him. She would develop into a prize, virginal, dedicated to him alone. He took her places to show her off. He gave her little gifts and pictures of himself to look over her. He had tried to hint subtly about her marrying him when she grew up, let her see him as her protector. Then he would have one of the finest women of the city to walk on his arm, and give him sons, and would at the same time be able to leverage her holdings to become one of the city's wealthiest men. But as she became an adult she had made it clear that she wanted no part of him. Subtly she moved away from him when he got too near, walking about a room so that she was keeping a piece of furniture between them. More and more she declined his invitations to accompany him to public functions. She didn't like riding alone with him in his carriage, or having Chien or Salete watching her. Whitehall helped reinforce this and fought him off, thinking she could protect the girl from him. Absurd thought.

LeFrank hated to be forced to take an action he had not been fully prepared to take. It was something that rarely happened. But Whitehall had encouraged an admirer of Elizabeth's to court her, and once LeFrank learned of it he saw the threat and was determined to eliminate it. He had Salete investigate the young man, Parsons by name, and quickly discovered what was afoot—Parsons' father was the owner of a couple of ancient and dilapidated sailing ships, and while he had a poorly run and struggling operation, he was acute enough to see the same opportunity LeFrank had seen. Parsons was a workingman with limited means and little in the way of prospects for improving his lot. His son, while handsome and able to put on a good appearance, was no better. He acted interested in everything she said and pretended to listen to her carefully, when all the while he had his mind on her money, his prospects, and her person, in that order. His appeal to Elizabeth, scant as it was, lay solely in the fact that he was unlike any of the others of her set, and while this was a paltry recommendation, he was pleasant, and in a way she was not really aware of, she liked the attention.

LeFrank weighed the benefits of simply removing the boy, but didn't know how many people knew of his involvement with Elizabeth, and did not want to become embroiled in a murder investigation, one the older Parsons would insist on should anything happen to his plan. He had acted quickly, sending the pictures of Elizabeth to O'Neill, deciding that if he couldn't kill the shark in the water, he would remove the blood that drew him. So she, herself, had decided what would happen to her; only LeFrank had meant to sell her, not have her drown. He hated to lose the price she would have brought, but more, he was furious at not having his revenge on her. Maybe he'd just use Jane Barr instead. Dress her up to look like Elizabeth and pay a visit to Father Barry for a mock wedding. Bring her down to O'Neill. Or maybe he would just bury her in Newport News and bring papers back with him, certifying her death, for the benefit of the bankers and lawyers and the courts. O'Neill could arrange all of that for him ahead of time—the man didn't care what he did as long as he was paid for it.

O'Neill watched the turmoil evident in the other man's face turn into a slight grin.

"How am I supposed to hold onto him?," O'Neill asked. "He's dangerous and he's insane about this girl. He'll kill me if I don't get her for him."

"He'll never know. I have another one just like her."

O'Neill looked about the small cabin, and he was so warm that despite the damp and chilly air that surrounded the *Luluwa* he was flushed and sweating. "What do you mean? A sister, or what?"

"I mean," LeFrank looked intensely at him as he spoke, "there is another girl who will pass. He'll never know. He hasn't met her. All he has is a picture. He won't know any different."

O'Neill was not so sure, but grasped at the hope this gave him. "Christ, I hope you're right, or I'm a dead man." He knew there was no worse criminal on the sea than Strell. Strell had seen to that, having his man get stories to O'Neill, illustrating how cruel and debased Strell was, how he became feverish when he hurt those that disobeyed him.

LeFrank shifted in his chair. "Tell him she was sick and couldn't make the trip, and that you'll sell him all of the rest of the cargo for half of the agreed price. Tell him she'll come with the next shipment."

On the pier, Lamp figured he had heard enough. He wrote the word on his hand to be sure he remembered it correctly. "*Hathor.*" Strell would be very interested in what he had overheard and he stood up slowly and brushed the wood shavings off of his britches. He stretched and looked around and then began to walk along between the pilings toward the bulkhead that kept the harbor and the land apart.

LeFrank didn't tell O'Neill the other thoughts that rippled beneath the surface of his mind like sea monsters in deep black water. He needed O'Neill. More than once he had taunted him by telling him there were others he sometimes used to accept his shipments. He told him that soon he would have several more ships at his disposal to work the coast. But in reality there was no one else so easy to manipulate, no one so close, no one he could be sure would take the women. He needed to keep on getting and selling the women. He liked having the actresses and then passing them on. He smiled to himself. How many of them had he "married" and then sold away? He couldn't remember them all. But they were easy prey. Most were easy to forget. Sometimes Jane introduced them to him and he told them he was in love with them and wanted to marry them at once. Sometimes he sent Salete, with his dark mysterious looks and charm. He overwhelmed these girls, whisked them away to the church outside of Boston and had Father Barry perform the ceremony. There was always enough money to convince the priest to accept what LeFrank had told him. These were LeFrank's protégés, he had said, women auditioning for parts in future productions LeFrank might be funding. He told the priest that no event was more charged with emotion for a woman than her wedding and that was why he used this setting to evaluate them. The mock weddings were carried on as if they were real, with Chien and Salete as witnesses and the priest playing his part and going through the whole liturgy. The women were overcome with it all and accepted what happened as their dreams come true. Their lives had been hard and this was their chance. They would love this rich husband who was going to see to it that they would have a life of fame on the stage. They saw themselves beloved by the public and by this wonderful man. LeFrank saw them as stupid, yet beautiful playthings. Playthings that paid well for a small, low risk investment.

With Elizabeth gone he might have to use Jane. With Jane gone he would have to find another like her to perform her role. It was easy to find jealousy and ambition in women like her. Someone would come along.

Barry liked the money. He didn't let himself think past it. Priests were always convincing themselves and others of something. This was easy.

LeFrank liked the taking without force. In fact, it was not even taking—the women gave themselves to him. They threw themselves into his arms and did everything they could think of to please him. These were beautiful, young, nearly perfect women whose faces and bodies and voices and talent brought throngs of people to the theater, happy to pay to see them. Chien and Salete stood as witnesses, but thought only of the days following the fake weddings, when they would go whenever they liked to the cabin on the *Hathor*, where women in horror scratched their names into the paint on the cabinet door.

LeFrank wanted to be known and respected by the people of the Boston business and society worlds, but even with the money that would soon be his, he needed to play in this other world and play with the people in it. Why live only one life at a time? Inferior people did that. He had been a slaver before he joined Harrison. In those days he sailed aboard the ship *Vainqueur* and the men under him obeyed him or felt the sting of his whip. It was always in his hands and he could use it to take a single hair off of a man's head or as easily lay open his back and kill him. He was still one of them. It was in his blood. There was no power like it. Selling one person to another. Murder was insignificant by comparison.

On deck Salete watched as Lamp shuffled along the quay. Salete looked down on him, sneering at this ragged bum, a young man who already looked old and tired and broken. Their eyes met for a moment and then Lamp looked down again. He had to concentrate on his walking. Make sure he did not be seen to hurry. Stay in character as a bent and pathetic figure. When he was on a back street away from the waterfront, he reached into his ragged coat and pulled out a purse weighted with coins and looked for a cab. He had to get to Strell as soon as he could, and tell him everything about O'Neill and his guest. Lurking along the quay had paid off.

Chien emerged from the shadow of a storefront and followed him.

CHAPTER 12

Murder

Newport News

Strell heard the commotion in the street. His man looked at him and Strell turned his head toward the window. Strell waited while he looked out of a crack between the shutters where a shaft of morning light was splitting the darkness.

"It's a crowd of some kind…something's going on." In the street the crowd grew. At its center was Constable Daniel Armistead. A Virginian through and through, he was formal, courteous, and a gentleman, despite what his occupation brought him in contact with. Today it had introduced him to a dead body, a young man without identification, whom nobody in the area seemed to recognize. People pressed in on all sides and some even jostled him in their efforts to see the body. It was something he never did understand—the fascination people had with misfortune. They had to see. They pushed. They stopped whatever they were doing. For the love of all that's holy, they even brought their children to see. What were they thinking? He muttered under his breath, "They're just happy it's not them, lying there in a pool of blood."

Just because he hated this part of his work did not mean he wasn't good at it. He turned to his two men. "Clear the area. Get these people to move back and start around the houses and shops to see if anyone knows the lad." His men started moving the people back. "Go on along now, there's no more to see. Let us do our work. Move, the lot of you." They had to say it over and over and hold out their hands to the more reluctant ones.

Armistead knelt beside the dead boy. He saw then that it was not a boy, but more a young man. Someone in between. It looked like someone had gotten him from behind and slit his throat. Whoever did it had done it before, that he could see. It was done clean, all in one motion, and the dead man, sure as could be, had probably never known what hit him. His pockets were empty, and if there had been anything in them, it was all gone now. Armistead stood up slowly and looked around the area. What was the victim doing here and why was he killed? Why rob someone who from the look of him would have had little or nothing worth taking? Of course people these days hardly needed a reason.

One of his men stood beside him. "What is it, Daniel?"

"It wears me down, Billy, these killings. People treating each other like dogs. I get tired of the meanness I see. And now this poor lad. He is ragged and unkempt, like someone with no home or people of his own. Why kill him, murder him, lay in wait for him?"

"Maybe they thought it was someone else."

Armistead wasn't too sure, "Maybe, Billy, maybe."

Armistead waited for the wagon that would take the body to the morgue. He had sent a runner to fetch the man but it would be a while before he got there. They never needed to be in a hurry.

Several doors down from where the body lay, Strell came over to the window and cracked the shutters wider so that he and his man could both see what was happening. Strell saw that the lawmen were coming his way. "Go out the side door and find what they want so we have an answer ready for them if we need one. The last thing we need is for them to ask us a lot of questions."

Strell watched the street. He saw his man as he slipped into the crowd from an alley a short block away. Strell admired his ability. He was a man no one would remember later, nondescript, unobtrusive, pulled inside himself. He and Strell often laughed at Strell's various sayings, like this one: practice being invisible, it's a skill you'll need later. It was a skill all of Strell's men had mastered.

While he waited for the wagon, Armistead took another look at Lamp and evaluated what he saw. He looked poor, but well fed. He had on a seaman's cap, but not the rough hands of someone who worked on a ship. There were, however, black marks like tar on his hands, and shoes, and in a few places on his clothes. And on the palm of his left hand was written a strange word, *hathor*." He looked closely to be sure that was what it said. And then he copied the word in his notebook, working the pencil carefully to be sure he had it right. He supposed it was a message or a code or someone's name.

Just what he needed, he thought, more of a mystery. In his experience, things like this initially made his job harder, but often, later, when they had tied the bits and pieces together, that bizarre item of information suddenly made sense and in some instances formed the keystone of their case, holding the other facts in formation, supporting them and making it all understandable.

Strell could see from his friend's face that there was trouble. Life can drain away from a face, and vanish like water tipped over onto sand. Strell's man stood there alive, but dead.

"What is it?"

The man leaned heavily on a chair just inside the door. "It's Lamp. Someone slit his throat."

The room filled up with silence.

"Armistead's there." Strell thought about that, how it might fit with what he was doing.

Strell's face was like stone. "Go out and wait. See where they take him. I won't go to the door when they come down here. I'm not going to talk to them…since it's Armistead involved. I'll deal with him later." As the other man rose to leave he said, "Ride to the docks and see what you can find out there. Lamp was staying close to O'Neill. If there is any hint that he was part of this…"

A tired and unhappy looking man driving an open cart came for Lamp. Strell stayed away from the window but his man watched as the body was placed onto the wood planks of the sad conveyance, next to another body, that of a young woman, and draped with a heavy dark canvas cover. Their feet stuck out at the end of the bouncing cart and they seemed to dance together as they were taken from the scene. For Lamp, unless Strell did something about it, it would be nothing more than a pine box and a place in a potter's field. No one would know his name or the story he had lived. He had been rendered a vague shape being carried away from his world, and not by an angel. It was Lamp's turn, one that had come far too soon, for him to truly become invisible.

Strell walked to the darkest place in the upper room and closed his eyes and stood clenching his fists in rage. Young Lamp had been important to him; he had been one of the ones that Strell had taken from the streets years before. Lamp had survived the horrible New York slum known as Five Points, had grown into a young man, and now this.

Later in the day Strell's man sat on a bench by the water, smoking a clay pipe and leaning his head back, like a man who had nothing to do but kill time while it was killing him. It's easy to do nothing. The only demand on you is that at every opportunity you complain about your luck, the rich, the law, what's wrong with the government, and everything else, especially the other guy. It's never what you do or don't do—it's always somebody else holding you down. He kept his eyes and ears open and noted what happened all along Water Street. Strell's man concentrated on the sounds. Only the breeze and the creak of thousands of yards of rope strung all about him, and man and animals jawing, only this chorus came to him. None of it told him anything he could report back to Strell. When he was getting ready to leave he saw the constable who had been looking at Lamp that morning. Armistead was moving slowly along the walk, stopping to ask questions of some of the men there. The farther he moved into the area, the fewer people there were for him to question; word of him moved faster than he did, and many of the players on the broad stage of the docks suddenly remembered things they had to do and other places they needed to be. Strell's man was no exception. Armistead could recognize him from the times Strell and the constable had had dealings in the past. He slipped back into a side street and moved steadily off into the shadows. He watched Daniel Armistead doing his job. If he was here asking about Lamp, which seemed likely, he had done well. There was no point in being questioned by someone who was as savvy as this fellow. Soon someone would notice Lamp's disappearance and talk, and the lawmen would have the answer they needed to focus their inquiry. Who knew what that would turn up or where it would lead. Yet, he knew also that it was just as likely, and maybe more so, that everyone the constable talked to would have a convenient loss of memory. At any rate it could make things tighter for Strell and his men. They needed to learn the identity of O'Neill's contacts. And Strell was looking for the woman. His man knew he was desperate to get the woman. He had watched Strell staring at her picture often enough and knew how important she was to him. Nothing was going well for them, he thought to himself as Armistead boarded a ship, several berths down from the *Luluwa*, to ask more questions. He would have liked to be where he could hear the questions and the answers, to learn about what had happened to Lamp, but there was no way he could see to do this.

Across the harbor, lying at anchor among some newly arrived ships, the *Hathor* was now concealed from view. LeFrank and Chien and Salete leaned against the taffrail. An array of ships hemmed them in.

Most ran under sail, but there were some steam vessels adding to the atmosphere of the harbor. Smoke swirled around and colored the air.

"Did you find out where he was going?"

Chien shook his head.

"Why did you kill him?"

Salete smiled to himself as Chien squirmed at LeFrank's questions.

"I couldn't risk following him no more. He was taking a long route, like he thought he was being followed. He took a cab at first, then got out and walked. I barely caught one in time to stay with him. Had to pay a lot to the hack to keep up for me." Chien looked expectantly at LeFrank, "Yes, a lot of my money. On foot it was even harder. The boy kept looking back. And doubling back. Like he knew someone might be there. We were all the way across town and suddenly he turned and came right back at me. I had no choice...he would have seen me when he got past me. Recognized me. The bastard. So soon as he came up I took my chance."

Chien grinned as he thought of what he had done. How well he had done it. The knife slicing through the windpipe and the weight of Lamp's body as he lowered it slowly onto the paving stones. Careful with his artwork. He lost track of the other two men with him. He thought about Elizabeth and that delicious moment when he was about to kiss her. Thoughts of Elizabeth and the dead boy gave him almost the same feeling.

LeFrank thought for a minute. "Maybe it's..." he trailed off, thinking of something else. How this could be connected with the girl. No one here could know anything about that. No, that was not possible.

"Where was this?"

Chien looked at him. "West, all the way to the end of the city. He went a long way around, but whatever he was up to, it was there he was going. Somewhere near where I got him. It's all just houses and small shops there. He was listening by the side of the ship, heard something. It's sure he didn't get to say what he set out to. I saw to that."

LeFrank seemed to forget what they had been discussing. He looked around the deck of the ship. He turned to look at Chien. "What I want you to do is leave here...now. Get out of the city. Take the train north, or find a ship, up to Delaware, and take a look around. Go up the Chesapeake. Buy a horse, maybe a wagon, like you're selling something, and stop at the stores and homes and shore stations."

He thought some more. "Find that lifesaving station. But don't go there, go to the ones near it. Those men travel between them. See if there is any word about us or about the girl. Did anybody wash up on shore. Find out where they live…the surfmen. Go to their homes. Find out about the young one, who said he saw a seal—I think he was lying about something. Then get on up to Boston and meet us there." He looked at the two men, stared silently for a minute, "Do you know the Inn of the Three Arrows?" They grunted assent. "We'll meet there."

LeFrank still could not help wondering about Elizabeth. Something was amiss. He had to know that she was dead and gone. For certain. This was a perfect opportunity—get Chien out of town and have him investigate things on his way back to Boston.

Chien squeezed the purse LeFrank had given him and smiled. As he hunched over in his seat aboard the longboat, his other hand closed around the other purse, the one he had taken off the dead man, Lamp, the one he had not told LeFrank about. They both had weight. He had his hands full of money. And now, even better, he had been ordered to find the woman. LeFrank only suspected she was alive. But Chien knew. He let the two bags rest in the inside pockets of his coat and hang heavily against his chest and pulled a handful of glass beads from his pocket and rolled them idly around the palm of one hand with the dirty trembling fingers of the other.

For once, LeFrank thought, Chien had done the right thing. Whatever this man had been about, it had not succeeded. But now they had to have even greater care for when the dead body was discovered someone might suspect him or connect *Hathor*'s presence in the harbor to the murder. LeFrank decided he would leave the port as soon as he could. He would get a message to O'Neill telling him to get their business done. O'Neill would not like having to contend with his man, this pirate that terrified him. He wondered if he had confronted the man yet. Well, that was O'Neill's concern, not his.

CHAPTER 13

"Coin Beach"

Delaware Coast

On the morning of the third day that Jack was at his cabin with Elizabeth, Ezra and George Kimball were walking around the station looking at the condition of the buildings and checking for maintenance items that would become tasks for the surfmen. Ezra was glad to be outside. He had spent the early part of the morning reviewing his log and bringing it up to date. Every surfman in his command had performed heroic deeds, risked their lives, saved the lives of others, hundreds of them. There were many rescues and most of the thick log was a record of their successful actions, of the people and ships saved. Sometimes they were accounts of simple acts—a surfman signaled a ship and it moved off shore to deeper safer waters. Many times they got a line to a sailor and pulled him to shore. There were the other times too, when their strength and courage overcame their fear and pain and they pulled men back from the edge of eternity. His log entries always started with the date and the weather and the time of day. Then he described what had been seen. "The brig *Molly*, with a cargo of molasses bound for Philadelphia, and a crew of nine, was driven toward shore by a northeast wind. The water was heavy and we could not launch the surfboat. We did get a line to her and brought the men to shore one by one. One of them drowned in the surf. Owen Troutman. We buried him inland in the churchyard. He had no kin to tell, his captain said. The ship was pounded by the surf until little was left...Ezra Stock, Keeper." Like other men, he knew what he knew. But once the stories flowed down his arm and out of him through the ink of his pen, they seemed strange, impossible. Stock had a hard kernel at the center of himself that said he could not be satisfied if what his surfmen did led to failure. You had to go out. You had to. You didn't have to come back, but they, the sailors you went to save, they did.

George and Ezra strolled down to the water's edge and looked back at the roof of the building. They were satisfied at the overall condition of the station, but living by the sea took its toll on everything and there was always something to do. Most of what was on their list was minor, but the list was a long one.

It was low tide and they were away from the buildings, their boots sinking in the wet sand as they walked. It was cool and the land breeze did little to warm them. The fine, broken water of light spray leaped like fringe from the tops of the three-foot waves and blew away from them, but they could still smell the rich salt air.

Kimball kicked at the sand, seeing a bright reflection there. It was the gold edge of a jingle shell picking up the flat orange morning light. Both men looked at it for a minute, both thinking the same thing. It could have been gold. Many of the surfmen had a small to fair sized hoard of gold and silver. There were so many wrecks along the coast that several places on the shore regularly yielded up bits and pieces of treasure to reward the men for their work. Some of the men had found large, valuable items and this offset the fact that they were poorly paid. In the years since Europeans first began making expeditions to the Americas, vast amounts of bullion and specie had plunged to the bottom of the ocean, down with the ships, never making it to its destination. The names of the lost ships were familiar, as they enriched the tales told again and again by surfmen and sailors: the *Enoch Turley*, *Brinkburn*, *Castel*, *Determine*, *Mascote*, the *Ruth Carliste*, the *Jan Melchers*, *Quattro*, the *Ella*, the sailing ship *Harrisburg*. There were hundreds of wrecks lost in the dark sand, nestled at the bottom all along the Atlantic coast. Many of them were very close to shore. One of the surfman said if they all rose up at once, a man could walk from Maine to Florida on their decks and alight on the warm sands there with dry shoes. The ships carried everything from oysters to pine lumber, but many of them bore treasure. Much of the money was lost to piracy, some buried and forgotten, but the bulk of it was taken back by the earth itself with the help of the wind and sea. Squadrons of ships made way across the water and squadrons of storms attacked them. Storms wrecked the plundering ships and storms threw some of the precious items back from time to time, like tips for the surfmen, who in their off-duty hours, walked along with their eyes down and hopes up. The prospectors on America's opposite coast were squandering their miserable lives chipping at merciless rock and living in the wilds in hopes of finding bits of gold ore; the surfmen here took leisurely strolls out their front door and sometimes bent casually over to gently lift up beautifully wrought treasures that rested comfortably at their feet. The days following a storm were the best times to search the rippling sand. A storm could deposit a plateau of new sand onto the beach and bring treasure with it or it could take some of the beach back to itself, uncovering something valuable that was already there. They called the stretch of shoreline where they lived "Coin Beach."

They continued their walk. Both made quick, regular looks along the horizon. Habit.

"I've been thinking about Jack." Ezra waited for the man to say more.

"Something's wrong, but I can't for the life of me think of what it could be."

Ezra answered his friend. "Tom would want us to let him be. For now. You know he wanted Jack to be able to do for himself, especially after his mother died."

"He might be sick, you know. Lying out there in the woods hoping we would come help him." Kimball looked to his side as the men walked, reading the look on Ezra's face.

"Old Gunn said he was feverish that night, but more like he was worried than sick. Course you know him, probably thought Jack was possessed by the devil."

They shared a smile at preacher Gunn's expense. Kimball was anxious about Jack and not willing to let it go. He did not feel, like Ezra, that they should wait. "I say we should go out there and check on him. I can go today if you say the word."

Ezra wasn't sure. In his mind Jack was a man now. Maybe time for them to tend to him was over. Or should be. "Okay, but let's wait one more day. Let's get the day's chores done first. You can go out there tomorrow. Better yet, we'll let the preacher go. He might be better than either of us and it'll do him good to get away from the work we have to do." His reluctance was like the sea's, who that morning was not giving away any of her gold. Only her surface was gold. She was a sheet of metal, buffed bright in the morning.

CHAPTER 14

The Burial

Newport News

Strell watched Daniel Armistead walk slowly across the grass. His breath streamed out ahead of him, parting in fading plumes as he walked through it, and Strell could see how the older man labored. This close Strell could see that Armistead looked just the way he remembered. He moved to his side, keeping out of sight behind a massive white oak that looked as if it had been in this ground since Jamestown was settled. Armistead was there to see if anyone came, but all he saw was two miserable men shivering in the chill as they leaned on their shovels and waited for the boss to come and tell them to go ahead and fill the hole. All his questions on the docks had gotten him nothing but evasion, hostility, apathy. What was another dead man to them. Nothing. The constable said a short prayer to himself. "Lord, let this poor soul find peace with you. Sure he didn't find any here. Amen." He didn't know what else to do and as he turned to leave he almost bumped into a robust young man in the black cloth of his vocation, coming to do a reading over the body, but for the departed soul. They nodded to each other and Armistead, although cold and tired, realized he should stay for the service, such as it was likely to be. He thought it sounded okay even though he was paying scant attention to it, and was thinking of all he had yet to do before he himself had rest.

Strell, however, was pleased, and even from his hiding place, he could hear parts of the earnest young man's simple prayers and musings on the life of someone he had never even seen. The hymn with which he concluded the service was one of joy, not sadness, and it carried beautifully in the dense autumn afternoon.

Strell remembered when he first saw Lamp. Back then the scene was the same: Strell standing in shadow, watching. It was in New York, at a market on the docks, and he stood stock still, nothing specific in mind, just waiting to see what would come his way. There went Lamp, nine years old maybe, no one knew, walking past him, also looking for an opportunity. At first Strell paid him no mind, just another waif trying to make it. Stay alive for one more day. Then the lad walked up to the baker's stall and smiled at the owner, who from experience was suspicious of all street urchins. Strell watched more closely and was amused when he saw the boy, in the split second that the baker glanced toward a customer, reach with both hands and grab two crusty rolls from the basket in front of him. In a swift, practiced move, he took the rolls and put one under each arm, and hunching his shoulders, crushed them flat. When the shopkeeper turned back he was still there. He smiled up at him again and talked for a few more moments, his hands accompanying his words, and then ambled casually away, along the bustling waterfront. Everyone around him was taller than he was and the crowd concealed him for a moment. Strell almost laughed aloud as he watched Lamp quickly eat one roll and drop the other down the front of his pants into a concealed pocket. "Christ," Strell muttered. The kid had moved like a magician. He glanced once more toward the baker's stall and when he looked back, the boy was gone.

The orphans and hobos who roamed New York City were like animals with territories. Inside the invisible lines they were known to others. They made their marks and learned where safety was and what the boundaries were. It did not pay to venture too far out into the city, away from the small area that, ironically, they thought of as home. When Lamp was living there he was one of thousands of orphans, desperate, trying to survive. Some authorities said there were ten thousand of them, some a hundred thousand. As Darwin had recently held out, the fit prevailed. Even the very young learned that while strength won some of the battles, cunning was a weapon with endless uses. Without the father-mother-sister-brother of family, these forgotten people never learned trust, love, the feeling of security. Any threat to a child brought the subconscious question to his mind: what's going to happen to me? There was no longing like that yearning for safety and protection that the young crave. But there was no true safety in the filthy warrens they inhabited. Some learned how to manipulate others; their counterparts were the used.

Strell waited until Armistead and the preacher left and watched the gravediggers take their shovels in hand. They weren't going to wait for the cemetery caretaker to come and give them the word. Let him complain if he wanted. It wasn't him standing in the damp and cold of the graveyard. What was he going to do, make them dig the box back up. With each shovel of dirt there was the chink of the metal on stones followed by the rap of the dirt on the lid of the coffin. It went back in easier than it came out and Strell kept time, counting in his head, as the men played a sad thumping lament of wood and steel and earth and death.

He walked back to the main road into the city and met with his man as he returned from making a circuit of the cemetery property. He looked at Strell, shook his head, and opened the door of their carriage. He too had seen nothing. As they rolled off, Strell told him that they would be leaving in a few days. He had a few more things to accomplish and then they would set sail. O'Neill had delivered the cargo—minus the girl—so there was nothing else to do here. Strell kept thinking about the girl. And Lamp. Lamp's death would be avenged. God help the man when I find him, Strell vowed to himself, not for the first time. And he was not going to give up on having that girl delivered to him. Her picture felt warm in his breast pocket. His plans included her. Required her. The rocking of the carriage made his head nod up and down as if the horse, the wheels, the world itself wanted him to agree to these things. Satisfy these desires. Of the girl and of Lamp.

CHAPTER 15

Theater Girl

Boston

She liked to be through the door before darkness crawled from the corners and took the stage. Often she was one of the last of the cast members to exit the theater because her costume for the final number and the curtain calls was elaborate, despite how skimpy it was. The less there was to them, the more involved they were likely to be, lest they slip or sag or fall off altogether. Hers was an assembly of straps and hooks and tight clear netting and tiny flesh-colored bands. Dance numbers for the current show were athletic ordeals and the blocking she followed had her in constant motion. The variety shows of the time were made up of skits, songs, big production numbers, the cancan. Much of it was far more bawdy and risqué than what she envisioned when she chose this path, but you had to take what you could get in the cold and danger of the big cities. Since leaving the small town of her birth and coming east, she had seen more poverty, prostitution, broken people, and orphaned children than she could ever have imagined existed in one place. The women were jealous of each other, the lot of them regularly acting like stupid schoolgirls. It is what most of them had been not long before. As one of the prettiest girls and one of the best dancers, she was envied and, as a result, ignored by the others. All of this, her isolation and sadness, had been noted, become facets of her selection, innocent facts of an innocent life, allowing her name to remain there alone on the LeFrank's list, first, as the others were eliminated one by one.

She started to go outside just as the theater manager put out the last of the stage lights and came her way. His footfalls cracked across the boards and alerted the darkness behind them. She went down the stairs into the sharp night air. No starlets and none of the starstruck revealed themselves. Only the old distant lights from the shell of the universe were there, the real stars, an audience high above, in indifferent attendance. She walked home alone. The alley was empty save for a carriage that lurked in black ink shadows at the turn into the lane ahead.

When she became aware of the man moving across her path at some distance before her she was sure it must be one of her troupe, for his movements were ballet. Closer, she still couldn't recognize him as he bowed gracefully and held out his hand, in it a gift for her. She drew up before him and took the gift. This was the first time anyone had sought her. Waited for her. Knowing which way she walked. She had seen it with the other girls plenty of times—on the arms of feverish young men they went, pressing themselves hard against strangers whose good looks or fine clothes they had seen for the first time only moments before, bound for places they had not seen at all. She looked at Salete's face. The small part of it that was revealed to her was handsome, as she imagined it would be. In the gift box was a gold clasp. She removed the gold piece carefully. It was an unusual gift, fine and heavy. It must be worth a great deal, she imagined. She inclined her head and smiled slightly in thanks, called on her training to help her be calm and make the proper response. She fought with her breathing as she imagined the plot lines waiting for her. Leading lady. That's what she was now. Oddly, the man moved to her side. Oddly close. With an intimate formality he spoke to the curls that laid comfortably around her ear, "My master wishes for the two of you to come to know each other."

Had she taken in his breath with his words? She couldn't tell.

"There was more to this…it's not you?" she said, almost aloud.

Salete turned and walked slowly away. Her eyes followed him and she could now pull the outline of the carriage from the darkness. Salete opened the carriage door, reached inside, and withdrew a long black cloak. When she came to where he stood he said, "This is the rest of the gift."

Its swirl showed the flash of a red lining. "Of course," she realized, she was to remove her modest coat and move into the red embrace of the gift. He had not met her or stood close to her or touched her hand, but whoever he was, this man was already changing her.

Into what, she wondered. When she had circled herself in the luxury of the gift, she understood the clasp. It fit at the collar, looping into the frogs stitched along both sides of the opening. She forgot her family and the theater and she dreamed, afraid, but wanting to open herself completely to this future. It might be her only chance.

It was a short ride in the darkened carriage to the large house overlooking the harbor. With imperceptible movements she slipped her hands from her gloves and stroked the finish on the red fabric that clung to her. For some reason she didn't want the man with her to know what she was doing. She loved the feel of cloth. It slipped softly against the skin on the backs of her fingers, almost unknowable. Like the skin of children, you had to look at it to be sure you were touching it.

She was surprised when the carriage stopped and didn't have time to fit her hands back into her gloves before Salete took them both in his and helped her down the two steps to the ground. His grace complemented hers as he held her firmly and yielded to her movements so that she descended slowly and landed softly. Her old gloves, holding the shape and warmth of her hands, fell unnoticed into the gutter. Salete led the way to the door and she followed him. The house was beautiful. It was old and grand and had its own smell and feel, masculine and musky. She had never been inside such a home.

In the first drawing room to the right she saw a fire devouring long, dry logs at a broad and high hearth. Redness filled the room. To its left stood the man she had come to see. He stared intensely at her, but he didn't move. She couldn't take her eyes off of him. With a swift deft motion Salete reached for her throat, released the clasp, and removed the cloak. As he withdrew he stated simply, "Monsieur LeFrank, I present the lady you have spoken of and longed to meet." She did not know it but she was the first of many to be so introduced.

"Sir, this is Anna Ulter."

CHAPTER 16

Elizabeth

Jack's Cabin, Delaware Coast

Anna Ulter. Her name intruded into Elizabeth's thoughts. She wondered what had become of her. How had she been taken, and how long ago? To Elizabeth, Anna was someone she had learned about just days before, but LeFrank had taken her years earlier. The others. How many more? She felt an obligation to them, to save them. There was nobody else who knew what had happened to them. Harrowing lines from the Book of Job crept up upon her, "And I only am escaped alone to tell thee."

But there was no one to tell. The thought kept recurring. Who to tell? Or trust? It did not seem possible that she could face all of this alone. But there was no one. She thought of the young man, Parsons, who had been courting her, but dismissed him as quickly; he was not a man to save her. He seemed more like a lovesick boy, and she didn't like him that much. She thought of Jack, the surfman, but he couldn't help her. Jack knocked softly at the door. Elizabeth opened it. "Sorry, I forgot to call you." She hadn't forgotten; she was delaying. He saw that she was dressed and had fixed her hair.

"It's fine. I had wood to load."

He carried the canvas sling to the hearth and knelt to stack the split logs to the side. It took him longer to arrange the pile than it normally would have. He was not used to putting things off. Elizabeth ran her hands through her hair and let her fingertips trace along her neck. She retied the sash of the apron she had put on. Jack looked at her, then looked away.

They were awkward together. They still half thought of the ships—*Mercury* and *Hathor*. Few words passed between them while they fried slices of cured meat for their breakfast. The grease in the pan sizzled up a welcome diversion. The heating coffee smelled good to them and they thanked each other for the food and the help with its preparation. Elizabeth insisted on cleaning the dishes herself. Jack didn't like to be with her when he felt the strain between them. The early morning together had been wonderful for both of them; then an hour, one small hour, had changed her mood.

Feeling better physically than she had in many days, Elizabeth was determined to begin the terrifying journey back to the place where her life had been. To do that she had first to break away from the surfman. On the beach she had begged, even demanded his help and protection. Looking back she could see that it had been a terribly selfish act, this insistence that someone change his life and break his oaths for her. She had won and he had lost. She owed it to this kind man to leave him, to protect him and let him go back to his life. Elizabeth realized that she had never expected to find the goodness and strength of character he possessed in someone who lived so simply. A man with nothing who had everything she did not. She pressed her lips together and smiled to herself as she remembered that she was the one who was supposed to be educated. He knew far more than she did about many things. His things now seemed more important than hers. Survival. Bravery and its partner, fear. She couldn't imagine what it was like to row out in a storm and risk your life to help strangers. She knew she was fighting the attachment she now felt for him. It was a new feeling, this nebulous yearning, one she thought she could ignore or at least hold off for now, until her leaving extinguished it altogether. There would be no peace within her unless she knew and could understand all of what had happened. To her, and Nana and to the life they had lived. In some ways she felt the greatest obligation to the women on the list. They were a burden she could not ignore. They had done to her what she had done to Jack. She felt like she should just forget everything else and spend as much of her life as she had to, never stopping, until she had found them all. She felt compelled to sort through what she knew, add things up, form a clear and simple plan. Then she would leave this place and keep it, and Jack Light, as a good, but sad memory. She fought tears again as she realized that now all she had was a collection of sad memories. Her chin trembled and she swallowed hard, keeping her face away from Jack. He could sense the turmoil in her and knew more than anything that he did not want her to pull herself away from him.

"Elizabeth?" It was the first time he had called her by her name. She looked at him.

"What is it you're thinking about?"

"Jack, I have to leave here."

"No, you don't. You can stay as long as you like, you can stay…"

"No."

His eyes searched the room.

"But you need to be healthy. Wait 'til you've recovered from all you've been through. You aren't strong enough. I'll stay here with you. I'll protect you. I can take care of you." They both understood what he meant by that. She didn't look at him and continued to wipe a pan that was already dry. He decided to change tack. "Where are you going?"

"North."

"North to where?"

She shook her head, "Just north."

"How will you get there? There are barely any roads here. You'll have to walk miles and miles—alone—before you even get to Lewes, the closest town. Maybe fifteen or twenty miles. And it's a very small place, at that."

"Then that's what I'll do. Walk." It sounded brave, but she was terrified.

He moved slowly, step by step over to the window, looked out, his left hand squeezing his right fist.

Jack knew how strong-willed and determined she could be. He was, unaccountably, mad at her. At the same time he was thinking how beautiful she was, and was becoming, unbearably so, as the time passed.

"Stay. For now. When you're better, if you still want to go, I'll take you."

She stood up straight and folded her arms.

"Jack, when I leave it must be alone. I have to go. Soon."

He turned around and stared at the planks of the floor. It was the last thing he wanted to hear. What would he do without her? His father at least had him when his mother died. He would have no one. Whatever his future held, there would be no happiness in it if he were not with her. Of that he was dead certain. He thought of following her. He thought of his father's words about duty. They were an unwelcome intrusion. Old Gunn said that you could find what was right if you prayed. Outside he had just been thinking about George Kimball and David Marshall—what they had lived through. He couldn't just leave all of this. It wouldn't be right. No matter which way his mind looked there was an expectation, a demand on him. Protect this girl. Keep her. Obey his father. Do his duty. Be honest. Honor his word. How could he, once more, betray the men, betray Ezra? George? He had already lied to them. That could never be undone. He was like Marshall, with a sin that could not be forgiven.

He wondered how many people had deep hurts in their hearts for things they had done and later regretted. Gross secrets. You hated, but couldn't stop. You wanted someone to die. Thoughts of the men from that ship entered his mind. Did he want them to die? God help me, he thought. You lied or were mean or hurt someone for no reason. Schadenfreude. You couldn't make yourself feel sorry for the other person, only for yourself for being unable to escape the guilt. Duty and honor and fulfilling one's obligations sounded easy when it applied to someone else or was without cost. What would he do when she was gone? He didn't have to do anything. He didn't have to work harder, or longer, or solve difficult problems. He wasn't poor, far from it, and he had the other surfmen. All he had to do was what he had been doing before the ocean threw her into his arms. Checking his traps and testing his aim and skill. Working a line back to his boat and seeing what he would have for his supper. Being a surfman. They were the things he had always loved doing. All he had to do now was to do without.

It looked like the hardest thing he would ever face. He couldn't see how he could live his life, just as he had a week ago, now that this had all happened. The service once was everything; now it didn't even seem important at all.

One night, as he and a handful of other surfmen and sailors listened to Marshall and Kimball telling their stories, he thought about how much time they had spent reflecting on the truths of their lives. Culling through events. Looking for something. Now he too had experienced violence and hatred and passion, coming to know the antithesis of all he had been taught. Kimball said something that night, a year ago, that had made little sense to Jack then, but that he now could understand. "I had to give up selfishness. At first it was hard. After all, I only had myself. But then, when I thought about it, it was easy."

Kimball looked around at the men. "I had nothing and I was nothing, and I realized it didn't make any difference to the world what I did. I was never going to be a ship captain, or a man of importance of any kind. What could I accomplish? I had no power, not even an identity. I had no past, and I had no future. I didn't want any more dreams. Dreams are too hard to live with. So what did anything matter?

"So I forgot everything but what I was doing at that time, what was right in front of me. My life was a sequence of tasks, the past a single task back, the future, the one task that awaited, just ahead. And no further. I think happiness is just knowing what to do next.

"I did so many things that soon my sorrows didn't mean as much to me as they once had. It was as if I once loved them, but now did no longer. You can find yourself cherishing sorrow, men, believe me, you can. Then I hadn't seen them for so long a time that I really didn't know them anymore. When I met them again, and they did come to see me sometimes, those old miserable sorrows, it was within my new life; they had become smaller incidents, little parts of a new, bigger life. They had faded back," Kimball looked out into the boundless sky, "almost to a vanishing point. Things seem to exist in limited supply. The more people there are, the less there is to go around. I mean, time, trust, love, things like that. Sorrow too, I guess." He smiled at the men around him. "Already there are too many men on this earth—anyone want to get off?" They all laughed. Marshall watched his friend and the men could see the admiration in his eyes.

Jack didn't know that men forget pain but remember happiness and pleasure. They remember that there was pain, but cannot truly recall it or feel it again. It was a saving part of their nature. If sadness and pain accumulated, the lives of men would become increasingly miserable, and accordingly, increasingly short.

Jack knew it wouldn't be easy, not for him. He couldn't accept losing her. And he was sure that what he felt would never go away. Maybe Marshall and Kimball could forget or feel the lessening of pain, but he wouldn't. He looked around him. There was nothing that he could see that would dilute the sorrow. She wasn't gone yet, but he felt the tight pain in his stomach. And he knew the sad irony of the words that were true for her as well.

She had to leave, but she didn't have to come back.

CHAPTER 17

Old Gunn

True to his word, Ezra agreed to let the "preacher" go out to Jack's cabin to see if he was alright. It was early afternoon and Gunn was enjoying his solitary walk through the ranks of dunes. The sound of the surf had stayed behind and in its place he happily substituted a hymn with the same tempo as the waves. It is easier to understand the words of slow songs, easier to reflect on the lyrics as they pass through you. Tones and meanings become the same thing as they enter your ears and fill your mind. Your own voice leaves you and returns through your ears and the circle thus formed marries man to song. His voice had a little of the quaver of age, but it was clear and on pitch.

He believed that God existed. He trusted Him to watch out for him, help him in this world and welcome him into the next. Some said He was a non-providential God. He just watched. He didn't answer prayers. And what of uneven prayers? The farmer prayed for rain while the man across the church aisle from him, soon to be off on a journey, prayed for sunshine and dry ground. Did God favor the one most sincere, the one who prayed the loudest, or test the better man by ignoring him and favoring the other. Or did God just let the sky do what it wanted to do. The world was awash in uneven prayers. Weighing them out, Gunn smiled at the thought, would be a daunting task, even for the omnipotent.

One of these days, God willing, he laughed to himself at the pun, he would find out. For today, however, he had to deal with the world of men. He felt himself responsible to his old friend, Tom Light. He had been a good man and the two of them had spent many hours talking about faith and the world. Tom had come to him to ask his help when Jack's mother died. Tom asked why. Old Gunn knew enough to simply listen and let time help him comfort his friend. Why? Why? Those had been hard days. That's when his faith had helped him the most. It came to him when he needed it to help another. Using his faith was the soft-slap confirmation of it. Nothing is as good as it is when it's put to its proper use. Of course there was no answer. A beautiful person died. It was not as if she had no purpose. She had a son to raise and a husband to love, returning the love he had for her. She knew the nobility of work, the most human thing to do. Her going left a hole in things. An unfillable space. Then it was Jack who turned to him. It was hard for a young man with no other family to lose both parents, first one and then the other. Gunn felt in some way gratified that he had helped save him also. Maybe save was too strong a word, but he hoped that was what he had done. He chose to see it that way. It is said that you are forever responsible for those you saved. That was just the way it was. He admitted to himself that there were times when he didn't want to be alone with Jack then. It was too hard, keeping up his strength against the sadness. But the test of love and friendship was, when the time came, doing what you didn't want to do.

This trip to see Jack, however, was made out of concern, his feeling of responsibility, not from any idea that the boy was really in any trouble. It was more to see if he could help and, mainly, to put his own mind to rest. So he held his head up, breathed in the pure fall air, and enjoyed seeing the hand of God around him. Jack's cabin was just beyond the bay and into the woods, but he had no boat to carry him across the water and had to walk along the shore to get there. The path was a slow, lazy arc along its edge. The sand was clean and flat, polished by the last tide. It was much easier walking here than on the beach between the stations. He remembered his days patrolling in the darkness, scuffing and stumbling along. Now Ezra kept him at home and he spent a lot of time in the tower. When he did patrol it was usually to the north where the beach was often better. There were no seats in the towers, an effective measure meant to keep the men awake and alert, so he was used to standing for long periods of time, but he was not in good shape for taking long walks. He stopped and stretched and then sat down by a patch of dry, round pebbles and crumbled shells. His back and arms were still strong, he had no trouble rowing, and his eyes were good, but he could feel his age when it came to walking. Knowing he was helping Jack offset the ache in his legs. He drew them up under him and leaned back so he could pull each leg, one at a time, up, heel to butt. He squeezed the blood into his calf muscles.

CHAPTER 18

Jack and Elizabeth

Yield to the inevitable. There was nothing else for it. Jack was going to go along with Elizabeth for now. He had to live in harmony with her for as long as they were together. Moreover, when he found her again in another place and time, he wanted her to remember him in a good light. He had made up his mind that he would find her, no matter what he had to go through to do it. He decided that the best course would be to live the few days left the way they were when she seemed happy. He had no idea how many days it would be. She still had physical injuries that must heal before she could go on. He started telling her about the cabin. Obviously, she too was eager for relief from the tension they had felt, and she warmed to their discussion. Curiosity was her weakness. She was fascinated with every aspect of how he lived and this island in the woods. Slowly they went, wall by wall, talking about what he had in his house and how he used the things there. Whatever he touched, handed to her, and explained, seemed a thing of joy to him. A rifle, a spoon, a saw, one of his books, they were all the same. You just used them at different times. The simplicity of it, the efficiency, was exquisite. She said that aloud and Jack questioned her. It seemed to her that maybe he had never heard the word said before.

When they were finished with the interior and the things in it, they pulled on sweaters and coats and walked outside. Elizabeth tied his mother's scarf around her neck. Jack liked seeing her do it, thinking it bound the two women together. They were much the same to him in their representation of beauty and warmth, although he knew instinctively that she was making a point of keeping everything between them on an impersonal level.

"Use what's available. That's what the settlers did. Most of this is from pine logs, although the ones at the bottom are oak. They hold up better, being down in the dirt. Pine is soft and easy to work, so cutting the notches at the corners wasn't that hard. You could build one of these without any nails at all. They probably didn't have any when they put this one up. This cabin was likely built by Swedes, or Germans. At least that's what the old folks always say. Whoever it was did the main room. Some others added on. There's nobody alive to tell what or when. See the top log. It's about as high as a man could reach. Most cabins wound up just that high. But other parts were added on later, like the loft, and my father and I built that shed on the end." Jack pointed to the building and Elizabeth walked over to it and looked at it with true appreciation. "The craftsmanship is obvious. How the wood fits. I'm sure you and your father were proud of it. This door looks different…" She turned her head, frowning slightly, to look back at the main cabin.

"That's an Indian door." Jack pointed to the entrance to the cabin. "Added later. After it was first built. The spikes through it are clenched and it's more than twice as thick as a normal door." She walked back and examined it carefully. She opened the heavy door and inspected it on both sides, repeating the process and swinging it on its hinges. He was fascinated as he watched her move, gracefully, leaning in and out, extending a pointed toe as she stretched her body and craned around the edge of the door. Eyebrows raised, she looked at him and slowly closed the door, making it shriek in agony.

Jack laughed. "Yeah, I know it squeaks. I could put some fat on it, but this way the door tells me if someone comes in who's not supposed to." He almost said that she couldn't get away without him knowing it, but caught himself in time. "The Indian door, when it was barred and locked, was there to keep Indians out. They could chop at it with their stone axes and it would take a long time for them to break through. Long enough for the settler to load his gun and wake everybody up to fight. Jack looked back at her. He could tell she was remembering everything he was telling her. In a short time he had learned to read her expressions and moods. Her brows moved down and her forehead would wrinkle when she was working something out in her mind. When she raised her eyebrows in surprise the line of stitches on her brow almost formed a question mark. They walked around the clearing and Jack pointed to the things they had built, telling her how they used them.

Old Gunn left the beach and began following a well-used path through the woods towards Jack's cabin. He continued to take his time, looking out beyond the trees at the marsh grasses, listening, watching for birds or deer.

Jack took Elizabeth into the woods and showed her some of the trees, the ones with beautiful shapes, and some of the plants and shrubs, ones he recognized even now with their leaves mostly gone. There were trees, he told her, that looked best in barren winter, ones with a certain growth habit, who sculpted themselves into beautiful free forms. He thought of seeing them, climbing them, sitting in their shade; she thought of their shapes and proportion. He told her what they were and if they were useful for fuel or food or medicine; she knew he liked them because all men liked the things whose appeal was based on a harmony. One line related to another.

Was it absurd to think that appearances could hold such sway with one? How did they look, the people that she knew? Nana, LeFrank, Chien, Salete, Jack Light? Five people dominated her life. One was almost certainly dead. One, Jack, was as naïve and innocent and good as the remaining three were the opposite of those things. Soon Jack would be left behind. There really was no one else. Even the servants at her house could not be trusted since they were in LeFrank's employ. The young suitor, Parsons, came to mind again, but somehow his way didn't seem true to her, especially now when she had spent time with Jack. When she left here only three people would count. Jack noticed her absence, even as he walked over to her and stood very close to her. He said her name.

He pointed to a leaning white pine. It was old, with its limbs bent down only to reach up at the ends, as if changing their minds and wanting to touch the sky and not the earth. He pointed out others. It seemed he knew every one of them. A few of the grand ones he regarded as old friends—ones you looked in on from time to time, to see how they were doing. Some were habitat trees whose various-sized holes signaled what lived there. Help for the hunter, he informed her. Her neighbors went to the market or had regular visits from the tradesmen. They didn't have to know where the animals lived or how to trap and kill them. It was very different here. There were fewer things to eat and they were harder to get. Except maybe for the fish. Of course, she thought, they were all free for the taking. She thought about money. She was—or had been—a very wealthy young lady. Now all she had were the clothes of a woman long dead, and the help of a man she barely knew. He had no need of money. There was no place to go and nothing to buy. All of her dresses and gowns and jewelry were far away. She couldn't picture herself wanting to wear them again. If Nana were gone, there were no friends to see, no one to trust. But she had to go back. The thought insisted that she listen and not forget it.

Jack was speaking to her.

"What?"

"Let's get our dinner. I have to go back to the cabin for a minute. Just wait here."

He saw the doubt in her eyes. "It's alright, there's nothing here that will hurt you. No lions or tigers." He laughed. She didn't. "Or, you can walk back with me if you want. We're going fishing, and I need our gear." He smiled, "You do want to learn how to fish, don't you?"

Elizabeth realized where she was. She was suddenly terrified. She couldn't move and Jack suspected what was happening to her and allowed time for her to make up her mind. "I'll wait," she managed. He smiled at her again and turned back, walking off through the trees. Her eyes stayed on him until he was gone from her sight. Elizabeth sobbed. She pressed her fingertips to her forehead and squeezed tears from the corners of her eyes, shivering. She looked around her, turning her head from side to side, as if she thought someone was watching her. How could she get all the way to Boston, alone, with nothing, if she was afraid to wait a few minutes for Jack to come back? She had to admit that she felt safe when he was with her. Once she left him, everyone she would encounter would seem to threaten her. She knew Boston and, before this, felt confident and safe on its streets. Some neighborhoods were quite dangerous, she knew, but ladies did not go to such places, rarely went anywhere without chaperone or escort, for that matter. She tried to remember being alone in the city and realized that only on a few occasions had she ever visited a shop or gone to a reception or performance alone. Even then her carriage and driver and footman had always been nearby. Too, there was always someone expecting her to return by a certain time, someone who would look for her if she didn't arrive at the agreed hour. Traveling alone from here, through wilderness, and then through Philadelphia and New York, would be a test of courage she would rather forsake. Each had its own terrors for her, but though it was completely foreign to her, this wild empty place with its owls and deer and forest was becoming less fearful, less so than many parts of her "civilized" Boston. There seemed little here that could harm her, certainly nothing greater than the despair and reluctance within her.

She took a few steps along the path then turned back, stopping and turning, moving her eyes, making a perimeter of trees. She had drawn a circle around herself, but saw nothing, no one moving within it. She stopped crying and dried her tears on her sleeves, giving herself a little nervous laugh at how silly she was being. Her feet paced back and forth, but the long minutes could not be made to move more quickly.

Old Gunn was startled when he sensed the movement in the woods. There was someone there. It was a flash of white. Or was it a deer showing its white tail to signal danger? A bird? Maybe just the wind blowing through the brush, exposing the silvery underside of a maple leaf. He waited a minute and then walked in that direction. He hadn't expected to see another soul out here today. Jack lived a long way from anyone. Maybe it was Jack. After he had walked a little further he called out, "Hello? Who's there?"

Elizabeth lost her breath. She was unable to move and began to shake uncontrollably. It didn't sound like LeFrank or any of the others, but she couldn't be sure. The wind and the water made things sound different. Had they sent someone else to find her?

Whoever it was called out again. Elizabeth knew she had to hide. She looked for Jack, but now wasn't even sure which direction he had taken. She took several uncertain steps off the path and crouched down in the brush. The vegetation was sparse and scrubby and she turned her back to the path and pulled at her coat so that it covered her shirt. The pulse in her neck moved so that she could feel it. Almost hurting her. She was very uncomfortable and was about to settle herself into a better position when she glanced back and saw a man coming toward her. His presence seemed to double the pain gathering in her legs and neck and arms. Her head throbbed. She closed her eyes, but she could hear his steps crunch through the sand and pine needles. He stopped and looked down at the scuff marks on the path. They looked recent, damp earth showed dark against the dry, faded needles, and there seemed to be two distinct sets of prints. He was puzzling over this when he heard a noise and looked around to see Jack walking toward him.

"Hello, preacher."

"Well, Jack, it's good to see you up and about and looking well."

"I'm okay."

"You had Ezra and me worried, taking off like you did. Leavin' and not saying anything to anyone. Not like you."

Jack tried to think of what to say. It was hard knowing that Elizabeth was probably hiding nearby. At least he hoped she was. This was where they had parted. There was no way for him to explain her presence here. He moved closer to his old mentor, keeping him from having a long view of the area. He wanted to get Gunn on his way as quickly as possible, but knew from experience that that wouldn't be easy. The man loved to talk and now that he had seen that Jack was okay, a lesson was not going to be far behind. Jack was betting on something from the Book of Job. The old man liked Job. Maybe the part that said that if you accepted good from the Lord, how could you reject the bad. Followed by him saying, "Selah." Jack had never learned what that meant.

The preacher looked at the fishing rods Jack was carrying and scratched his head.

"Fishing with both hands, Jack?"

He feigned surprise. "Habit, I guess, from carrying them for dad and me. I like to have two lines in the water sometimes." Louder than he needed to, Jack said, "Come on back to the cabin. We can have some tea to warm our bones, and I'll get rid of the fishing poles and when you're ready, I can row you across the bay. You did walk around the shore, eh?"

"Mm. Nice day for it. You could see God out there today, you could."

Jack walked slowly and talked loudly, making excuses to stop from time to time, hoping that Elizabeth was following and was not lost out there somewhere in the woods behind him. He did steal a look back a couple of times, but never saw her.

CHAPTER 19

The Black Mass

Lynn, Massachusetts

Father Barry was a small man. The black of his habit made him appear to be even less of a person than he was. The priesthood for him was a convenient place of refuge. From it he got his room and board and his freedom. He could skim a little extra spending money from the collections. Better food and better drink were welcome occasions of sin, but only small sins, ones he could forgive himself for. Yes the priesthood was the perfect place for him. There were few demands on him and no expectations that he meet goals or produce results. Faith was now, to him, just part of a daily routine, like dressing, washing, eating. It didn't mean anything; it was merely something you did. Motions gone through. Whatever he said from the pulpit or to members privately were just groups of words strung together in a certain order. They were empty gongs and unlit lamps. So, while he was somewhat nervous about it, he could not see any way he could get into trouble by acquiescing to the wishes of this man, Mr. LeFrank. Regardless of the risk, which he thought negligible to the point of nonexistence, the man's generosity was not to be ignored. LeFrank had visited him and made a strange request. He had given him time to think about it, indeed paid him to think it over with no obligation. The offering, as the man referred to it, was to help the parish in any way Barry saw fit. It was said with a smile, one of those odd, knowing smiles. But Barry sensed there was more to this. That part, and he could not imagine what it could be, need not involve him as long as what he did was defensible and the reward was substantial.

Barry knew better than to put anything in writing that could give the wrong impression so he sent a letter to the man telling him merely that he would like to see him again. This time, however, it was not LeFrank, but a man named Salete who presented himself and informed the priest that LeFrank was not able to come himself, but that he, Salete, could transact any business that was required. Salete sat comfortably in the priest's dark office in the rectory. Barry thought this is what it must be like to meet with one of those angels who, at the beginning of the world, fell from grace because of their own vanity. The man, doing nothing, only sitting there motionless, gave that impression. As they settled themselves, Salete took the breviary from the priest's desk and leafed idly through it, his long fingers handling it gracefully. He stopped and read passages here and there, curious expressions passing like clouds across his plain, handsome face. A few times he laughed aloud. He put the book back carefully and smiled at the priest.

"Are you ready to help Mr. LeFrank with his business?"

"Tell me again what I am to do and exactly why it is so important."

Salete paused. "Do you know anything about the theater?"

"Very little." He bowed his head slightly. A smile of self-deprecation accompanied his words. "I am a simple, poor country priest. With a very parochial, backward, and I must admit, a hardheaded flock."

"The theater is a place of emotion and control. There must be a balance. When dealing with artists," Salete coated the word with loathing, "you find this war of feelings and control to be one of exaggerated violence. Mr. LeFrank has the ambition to develop the talents of promising actors and actresses, with a view to backing the ones who can achieve fame and fortune. He is interested in both. However, profit is his main interest. This is not a charity; it is a business, and as such it has costs. Things cannot be known if they aren't tested. But the answer you're looking for can be distorted by the test itself, influencing it in a way that is unpredictable. This is where you may have a role to play. It should be easy enough. Mr. LeFrank will select a candidate he believes may have the talent level required. With your help he will put them to a unique test. He believes there is no more intense event in a young lady's life than her marriage. Once he selects someone, he tells them, at the last minute, that they will have to act out their own wedding, with no rehearsal and no script. The groom is LeFrank himself, an element that makes the test that much more difficult for the "bride" since she must face the man who will decide to take her on as a protégé or not. On a stage they are made up, behind lights, separated by distance from the audience. In this case they are inches away from the theater critic, touching him, made to say the words and stand with the greatest degree of composure. For it all to be effective it has to take place exactly as if it were real. The candidate must convince LeFrank that she is married to him. That is the most important part. At no time before, during, or after the mock ceremony are you to act as if this were anything but a real wedding. Or say anything to the participants or to anyone else for that matter. Of course, they will not really be married." Salete smirked. "Cross your fingers or leave out a word or whatever you have to do. But it must appear, in every way, that they are. If all goes well," Salete looked directly into Barry's eyes, "everyone will benefit."

"Tell your Mr. LeFrank that I agree to try this. For the benefit of all, as you say."

They both smiled at this.

They smiled at each other again the night Anna Ulter was ushered up the aisle toward Father Barry in his first role as an actor playing the part of a priest. Salete, as best man, stood to the side, and like Miss Ulter, was very convincing. Her heart was in it. Barry thought that LeFrank had found a woman whose performance ability was miraculous.

CHAPTER 20

The Cabin

Jack was trying to keep up with every fourth or fifth word from Old Gunn. That's all he needed since he had heard it all before. Nods and grunts back were enough to let the preacher know that his companion was listening and to keep him talking. All at once, through the drone of warnings and admonitions and advice, an alarming thought popped into his head. If they went to the cabin, Gunn would see the dishes and women's clothes and the bed, my God, the bed. With that realization came another. He could delay this, maybe avert it, if he could pretend to go out to check his traps. So he gradually changed course, like a ship tacking in the wind, and led the way, meandering slowly out into the marsh, not back toward his home. A number of trails crazed through the area. Off they went. Gunn didn't seem to notice. He was enjoying just being with Jack. Old Gunn often said to Ezra Stock, "People like to talk to me." Stock didn't point out that what people did when they were with the old preacher was listen, not talk. When they had checked the last of the traps Jack tried to suggest that he row the old man back to the other side of the bay so he could get in before it was dark.

"I can find my way in the dark, Jack. Lets go get that tea you promised me before you led me forty days in the wilderness." Old Gunn hadn't missed a trick.

With as much delaying and stopping as possible, Jack took the old man back toward his cabin. In the clearing he scanned the area nervously. There was no help for it now so he walked to the door and opened it slowly. It squeaked. He let out a long loud breath and resigned to walk inside. The place was in perfect order. "Bless her," his lips moved as he whispered the words. The tea was brewed in record time. He had made such a big fire he had to open the door again to let some of the heat escape. As the two men sat at the table and talked, Jack could not resist looking here and there for signs that Elizabeth had been there. There were none he could see. She had done well. Even the bed, with its board, was covered with the counterpane and had clothes piled on it, hiding the board, making it look like nothing was out of the ordinary. He figured she would be someplace outside, nearby, watching and waiting for him to get his guest on his way, and he relaxed somewhat. He was pleased to hear Gunn talk about the men and to learn that they had had a few uneventful days. He realized how much he missed their company. At the end of what seemed like an unusually long lecture on piety and health and well-being and the dignity of hard work, the preacher got up to leave. He walked around the room, looking at things, stopping to peer out of the windows. He stopped by the bed.

"What should I tell Ezra? You seem fit for work. When will you be coming back?"

"Just tell him soon. I am feeling better and should be good as new soon."

Gunn left it at that and started out the door. "Since it is a bit late, I'll take you up on your offer to row me over." In a day of ups and downs it figured that this would happen, Jack thought, not without some appreciation of the humor of it. He left the old man on the east shore of the bay with a wave of his hand, and watched him venture off into the fading light. Jack, using the muscles of his arms and back and legs to move the small boat as fast as it could be moved, appreciated the help the earth was giving him, for the water was smooth and yielding. The boat seemed to be gliding down a steep hill, the bay tilting away from him. He jumped from the boat and dragged it up onto the grass, going in an instant from standing still to as fast as he could run. Smoke and light greeted him in the clearing. There was a candle in the window. Jack grinned. He started singing. "When I came home to Portland Town 'twas as I said before, a candle at the window and my love at the door…" When she heard him she opened the cabin door and said, "You're in time for supper." There was a hint of a self-satisfied smile on her face.

"Did you see us?"

"I saw him. He was calling out in the woods, after you left. I hid and he was just about to find me when you came back." She stopped, not wanting to admit how scared she had been.

Jack moved closer to the fire, seeing that she had laid it out as he had with the same piling and mix of logs. There was a fresh load of wood in the carrier, her preparing for the chill of the evening. He emptied it and stacked the wood carefully.

As he worked he asked her what had happened when he left. "Where were you?"

"I don't know…just a few feet away from you. I heard you talking. I was sure you would see me. Who is he, another surfman, like you?"

"Yes. But not like me. They call him the preacher since he's always talking about the Bible and keeping after the men. He's the conscience of the group. Sometimes he makes the men mad, but we all love him like a brother. Maybe more like an uncle or grandfather. I like him since I learn so much from him. Like I do from you." He glanced at her, saw no reaction, and kept talking. "And he helped me a lot…over the years."

"With your loss. In your family."

"Yeah."

She went back to the table where she had laid out part of their meal.

"What's that good smell?"

"I was browning flour for the gravy. It burns it a little. It's funny how everyone seems to like the smell of things burning. I made us a hearty meal. I hope you're hungry since I maybe cooked a few too many potatoes."

As they ate they talked about things neutral. Jack promised to take her fishing early the next day. Before they finished the day, Jack fashioned a straw mattress near the fire, and while they were to sleep close to each other for many weeks to come, there would be not be another wonderful morning like the first time. She surprised him by asking if they could go hunting so she could, as she put it, learn to shoot a gun and, she added, become good at it. She'd spent much of that day alone and was beginning to build a plan in her mind. When she withdrew from the emotion of it, the way ahead became clear, and she could account for most of what must be done and a little of how she would go about it. She knew Jack was the source of most of the emotional turmoil she felt, even compared to the hideous assault on her and the days of her captivity and her escape. Those things were past, over. Every day they moved back in time, losing some of their reality. In her subconscious she entertained the idea that in the future, far enough, they will never have happened. Jack, she feared, or at least her thoughts of him, would never go away. More than just fearing it, she knew it. She'd been glad to be away from him for part of the day. It helped her to see. Jack, on the other hand, was as tormented by leaving her hiding in the woods as he was relieved when he walked into his home with Old Gunn.

A few days later Jack returned to his work as a surfman, never staying away for more than three or four days at a time, always going back to check on her and to be with her. The days he was at the station were, for him, lost days.

As the weeks passed, and October turned into November, she learned about her body and its strength and skill. Until now her body had been a mechanism that did little more than transport her arms and hands and senses. She saw, heard, and smelled, spoke and sang, read, played her hands over keyboards and pulled thread through fabric. What happened was at the extremities of her; now she felt her core. The pleasure of using her shoulders and back and thighs was addictive. Once Jack showed her something she insisted on doing it herself, over and over until she could feel the muscle memory of it. Then she insisted on going out alone. To climb a tree and watch for small game and to shoot it and bring it back for them to eat. She learned to crouch in the understory growth and wait by a path. They fished together, spending long hours of quiet in the boat or along the shore. Then she went alone again. She practiced with rifle and pistol so much that Jack was afraid he would run out of powder and shot. When she held the gun in her hand and looked over the front sight she had a singular expression on her face that was unsettling to him. She was so very intent and grim. Sometimes she pulled her arm from her coat and shirt and looked at her hand and forearm muscles just before she pulled the trigger. She flexed her wrist and turned the gun from side to side, rocked it to balance it, and ran her fingertips along the barrel to feel its heat. She began to like the pleasant pain of soreness. Her manner through all of this was serious, but she did have to giggle uncontrollably when she caught her first fish and struggled to hold it and get it off the hook. Jack loved watching her when she was being herself. Those were, however, times of lapse, like memories that popped back into reality, only to be quickly returned by her, chastened, into the fading past. Every time he came back to the cabin she had changed again. More and more she was becoming a stranger. She was not the woman she had been in Boston, or aboard the *Hathor*, or on the beach, or in his bed. She was transforming herself, purposefully, into someone else.

CHAPTER 21

The Tombstone

Newport News

Armistead decided to go and see for himself.

The day Lamp had been lowered into the earth of the Newport News Cemetery the constable had asked Billy to leave word at the caretaker's office that he wanted to know if anyone came to ask about the dead boy. He loved a mystery. Dealing with them was, after all, his life's work. Unlike so many other people living in the world, he had, and thrived on, the endless flow of challenges that ran through the years. He swam upstream all day, every day. Every day there were more puzzles to solve, pieces to fit. Some days there was a waiting list, crimes lined up like passengers on the platform waiting for the next train. Some were easy, some a lot harder. But he did not like the ones that were impossible. Those he hated. He reasoned that he should be better at crime than the criminals; they were stupid, amateurish, while he had earned his professional credentials through long study and hard work. Usually they were people too lazy to work. Most of them committed only a few illegal acts, while he had solved many. When he thought back to his early days he sometimes wished he had kept count, written in a diary each day and cataloged the ridiculous deeds that had come to his attention and demanded his involvement. He never got over his astonishment at what men—and women—did. Did their minds arrive somehow at the conclusion that it would be a good idea to murder someone in order to solve a problem? Were hiding, lying, and running away usually successful strategies? Was theft a desirable vocation? Stupidity, ignorance, drunkenness, rage, lust, greed, laziness. Were these what you wanted to guide you through your life?

Admittedly, you didn't always find the answers, and sometimes you had to let some go and drift off into memory—or forgetfulness—without any resolutions to satisfy you. Even when you made an arrest the courts often failed you. But some things stuck. And the appearance of the dead boy and the word written on his hand just stayed in the man's mind and he knew it would gnaw at him for a long time if he couldn't find out more about him. When Billy showed him the envelope bearing the seal of the cemetery office he grabbed it and tore it open quickly. Billy took a step back and frowned at Armistead. He pursed his lips as he read.

"I'm going to be away from the office for a while, Billy, but I'll be back before dark. If any of the men need anything, you handle it."

The deputy began to remind him of the plan they had made for that day: watching a warehouse where there had been complaints of recent thefts, and interviewing the tavern girls who saw a fight and murder the night before. "You take care of that, Billy, and I'll find you along the way. And not too long with the girls. I don't want you to get into any trouble." The old man smiled at this, but Billy looked at the floor as blush colored his neck and face. Armistead shouldered his coat around him and left with a firm closing of the door. Billy went to the window and watched him clatter off, moving faster in his carriage than usual. He began to pace back and forth in the quiet office. He looked at the clock and adjusted his coat and smoothed his hair and pulled his tie up tight.

He kept thinking about that one girl, the pretty one who had put her hands on his arm the night before and told him how frightened she had been when the men had started to wrestle with each other. "And then I saw the knife. I couldn't move and then the small man with the dark coat raised the knife and brought it down again and again..." She was close to the dying man and blood from his wounds was everywhere. Billy took his handkerchief and cleaned a drop from her hand and sleeve and at that she cried, pressing her face into his chest, thanking him as if he had been there in the melee and saved her life. In truth he hadn't slept well last night and he wished Armistead was going to go with him. Maybe he would show up. Billy decided to take his time with the other business and visit the tavern as late in the day as possible. He was anxious to see the girl, but for some reason not clear to him, was timid about going there alone. She said her name was Joan Markley and he kept thinking about her name. It was a song with two words, stuck in the front of his mind.

Armistead made bets with himself as he raced through the streets to the cemetery. The boy was a visitor to the city. He was lured off a ship. He had deserted from a ship. He was a messenger, killed for what he was carrying. He was just another unfortunate, in the way of something he couldn't even understand. Yes, probably the last. That was what he had found, too often, to be the case. If he had to put money on it, that would be his bet. What a sad business.

He began to regain some of the excitement he had felt when he first saw the note, once the graveyard came into view. It was a piece of rolling ground, sprawling through trees and brush, but contained into a rough rectangle by a four-foot-high wall of fitted stones, with only friction and gravity for mortar. With the rapid population growth in this small Virginia city, the churchyard burial grounds had become filled, and sanitation concerns had prompted the government to establish poorhouse cemeteries. This one didn't even have a chapel and the keeper lived there in an old house that was adjacent to the gate. Armistead went from his carriage directly to the front door and turned the handle in its center, ringing a small, high-pitched bell inside. James Kensel, the keeper, answered promptly and had his guest in, and offered to share his morning tea with him. They sat in the modestly furnished front parlor, the one usually reserved for use only for those special family occasions: weddings and wakes and the announcements of good news or bad.

"I'm surprised to see you so soon."

Armistead looked at the man and waited.

He went on, "You and I being in the same business, as it were. We both have a lot to do with the ones who die, not, so to say, from natural causes. And so forth. You take my meaning."

Armistead didn't.

"So, you must be as surprised as I was, the lad seeming to be as he was."

The constable summoned more patience.

"Of course, it goes without saying. Even though I do say so. But being poor and not having anyone and being found dead. Well I am speechless on the matter. More or less, that is. If I were inclined to think about it—and like you I do not have a lot of extra time to ponder such matters, the state of man being what it is—I would say something is very unusual or maybe even wrong with this. But who am I to say. Surely you find the same in your line of work. Quite often, I suspect. Maybe even more often than I do myself. More tea?"

Armistead politely accepted, thinking he might as well have something to do while waiting for the man to get to the point. He prompted him, "So what has happened?"

"Of course, you don't know, do you? I see. You have no way of knowing what has happened. My wife, bless her, used to tell me that I assumed too much. Imagine. I knew enough not to contradict her, not my wife, no, no, no. Let her think what she wanted, that was my motto. You don't often change a woman's mind now, do you?"

His visitor was glad at last to have something to agree with and nodded his head knowingly. He pictured his wife, Harriet, and smiled to himself. Kensel was encouraged by the assent and talked faster. "Died two years ago. My wife." Armistead formed his lips into what he hoped was a sympathetic line and had the uncharitable thought that she might have taken her own life. "I miss her. Thankfully, I have my work. So you don't know what's happened. Why I sent you the letter. Well, it is just that it is so unusual. I can't even say unusual since it has never happened before. The word wouldn't truly apply in that case." He waited for the constable to comment.

"What is it that has happened, sir?"

"Maybe it would be better if I showed you, rather than telling you, a picture and all the words as they say." They left by the rear door of the house and walked up a rise to the place where Lamp had been laid to rest. The cold drew around them. Dew lingered in the shadow places. Armistead understood now what the caretaker had tried to describe. The mound of dirt had not sunken at all, but showed surface channels where rain had washed some of the loose soil away. Orange clay and small rocks peppered the top of the grave. At its head, however, was a huge monument, the biggest in the place, one could easily tell, since everywhere else in the yard small wooden crosses were all that told what was below. Armistead went to it and bent down. He ran his fingers into the cuts made in the stone. They were fresh and deep and their edges were sharp as knives.

The inscription was simple. "Lamp, An Orphan." Centered below that, "Found, Then Lost Again." The final line said, "Become Invisible Too Soon."

Remarkable.

All that money to say so little. And for an orphan who did not even have a first—or was it a last—name. The caretaker stepped back, as he usually did in the presence of grieving family members, and waited for his visitor. Over time he had observed the various moods of mourners. He could tell who was sorry and who was glad. There were more of the latter than many would think. He could spot them easily, the shifty-eyed ones, the wailers, the poor relations who would not get a cent from the deceased. A lot of people who, truth be told, were delighted the old bastard or old bitch was gone. And hopefully not gone up, but down.

Armistead took a packet of notepaper from his coat and copied the mysterious epitaph. He compared his note to the hard gray stone to be sure he had it right. When he finished he asked the proprietor how and when the stone had been delivered. "I don't know exactly, just came out and there it was. I don't think it was here yesterday. It is a shame, too, the only stone in the yard and I didn't even get to see how they handled it. But it is in the ground solid. It's not going anywhere. None of my men saw anything either. I was in town buying shovels. We do go through shovels here, I mean to tell you. But since you left word when the lad was laid to rest, I sent the message right over to you."

Kensel smacked his hand on the stone. He pronounced it solid and heavy and pondered aloud about how many men it must have taken to carry it there and lift it into place. Armistead pointed to the wagon tracks and several sets of footprints and let the man come to his own conclusions. The realization stirred suddenly in Kensel's mind. It pleased him to say, "That's why you're the detective." As the two men walked down the hill together, pacing slowly as if they feared disturbing the dead, or out of respect for them at least, Kensel ventured a guess about who could have done the grave marker for young Lamp. It must have been the large shop near the waterfront that did tombstones as well as ornamental work for the building trades. He was correct in his guess and when the constable went there and identified himself, the owner was summoned and welcomed him into his office. His name was Peterson.

"The order came by messenger. I don't know who actually paid for the work. Certainly not the boy who carried the envelope in here. It had instructions with it, and quite a bit of money, actually. About twice the usual fee. Stipulating that it be done at once. Odd inscription, but I've seen stranger."

"Were there any dates with it, you know, birth and death?"

"No, I am certain there weren't. I have the record if you'd like to see it." He looked over his shoulder as he left the office, "What's this about?"

"An investigation. Boy was murdered. We don't know much more than that."

When Peterson returned he was shuffling through a neat and thick sheaf of papers, work orders and invoices. He looked down his nose and hummed a popular tune for a minute, seeing for himself, then handed several crisp sheets of paper to the policeman.

Armistead took the paperwork and looked at it carefully. He acknowledged the man's speculation with a nod and looked with great concentration at this new bit of evidence. "Can I take this with me? I'll return it after I have examined it more."

Peterson agreed. He couldn't see what could be learned from it, but Armistead knew that if you looked at something over and over and even slept on it, sometimes something popped up that you missed the first several times through. This lacked promise, he had to admit, being a plain piece of paper with a simple, direct, clearly written set of instructions. There was how, what, where, and when, but no who or why. It was what he needed most, the reason for all of this and the identity of the poor young man lying cold in the grave. Day in and day out he became less real. Armistead knew this all too well. It was why he liked to talk to witnesses right away, when things told might at least resemble what actually took place.

Everything meant something; even nothing meant something. Like the fact that the writer wanted anonymity so much that he, or she, as the case may be, used plain pen and ink and paper, and insulated themselves further by using a messenger to make the purchase. To take such steps meant it was very important to someone to conceal what this was all about. He looked at the writing again. Strong. Direct. Probably written by a man, maybe someone in a position of authority. This case began to be what he considered compelling. It was something that demanded action and results. Yes, he loved mysteries. He would not forget this one.

It didn't take long to ascertain that no one at the shop remembered the boy who brought the note to them. A predictable dead end. The two men exchanged pleasantries as Armistead prepared to leave. Peterson looked out of his office window at his yard full of blank markers. Somewhere, at that moment, there was a living person who would soon have his name put thereon, a lighthouse marking where he would remain, like a rock on the coast. The bubbles and wrinkles in the window glass bent the stones into threatening shapes. He folded his arms and turned his head toward his guest.

"What makes me sad is the dates—how close together some of them are. The older the stone the more likely it marks the place where a child was laid to rest. Born and died in the same year. Now folks live longer, but still no one has anything to say on their headstones, just when they were born and when they died. It's bad for me—not so much business, you see, just writing dates—but it is worse for the dead man. Lived and died and nothing to show for it. Not even a few words. Like it didn't count at all." It was precisely this that made the mystery of the young man named Lamp so intriguing.

"As you said before, my work begins after someone has gotten themselves in trouble. No one has figured out how to prevent criminals from doing what they do. Never will, if you ask me. Is there anyone out there who can say he really doesn't know it's wrong to do these things? A lot of them, you know, are good fellows, driven to do stupid things. But make no mistake, there are a lot of bad men in the world. They don't care for anyone but themselves and never will. All these years and I still don't understand it. Not at all. I can't stop mine and you can't stop yours." They smiled and nodded in unison.

"Well, thank you, Mr. Peterson. I'll bring your papers back before long. It has been a pleasure meeting you."

Peterson expressed his agreement in as courtly a manner as did his fellow Virginian. They shook hands and walked to the front of the shop together. Armistead looked at his pocket watch. Billy should be at the tavern by now, he figured, so he went in that direction.

"I'm glad you came back to see me. Last night in my bed I was still afraid, but then I thought about you and it made me feel better."

Billy gulped at the girl's words. He had no idea what to say. It occurred to him that he was nodding like a fool. He looked around the dim interior of the alehouse and tried to think of questions to ask. At this point he didn't care at all if he found out anything about the one man who had stabbed the other man. He just felt himself in a fix and wondered what to say to get himself out of it without appearing to be a complete moron. As much as he liked to have the girl standing near him, it made him too nervous and he suggested they sit at a table and go over some of her story.

"Tell me again, Miss, what you saw happen."

She leaned toward him and rested her arms on the table surface, her hands near his. She wore a black skirt, puffed full by petticoats, which reached almost to the floor, but her top was a low-cut white blouse, not frilly, not tight. Around her neck she had tied a dark red ribbon, just above the hollow place. Her sleeves were pulled up above her elbows and Billy looked down at her arms. They showed lines of description, predictions of her, the skin wonderfully pale and delicate, the muscles below long and showing her strength.

He listened, hearing the words, but seeing her eyes, her lips, her hands, her fear. "Tell me again what the man looked like."

"Did I tell you my name, it's Joan. Your name is Billy. I found out from the older gentleman." She was anxious to impress him with that bit of knowledge. "I never noticed him until the fight started. The dead man was much bigger and I thought he'd be the winner, for certain. And he would have been, except for the knife. You want to know what he looked like. The bad one. Well, he was small, quick like. Dark. His skin and his hair. Like he was a sailor and was out in the sun all his life. Had a full mustache. All the ones come in here look about the same. They get their share from their voyage and come in like they want to see how fast they can make it all go away. They gamble and drink and go after the girls…" She looked around the gloomy room, "It's what some of the girls do mostly, for the money—but not me. Not me…no, I never… You didn't hear that from me, did you? Please don't do anything to the boss, he's a good man and good to us girls. Some of them make a lot of money. Have regular customers. And not all sailors, no. Gentlemen stop in for certain ones of the girls. If you charge him and shut him down, we'll all be turned out."

Billy's head was spinning. He remembered to jot a few notes about the killer. She described again how he had stabbed the victim and run out of the door before anyone could do anything. "Like we were all frozen. Like statues. Then everybody started yelling and running. Some of them got out without paying. Some decided not to be here when you came, their being known to the law already, probably." As she repeated the whole tale he began to relax and he listened once again and then felt it best if he went on his way and met with Armistead.

"You've been a big help, Miss, and we'll do our best to track this man down. If he comes here again, just send word and I'll come right away."

"I'd like that…seeing you, I mean," she said.

"I would…as well," he managed. "And don't worry, I won't tell."

"Won't tell what?"

They both jumped at Armistead's question. They had been whispering like the conspirators they had become and his voice boomed out at them. Neither of them had seen him come in and walk up to their table.

Billy rose. "Can we talk about this later, sir?"

"Why not now?"

"It's about the case…"

"Not about this pretty young lady?"

The young man stepped back and knocked his chair over. It cracked loudly and he scrambled clumsily to pick it up. Armistead took it from his hand and pulled it around and sat in it. It was rough and heavy and it made a noise like a troubled stomach as he dragged it up to the table. The girl was directly across from him and she withdrew her hands from the tabletop and covered her lap with them. She pulled at the edge of her blouse, raising the neckline. He smiled at her and asked Billy if he had finished questioning her. This got him, over his shoulder, replies and assurances that he thought seemed a little overzealous. In front of him the girl watched, eyes dancing a fast jig from one man to the other.

"Tell me please, Miss, the one thing that stood out in your mind about the killer."

"The fact that he had only one ear, of course."

Billy tilted his head back and squeezed his eyes shut tight.

Armistead was pretty sure that this was something they hadn't gotten around to, the distractions being what he knew they were. The shuffling and swallowing he heard behind him and the wide-eyed look the girl was giving Billy converted his suspicion into fact. "And this is what you told Billy?"

"Oh, yes, it was the first thing!" She stared at Billy, her eyes wide with alarm. The constable thought it might be fun to ask which ear while looking at her, but calling the young man by name. He thought he might hear the words right and left spoken at the same time.

"What else did you tell Billy?"

"They were arguing about the cards. When the fight started some extra cards fell from the big man's coat, so he was cheating, sure. Later someone said the man was right to kill him for that."

"What do you say to that?"

"I say you call the coppers and let them do what needs done." She smiled at both of them thinking she had been smart about that.

Armistead made silent calculations. A man with one ear stabs another man over cheating at cards. Not too hard to understand. He had seen it or a variation of it many times before. The drawers in his filing cabinets bulged with cases like this. The judges at the courthouse yawned over them. Look for a man with one ear and some bruises and it's all sewed up.

It bothered Armistead but he had to be honest about it: he was unable to summon up any sympathy for the dead man. He deserved at least the full attention of the law. Someone should care about him and work tirelessly to apprehend the man who murdered him. Maybe Lamp was worse than the card sharp. Maybe he was the worst criminal Armistead had ever come across—he was not betting on that—but it was possible. Was the boy's killing a slaughter or a sacrifice? To the killer he had been an animal to be slaughtered, whatever the reason. To Armistead it seemed that Lamp had been sacrificed. He would bet on it, but he had no idea why. When he wagered he usually won, but he usually only bet on sure things. Why not use his time on the man with half his ears gone? It was a game with better odds.

The way out of this came to him. "Billy, this case is yours. I have things to do that might take up a lot of my time." He looked at the two young people. "Get all the information you can. Maybe this young lady will help you when you talk to the other girls. The innkeeper was in the back room at the time of the fight, so unless he knows the man or how to find him, you won't get much there." Billy didn't know if this was a good thing or not, but moved his head in agreement. In the evenings he could be there officially, so to speak, checking on the clientele. He looked at Joan, who was smiling a bevy of thank yous across the table to Armistead. The old man knew what he was doing.

CHAPTER 22

Reflections

Strell watched the sun off to starboard. It came at him, painted a blazing stripe on the water that cut across his ship, inked a long shadow of it, and traveled on. The ship was dark and light. The sun lit one side like fire, the other it left black. The name of the ship, in raised letters across the stern, was held back in the shadows. His heading was east northeast, toward the Sargasso Sea. No matter where Strell was or what he else was doing he was always about his business. Though at the moment he appeared to be idling, he was still thinking. Waiting for an opportunity. The ship was laden with the stores he would need for a long voyage, some of the goods he had bought from O'Neill, and heavy with ballast. She ran fastest when perfectly balanced. Until he was sure of what he was going to do, he would sail on, use the currents that ran to the northeast, and vanish.

Hathor had left Newport News two days before Strell and labored north in rough seas, bound for her home port of Boston. The Atlantic was easily provoked and, as always, more active than passive. The big ship stayed in sight of the coast, though not so near it as she had been when she was caught on the bar during her cruise south. The first mate had doubled the watch and had a line dropped repeatedly to be sure they stayed in deep water.

LeFrank sat in his cabin and looked at himself in the picture he held in his hands. He sat still now, just as he had when the picture was taken. Stillness helped him to think. LeFrank could not tolerate uncertainty. He thought and planned and made sure things were as he wanted them to be.

Now he had a number of alternatives to consider. Once he was sure Elizabeth was dead he could do several things to secure the ownership of the ships and the business. He didn't like things as they stood, however—open ended, with the possibility of unpleasant surprises. For the present he had to wait to see what Chien found out in Delaware. LeFrank considered Chien to be a scheming little snake, but he usually did his job well, especially when he was getting paid to hurt other people. His terror of his employer was, as it was with most people who knew the man, full and constant. Guillaume LeFrank couldn't, indeed didn't want to do everything himself, so he used his specialists. Salete for his smooth charm, Chien to shovel out the garbage.

His presence doubled in his hands as the shaft of light from the swinging lantern overhead sent back, over the picture, an image of the living, watching LeFrank shining off of the glass that protected the photograph. "So now there are three of me," he said.

Jack delayed returning to his work, and only went to the surf station when he couldn't stay away any longer. Elizabeth had established a separation between them and wouldn't allow him to cross it. She ignored anything he said about her staying or letting him help her. No matter how he approached the subject, she refused to acknowledge what he said and would not answer.

Each time he left their conversation was the same, "I have to go to the station."

"That's a good idea, Jack. I'm sure they wonder what's happening."

"I will have to stay for a few days, at least."

"I will be fine."

"You'll be here when I get back...?"

"How long will you be gone?"

"I don't know."

"Then I can't say."

"Please don't leave until I get back."

"It is not what I plan. But I am going, and very soon. As soon as I'm ready. That has not changed, and won't change."

From watching his father and listening to Old Gunn and Ezra Stock he knew things were supposed to wind up, as they said, "fair and square." Both sides of a contract got what they were supposed to. "Fair is when everybody pays his own way," his father often said. Jack didn't think he and Elizabeth had even shares in this, however. One day Elizabeth would regain her place in the world, and he would lose his. Yes, he was sure of it, she would have to fight and suffer, but at the end of it she would climb up into her place of status and privilege while he would descend back into his. He had no desire to live for years in misery, like Kimball and Marshall, and when he was too old to do anything with his life, subsist on the high regard of others. Sainthood was not all that appealing.

Jack was not such an emotional fool that he couldn't admit to himself that he was being unrealistic. How could he hope to possess someone like her? He wanted to marry her, make love to her, have them raise a family together. His want was crushing. It was what was started but never finished here in this cabin with his parents. They never had the chance to see things through. Live to old age, have grandchildren. She could never live here with him. Too much was lacking. He turned his back to her and looked out into the clearing. A faint impression of her was on the windowpane inches from his eyes. It was small and when she moved over to the fire to warm her hands, it disappeared altogether.

"Remember, Jack. I asked you to get me safely away from those...from...that ship. You did. You have revealed to me your honor and goodness. My staying would only take those things away from you. Someday, when I have solved my own problems, I promise you I will try to make amends to you...for everything."

She came closer to him. It hurt her to shut him out. "If things could be different," she made herself say it in a way that would show her affection for him, but let him see its limitations, "I would be happy not to have to say goodbye to you."

He didn't know what more to say. She had shown him that she knew what to do to take care of the place, and of herself. She brought food, kept the fire, cleaned, and even chopped wood. She learned everything at one pass. It was only practice and repetition that she needed for most of what had to be done. Nevertheless he spoke to her again and again about safety. Care of the fire, the lamps, the pistol, and rifles she often carried, watching for strangers. How to lock and bar the door and windows and where to hide the key when she left the area. He told her to be sure she was warm and dry when she went outside and how to make a shelter and how to conceal herself. She nodded thoughtfully each time, as if hearing it only then, and giving it the greatest consideration; she was learning that there were certain differences between men and women, besides the obvious ones. It was a pleasing learning experience. She smiled inwardly, but gave him his due.

Every time he left for the station they walked outside together. He had a sack slung over his shoulder holding freshly washed clothes.

She had dried them outside to give them scent and folded them carefully. He saw the pistol tucked into her belt. She watched him walk away. As he neared the edge of the clearing he looked back. She was bending over a rain barrel, seeing her face on the water. She had been doing this every day, seeing the cut and marks on her face fade away. They were almost gone, but the memories of them were not.

Jack knew she did this as one way to judge when she'd be ready to leave him. Now it didn't make any difference. One day he called out, "There's a mirror on top of the bookshelf if you need one."

As he was taken into the darkness of the trees and she lost sight of him, she said aloud, each time he left, "Goodbye, Jack Light. Thank you. I will not forget you."

CHAPTER 23

Cassiopeia

The Atlantic, November 30

Ellen Brahe moved to the center of the cabin where the light was better. The tossing of the ship was unsettling, but the damp air added a nice workability to the thread she was pulling through her needlepoint canvas. It wouldn't be until she reached her home in Nova Scotia, many days hence she thought, that she'd be able to tell if the salt had damaged her work, or made it impossible to block, or stolen color from the material. She did regret that she hadn't been able to spend more time on deck. The weather had not allowed that luxury and now it was the end of November and the cold and wind and overcast skies were not welcoming. She had brothers and cousins who sailed on spouters and warships and fishing vessels, so she understood the dangers of the weather at sea.

In all, the trip had been a wonder. She had never been to South America, would surely never go again. Sailing to the underside of the world had turned out to be like a stroll down a city street. The weather had been fair, as invigorating then as it was foul now. They met ship after ship along the way, pausing and exchanging news and mail with many as they passed. Each encounter was like a social event. There was a procession of commercial ships, carrying a great variety of cargoes, interspersed with the regular appearance of greasy whalers bound for Nantucket or New Bedford.

Best of all had been the nights. As they neared the equator the evenings were warm and the sky was breathtaking. It was impossible for her to take her eyes off of it. To her it was even better than the sight of the islands and clear ocean water and reefs that beguiled the passengers on their way. For Ellen the jewel blues and greens and glittering sands were outdone nightly by the colorless black-black, and the all colored sparkling whites of stars calling her from endless space.

She was sleepy most days, having stayed up late each night to enjoy the heavens. She was as upside down as the world she was entering, a place as opposite to Nova Scotia as it could be. Now the world had righted itself and she was, as the captain had announced to her and the other passengers at dinner the previous evening, about midway up the U.S. coast. Soon she'd be in cold, barren Nova Scotia.

No matter, she realized, it would be good to return to her home in Halifax, see her friends, and get on with her life. This hadn't been real life; this had been a vacation from it. She would keep the adventure, the year and a half spent away visiting relatives, in her heart as the best time she had ever had. But home was home and every hour that passed as the *Cassiopeia* plodded north brought her closer to it.

Ellen parked the needle at the edge of the canvas, smoothed it and held it out at arm's length to admire her progress. Her cousin Isabella had written to her asking her to come. After many of these requests, Ellen had agreed. She had an adequate income from her parent's estate, and at thirty years of age, believed she was in the now or never stage of her life. She thought that she might as well go and see more of the world than just the rocky crags and many bodies of water of her home province. Hosts of unknown relatives greeted her during he stay and she traveled with her cousin and absorbed the foreign atmosphere of the places they went.

Less than a league away, *Mithras* lurked low in the water. She had no sail on or banners flying, and was barely visible in the mist and spray. Anchors dragged below her, keeping her stable in the unsettled sea. Her captain watched through his glass, thinking, thinking, feeling. His men were ready. The ship always had an empty stomach and was hungry to replace the supplies it used every day and to take whatever could be had from someone weaker. In his glass he saw a slow, fat ship—slow compared to his, that is, one he could easily overtake and capture. But did it have anything worth taking? There was no point in risking his life or having a Cutter Service ship show up, if there was nothing aboard he wanted. Much gold floated on the water from the south toward the ports of Spain, but this ship seemed in its tiresome tacking to be going due north. If bound for Europe, it would have moved more to the east by now and taken advantage of the currents that carried that way in early winter. There was no gain from risking a fight if the ship was full of timber or asphalt or some commodity that he couldn't handle or sell quickly.

Cassiopeia turned and flowed down a swell. The captain saw it. The British Red Ensign. It flew from the topgallant masthead. It was all he needed. The ship was Canadian, full rigged, and from her cut, it was likely a ship with both passengers and freight aboard. Passengers meant money. Maybe women. He let his eye ride the horizon again. No one around. A short chase. Easy pickings. While she was capable of more speed, the *Cassiopeia* was being held back by her officers. They were being cautious and had most of the sails reefed. They were content to yield up a little speed and work a little harder, just to keep control and travel safely. The captain of the *Mithras* gave his men the order to raise her anchors and put on sail. There was no need to goad the crew to action. Every head had been turned his way, watching, hoping. They all wanted to get their hands onto what lay ahead of them, in easy reach.

He felt the skin between his shoulders twitch and writhe as he bent down and looked across the plains of the sea. *Mithras* crouched low and then began to creep through the wave troughs toward the weaker vessel. The chop sent lines of spray into the air and helped camouflage her approach.

Ellen was the only one of the five children in her family who had not married. There seemed no particular reason for it; it was just that where she lived there were no men. The women outnumbered the men and of the few men she knew in her village, none were a good match. As such she was used to taking care of herself.

When you are often alone you hear better. The shot didn't sound right to her.

Were some of the crew shooting at a bird, or a shark? Surely not on a day like today when most of them huddled below decks trying to stay warm and dry between watches. Then there were more shots and she started up from her chair when there was a loud boom and a great splintering crash that cast the ship to the side and her to the deck. She lay face down and confused. She waited until the ship rocked back to try to get to her feet. It was quiet for a moment and the ship creaked and squealed and then there were more shots. Volleys of them. Men yelled. A cannon fired. Ellen made it to the bulkhead and held the foot of her berth while craning her neck to see what was happening. When she got to the hull and looked through the porthole she saw only the gray chop and soiled white spray. Then she realized that they had been attacked. This was not an accidental collision; it was piracy. The shooting confirmed that. Ellen had heard about this, but had never believed it could happen to her. She knew what was done to women when things like this happened. Her brothers had explained this to her.

Time would be short. She thought first of hiding. What of her three lady friends aboard the ship, the other men and women? She wanted to get to them, see what they could do to protect themselves. She looked around the cabin, thinking the ship might be sinking, wondering who the attackers were. Her brothers had warned her when she first told them she was going to take such a long sea voyage. There were privateers working for their own governments, and slave traders and pirates, and God knew what other savages might be out there. Out of sight of land morality perished. Laws consisted of whims. She hoped the men on her ship could protect them, but they were not armed with more than a few swords and pistols; they wouldn't last long against pirates. At her cabin door she couldn't hear anything, so she opened it enough to lean out and try to sort out the noises that were not wind or sea. It was quiet, except for some odd sounds she could not identify, then more shouts, and some screaming and yelling, and she slowly climbed a few steps up the companionway, just enough to be able to see what was taking place on the main deck.

The scene was more than she could take in. The crewmen of *Cassiopeia* were, to a man, dead or near it. A few fought vainly, but were surrounded and wounded. Hunched over the bodies of fallen crewmen and passengers, their murderers worked like madmen, stripping them of their clothes, searching for valuables, hacking at them with their swords and when finished, kicking some of them, or parts of them, over the side. One man had been decapitated. Horrified, Ellen clenched her fists and scowled at the invaders. She looked at the men she had met on this ship, naked and mutilated and thrown away without dignity. She had dined with them, made pleasant conversation with the surgeon, the mates, occasionally some of the hands who were out on deck when she was. She could see that the remaining passengers were being brought up on deck. She backed down the passageway, but couldn't just leave the others. She had to stay, hiding in the shadow and see. Watching was a way of supporting them, not abandoning them. At least if she lived, she could tell their loved ones what had happened to them. Behind her she heard a noise and jerked around in panic, coming face to face with Cora Trussel, a young girl looking confused and frightened.

"Stay back," Ellen whispered, shushing her with her finger crossing her lips.

"What...?"

Cora was slight and fair, in her early twenties, her eyes wide with questions, but knowing in her heart that she was in great danger. She was traveling with her brother and they had boarded the ship in Nassau. The young man had fought with the pirates and Ellen had watched him being chopped down with a sword.

Ellen hugged her, whispered the horror of what was happening in her ear. Cora cried and squeezed her and she could feel her shaking. Ellen pushed back, looked over her shoulder toward the deck, and winced as she heard one of the men screaming in his dying agony. There were more shots. She put her hands on Cora's shoulders and shook her and tried to stop the girl from breathing so hard she would faint. She took Cora's hand in hers and crept up the steps again. She counted. There were still two men and one woman passenger she couldn't see or account for. She quickly decided that there was no help for it and that she must do what she could for the two of them. Then she saw the other woman.

Before boarding the ship the pirates had fired heavy guns and the ball struck and took down the foremast of the *Cassiopeia*. Rigging and wreckage had been blasted everywhere. A spar had penetrated the deck and a hole gaped where the wood had shattered. Its end pointed toward an uncaring heaven and Ellen realized that the other end must have gone through the hull. In the tangle of cordage and canvas and broken boards Martha Rampele was cowering, trying vainly to hide, her eyes darting around her. Ellen could see her shivering as the salt spray and lines of water running across the deck soaked her clothes. She pushed Cora back so that she wouldn't see; she didn't resist and cast her eyes down and repeatedly pinched a pleat in her skirt with her free hand. She plucked at it to pull it out and then smoothed it down. Over and over. Ellen grimaced as she watched the leader of the thugs, the pirates, or whatever they were, reach down and catch Martha by the hair and drag her to midships. He laughed as she tried to get away and slapped her viciously when she fought him. Her arms swung wildly. Most of the men began to gather around their leader. Ellen could not see his face. His clothes were dark and he had his hat pulled

low. He grunted at one of his men and stood back to watch as the
others surrounded her and threw her down onto her back and held her
wrists and ankles. The man knelt between her legs and grabbed the
collar of her dress. He put the point of his long knife against her throat
and yelled something to the others. They cheered. Then he dragged the
point the length of her, halving her dress and corset and petticoats,
sawing and slicing the white material until he had taken away all of her
clothes. She was alive, but bled in places along the lines the steel tip
had followed. Her belly shone white, and heaved with her frantic
breathing. Rich red blood streaked from long cuts down her chest and
thigh. Like predators around a kill they pushed and snarled and fought
each other to get at her. Ellen watched them, one after another, like
animals, taking, taking, taking. Each time it seemed there was less of
Martha's soul left to care. Martha may be dead, she thought. Ellen
hoped she was. It was hard to tell since the woman no longer made
any sound or movement. Her eyes were open and she did not blink.
Maybe now the last sliver of her soul had been ripped away from her.
If she lived, Ellen knew, she would never recover from the vile way
she had been used.

"You're hurting my hand."

Ellen released it and turned to Cora. She thought about the
layout of this deck. Since her cabin and a few others were astern near
the captain and junior officers' quarters, she knew there was a
passageway used by the stewards to bring food and drink to them.
They couldn't go up on deck. There was only one way out. "We have
to hide. Stay with me. You have to look at me, Cora. Cora! Our only
chance is to go below, through the galley and find a way down. From
there we can go forward and try to find a place to hide in the hold.
Look at me. Do you understand? We can't stay here."

The girl nodded through her tears and wiped wisps of straw-
blond hair back away from her face. They fell back again. Her eyes
were red and she kept biting the side of her bottom lip. Ellen pushed
her toward the door. Then she ran back into the cabin and turned
over chairs and trunks and dumped her things on the deck. She
kicked the things to scatter them. "Maybe they'll think they've already
looked in here," she hissed to herself. With a last look at the
unfinished needlepoint lying amid the mess, she grabbed Cora and
dragged her along the narrow passage.

Noise erupted from nearby cabins as they were being looted. She
figured that everyone else was dead and that they were going through

the ship, to steal whatever valuables they could find. Footsteps seemed to pound all around them and they looked at the bulkheads and ducked down as they ran. Each doorway they approached paralyzed Cora, making her stop, and Ellen had to push her on and tell her to hurry. As they ran toward the bow of the ship they saw light where the huge spar had brought destruction to the center of the vessel, like a spear through its heart. Pulleys and turnbuckles dangled from ropes that were tangled with the splinters of the mast. The debris lay about at odd angles and the shreds of a sail writhed around. On a taut line a spreader sawed back and forth, lowing like a cello. Both women inched carefully around the long shaft of wood. From above them blue water and grey light poured in together. To her right Ellen noticed an opening in the deck and looked down. The hatch was an access to another stair down. It was steep. Neither of them hesitated. Down they went. They came to the orlop deck and tried to go forward. They were only able to go so far and then were blocked. Below that was the bilge and through another open hatch they could see the water there. To Ellen's untrained eye it seemed like a lot of water, too much water. It was cold and very dark on this deck. *Cassiopeia* pitched far to the starboard and *Mithras* scraped along her side, pulling more of her rigging down and bashing against her. The water in her mourning body fell to the other side of the keel and splashed with a heavy sound as it poured against her side. The smell of the bilge water was staggering. They had to retreat, back up the steep stairs, through the crew's quarters and down another companionway, into a cargo hold. There was hardly room to stand up straight and barrels and boxes slid with the irregular tempo of the waves. All the way forward, in the dark they crawled until they could go no further. They wrapped their arms around each other and dragged some rope up over them and buried themselves against the ribs of the ship. A few inches away from them the ocean pounded against the prow of *Cassiopeia*, trying to get in. They lay on their sides, facing each other in the blackness. Cora's face was pressed against Ellen's neck and they cried together for a while and then pulled each other tighter and closed their eyes and waited. The sounds of the men yelling and hooting grew louder. They had found wine and ale and the things they were stealing added to their feelings of intoxication. More sounds came towards them. They could hear voices. Cora sobbed.

"Shh, shh, easy, Cora. Lie still. Soon they'll be gone. Lie still."

The women shivered; the men were close now.

CHAPTER 24

The Sutler

The Delaware Coast

"They don't come to me, so I come to them. That's what I do."

Matthew Hastings sat quietly smoking his pipe and listened to the sutler harangue his station keeper. "The end of the war was almost the end of us. We carried the army on our backs, all of us. The men had to have supplies and we were there, Johnny on the spot. You could say we won the war. You could."

Station keeper Will Vickers knew better. Most of the sutlers in the war sold their supplies to the soldiers at very high prices. Sutler stores stood shoulder to shoulder with the other buildings on most military posts and across their counters passed the tobacco plugs and pipes and games and knives and tools the men wanted. Back across those rough boards came a lot of money for the sutlers. Often whole paychecks. War took its toll on the men, their uniforms, their equipment, their souls. They bought buttons and thread for their clothes, and tobacco and candy for their weary selves, and Bibles and games of checkers for their souls.

"So I'm traveling now, still helping the men in the service, you know, and taking orders for any goods your men might need. So out I go. I can take your orders today. Pay right now if you want. When I deliver your orders I'll have my wagon with me."

"Why don't you visit us when you come this way again. If we need anything, we can see to it then."

"Oh yes, I'll come back and do that, just that. But while I'm here tell me, if you would be so kind, about what you do here at these stations. Are there many of them along the way here?"

He said the last as if he had forgotten that just moments before he had told the keeper that he was going to travel the coast, stopping every five or so miles to visit the lifesaving stations. It seemed unlikely that anyone who could read would not know about the service. There were by now almost two hundred installations dotting the coasts, and everyone also knew of the lighthouses and light ships that were warding off death where she waited for ships and sailors. Newspaper writers and editors lived off of the misfortune of others and the loss of life was especially dear to them. Shipwrecks were better than fire and theft, and even murder—unless it was especially sordid or featured someone famous—since with a sinking ship there was so much drama and danger to describe. Life at sea was full of romance, as everyone who had never been there knew. And the added benefit to the writers and editors was that so many people could perish at once. Or be lost to fates unknown. Then the writers could speculate on the terror of those eaten by sharks or guess at what horrible thoughts must accompany the water sucked into the silently screaming lungs of those who were drowning. For most Americans the sea was a place of fearsome mysteries. Only the firmament was deeper than the sea.

Vickers was suspicious, but patiently replied to all of the man's questions. They were all over the board. He asked the names of the men, where they lived, about the other stations. Had they had many ships to save recently, did he know the names of them, had anyone washed ashore?

"Do you get to keep what you find?" He winked and inclined his head toward the beach.

The surfmen standing by the stove, watching and listening to this, all wondered if the man was mad, saying things that made no sense. Vickers too wondered about him. Sutlers had a variety of things that people living on the frontiers needed and could not buy easily. Washboards and flyswatters and lamps and coffee and guns and drugs and scissors and axes and every item of clothing from caps to boots. The little the surfmen had got used and worn and patched until they could be no more. Things needed to be replaced. But this ugly little man with his scruffy beard and thick accent was no longer interested in blowing his own horn. All he seemed to want was the answers to a stream of random questions. Then the noise stopped as abruptly as it had started. The strange man was gone.

Shaken heads and rolling eyes added succinct footnotes of commentary. The surfmen went back to their waiting. One of them played his harmonica, pushing the air through the reeds, vibrating them in a soft, shapeless melody. They watched the stream of smoke that the salt air had pulled out of the wood stove.

As soon as he was out of sight of the station Chien pulled himself up into the saddle and walked his horse west, away from the ocean, and then angled to the north. Somewhere inland from the next station was the home of Jack Light. The old keeper had told him most of what he needed to know. It was easy. It had taken him weeks, but he had come up the Chesapeake, crossed the narrow stretch of the peninsula, and spent a little of LeFrank's gold on a horse and a smattering of goods, just enough to make it look like he was some pitiful huckster, forced to wander about, selling pots and pans to those just barely worse off than he was. When he was out of sight of the station's rooftop lookout tower he tossed the sack of junk, his sample bag, off into the scrub brush. He wouldn't need that any more. All he needed was to be alone with Elizabeth Harrison, to decide just how he would take her and how he would keep her. Thinking of the handful of little telltale beads shifting back and forth like blind eyes in his murky pocket made him sneer. It had been good of her to leave him a trail to follow. He would take his time looking for the cabin, being sure this time that he would have his way. Just as he had promised her. LeFrank and Salete, the bastards, they would never know.

CHAPTER 25

Hope

The Cassiopeia

Rats crawled over the two women. Cora screamed uncontrollably. Both of them kicked and clawed at their hair and face and arms with frantic motions. The vermin skittered off of them, but stayed near, scratching and twitching. The women could feel their tiny black marble eyes watching, and longed to escape them, shed their defiled clothing and bathe, to rid themselves of their stench. Ellen knew what was happening, why the rats were as scared as they were. She had smelled the smoke earlier, but wasn't sure what it was. There were no good choices to make now, but she decided they should not let themselves stay and be trapped here if the ship was on fire. They made their way, stopping often to listen, back along the route they had taken earlier, all the way to the stern and into Ellen's cabin. As they crept through the wreckage they saw smoke trailing this way and that, undecided as it probed the ship. It was black and had a peculiar odor, she was not sure what. It followed them aft. There Ellen climbed the companionway once more, stopping half way, just high enough so that she could peer along the deck. Her movements were slow and deliberate and she braced herself as her head cleared the top step. She couldn't see anyone on the deck and slowly climbed the rest of the way up so that she could look over the bulwarks. The ship heeled over with the roll of the waves and she held on and ducked down. When she looked again she could tell what was happening. The attacking ship had pulled away and was slightly behind them on the starboard side. She could see some of the crew climbing the rigging to unfurl the ship's sails. Two men hung from ropes and looked at the ram on the bow of their ship, checking for damage. She tried to study the ship, learn some feature of it to tell the navy. She tried to make out its name, but couldn't tell what it said. Forward, *Cassiopeia* was being tormented by smoke and flames. On the port side the world faded into a mist that swallowed the horizon. Sweet, safe land lay there, how far away, unknowable. What you want most is often hidden. It was a thought that sometimes visited her when she was by herself, at home, lonely for a different future. She wanted to see if she could stop the fire, but knew she first had to be certain the other ship was gone from sight. If they saw a woman, she knew they would come back for her.

She returned to her cabin. "Cora, they're sailing away from us. We have to wait until they're so far away they can't see us before we go on deck. For now I want you to stay here in my cabin and try to put things back in order. I am going to the galley to get us something to eat and drink. If they've left us anything. Don't go up on deck, no matter what—I'll be right back." She feared that if the girl saw the butchered bodies and the blood and offal smeared above them that she would collapse completely. Cora was weak, and might be of no help, but there was an element of comfort in having her there. It was more than just not being alone. To care for someone other than herself was giving her strength. It consoled her as she took on the role of mother to the distraught young woman. She ran forward.

When she got to the spar that pierced the deck she pulled her skirt up around her and found a foothold on one piece of it, and by grabbing at the tangle of lines swinging around her, climbed onto the deck. The sailors had made it look easy. It was not. She crawled forward on her stomach until she was close enough to see what was burning. The pirates had made a pile of wood and rope and the remains of a lifeboat blasted from its davits when the mainmast fell. To fuel it they had thrown barrels of tar on the pile and around it they had laid lines of oakum. It was the strange smell she had noticed earlier—oakum—hemp soaked with creosote, kept on wooden ships to stuff into cracks and keep the water out, but now being used to destroy the vessel by fire. The fire and its ancient enemy, water, fought each other for supremacy. The wind helped the fire and the mist and splashing waves battled back. It smoldered and smoked and flared up in spots, only to have its rebellion put down again by a curtain of seawater sloshing over the bow of the ship. Ellen realized that for the present there was nothing she could do. Burning and drowning were preferable to falling into the hands of the men on that ship. The fire would have to wait a little longer. She climbed back down and searched for something for them to eat and drink. She found enough food to last them several days. She made Cora drink some wine and they ate some cheese and meat.

"My brother...did you see him?"

Very softly Ellen said, "Cora, he's gone. I'm sorry. Everyone but us. We have to save ourselves. But the other ship...by now they must be far away. We have to be thankful for that. I'm going to make sure and then I have to try to put out the fire. That's first. I don't think it's too bad, but I've got to be sure. The waves breaking on the front are stopping it some. I want you to go through there to the captain's quarters and search it. Do it carefully. Look for his charts and log and any compass or telescopes you can find and bring them in here. We'll need them to sail the ship." Shoulders hunched, hands clasped in front of her breast, Cora jerked her head and looked frantically around the cabin, as if to see if there might be someone else there. "We can't sail the ship! How can we do that? It's sinking anyway, isn't it? I saw all the water, same as you. Where can we go anyway?"

"We can steer it. Just steer it. That's what I hope. And we'll go west, toward land. It can't be that far. Get close enough for someone to see us or for us to get in a lifeboat and get to shore that way. The one on the port side is okay. I saw it just now when I went up. That's why I need you to find a compass. There's still enough sail to push the ship along."

Cora once more looked around the cabin and started to cry. She worried the cloth of her skirt.

"I need your help, Cora, just do those few things I asked you to do. Clean up the captain's cabin, do a good job, just like you did in here. Why don't you change into dry clothes. Take whatever of mine you want from the wardrobe or trunk there. Please do this for me, will you?"

The girl nodded and stood up and ran to Ellen and hugged her, crying but thanking her between heaving breaths. She began to take off her wet, torn dress.

Ellen went back up onto the deck, mounted the quarterdeck, and crawled all along the rail, lifting her head carefully and scanning the seas around her. She took her time. And then she was sure. She let out her breath in a long sigh. They were alone.

She ran forward and looked at the fire. Thankfully it had not spread, but it was hot and smoldered fitfully, and flames stuttered from it in several spots. The heat it sent to her felt good and made her want to stand close to it and turn around and around. She decided to see if she could steer the ship. She surveyed the rigging above her. There was still some sail overhead, flapping and luffing. Some was torn, but there seemed to be enough to make the ship go, if only she could steer it in the right direction. The wind was strong and seemed to be driving them backward, but she couldn't tell for sure. The wind and the water swirled, making it impossible to tell which way the ship was moving, if it was moving at all. Before she did that, however, she had to do the one thing she had been putting off—moving the dead to one place and covering them. Cora would not be able to come up to help her if she ever saw the wreckage of the men and women that had been left behind by the savages from that ship.

She began to drag the people and shards of people to the center of the deck so that she could cover them. Her hope was that they could get to shore and these people could be buried properly and their loved ones be able to visit them and at least know where they had been laid to rest. Some imperative of natural law demanded that she do this unimaginable thing. She couldn't not do it. She used a piece of torn clothing or sodden sailcloth to cover each person as she handled them. Most were too heavy for her and she covered them where they lay. She gagged at the sight of some of them and had to go to the rail and wait for a wave to splash her and bathe her face and mind so that she could continue. The cold was helpful as it shocked her, but wet and sick as she felt, she couldn't stay out in it much longer. When the grisly task was nearly done she went forward again to look at the fire. It had not advanced, nor retreated. She prayed for a rainstorm.

None of the pieces of canvas she found on the deck were big enough to cover all the bodies. It was necessary to gather several smaller scraps, overlap them, and weigh them down with broken casks and cargo boxes to secure them in the ever-present wind. As she picked up a large section of the canvas a hand snaked out from under it and fastened itself to her ankle. It pulled and she lurched away at the same time, screaming and falling backwards onto the boards. Her head banged on the deck. The hand released her and she scrambled away from it.

Then she saw what it was. It was the bloody twitching hand of Martha Rampele. Ellen went to her.

"Oh Martha, Martha, it's me, Ellen. Oh Martha."

She looked at her friend, naked and bleeding, and knelt and put her arms around her. Now it all was more than she could bear. She cried and cried, thinking she would never stop. They had to get below. Ellen rolled the woman as gently as she could onto one of the sail fragments she had gathered. There was no other way. She had to drag her to the companionway. There was a bizarre encouragement in the woman's moans as she bumped over some of the chunks of wood and knots of line that littered the deck. At least she was alive and able to feel pain.

Cora helped get Martha dried and warm under the comforter in Ellen's cabin. She even took some wine and ate a little bread. The two women cleaned her with great tenderness, swabbing the ravaged center of her, and wrapped the cuts on her body. Martha smiled vacantly at them and nodded and even said thanks to them a few times, and then drifted off peacefully to sleep. The chart Cora had found showed their progress as of the previous day. Assuming they had not gone too far, Ellen reckoned that they were about due east of Philadelphia or maybe even New York City. If she could turn the ship that way, west that is, they would have a good chance of seeing another ship. Or running right up onto the land. She didn't know what would happen to a ship if it did that. If they didn't sink or burn to the waterline first, that is. She got a slicker from the captain's cabin and went back to the task of covering the bodies. Short of breath and about to succumb to weariness, she used less care in dragging the rest of the remains to the side of the ship.

There was one last thing to do. It took all of her strength to move the helm. When it finally turned it took the ship the wrong way. The ship circled, east then south. After a half hour of fighting, *Cassiopeia* gave in and took the wind across her starboard side and the sails filled and drove her to the west. One benefit of the tossing and rolling was that some of the burning wreckage had been jettisoned off into the sea and the fire was smaller. The barrel holding the tar had burned away and the soft liquid was oozing across the front of the ship. Only the cold and occasional wave pouring over the bow was holding it back. Ellen looked at the compass and verified that the wind was from the north and that they were on a western heading. The world faded away; only the insistent flames at the front of the ship remained. She tied the wheel as she had seen the sailors do it, looked a prayer up into the gray sky, and went below.

CHAPTER 26

Rescue

Delaware Coast

Will Vickers enjoyed the ride. His horse, Lady, was tall and strong and she too seemed to think a leisurely walk along the coast made a pleasant start to the day. It was fairly clear and just the right amount of cold. Tea by the fire with his old friend awaited him; these visits, every ten days or so, were times he looked forward to and looked back upon with pleasure.

"Captain Stock."

"Captain Vickers."

The former showed the latter to his chair by the stove. It was the chair of honor, only insofar as it was a few inches closer to the nice warm stove, and had a little better view up the beach to the north. Together they looked out the window and watched Ben Wolcott take the horse for some water behind the station and out of the wind. Wolcott was an animal lover and he would make sure Lady was comfortable. One could say he was happier to see the horse than to see her rider. Vickers settled in and slurped his tea.

"Did I ever tell of the night I fought the octopus?"

Ezra shook his head and laughed. No one who knew him could keep himself from laughing when the old man started with "Did I ever tell you…"

"You laugh, but it wasn't funny to me, having to save the whole ship and crew, and all the time holding my breath."

The men in the boat room grinned at each other and gathered around the doorway to the kitchen. They knew what was coming. It was a long and unlikely tale in which Vickers wrestled an octopus and left it with knots in all of its eight arms. None of the men had ever heard old Will Vickers tell that one before. There was no telling where he got his tall tales, but he had a lot of them. They joked with him and complimented him on his quick thinking in battling the octopus. Vickers' mouth went wide and his teeth shone through his long white beard.

"Ezra, tell these young men about Kraken Island."

"They've heard it, Will. A dozen times, at least."

"Did you tell them about the time you were captain of that ship with the big masts? Did you know that, men? Old Ezra, your captain, once sailed a ship so tall he had to put a hinge in the mainmast so it wouldn't hit the moon. One night he forgot to lower it and that's how that big crater got there."

Ezra smiled in resignation and waved the men out of the room. Only Kimball and Gunn remained, ready to participate, as they always did, in the serious side of the visit. One of the reasons for these meetings was to exchange the brass patrol checks, returning them to the proper stations. Mostly they talked about the rosters, and what had happened at the two stations recently. Ship traffic. Patrol schedules. Beach conditions. Repairs. Service rumors. Routine business matters.

The final topic was news from the service. There had been some more scuttlebutt about Congress giving the service official standing, establishing a budget, and improving the manpower and equipment situations. These things varied by state, and some of them were much more organized than the others. Like station keepers and the experienced men of the lifesaving service throughout the country, these four knew that many improvements were sorely needed. Considering the pay, the hours, and the isolation, it was easy to understand that not everyone would be attracted to, or content to remain in, this way of life. For some, however, it was ideal, and the four agreed that those men deserved to have a better reward for what they did, and better equipment to do it with. The big news was that it seemed likely that things would improve soon. Rumors were like life preservers sometimes, things to hang onto and give hope.

Ben Wolcott burst through the door.

"Captain, there's a ship out there. On fire."

"George, get the men together." Without a word Kimball left the room and called to them to suit up and open the boat room doors. Vickers and Stock ran out and stood next to each other on the beach, both with their telescopes held straight out.

"Can you see anyone?"

"When the smoke blows around…no, look at the helm…there's no one there."

"I don't think it's turning. It's going to run aground."

"If it doesn't burn up first."

Ezra turned to Wolcott, "Ben, go up to the tower and tell whoever is up there to stay there and look in the water for lifeboats. I think the ship's abandoned. Not surprising, with that fire. What do you think, Will?"

Vickers wasn't looking at the boat. He was looking south along the beach toward his station. Sure enough, he could see some of his men running toward them. The black, twisting smoke column would have made it easy for them to locate it. On its heading the dying ship looked to come near shore at a point anywhere from where the two captains were standing to one about equidistant from the two stations. Kimball had taken it on his own to have the men heave the surfboat out onto the boardwalk and start moving it toward the water's edge. There were some gusty wind swirls and riffles on the surface and long-period waves rolling in. Two to three feet high. Easy was not a word for what the men had to do, even on the best days, but they all watched the water carefully, calculating what it would be like, thinking they had seen worse, much worse. Uncertainty was what they did not like. With people in danger there was always a focal point and the strange sight before them, this ghost ship, made them uneasy. It moved, it seemed, with intent. Despite their caution they would, as always, trust their leaders and do their duty. You had to go out.

Cassiopeia did not waver from her course. It was plain to see that the ship was going to run aground. How close she would get to shore was unknown. Sandbars moved where the ocean told them. The wind was still blowing from the north, right across her beam, and she made good speed.

"Look how low she's riding in the water. She's leaking. And no one there to man the pumps. Burning and sinking, God help anyone who's still on board." It was Edward Chase saying aloud what the others standing on the beach were all thinking. Old Gunn, standing among them, had been praying all along.

"Ready men. Put the boat in the water, but stay here, don't go out yet. She may just come all the way in." Stock looked along the beach. "Will, maybe your men can spread out that way and be ready to help if someone is still on board. They might jump. We might have to wade into the surf to get them."

Vickers told Matthew Hastings to move the men from the other station down the beach and watch for anyone or anything in the water. Any information they could get would be of help since many ships were lost and no one ever knew what had happened to them. The ocean could keep a secret and anything with a name or other identifying marks on it would be of use. The men knew from experience that the wind could change or the seas pick up and in a minute this ship could pull away from them and become a wreck no one would ever be able to find. It would be welcomed to join thousands of others torn and scattered and slowly wasting away on the seabed. The floor of the Atlantic was a vast expanse of desert, cut with black trenches and interrupted by mountain ranges, Saharas and Himalayas hidden under miles of green and blue water. The men also knew that the fire might flare up and make it impossible for them to do anything at all.

"Usually we go to them. This one seems determined to come to us." These words went through Jack's mind as he stood atop the ridge of sand that belonged to the last line of dunes, the sentinel that kept the ocean and the bay apart. It was not what he expected. On his way back from his cabin he thought he'd be joining the others for a normal day of training and would be worrying about explaining himself. He got apprehensive about it every time he neared the station, even though after almost two full months of having Elizabeth hidden at his cabin his frequent trips there were rarely ever mentioned. He welcomed the scene before him—a proscenium of the station, to its right the men standing by the surfboat, and a line of others, all transfixed at the sight of a ship, huge in aspect as it came close, burning, and as he could see even from where he stood, abandoned. Every back was turned to him. He would not be the center of attention, not today.

Ezra ordered a Coston flare be lit to attract the attention of anyone on board. It stirred Jack to action and he ran down to the station and picked up his gear. When he reached Ezra there were some waves and nods from the other men and Ezra told him he was glad to see him. Kimball smiled and that helped settle him. Jack stood with the other men as they scanned the deck of the ship and the water between them and the dying vessel. Nothing.

"Why the gulls?" Vickers muttered the words and Stock answered, "What I was thinking too."

For although the ship looked to be empty, and the sky and land and sea displayed their complete indifference, the birds seemed feverish to form a coterie with the fire on deck and the water in the bilge to hasten her perishing. Like the weight of them alone could sink her. Ring-bills, herring gulls, and laughing gulls stormed the deck at midships, diving and fighting and squawking like madmen. Gulls often followed ships, like sharks, opportunists trailing along, looking for anything edible that went over the side. Occasionally they used the cross trees as a nice perch for a rest or a free ride, but never in this number, not even when the ships were close to shore. There were clouds of them and more arriving all the time. A heaving blanket of white billowed over the center of the ship. Crows too began to show their interest in the death throes of *Cassiopeia*. One would have expected the birds to avoid the fire and the black smoke that streamed out this way and that, sporadically combed with licking flames. But the temptation was too great.

When *Cassiopeia* hit the sandbar it jarred the women and scared them badly. Cora was barely holding her emotions in check and Martha Rampele was awake, but still removed from reality. Ellen once again took charge and told them to stay in the cabin while she went above. One of the men saw her walking across the deck and called out. Soon Ellen Brahe had a large audience of surfmen training their eyes on her and watching her waving back at them. She clapped her hand to her chest and in broad gestures indicated that there were two others aboard. It was obvious that they couldn't use a breeches buoy to affect a rescue that would be the safer, preferable thing to do.

"Go!"

Kimball waved to Jack and he vaulted the side of the surfboat and he and Kimball and the five other men began to move through the breakers. Kimball took the tiller. It felt good to Jack to be with the men again. It seemed like a long time since he had done this. His muscles took to the rowing as if they had minds of their own and were enjoying every long stroke of the oars. They parted the water smoothly. Once Stock saw them underway he ran along the beach shouting out orders to the men to sharpen their eyes and be ready if they were needed. His commands put them on a higher alert and their necks strained out and their eyes shot this way and that. Undertow and longshore drift could take someone or something in the water a long way along the beach. The surfmen all continued to scan the surface. When Ellen saw them launch the boat she jumped up and down and waved before returning to her charges below. She tried to think of the best way to prepare them to see a group of men they didn't know boarding their ship and carrying them away.

"We're saved. Cora, Martha. In a few minutes a lifesaving boat will come here and take us to shore. It's going to be alright. We can go home. To our families." She tried to smile. There was no reaction from Martha, and Cora cried. It seemed to Ellen that the girl couldn't have any more tears or despair left in her soul. She reflected that in an odd way they had helped. They had kept her busy, made her single-minded and strangely unafraid. Women helped women. It had always been that way. Maybe her optimism was what did it. Maybe she was just numbed from what she had witnessed. Whatever it was she was glad it was almost all over. After this, finding a way home, getting word to her family, borrowing money, regardless of what lay ahead, it would be easy. She determined that she would go by land. It would be a while before she would have the temerity to face the dangers that lived on the sea. There you were too much alone, always in peril, defying God, fate, common sense.

She waited until the men in the boat pulled close before she took the others up the companionway. The birds saw them. The host of gulls rose and fell, shredding the sky with a rumble of wing beats and harsh yells at the world and each other. The slosh of the sea and its slap against the ship's sides was drowned out by the screaming and tumult.

George Kimball was the first man to climb over the rail. He saw Ellen, fixed to a spot, staring at him. More than thoughts of rescue passed between them. She was holding both women tightly against her and her hands were firmly on the backs of their heads, pressing their wet cold faces to her neck so that they couldn't look around them. George didn't even see the two other women. It took a moment for the two of them, their eyes touching across ten feet of space, their bodies electric, to move. They came close to each other. They smiled at each other and shut out everything else.

"Is there anyone else on board?"

She shook her head. He reached out his hand and took another step toward her.

Jack climbed over the side and immediately started toward the bow to get a look at the fire. Saving a ship was always a priority. Massive amounts of money were at stake and if she could be repaired and the fire extinguished, she could be anchored safely offshore and her owners notified. The value of the cargo could also be considerable. He looked down the gaping hole in the center of the ship, kicking at the teeming birds to clear a way so that he could see. The point of the spar that had gone through the hull had acted as a plug, wedged into the thick oak boards and slowing the leak. When she got to the shallows, however, it was that same spar that struck first and it had ripped a long gash alongside the keel. *Cassiopeia* was not going to survive this, even if the fire could be controlled. He saw the water rising in the hold and jumped back, kicking at the flocks of birds in frustration. The gulls screamed and Martha abruptly began to scream with them. She pulled away from Ellen and scrambled backward, stumbling over ropes and debris. Jack saw that she was about to go over the side and ran to catch her.

"Stay away from me! Beast! Beast!" Jack was shocked at her anger and accusations and felt hurt by this stranger and her horrible words. "Animal! Animal!"

"Young man, wait. Stop!" Ellen's tone told him she knew something he did not.

He held his place, shrugged a question at Kimball. Martha continued to retreat, her eyes burning into Jack's.

Kimball looked at Ellen Brahe. "What is it?"

She still held Cora, but craned her neck toward him.

He leaned close and she whispered in his ear. "She was attacked. Brutally...by many men...you know what I mean?"

With his lips drawn in a grim straight line he stared into her eyes and gave her a single nod. "How can we get the three of you off the ship? We have to do it now, right now." He looked around, sensed the pitch of the deck, exaggerated at intervals by the bumping keel and wind and swells. They all unconsciously kept adjusting their feet to maintain their balance. Smoke stung their eyes and both the men and the women felt tears creeping down their cheeks, crooked lines furrowing the soot gathering on their skin. The birds bunched and piled at the same spot on the deck.

"This is Cora. She should be alright. Stay here Cora. Just for a minute. Will you do that for me? I have to try to get Martha, there, to come with me. Try to keep the men quiet. Tell them not to talk to her or even look at her."

The two men remained where they were and Ellen released Cora and walked Martha slowly to the side of the ship, whispering to her, trying to soothe her. When Martha looked down at the surfboat bobbing along side she lost all control of herself, broke away from her friend, and lurched off like a madwoman forward toward the fire. Jack thought she was going to throw herself onto it and indeed she might have if he had not run after her and grabbed her, and using all his might, carried her back. She fought him viciously. He was behind her, his hands clamped on her wrists, their four hands wrestling against her breasts, and she kicked at his legs and tossed her head, trying to reach around and bite him. Her screams choked through her struggling, her voice piercing the mixed chorus of vicious crows and insane seagulls.

He squeezed her as tightly as he had longed to hold Elizabeth, and in this desperate embrace with yet another strange woman he forgot, for the first time in many weeks, to think of her. Not for a moment in the time since he first saw her had she been absent from his mind. Until now. He looked at Kimball and the other women. The one in control stood close to Kimball and spoke quietly to him. His face agreed with her decision.

"Jack, take her over to the boat. You'll have to hold her until we can get her ashore. Do whatever you have to do. Just keep her safe until she's on land."

Cassiopeia was now riding so low in the ocean that her deck was only a few feet above the surfboat.

They watched the terrible struggle as the men helped Jack get her into the boat. It was all the crew could do to control her. Her energy seemed not to wane, but grow furiously. No one had ever before tried to get out of the surfboat. They only clamored to get in. When George and Ellen turned back to get Cora they found her wading through the gulls. During the night the wind had blown some of the covers off of the slain men and women. Cora had stalked through the clamor of birds and had found the mangled corpse of her brother. She could not stop them from picking at the flesh of his face. She called, "No, no, no," over and over. Ellen grabbed her and tried to get her to move away from the bloody scene. With her hands over her face and her shoulders heaving, she let them take her and lower her to the boat.

Only the two of them remained on the wreckage of the once proud ship. *Cassiopeia* seemed to hang her head in shame. George looked with calm and sympathy at Ellen.

"Let's get you safe, Miss."

"What about the bodies? They were butchered. It was horrible. I saw them, a ship full of men with no humanity in them. Men with no souls. They were stripped, some of them had…they had their heads and arms…cut off…to get a ring off a finger they just cut…" She shut her eyes tight, swallowed painfully. Pressing her hands, folded as in prayer, against her lips, she begged Kimball in a way that he could not have resisted, "We have to bury them. Care for them. It's not right, to leave them."

She walked up to him and he took her in his arms and let her weep softly. Her cheek loved the feel of his wet oilskin coat. Its smell was oddly pleasant. He spoke softly to her, his lips forming the words against the wet curls on the top of her head. "I don't know what we can do for them now."

Ellen leaned back, grabbed his rough hands. Hers were cut and sore from the cold and from trying to fight the fire. With them she gave back a soft pressure, holding his large hands as she answered the light touch of his fingers around hers. "Send them off. We can hardly fit in the boat as it is, with them holding Martha and Cora. Get them to bring back another boat, or use the lifeboat there to carry these people to shore. They deserve that. Their families deserve that."

Kimball let go of her hands and told the crew to shove off.

"You can't stay, George, this thing is about to lay over or go straight down. Look at how low it is. The water's pouring in. And you can't stay in the smoke and fire…"

"The sooner you go the sooner you can come back for us. Jack, there are bodies here, and we shouldn't leave them. I am not going to leave them. This is for them. What the three of them have lost, and what they had to see. Tell Old Gunn you've seen a miracle; it is one, that these women have survived. Hurry."

Jack took charge of the surfboat and brought it about. The men were glad to be moving away from the ship, but rowing, facing the stern, their eyes were fixed on George Kimball and the woman. Martha and Cora had finally given up their struggles and went limp with exhaustion in the arms of the men, but Jack stayed ready in case one of them had another episode of fear and panic. It had been very upsetting for him to witness such overwhelming dread. He could imagine what might have caused it as he thought about LeFrank, standing close to him on the beach, sensing how much Elizabeth feared him, and watching his black ship skulk off into some unknown realm. A familiar tightness came like an uninvited guest, squeezing his heart and lungs. He realized he was panting.

Stock and Vickers did not like what they were seeing. Kimball anticipated this and mounted the quarterdeck and sent them a semaphore message. They signaled their understanding. He knew what they were thinking.

CHAPTER 27

Boston

When *Hathor* slid smoothly into the tranquil waters of Boston Harbor the wind barely wrinkled the surface, and the air moved the big ship along at a soft, easy pace. News of her arrival reached Jane Barr soon after the ship was secured along the quay and LeFrank was not surprised to see her carriage thunder over the expanse of paving stones between the row of warehouses and the filthy water. It came in and out of view as it made its serpentine way around giant stacks of bales and barrels, past carts carrying boxes and trunks of goods from around the world. She stormed up the gangplank, shoving aside an official who had just completed his meeting with the captain, noting the arrival of the vessel and securing a preliminary manifest. The man didn't seem to mind, hardly even noticed the look on the face of the beautiful woman as she passed. His thoughts were on the money he had just been promised, a large sum, all that for the simple act of looking the other way. He could think of nothing better than getting paid, handsomely, for not doing anything. He couldn't get caught, no one could prove anything, and he had further cemented his relationship with Mr. LeFrank. You had to keep your best customers satisfied.

"Where have you been?"

He descended the stairs by the quarterdeck, not looking back, knowing she would follow him to his cabin. She knew the way. Inside, she pulled off her bonnet and shook out her long black hair, running her hands impatiently through it. "Well?"

LeFrank looked sideways at her as he poured himself some brandy from a crystal bottle on his sideboard. He took a small sip and held it in his mouth before swallowing it.

"You left without telling me. You said you were coming to the theater and we would be together afterwards."

It was another of her emotional scenes, something that happened often, and he maintained a shrewd silence.

"I want to move into the house. Now. Right away. You said when she was gone, when it was empty, I could have it. That's what you promised."

He seemed intent on infuriating her further. He only took another sip, savored it.

"Goddamn you, LeFrank, talk to me."

"When you're ready to listen."

She huffed at him, "I'm ready."

He waited a minute. She didn't say a word, but her quiet was loud, seething just inside of her skin.

"I had business." He held up a cautionary finger and she closed her mouth. "There's not always time to attend to every minor detail when I have something important come up."

"I am not a 'minor detail,' LeFrank, or 'unimportant'!"

He kept the smile inside, pleased that he had achieved the desired effect. For the time being he needed Jane Barr, so he let her go on. Listening to her carping, his whip hand itched. He would have dispatched any man who acted this way around him. With Jane, however, he knew he merely had to be patient for a few minutes. She proved his point by coming to him, her pride evident in one last stomp of her foot, and then threw her arms around him. "Oh, LeFrank, why do you act like this? Well, you're back now and you can help me move into the house. Like you promised." She kissed him, coloring the moments, telling him without words what she wanted from him.

"Everything has to be in place before we can do all the things we want to do."

"What are we waiting for?"

"The details aren't important, Jane, leave that to me. Believe me," he nodded thoughtfully, "I want all of this to fall into place as much as you do. I can't do what I want to do without you."

"It doesn't seem that way. I can't wait forever to go to New York. There is the matter of age, you know…no matter how good you are they look at how old you are. You promise you'll marry me, give me the house here and a hotel suite in New York, and get me onto the stage there, but nothing's happening. I have talent, too much to waste on the wrong person, not to mention this sleazy town. If you won't do it, I'll have to find someone who will. They come around my door every night, you know, the rich old guys, looking for me. I can get any one of them to do whatever I want."

"I managed to get some excellent wine on my trip. Would you like some?"

"You know I have to go on tonight. I can't be drinking your precious wine. I won't be put off, LeFrank. I went to the house. They're all gone. I saw the notice on the door. Show me you're serious—clean it out and let me move in. Let us move in." She studied his face, her eyes wide and her lips slightly parted.

"I told you I would. When the time is right."

"And when will that be?"

He stared at her, waited until he knew she was just about to burst into another tirade, and said, "Soon."

CHAPTER 28

Hunting

Hundreds of heads turned at the boom that exploded from her shotgun. Many of the birds nearby merely started at the abrupt noise; others took off to find safety on one of the many small ponds farther inland. With nothing in the landscape to hold it or throw it back in echo, the sound thundered briefly in all directions and vanished. The folds of cloth she had sewn into her shirt cushioned the recoil nicely. She didn't think Jack had noticed that she'd made that and other alterations to his mother's clothes, the ones he said he must have saved for the time when Elizabeth would make her strange entrance into his life. That statement was one she was sure she would never forget. What made someone think of something like that? Did he really believe it? Did she? The clothes were hers now and she felt good in them. Warmth and ruggedness were luxuries she appreciated. Although she had worked, performing chores and learning skills at Nana's urging, in truth they had taken up little of her time and she was, until her abduction, a soft and delicate person. Now, however, she was feeling the pleasure of using the muscles in her body. She had always been slender, but the weight she had gained since being with Jack was hard weight, muscle, and she reveled in the use of her new found strength. Climbing trees and leaping puddles was indeed fun. Men's lives were assuredly better than women's. She remembered the first time she fired a rifle. Jack had been right beside her, but she hadn't let on about the pain she felt when the explosion slammed the butt of the gun hard on her, throbbing into her bones. Now she knew to have it pressed firmly against her. At night, when she dressed for the time she would be in bed, sleeping in the same room with him, she inspected the gross bruise on her fair skin, an ugly stain spreading itself intimately onto her, replacing the one on her face that was fading slowly away. She hadn't told Jack any of this.

She wondered if he was aware of it. God knew he watched her enough when he was there. Though she tried to appear as if she was indifferent to it, she loved the feelings she had when he was showing his care for her and doing everything he could to protect her.

Although he couldn't tell exactly where the noise had come from, Chien let his instincts lead. He turned his horse to the west and walked it slowly toward the stand of trees ahead of him. Finding Jack Light's cabin had not been as easy as he expected it would be. The odd looks he had gotten from that old buzzard Vickers had made him careful not to ask too many questions, not to tip anybody off. He had wandered through the woods, around the bay and the salt and fresh ponds, and slept out two nights in the woods. The old surfman with the big beard said that there was no one else living out here, so the shot he heard must have come from the cabin. Someone hunting birds from the sound of it. Maybe deer. Someone was close and he had a gun. He moved in carefully.

Both ducks were in the water, within reach of the stick she had brought along for the purpose. She scooted them over and picked them up, proud to have proven once again her newfound ability, as well as looking forward to a nice dinner. She thought about Jack, how this was as commonplace to him as it was exotic to her, and wished he could see her now. She enjoyed the occasional smack of the cold fall air against her rosy cheeks as gusts of wind played in the low grasses and tall white pines. Food for the day in hand, she relaxed as she made her way back into the woods.

Chien and Elizabeth walked parallel lines toward the cabin. Both made frequent stops to listen and look around. When she came to the edge of the clearing she dropped the two mallards she had shot and settled down in the concealment of thick brush to wait for a minute, take the measure of what lay before her, and get her breath. Something stirred up an argument among a handful of crows up in the trees and they sounded as if they needed to be oiled. She was alert to see what had spooked them.

The horse snorted softly as it moved into the clearing. Elizabeth froze. Her eyes went wide and she felt the stinging nervous jolt of adrenaline fly through her arms and chest. She couldn't see the face of the rider but she could tell he was tense, swiveling in the saddle and leaning back and forth, searching the area. There was a gun in his hand. The hood that protected him from the cold also concealed his face. When he made his move she made hers. With his eyes on the door to the cabin he climbed down from the horse. At the same time she pulled the pistol from her waist and laid it on the ground in front of her. Ready. He ducked under the horse's neck to move closer to the cabin and she moved the shotgun up, resting the barrel in the crotch of a groundsel tree. Her wait was rewarded when the horse snuffed again, masking the sounds of the forest and allowing her to pull back both hammers.

He was not a tall man. She could tell that much. Instead of going to the front of the building as she expected, he moved toward the rear. She took the opportunity to reposition herself and cock the pistol. Her hands caressed it. She replaced it carefully in front of her, never letting her eyes leave the cabin. It was hard to be calm, but she was not going to run, no matter what happened. Her breath raced and her head hurt and her hands shook. After what seemed like a very long time the man emerged from the woods on the other side of the cabin, having obviously circled it carefully and given it a wide berth. He approached the front door and bent over the rain barrel, looked at his reflection, and pulled back his hood. He scooped a palm full of water and drank. He took one last look around, scanning the edge of the clearing.

Over the front sight of her shotgun Elizabeth looked into the eyes of Hillaire Chien.

CHAPTER 29

Salvaging Souls

They worked well together. Ellen kicked at the gulls and crows, and searched through the grotesque alloy of blood and limbs and shreds of bodies. George helped her take them one by one to the port side of the ship and ready them for transport. As *Cassiopeia* sank further into the water he was able to cut the lines holding her lifeboat in its davits and let it slip the last few feet to the water and float alongside. It settled gently. They loaded as many of the bodies, the whole ones, as they could and then prepared to leave.

"Wait. I need to get something."

"Let me go."

"No, I'll be okay."

He stood up in the boat. "I won't let you go without me."

She smiled how much she liked him saying that and led him across the deck and down into her cabin. As the ship rocked, the ocean began to claim her. The fire hissed its disapproval, knowing it was going to lose the fight. They ran to her cabin and he watched as she gathered up her needlepoint.

Her face turned to his, looking to see what he thought of her rash decision.

"It looks like you. Something you should keep with you."

She showed him some of the captain's papers and he gathered them and stuffed them into the front of his shirt. He took her hand, "Now, let's go." Even as the water raced across the deck and poured down the companionway, washing over them and scaring her a little, she was immensely happy. She could not remember anyone ever telling her that she was beautiful, although in the honesty in herself she knew that in a simple way she was. Kimball leaned hard on the end of a long oar, pressing it against the oak of her sides and they pushed away from the tragic ship, he watching it carefully and she looking over her shoulder toward shore.

The lifeboat was more than one man could handle, but George pulled hard on one set of oars and managed to move it to the south. He wasn't getting closer to shore but wanted to be out of the path of the large dying ship that loomed over them. The waves were moving her closer to the beach, and as he expected, the spar and her keel suddenly dug firmly into the bottom and the water and floating cargo in her holds shifted abruptly. The Atlantic was writhing in expectation. And then with a great heaving, *Cassiopeia* heeled hard over and poured herself out into the sea.

The masts and sails splashed into the water and he was glad he had managed to get out of their way. Her tumbling body heaved a large wave toward them and they rocked as it lifted them furiously and then passed, dropping them peacefully on its way ashore. As taut and salt starched as they had been when straining to bring the ship to land, the sails were now supple and freed from strife, undulating comfortably on the surface of the Atlantic, retired from service.

All along the shore the surfmen watched transfixed as the inevitable happened, the shuttering gasping drowning death of a ship. It was something they had seen before, though rarely on a calm, sunny day with light, mild winds blowing around them. They stood up the beach from the last line of the spent waves, climbing dunes when they could, the better to see what was in the water. There was no need to go out or worry about coming back. Soon they were busy running back and forth, fishing things out of the surf. More than boxes and floating scraps of wood were now spread out along the sand. In less than an hour the remains, or worse, partial remains, of many of the passengers and crew were hauled from the cold ocean and carried to higher ground. It was a sickening, grisly sight and the surfmen agreed later in the telling and retelling that it was the worst thing any of them had ever seen or had to do. Carrying a person was one thing, carrying an arm or leg or hand quite another. It was universally felt and understood that a man or woman should be whole. In life or in death.

When they reached the safety of the land, George pointed to the guesthouse. "The other ladies are in there. You should see if you can help them get settled. It's the house we use when our families visit, but there's no one staying there now. You'll find blankets and beds. I'll bring some food." He looked up and saw smoke coming from the building. Captain Stock had gotten his semaphore message and had had one of the men warm the place and carry water in for the three women, now refugees, to use. He sent Calvin Massey to his nearby home to see if his young wife could come be with the women and bring some food and clothing.

Most of what was going to escape *Cassiopeia* had already done so and the sea between her and the shore was a stew of the ship's debris and the dead. Whatever would float bobbed and jerked in the shallow chop. The Atlantic shrugged this off, preening herself as if she did not like the clutter of people and things obscuring her ice-cold beauty.

Vickers looked to the women, he and Ezra both thinking that as a much older man he would not seem to threaten them as much. Stock left the station house, surveyed the beach, and beckoned to Matthew Hastings and George Kimball and Jack Light to join him. His sad, grim face questioned them.

The younger men looked to Kimball. "We have to bury these people as soon as we can. Now. If we don't...if we don't, they'll begin to smell so bad that it'll be hard for any of us to get near them. There's no other way, Captain."

It was what he expected. "Can we identify them, to mark the graves?"

The four men looked to the south as more poor souls were dragged up from the surf. "I don't know. Maybe a few who still have uniforms on, crewmen and such. Not many."

Stock looked at Kimball. "What about the last one, in the boat with you?"

"I'll go ask her if she can do it. I don't think many of us men could have gotten through what she did. But it's a lot to ask her." He thought for a beat, "You know, though, I think she can. Strange to say, but I think she'll want to." He waited until it seemed the men had gathered most of the remains onto land, and Ezra supervised them as they arranged them the best they could. Ellen was glad to see him at the door of the guesthouse. "I have a coat just like yours now." He looked her up and down, she swimming in a surfman's shirt and britches, wearing a weather coat. Even then she still shivered slightly and she had a towel wrapped around her wet curly hair. He couldn't summon a smile, coming as he was to ask her to go through yet more horror.

"What is it?"

"We have to bury the people from the ship. It's something that can't wait...and we don't know or can't tell who any of them are."

She stopped his halting apologetic speech, "Wait until I get a blanket to wrap around me. I can't seem to stop shaking. You'll stay with me?"

"I'll be with you...close."

The men kept their eyes downcast as she passed them. Tears sparkled the sun-browned cheeks of several of them and they wiped their eyes and noses on their sleeves. She held onto Kimball's hand throughout, and with the papers he had taken from the ship and her memories, tried to give names to the bodies resting on the sand. Hastings and Gunn followed along, writing a book of the dead.

"Name, name, name, I don't know, a crewman, this one's name was James I think, that man was the cook, I don't know, name, name, name..." and on she went, doing her best for those past care and for those who survived them. Old Gunn was thinking about the living, the people who looked daily out to sea, or waited for letters, or wondered where their loved ones were and what they were doing. *Cassiopeia* would be there soon, they told themselves. At this moment they didn't know what was happening on this remote Delaware beach; they were happy, still married, not yet orphans... Before she had finished walking to the end of the line of dead men and women, the surfmen had taken the first of them, the ones whose identities she knew, and carried them off. Over the dunes was a cemetery, a sterile garden growing year in and year out with each planting of the dead. Close to half of the graves were marked with plain white mute crosses. No one would ever know who they were. Strange to be a surfman. Sometimes more undertakers than savers of lives. Watch, signal, shoot the gun, row, pull, dig. They drilled and practiced everything but the digging.

"Let me take you back now. We'll bring food and you can all rest. The men will keep the fire going, so they'll be in and out. One of the wives is coming to help you. The men know to stay away from the others." He looked her in the eyes. "Are they any better?"

"No. Tomorrow maybe we can write letters to the families and the ship owners."

"Okay. Tomorrow." He tried to smile, but was like her and the others still shocked at what they had all been through. She was glad that she was no longer alone in all of this, that others knew some of what had happened to them. Sharing it with them thinned it out, diluted it so that it wasn't so heavy upon her. Its reality was going by, heading for her past, and now that it no longer blocked her vision, she could see a future. To live was, after all, to surrender to the allure of anticipation or submit to the inexorable pull of dread.

"Later, tonight, when they settle, I'd like for you to come to the house, to talk to, to sit with me for a while."

"You know that I would like that." He held both her hands.

She took a deep breath, looked at his face for a second, let it out in starts so that it shook slightly, gave him the barest nod, and stared down at her hands. He couldn't tell but it seemed to him that she was talking to herself as she walked along the shell path that led to the guesthouse.

Jack Light watched the two people part. In hours, in minutes really, they had known that they could take from each other the rare joys of attraction, understanding, fondness. He had witnessed it. The way they stood and the looks on their faces told him that their parting was one that held promise, unlike that of his and Elizabeth's. She may already be gone from his home in the forest. His head turned toward the west. He remembered. It seemed a long time ago that she had buried herself in the sand under the same house that the three women now occupied. It seemed a long time in fact since this morning when he left her outside his home to return to his duty. Could that have been today that he left her, he thought?

For several days debris from the ship washed up on the beach. Then the Atlantic carelessly disassembled her and there was no longer any sign that *Cassiopeia* had ever sailed upon her calm rolling waves.

CHAPTER 30

The Deputy

Newport News, Virginia

One thing would lead to another. Billy, washed and refreshed and nervous, walked toward the tavern. Its sign, a silver fish jumping against a blue background, was illuminated by a host of lanterns hanging above the entrance. The fish was, to Billy's eyes, kind of stupid looking. There was no reason for it to jump, with a big smile on its face, frolicking over the door to a place where people got drunk and danced and put their hands up girl's skirts and fought each other—at least in one case even to the death—and sometimes ate fish for dinner. The words "The Happy Fish" were painted in red letters across the bottom of the large wood placard. No matter. Not five in a score of its patrons could read anyway. But they could all remember what the sign looked like. "Meet me at the sign of the red horse," one man was likely to say to another. Most people couldn't read their own names, but a majority of them knew their colors and what a horse looked like. Billy went inside and at once Joan appeared at his side. He smiled. "You haven't seen the man with one ear again, have you?"

"N...no. I guess we should talk about it some more. See if I remember anything else." Then she said something that caught him completely off guard, "That man is not going to show his face here again. Add to that two things: he's easy to recognize and he likes to gamble. So we should take a little tour of the other inns 'round here. People don't have that many haunts, you know. I know a lot about them, these sailors and drunks and crooks. I spend every night with 'em, I ought to. They don't stray too far from home."

"I think that's too dangerous, Joan. To go into those places..."

She cut him off, "I work in one of 'those places' every night, Billy, and you're going to say next that he might recognize me and he'll know you are a lawman, and so on. I can take care of a roomful of drunks and thieves by myself with no problem, and if you don't know, I'll tell you they don't none of 'em look much at our faces. They tell us how brave they are, where they've been—all over the world, they say—all about their ships. 'I am mate on the warship such and such.' As if we care. And you should hear the names. Who names these ships? *Lulubelle*, *Victory*, *Mary B.*, the *Cloud*, the *Snow*, *Hathor*, whatever that is, *Clermont*, all states and cities. I can get it if they name it after their sweetheart, but *Hathor*? What kind of name is *Hathor*? They go on and on, 'I hunt sperm whales. I've been to the bottom of the earth. You're the prettiest girl I ever saw.' Mostly rubbish, I say."

Billy suggested that they just go for a walk.

So they walked through the streets, far from her place of employment and its grinning fish, in order to make a long lazy circle through the town. He said little, not knowing what to say. She made up for that and he found he liked hearing her voice and answering her questions. She was interested in him, very interested. That much was obvious. Soon she was laughing, clinging to his arm in a two-handed, one-bodied grip, and acting like they were long time lovers. He was embarrassed about what she did, touching him with familiarly.

"Billy."

He stopped walking, turned to her. He was several inches taller than her and the way she said his name made him incline his head and lean toward her.

"I'm making you feel funny, ain't I?" He didn't respond, not knowing what to say, and worried that he had done something wrong. He wanted to be with her, but he didn't have any idea how to act around her. In his mind there were no words to help him.

"I can see it, Billy. I'm afraid too."

He started to say he wasn't afraid of anything but she stopped him. "It's us together—all at once. I like being with you. You like it too, right?" A little smile on his face allowed that he did. "But we don't know what to do, neither of us. Billy, I've never had a boyfriend, not that I'm saying that you are, but I'd like you to be, really a lot, and I don't want you to go away. Do you know what I mean?" He couldn't say a word, ducked his head, but then raised it and nodded a little.

"Bend down." He leaned over and she grabbed his shoulders, pulled herself up on tiptoes and kissed him on the cheek." He wondered if this is what it felt like to be shot. One of the old timers at the police station always talked about being shot when he was a young deputy and how it burned his skin. Then she pressed her cheek against his chest and hugged him. He draped his arms around her shoulders and hugged her in return. He had the strange inclination to squeeze her as hard as he could. Its onset was sudden and almost irresistible. Of course, he realized that using his considerable arm strength he could practically crush her, so he held her tenderly. Yet he could feel the mysterious urge to use all the force in his chest and shoulders and arms to engulf her. It was a feeling he had never experienced before, and it was unsettling. His limbs seemed to quiver with it.

She withdrew her arms and smiled up at him.

"There." She said it with finality. Like this answered all their questions and everything from now on was all set.

Not knowing what else to do he said, "Thanks."

They walked on, talking and enjoying each other's company. Eventually she led him to the shabby boarding house where she rented one small room. It was down the street from the Laughing Fish and looking that way he could just make out the shape on the sign. Her hand pointed toward a crooked window flanked by unpainted shutters with missing slats and rusted hinges. One hung precariously to the side, held in place seemingly only by the dirt around it. "That's my window, up on the side. If I'm not working, I'm right here. You can always find me if you want to."

"I'll find you. Can we, maybe spend another time together. Not when I'm on duty that is?" It was the question he had brought with him to the inn, a few hours ago. Thinking of saying the words had almost paralyzed him then. It didn't seem very hard to say now. Not at all. She smiled and squeezed his hand and went to her door.

In her bed she stretched and smiled, thinking herself a princess who had been rescued from danger and betrothed to be married to the proudest, handsomest lord of all the lands. His smiles, a short while later, rested on his face in the same way, even if accompanied by less fanciful imaginings. He still had the sensation of the force in him that wanted to hold her tight, stand guard over her. It left him slowly and he drifted off to sleep.

CHAPTER 31

Confirmation

The Delaware Shore

Elizabeth's body had mashed the grasses flat. It ached. For half an hour after Chien rode off she stayed still, cramped and marked in her soul with physical and spiritual pain. She knew. They knew. They were after her. There was no longer any doubt, and so, little room for hope. Unconsciously, her hand strayed to her neck. She rolled slowly onto her side, the movement making her aware of the wetness of her dress, under her arms, and down her back. Between her legs there was a slight dampness where, unaware of it, she had lost control of herself at the moment of first seeing him and knowing who he was. For a while she stayed there, stretched out like a sacrifice to the world. She pictured herself on a raised stone altar with everyone looking at her. Cut her open, examine her entrails to see if they are pure and clean, worthy, and then eat her flesh to atone for…for what? What had she done? Had she hurt anyone, been unkind, unfair, neglectful? "I have no parents, or friends, or home. I have been stolen. I have been stripped, mocked, locked up like an animal. I have thrust myself into the hands of a stranger. A perfect young man. Handsome, strong, smart, alive. Yet now I have endangered him, and to hear him say it, in not so many words, ruined his life. He's fallen in love with me. He's made it plain. There, now I've said it. He loves me and I will hurt him with his own feelings. And I…" She would not admit it.

She collapsed on herself, feeling tired and wanting to go to sleep. Blood smell from the pellets piercing the skin and feathers of the ducks stung her nose. Dead things and live things, she thought, so different.

Elizabeth cried for a long time. Her body was protecting itself, taking her to exhaustion with the effort, in order to make her give up and yield to rest. She stayed where she was, trying to regain her strength. Her thoughts tried to drag her down, but it was her body that triumphed. A chill came and a twisting in her stomach stirred her to action. She sat up in the grass, looking and listening. Her instinct told her to stay where she was for a while longer and she obeyed it. There was still some dried meat and cheese in her carry pouch and she took small bites and savored each piece just as Jack had showed her. At this hour her table at home would have been laid perfectly, adorned with flower arrangements, rich place settings, and pressed napkins embroidered with the family monogram. Candlelight, seductive scents from the butler's cabinet, the glitter of crystal and silver, the encroachment of the bouquet of the wine into her mind— these were the hints and enticements that foretold of the experience to come. Each dish would have been a delicacy. She thought of the biblical terms: lights and perfections. Now, crouching in fear in a foreign place, she was tearing apart small chunks of dried food, and was grateful for them. She had nothing to drink, but the food helped refresh her. She realized that there was a foul taste in her mouth, like there was blood at the back of her throat. She ran her tongue around her lips and cheeks to see if she had bitten herself.

She wanted to return to the cabin, but had to be sure Chien had left. It appeared that once he had looked in all the windows and tried the doors and inspected every outbuilding he was satisfied that he would not find her at this place. After he'd looked in her direction he had turned around a couple of times, watching and listening. Indeed, he had twice walked a circuit of the building and then the limits of the whole clearing. She had tensed each time his line of sight crossed hers, but she never flinched and he obviously did not see her. He looked into some of the open sheds, looked for footprints near the doors and all over the clearings, but evidently saw nothing that alerted him to her presence. It occurred to her that now there was only one thing for her to do: track him. He was cunning; he had almost found her. He could easily be trying to trick her, make her feel safe and return to the cabin. A fire, a light, a noise would be all he would need. Inside, she would be trapped. The Indian door would not stop him from coming in the windows, burning the place down with her inside. She wondered if she could risk returning there for supplies. A blanket, food, warmer clothes. Water, she craved water. She decided against it.

When it was nearing twilight she made her way to the northeast, the direction she had seen him take. It was a long and painstaking effort. Over and over again she took advantage of things Jack had taught her. Here was a plant you could chew for moisture, there some berries missed by the fall warblers, dry, but edible and nutritious. She avoided open areas, keeping to the shadows of the edges of growth. After an hour of stopping and going, stooping and bending, she crossed his path. It was easy after that. His horse obliged her and left nice deep scuffs in the sand. Horse manure on the trail, fresh and fragrant, told her he was not far ahead of her. She held her hand over it and sensed its warmth. She moved more cautiously, with greater intervals between risky peeks along the route he had taken. Since there were almost no established paths or trails anywhere on this part of the shore, he was meandering where there were open areas, around dunes, along flat stretches and in spots where he could sit upright on the horse, without constantly ducking under limbs.

Chien. There he was. Looking for her, but she had found him instead. She stayed very still and waited.

They settled in for the night, he eating by a bright, warm fire, she huddled down in a low place cradled by small sand dunes. She concealed herself with leaves and pine needles and slowly ate the rest of her food. It was okay except for the occasional gust of wind that found a way to get to her. A faint smile crossed her face as she remembered her first day on this land. Less than a half hour after staggering up from the surf she had buried herself in sand, just as she did now. She shivered. She could see him plainly. He was lit from the side by the fire, and she watched in disgust as he pissed on the ground right beside it. He checked the horse one more time and then rolled himself into his blanket.

Now there was only one thing she could think of. The rifle by her side. How easy it would be to take her time, aim, check her aim, and then end it. This close the shotgun would be devastating. Every pellet would pierce the bedroll and lodge in him. Walk up and use the pistol to be sure. Shoot every shot. Leave him for the scavengers. Sometimes the air over the cabin was cloudy with vultures. Let them have a feast. Her compliments. Set the horse free. Someone would be grateful to find it. Of course his failure to report back to LeFrank would guarantee that he and Salete would come after her. She would not be so lucky the next time. No, she had to let him go.

But the question remained. Would she do it if she could? Could she use her newfound skills to end his life? Anyone's life, even one as worthless as his? Back at the cabin, when she thought he was looking at her, if he had approached her, there was no doubt. She would have shot him, killed him. Easily. Threatened, she would fight. She was not, after all, the one who had brought all this on. But shoot a hideous creature in its sleep? She didn't know and was afraid of what the answer might be. Yet how was it different? The same beast, awakened, would do her harm, maybe kill her. It could be that he had been sent to do just that, kill her. "God help me, I like the feeling I get when I think of shooting him, doing away with all of them." Her lips moved as she said this silently to herself.

Her education had taught her responsibility, compassion, virtues to oppose the vices. It said turn the other cheek, not place it with grim intent against the stock of a shotgun. Part of her said always and never; a larger part said except for this one case. Then she thought once more of the silent screams scratched into the wood of the ship. They were voices she might never hear from lips she would likely never see, but the words insinuated themselves into her thoughts. They were like perfect poems, conveying the most passion in the fewest number of words, limitless emotion in the meter of childlike scratches. She touched the barrel of the revolver. "I will use it if I have to," she pledged. "I am going to fight."

She dozed and woke throughout the night. Chien, without care or conscience, slept like a contented child. His snoring woke her a couple of times, but in all she did get some rest. She had no fear that if he made any move at all she would be instantly alert. As disturbing as all this was, it was also a relief to have things put into play. It had been all this while inevitable. Lying to herself and hoping for another way out had been mechanisms she was using to delay things. No longer. She would have to act—leave Jack, as much as she dreaded it—and begin the frightening journey to the north.

Chien climbed onto his horse and started on his way and she waited for a while before following him. The morning was gray and cold and she was hungry and she and her clothes both had a very unpleasant smell. Some bread crumbs and a crust of cheese were all that she could scrape out of her bag so she foraged for a little of what remained in the woods. There were some beach plums, hard as pebbles, but she filled her mouth with them and waited and they finally gave up a little of their flavor and sweetness. A few persimmons clung to their small trees, but she avoided them. She backtracked and got to the edge of the bay and looked for shellfish in the flats. Jack had told her how the gulls would show you the way, and she saw one pluck a clam from the wet sand. The tide was fairly low and she waded out and found some breakfast without getting her feet too wet. It was salty and savory.

It was a long day. Chien walked an erratic path northward, not paying particular attention to route or direction. She realized that once she was certain that he was not going to loop around for another look, she would have to cover that same distance again. Hopefully, she could bag some game along the way, once he was out of range. She needed to eat. A couple of times, when his prints showed her that he had dismounted and was resting his horse, she hurried up and moved to where she could see him and gauge his actions. Giving him a long look, Elizabeth pondered what was in his mind. Her capture, her death, his promised claim on her? It was disgusting, whatever it was. She remembered that he had admitted that he watched her as a little girl and once more she was filled with hatred for him. She aimed her shotgun at him and touched the trigger, but then lowered it again, shaking and sweating. Finally she was convinced by time and distance and his behavior that she was safe, and she turned around and headed south. He had given up here and was going to go tell LeFrank what he had found. She stretched and yawned and pulled bits of grass and pine needles out of her tangled hair as she walked along. It had been a long twenty-four hours and she was bone tired. The cabin was dark and cold when she arrived. If Jack was not here by now, he probably was not, she reasoned, coming back tonight. So, just to be sure Chien had not fooled her, she got some food and water in her, covered herself in several layers of blankets, and slept on the floor in the back corner of the room. She craved the luxury of a hot bath, but that would have to wait until tomorrow. The pistol was in her hand as she fell down, down, down.

CHAPTER 32

Journeys

"Every one of us is on a journey." Old Gunn let the words hold the people for a minute. He wanted them to consider their own lives, not the ones lost. "For these people we lay to rest today…theirs is over. We hope they find peace and we will pray for that peace now, together." Jack looked closely at him. There was no diminution of his body or spirit; he stood as a rock, radiating strength to the strange congregation whose members faced him across a long row of fresh graves. One brave woman was there, standing amid the group of somber men. Gunn believed that the people from the ship were already united with God. This service was not only about them. He never let on to the men his real belief—that all men are accepted by Him—and kept up his stern warnings, lest he be wrong and one of them did not find salvation at the end of his life. Besides, he liked to fuss over them. It gave him joy and purpose. Today he wanted to pray for the dead, but most of all, encourage the living, and show praise for his Creator. When he sensed that they were thinking about their own lives, getting the idea, he began to sing.

"Oh God our help in ages past,
Our hope for years to come,
Our shelter from the stormy blast,
And our eternal home."

They sang the lines twice, the sound fuller and better the second time through, showing Old Gunn, and he believed, God, that they truly meant it. He knew that people want to hear the things that they know, so he read some soothing and familiar selections from the psalms.

Before he finished, the preacher addressed the people they were honoring. He read out their names as they knew them, from what Ellen could recall. Some of the crosses had only a first name lettered on them, some had none. They were simply marked "Mariner." He said to the sky, not casting his eyes down toward the sand graves, that all of them standing there were happy for those who had perished, now that their trials were over, and that they were with God. He promised them that those who remained there on earth would try to give comfort to their relatives and friends and he asked for their prayers.

When they finished singing a second hymn they looked to the preacher. He looked back, the wind rustling his thin gray hair and lifting the lapels of his dark coat. Some of them shifted from foot to foot. He said again, "Each of us is on a journey. As we travel let us say the words that the lord taught his disciples. I can't see how we can go wrong with them to guide us." They said the Lord's Prayer together, but as they spoke, every one of them pictured him with a different face. Gunn saw him with a smile to match his own. He was happy. He loved God and he loved his fellow man. None of this had been pleasant, but he was gratified that he had been able to be of some help. He was an old man by the standards of the world at the time, and it felt good to think that maybe he had given hope and guidance, no matter how little, to some of these people. Surfmen were stoics—isolated, a little withdrawn at times—but he knew his words had affected some of them. It was on their faces, but he would have known it with his eyes closed.

With small waves and few words, Vickers and his men filed slowly to the south, back to their station and their routine. Most of the rest walked quietly over to the boat room. They showed the odd respect that the living show the dead, keeping quiet around people who can no longer hear. George Kimball saw Jack standing up the side of a dune, alone, and asked Ellen to wait for him for a minute and climbed up the soft sand to talk to him. She nodded absently, looking over at the whitewashed house where Ezra sat waiting for Martha and Cora. The two of them were still asleep, huddled together in the same bed. She had slept across the room from them and tiptoed out to join the men for the prayers. Before they were up, needing her attention, she wanted to have some time alone with George, to pinch herself and be sure that what had taken place between them was not just a dream. Even though she was certain about their miraculous sense of each other, she had to see it one more time to believe it. She had attached herself to him for now and for the future. No matter how impossible it might look on the face of it, she was sure that they would spend the rest of their lives together.

When she looked back she saw him, the man she had committed her self to, talking to the young surfman, the one he said was named Jack Light. George was doing almost all the talking. The young man shrugged, looked off to the side, shook his head, but only spoke a few sentences just as he and George parted.

George walked beside her, "He's an orphan. The son of one of my friends. Some of us here, Old Gunn and Ezra and I, have had a hand in raising him, looking after him really, since he spends most of his time here with us. He's done all the things we do pretty much since he could walk, and he's a big help to everybody. I'm not sure what's bothering him, but it started before this all happened," he looked at her, "right after another ship ran aground here a couple of months ago. Something's changed in him. We can't figure it out. But he's young and I guess he'll get through whatever it is. It's just something you don't want to see, the ones you care about being unhappy." George looked back at Jack, who was in the same spot, still staring into the distance, "You don't often meet a man like Jack Light. He's one of the good ones. Like his dad. I'd like to work it out of him, keep him so busy he wouldn't have time for this, but Ezra thinks we should let it be for now." She nodded her interest, but didn't know enough about the men and what their lives were like to offer any help.

They reached out their hands at the same time, his saying he cared about her, hers saying that she too was by no means unhappy.

"What are you going to do today?"

"Stay with you for a bit now. As long as I can. Then I have to spend some time with Martha and Cora. We'll write some letters home. Begin to make our plans. Soon I think they'll turn to each other. They're closer in age and might talk better together than with me. But they will need some care from an older woman for a little longer."

"I think you're just the right amount older—for all concerned." It got him a nice smile.

"Can you get time off…are there duties you have…?"

"Ellen, it's funny, but we get time off and I never take it. I have a lot of leave time due me, and now I have reason to use some of it. Today, though, I should make sure that Ezra gets some help with the men. If I know him, he'll let them be for a while and then he'll get them busy with something. It's best, keeping their minds occupied and letting this all go away slowly. These men are strong in many ways, with what they have to do and what they see, but something like this... It's not all about time, though, it's more about what you do with it. He's an admirable man, him and Vickers both—the one with the big beard—and they know how to lead men. I'm lucky I landed here when I did, and fell in with Ezra. He helped me a lot, no questions asked. Now he knows my story, all of the men do. It's something I have to tell you also. Important to me...and to you. And I have to know about your life. I'm looking forward to it...while we have some days...here together."

"I don't know what could be in your past that would concern me. I can see, the way you say it, it does you. In that way, then, it is something I care about, will care about. Whatever it is, it has made you a peaceful person, and that is what I see and what I like." They looked at each other and kept walking along the water's edge.

CHAPTER 33

Home

Newport News, Virginia

"Retti!" She heard him, but pretended not to. Armistead called out again, but once more got no answer.

It was warm inside and he placed his heavy coat on a hook on the wall. It took its place in line with the others, coats for the seasons. Below them was a row of boots and shoes, an army standing by the door, ready to march. He was often teased by his wife and two sons about the number of coats he had, but he pointed out that he wore them all at one time or another, and it was an innocent luxury to have a small collection of garments, most of them long out of fashion. It was not that he got so many new things, it was just that he couldn't seem to throw away any of the old ones. His daughter went out of her way to remark to him about how natty he always looked. Everyone in the family knew these were more expressions of affection than honest compliments, including her father.

There she was, in the kitchen, shoulders slightly hunched up as she clutched the wooden bowl in one hand and stirred vigorously with the other. He walked up behind her, put his arms around her waist, and kissed the smooth skin at the base of her neck. He loved to look at that part of her, he didn't know why, but it seemed beautiful to him, always had. He kissed her again, fingers and thumb stroking an escaped wisp of graying hair. She was still for a moment, enjoying his attention, then resumed her mixing.

"How's my Retti?"

"I'm sure I don't know about all your other women, but your wife Harriet is fine."

Armistead had a long list of pet names for his beloved wife, and she made it a point of never answering to any of them, although she did look at him as if he was crazy when he used some of the more unusual ones. Her looks brought out fantastic explanations of how he arrived at them and invariably egged him on.

"I love you, Harriet."

She put down her things and turned around and put her arms around him and kissed him. "I love you, Daniel." She searched his eyes, learning about his day with her practiced glance, and have him a long warm hug before turning back to her dinner preparation.

"You hungry?"

"I am ready to eat. Whatever you're having is what I am hungry for." She was a good cook and he was a good eater. They always enjoyed nice meals together. Family meals. They both thought it was one of the reasons for the way their children had grown into fine adults.

"Can I help with anything?" As always, she asked him to set the table and help with cups for them to drink from. Armistead sat and savored the warmth, the smells, the sight of Harriet there with him and thought about the cozy glow of his home. All of this was a part of a thirty-year-old ritual. He was the richest man on earth. Someone had told him that the best thing in the world was to be happy to go to work in the morning and be happy to go home at night. Based on that he had wealth to spare.

When they'd cleaned the dishes and taken a short walk together in the brisk evening air they set the fire and went to bed. They talked about the day, all but gone now and only surviving the blackness outside with the help of a bedside candle. She had gone to the market and visited a neighbor and had a letter from their oldest son. She propped herself up on one elbow, leaned toward the light, and read it to him. It was news of his family, how his wife and children were doing and about his work in the big city. It was hello and love and doing well but, of course, missing you. It was what parents want to hear. They had done the same when they were newly married and making their way in the world, living their own lives, but remembering how important they were to others. They made plans for the next several days, noting things they needed, or wanted, to do.

"I have a mystery that keeps nagging at me. A lad. Named Lamp. I think I told you when it happened. He was found murdered and things don't add up. There's something wrong with it all and I can't put my finger on it. I'll wager I find out more one of these days. Only thing is, I can't get it to stop popping up. Experience tells me there's more to it. It also tells me I have to go over it all again and see what I missed. Look and look again. My eyesight is not as good as it used to be…course I know a beautiful woman when I see one." She folded the letter and let it slip from her fingers onto the floor and turned back toward him. "Why don't you let Billy do it? He needs to do more so you can do a little less."

"Billy's got a girlfriend."

"Well, that is news. Who is she, someone we know?"

"A tavern girl.

"Don't give me that look, she is a nice, innocent, young one, just right for him. It was sort of my doing. He is so bashful he'd never talk to a girl, so I sent him to interview her about a crime. She saw someone killed, so it was perfect for her to look to him and him to feel he ought to protect her. You should have seen them, Billy fumbling and stuttering and her blushing. If they go on seeing each other, maybe something will happen. Course he could stick to his bachelor ways. If not, she'll end up leading him around by the nose, just like you do me."

"Hmmm."

She shrugged the covers up to her chin. "Tell me about the boy, Lamp."

He told her about it in detail. The boy looked wrong for his clothes, where he was, how he was killed, the strange word, "*hathor*," scrawled on his hand. The way all the men at the waterfront had denied knowing anything about him, speaking quickly, looking about, told him that they all knew who he was. Or knew something or had heard something. Every one of them wanted nothing to do with whatever was going on. He had tar on his clothes, like a deckhand, was dressed like a street arab, but had clean hands, not like any sailor or laborer thereabouts. She told him that "*hathor*" sounded foreign so he should ask someone who could tell him about languages. He agreed with that idea and they puzzled out if there was a teacher at the school who might know. Armistead knew many people in the city and he was sure someone would know how to put him on the right track. He would probably have let it all rest, he told her, if it had not been for the tombstone.

"Lamp, an orphan. Lost then found again. Become invisible too soon."

"That was on the tombstone?"

"That's what it said. I talked to the man who made it, thought I was onto something. It led nowhere. Someone paid a lot of money for that stone. Someone who cared about him. Peterson, the stonemason, showed me the invoices. And for an orphan? A young man living on the docks...no, something else is at play here. But I'm baffled so far. Who writes mystery poetry on a headstone for some bum off the street?"

"I'm sure I have no idea what it is, but I know you and I know you'll probably find out before it's all over." She puffed the candle out and burrowed under the coverlet. Her encouragement was helpful, but was a measure stronger than his confidence.

CHAPTER 34

The Leaving

The Delaware Shore, December 9

They were anxious to see each other, Elizabeth and Jack. Jack had watched Kimball and the woman from the ship for several days now, walking and talking, their heads together, planning their future. It made him consider his own, what lay ahead. Elizabeth too had been obsessed with thoughts of the days that waited for her. Seeing Chien had renewed her fear, but more than that, hardened her determination. Every day Jack thought about going to his cabin to be with her. She longed to see him, and caught herself looking often toward the woods, even walking the edge of the bay and peering out over its shiny surface several times a day. He wanted to see her to convince her to stay; she wanted to see him and say goodbye. There was a strong feeling in her that she must first brave that meeting, resist his pleas, suffer the look in his eyes, and bear the sting in her breast, before she left for the north. At first, leaving the safety of his home had been what she feared most. Now she was afraid that the longer she stayed the worse everything would be for her. It felt odd to her that she seemed to need as much courage to face him, the man who had saved and sheltered and fallen in love with her, as she would to return to Boston. He was all she had, but she had to leave him. She wanted to know him fully, and see him, and talk and laugh with him every day of her life. Teach, learn, spend time, love. But that could never be. It was impossible. She would miss him terribly.

Edward Chase was the one who convinced Jack that he could wait no longer, but had to return to his place. To be with her. The big man was playing his little squeezebox organ, singing a nonsense song. Chase finished it, dashed through a piece about a daring soldier, and sat down on a bench. He caught his breath and said, "Here's to George Kimball and his lady, out there right now, mooning on the beach." The men laughed out loud and looked out the doors of the station. He began again.

"O fare you well, my own true love,
O fare you well for a while;
I'm going away but I'm coming again
If I go ten thousand mile."

Chase allowed the last note of the long song to linger sadly and trail off, whispering away with the last air in the bellows. He looked up and stared at Jack, "Hey, lad, you're supposed to smile at the words, not frown. It's about true love, you see, and how the two lovers, though parted, will surely get together again. Lovers always find a way to get together."

Jack smiled. They thought the expression on his face meant one thing, he, another. That night he checked with Ezra and said he wanted to leave early the next morning, to return home for a day or two.

"Sure, Jack…you doin' alright?" He saw the young man nod. "Good. Check the duty list and be sure you get back on time and you're rested."

His body and soul were empty, but his mind was filled with dread. Pulling at the oars of his skiff, usually a satisfying communion rhythm of mind and body that Jack could feel in the core of himself, was for him this early morning a chore, unwelcome and painful. Going somewhere he didn't want to go, accepting something that would make him unhappy. He was desperate to find some way out, find an alternative. But of course, he knew there were none. The rowing made his shoulders hurt. The oars were wet and the roughness of the wood picked at the calluses on his hands. His headache listened carefully for each clunk of the pins in the oarlocks and pounded in time with the strokes, one stroke after another.

Elizabeth wondered if today would be the day. She hoped he would come. She needed to talk to Jack about a few things and then she could go. The first part of her plan was fixed in her mind. She had decided to break all ties with him, end that pain for both of them, and leave the beauty of this area along the shore. Once she got to Philadelphia she could get a train to Boston. What would happen then depended on what she would find when she arrived. There were too many unknowns for her to make plans beyond that.

Concerned that he would frighten her, Jack called out in a soft voice as he entered the clearing. "Elizabeth. Elizabeth. It's Jack."

She came to the door of the cabin and they looked at each other like a married couple, the husband coming home and the wife there at the door to greet him. She smiled at him and stepped back to let him in. One look at her told Jack that he should forget about arguing with her. It was pointless. Rather, he should resign himself to it all and do what he could to help her. He'd been thinking about that also. Surfmen, he had learned from his father, always looked for a second way out. "Don't let yourself get trapped on a sinking ship. Have a spare rope, a knife ready, room in the boat. Preparation, that's what saves you." He sat on the bench and dropped his satchel on the floor by the hearth. She had a small fire burning and he held his hands to it and took a minute to catch his breath and warm up. He waited for her to speak.

"I was hoping you'd come today...so I could say goodbye." She smiled, "Also, I have to ask you for help, where to go, how to get there. What I can take."

Jack nodded.

She didn't know what to make of it. She had expected an argument and now he seemed ready to see her off, no questions asked.

"Today?"

"Yes, I'd like to go now. Soon, while it's still early."

"Sure. Let me think a minute about the best way to do this, the way for you to go." His father taught him to be helpful, make the best of things, treat people properly and courteously. Jack was determined to make this easy for her.

His easy manner and cooperation hurt her. Didn't he care for her the way she thought he did? His strong feelings for her had come first, she was sure of it. Her affection for him had followed. Maybe. Maybe what? She didn't know what.

"Come outside for a minute." He held the door for her.

Pools of light spotted the floor of the clearing on the side of his cabin. He stood by a large such area and cleared the pine needles from the ground. His sweeping boots exposed a dark, damp patch of newly made soil. Tiny pieces of needles and leaf litter gave it a bristly texture and it smelled of the earth. He waited until she crouched down beside him and scratched out a map of the area with a stick. "I was thinking of this before, having you follow the beach, but you've taken to the area so well that I think you can go inland. It's a better route. You won't be seen, there aren't that many dunes to climb or go around and there's shade and cover." He stood and looked north, then down at her, in his mother's clothes, one foot flat, her other pointed out behind her as she rested her knee on the ground. He had seen the attitude before—intense concentration as she memorized something, her face without expression, only her eyes telling what was happening in her mind. When she was finished she stood, whisked her hair back away from her face, and turned to him. She brushed at some leaf bits that stuck to her skirt. "From Lewes you can get a boat up to Philadelphia. Then a train or whatever you want to get back home." She listened, but said nothing. He led her back inside. She frowned at his actions as he barred the door, and lit lamps, and then looked carefully out the windows before closing the shutters. He went over to the bed and glanced at her. Then he pushed the bed aside. It scratched a noise over the boards of the old floor, the marks it made joining many others. He counted to himself, tapping his knuckles down the wall, and when he found the spot he was looking for he hammered it with the heel of his hand, dislodging a board, which fell noisily onto the floor. He felt around inside the opening and pulled out a black cloth bag. It was obviously heavy and Elizabeth understood what he was doing at once. "Jack," she protested.

"You asked for help, Elizabeth, and you're going to get it. I insist. I wont allow you to go without preparation. It's easy for me to do this and it's the best way to see you safe. I have to know that you'll be safe."

She said nothing, just nodded in the gloom. She was tempted for a minute to ask him what he was going to do to prevent her from leaving, but realized it would not help her situation. When he carried the bag to the table, she quickly wiped the tears from her eyes and bit on her knuckle to choke back what she was feeling. She knew it would be awful for him if he saw her crying. She also knew that nothing had changed for him. No, he felt what she felt. He was protecting her, seeing her off with all the care he could give, or that he knew she would allow him to give.

He emptied the bag onto the table. He made stacks of the gold and silver coins. There were a lot of them. To the side he mounded up a small pile of gemstones. In all it was a considerable amount of money. "When I found them I was as surprised as you are now."

She sat on the bench across the table from him, looked at him, the wealth before them, and then back at him.

"After my father died and I was alone, I took extra care to inspect the cabin regularly, making sure everything was in good shape. One day I saw a mark on the wall outside, something I never noticed before. It was the number twelve. Carved into the log. I went inside and looked at about the same spot and saw some scuffs on the wood. Behind the bed. I wrapped on it and hit it and stumbled onto this. At first I thought it must be stolen, but my father and mother would never have been part of anything like that. And I knew they didn't inherit anything. It scared me. So I kept it there and never said anything to anybody about it." He picked up a large purple stone and held it at arms length so that he could see the firelight through it. The flames danced wildly inside the amethyst. He gave it to her and she did the same, squinting one eye closed and angling the stone back and forth before placing it carefully back on the table top.

"One day Old Gunn—the one that came out here that time—asked me if I had the money my father left for me. I told him yes and let the matter drop. Later, one of the other men, Matthew Hastings, a friend of mine from another station, told me he had found a dagger, with gems in it, to add to his collection. He said he had some coins and a silver cup. He laughed about some of the men who had never found anything, but said it was just luck. We aren't rich...the surfmen...don't get paid that much, but some of us have things we find in the sand...from all the wrecks. Little by little I heard men mention some of what they had found, what they had. It was money for their old age. They knew my father had found things and all of them must have thought that I would have known about it. I knew the men went searching at the water's edge, but never thought much about it."

He looked at her and said, "I only ever found one thing on the beach...a thing of great value."

She lowered her gaze and turned her head away and stared at the fire. No more was said.

"Take these coins," he pushed a stack over to her, "and carry them in your purse. This stack, you should sew into a belt and place it against you, inside all your clothes." He laid out the second stack into a neatly spaced row, alternating the gold and silver pieces.

She saw the wisdom in what he was saying. "It's a lot of money, Jack, will I need that much?"

"I don't know what it costs to stay in a big city. Better to have too much than too little. Take these stones, for an emergency. Sew them into your hem or hide them somewhere. If you need to, you can sell them for more cash. Get paper money from a big bank. My father always said to trust the big state banks. For the clothes, take whatever you want, what you can carry. They'll be a good disguise—for whatever you are trying to avoid. What you don't take, I'll keep here."

"It's already all set aside. What I'd like to have. Those things by the door." She pointed to a small neat stack of clothes and a carry bag she had sewn from new cloth. It had a strap to cross her shoulders and she had made it to be perfect for her size. "I also want the gun, your mother's pistol. I'll feel safer with it." She looked worried, but saw with relief that he just shrugged. "A little food to hold me?"

"Whatever I have is yours."

"Jack, I will repay you, somehow, I swear it."

"You, Elizabeth, have already given me a great deal, and I'm the one who owes you. I don't think you understand. The more of what I can give that will help you, the better it makes me feel. This giving is something I have to have. No paying back. You have to let me do this." He was holding up under the exchange, she was not. She stood abruptly and went over to the fire and threw a log on so hard that a shower of sparks sprayed out over the floor. She kicked them back onto the stone. Jack rose and pushed the remaining money back into the bag and placed it into the niche in the wall. He pounded the cover board in and slid the bed back into place. He saw from the rumpled covers that she had been sleeping on his side.

"The mark on the wall, outside, the twelve? I figured my dad made it so he could get to the money from there, chopping through, if there was a fire, or something. I don't know that, but I knew him. Later I realized that it was twelve boards down to the loose one inside."

He stared at the pile of things by the door then cocked his head at her and spoke in a matter-of-fact tone. "If you're going to take off today, you should sew that belt now, and make a nice tight purse to carry. You can get to Lewes before dark."

Jack ate a little food while she arranged the coins into a band of cloth and folded it and sewed it together. The small darts she stitched between the coins kept them from clinking and giving themselves away. She stood behind him and watched him eating as she took off her shirt and tied the belt around her waist. Her body was lean and there was some smooth firm muscle in the middle of her, muscle that had never before been used or developed. She liked running her hands over it. It was symbolic of her creation, a new Elizabeth Harrison, made to replace the old one who had been stolen from a distant dead reality, and was gone forever. When she was dressed again she gathered the food she was taking and packed it into her carryall. Jack just stood there watching. It unnerved her that he wasn't saying anything, just helping her, just giving her up, letting her go. She knew what he thought, but in a way just wanted to hear him say it again. Taking one last look at the place that had become her home, her first real home she realized, she went outside. Jack followed.

He looked at her, but didn't stand close to her. What he saw was what nature aspired to. She had a purity of evenness. Her body was long and lean, the weight she lost regained, and more. When he studied her face, he saw that her skin, now colored by the sun, was clear and smooth. She had a long nose, lips that smiled when they were relaxed, and dark eyes that were like her hair, shining and rich. The bruising she brought with her was gone and the scar he had stitched was fading. She had fixed her hair to drift down over that eyebrow to minimize its presence. While he memorized her, she was doing the same to him. Like telepaths they looked at each other. She saw the same man she had first clutched at the beach. Now, however, he was careworn, thinner, diminished, all because of her, she knew. It made her sad. He was the inverse of her as men are to women, she reflected. He was broader at the shoulders as she was at her hips, his weight high, hers low. Together, their arms around each other, she thought that they would have been just right. Today he was not the same as he had been. His wide face was clear, as were his dark eyes, brown like hers. But no smile flashed brilliant against his tanned skin and his wide mouth was sad and set, pressed against his teeth.

Elizabeth took a step closer to him. He stayed where he was. His eyes wrote love songs to her. Hers begged him to forget and not forget, telling him all that she felt, but could never act upon. She longed to accept his offers, but could not. They'd gone over this before and neither wanted to feel again the dark matter of emotion that spoken words would reveal to them. So they said them one last time. In silence.

They said, "Goodbye," just that one word, at the same time. Hers was little more than a whisper, his low, the last sound hardly making its way in the wind.

She turned to the north and walked away.

CHAPTER 35

Ellen Brahe

Delaware Coast, December 9

The last thing she wanted to do was to leave George Kimball. Whenever he could he had been at her side, learning about her, getting to know her, and being sure she had what she needed. All she wanted was to be with him; there was nothing else in her mind, and she dwelled on him, and on herself. She realized how strange it was that she had never spent much time examining her own life. Once in a while, at home, she felt lonely and sorry for herself, but she liked many aspects of her life, and was, on the whole, satisfied with it. Being busy was not being in love, however. The other person. That one other person. What satisfied and complemented and fulfilled was the giving of time and attention to that other person. It surprised her also to feel all of the physical comfort and emotional exhilaration his care and gentleness aroused in her. She began to understand the mystery of giving and receiving, how they took roles opposite of what she would have expected. Wanting to give made being willing to receive necessary and understandable. Sometimes she wondered about the way they came together—did you have to have an abrupt and repulsive intrusion into your life almost destroy you before, surviving it, you chanced on the one person who fit inside you perfectly, complementing you, filling you up and emptying you out? Nothing like this had happened before, so she didn't know. Was there a price to be paid for this, for finding him? Had she already paid it or was there more to be demanded of her? No matter. Nothing could match what she had been through, and with George, no price in the future would be too high. He, from what she had learned of his past, had come to this point in his life at great cost as well. They had spoken of the fact that they were, in this moment, together, about to enter into another, new lifetime. It would be the third one for her, the fourth for him.

She was preparing to go home. There was not that much to do since she had little to take with her. She had a small bag, a few clothes, and her needlepoint. Kimball was going to take her to Lewes and see her safely on board a boat to Philadelphia. She wanted to travel by land as much as possible and would go most of the way home by train. The other women were no longer a concern. Cora and Martha had found companionship in each other and the Massey woman, and even felt safe around Ezra or Gunn. They liked Gunn's readings and hymns and he loved having new "parishioners" who paid attention to his sermons. Ellen knew that it would not be long before their families arrived to take them home. She hadn't heard from anyone in Halifax, but it was scarcely enough time for their letters to reach her. It was possible they had not even received hers yet. The sooner she left, the sooner she could return. For the present, they had agreed that she would move back to Delaware and be with him. But she had to go home first, be with family, get them used to the idea of her being away from them. Probably for good. It would be difficult for her and for them—they spent most family occasions together and she was a favorite aunt to several of her brother and sister's children. It helped that her long trip to South America had prepared her and her family for the separation. The children were already used to it.

They had not actually said the word marriage, but she was certain they would take vows soon after she returned. Calvin Massey was the married surfman who lived closest to the station and he had arranged for Ellen to stay with his wife and small children when she came back, so their plans were made to that extent. That Ellen had already met her and seen how pleasant and helpful she had been would make her return easier.

Through the rippled glass of her bedroom window she saw him, the stranger, for that is what he truly was, talking to Ben Wolcott. Ben was paying more attention to Lady than to George, rubbing her legs, combing her mane with his fingers and running his hands slowly along her neck. Captain Vickers had the idea of giving them his horse for the trip north and Ellen had enjoyed their practice ride together, with George mounted in front and her arms tight around him. He assured her that they would go slowly, take as much time as they needed, walking some and riding some.

Ellen walked across the soft glowing white sand and entered the boat room. There she found Edward Chase, Jonas Hope, Calvin Massey, and Thomas Steele, sweeping up the floor and wiping down the surfboat equipment. She spoke to each of the men, thanking them, promising she'd come back and sew for them and bake treats for them, telling them she would pray for them. She climbed the stairs and did the same with Mark Tulley, who stood in the tower, watching the sea. She was sorry the young man, Jack, wasn't there to tell him goodbye. Outside George lifted her onto the horse and they waved back to all the people at the station as they walked slowly away. Cora and Martha were side by side at the door of the guesthouse, standing close to each other and holding hands, and Ezra and Old Gunn walked down to the surf to see them off. George took the lead reins from Ben and walked in front of the horse.

When they were out of sight of the station she asked him to get her down, saying that she would rather walk for a while. His hands were tight around her waist as he placed her gently on the dry sand. "There isn't anything like this, is there? Being in love. I do love you, Ellen. It doesn't take any time at all, does it, to love someone, if it's the right...if...you know?"

"Those are the same words I've been saying to myself. At first I was worried it was just the fact that you rescued me and took control of my life under the worst circumstances, but I know, I'm sure, we are both right about this." Her eyes danced, "And I do love you." They looked toward the town of Lewes, to the north.

The sky was blue, the sun was yellow, the sea was green, and the wind was fresh. A busy knot of sanderlings escorted them up the beach.

Elizabeth was making her way carefully, staying in the shade of the pine and holly and hickory trees. One foot after another, toward Lewes and fate one step at a time. Looking over her shoulder, to the side, ahead. Even with their leaves gone the thick stand of deciduous trees, keeping company with the proud older evergreens, afforded shade and held the fragrant, cool air. In places the vault of the rising tree trunks formed cathedrals of space; in others, thick branches made low, foreboding tunnels with small circles of otherworldly light waiting for her at their ends. She had to bend at the waist to traverse these dark tubes through space. Little light came from above. Her thoughts raced from Jack to LeFrank to nothing. And back again. For long stretches of time and distance she was blank, receding into a faint existence, just a person walking over roots, around aggressive old blackberry canes, ducking under dying honeysuckle vines. LeFrank had sent Chien to look for her, so they knew she was alive. In a way, LeFrank was now the only person who mattered to her. Their knowledge of each other kept her alive. She was sad about what had happened with Jack and worried that she'd never meet another man like him. But their knowledge of each other would eventually be a dead thing, cataloged like a Latin text that could be examined and memorized, but never added to or changed. She thought in circles, while her halting steps took her straight toward the town of Lewes.

Lewes, Delaware, was a small isolated town with a brief, albeit rich and varied history. Indians from the area gave it its first eponymous name, Sikomess. That name was followed by Swanendael and, later, Hoorn, ill fated Christenings made by Dutch settlers in the early 1600s. The English called it Whorekill in 1664; then Deale; and finally, in 1682, Lewes, after a town by that name in Sussex, England. In its annals were stories of a failed whaling venture, a massacre at the hands of the Indians, privateer raids, the birth of statesmen, a limited stint as county seat, and an ineffectual bombardment by British warships in the War of 1812. In the sands of nearby Cape Henlopen, the legends said, were buried chests of gold hidden by the pirates Blueskin and Captain Kidd.

Now the town was growing in size and importance. The nearby lighthouse guided and warned, the harbor was filled with ships, and commerce in the port of Philadelphia brought a wealth of traffic from all over the world past her docks. It was the ideal place for ship's pilots to set up shop and be available to guide traffic up the Delaware Bay to the busy port. To the west, away from the coastal lands, small farms were being established. Whatever great force had scraped off the eastern shore of the Chesapeake Bay had used level and square and sighted a transit on the stars. The land was impossibly flat, easy to clear because there were no rocks, and ideal for certain crops. Abundant game and plentiful fish supplemented the diets of the settlers and made it possible for them to live comfortably off the land.

When they were a couple of miles from Lewes they were able to travel a hard clay road used by farmers to take their wagons in to the market and onto the docks. It was paved solely by its use. Today they had it to themselves. Ellen sat in front of George and leaned her head back against his chest. They were used to Lady's easy gait and moved rhythmically together with her, holding on only to each other. His hands reached loosely on her hips and hers rested, with fingers spread, on his thighs. She lifted his hand to her lips, held it there and took it slowly down the front of her. She hummed idly and had her eyes closed.

George had been to the town often and knew the men at the Life Saving Station. The introductions he made fooled no one. He said he was bringing a friend to see her off aboard a boat to Philadelphia, but they could all tell from his manner with her that this was not just an acquaintance. He left her to rest at the guesthouse behind the station, found a stall where Lady would wait for Ben Wolcott to come and get her, and went to the harbormaster to find out more about available transportation. It was late afternoon and there were no boats available. They'd have to spend the night at the Surf Station.

A few blocks away Elizabeth mumbled her way into renting a room at a boarding house for ladies. The owner was suspicious of her, with her head down, odd assortment of clothes and homespun satchel. In her business you got everything. But still, she thought, the ones who won't look at you, well then, you need to look at them. The coins the traveler used looked very good to her, though, so enough questions, as long as she behaves. No men or other things going on in her house, she said to herself as she so often said aloud to her tenants. Coins or no. Elizabeth checked the door of the meager room over and over, making sure it was shut tight, and peeked around the edges of the old yellowed curtain, looking up and down the street as far as she could. The owner said she'd be able to get passage north tomorrow, or the next day at the latest. She decided to stay in her room, eat some of the food she had with her and not risk being seen for as long as she could. Her eyes compared the faces of passersby with the ugly images lodged in her mind of Chien, Salete, and LeFrank. She realized how pitiful it was for her to think constantly of them and had a painful start each time someone approached who even vaguely resembled one of them. It grew late and the power of lamp oil was no match for the darkness of space. Save for the small pockets of yellow dimness outside the public houses, and little candle flames peeking spark eyes through the smudged windows of nearby homes, Lewes sank into black. She slept in her clothes and kept her pistol on a chair beside her bed. The town, even in the dark, was noisy early and late. So much for civilization.

George and Ellen rose early the next morning and went hand in hand along the docks. He showed her the ships, explaining their various parts, how the lines and sails worked together. At the same time, Elizabeth slipped out of the boarding house and walked toward the waterfront.

Not far ahead of Elizabeth, George was telling Ellen his story a little at a time and recounted how he and Marshall had studied for their exams, driven by the fierce desire to be naval officers, a pursuit that excluded all else during that time in their lives. They couldn't serve as sailors and simply learn from experience. They had to know everything about ships, navigation, the military, the world itself, and all that before they could even think about taking command of a vessel. And they had to do it all at once. On her voyage, however, Ellen had looked outward, always outward, to the beauty of the blue water, green islands, and the black and white night universe all around, never thinking that none of that counted as much as the boards beneath her feet. Those mighty oak ribs and planks, that keel and rudder, from bowsprit to transom, and those towers of masts— they were her land, like rock and soil, sure and safe.

"I remember!"

"What is it?"

"That ship. I can see it now. On the stern. It was called *Mithras*. That was its name. I saw it when it was sailing away. Tell the Service—you said your officers work with the Cutter ships?"

"Yes. Good. Are you okay?"

"Relieved. I think it was in the back of my mind, that somehow I knew that name. It's bothered me. Tell Ezra, it's *Mithras*."

"I will. It'll help. *Cassiopeia*'s owners will use it, maybe put out a reward. I'll write to them and tell Ezra and the men. The Cutter Service will watch for that ship. I promise you I'll see to it."

A crowd had gathered on the dock, shuffling bundles and packages from hand to hand, waiting to board the small steamer that would ferry them up the Delaware River to Philadelphia. George and Ellen made their way into the middle of the group and prepared their goodbyes. They looked at each other, up and down, and softly stroked each other's faces. They talked in soft, slow kisses and hard hugs. They told each other to take care. They said, "I love you." She watched a few children walk by. People began to board. They scuffed along the boards toward the gangplank when Ellen noticed that George hesitated and was staring intently at the boat, or rather, at a woman who stood at the rail looking back at them, studying the faces in the crowd. "What is it?"

"That woman, in the straight brown skirt. I swear I know her. But it can't be. It's just that she reminds me of someone...Jack's mother. Jack Light, the young surfman. She died years ago. There's something about her, though. Not her face. Her hair, maybe, or her clothes." He decided to talk to her when they got onto the boat. Ellen's playful yank on his arm got his attention back. "I haven't even left yet and already you're looking at other women."

He shook his head. "It took me all my thirty-eight years to find you, Ellen. There's not enough time left for me to start over, so I'll just have to settle for you."

"Settle?"

They boarded together and George went to the wheelhouse and spoke a minute with the skipper, who agreed to watch over the special passenger during the short trip upriver. After he disembarked he did take one last look back at Elizabeth. He had forgotten that he wanted to talk to her. She looked his way. Something was not right about that woman, how she looked, how she darted her eyes around, like a hunter, or the one hunted.

Her heart thundered in her breast. There was the coat and hat, the same as Jack's. It was a surfman. He was staring at her again, mouth slightly open, rubbing his thumb along the side of his jaw. She wondered at it. Could Jack have told someone? No, he said there was no one he could tell. She was sure of that. Had they been found out? She hoped he hadn't gotten into some kind of trouble. But there was no help for it now. The thud of the stern bouncing off a fender brought her attention back to the boat. Its whistle blew and smoke rushed around them as its engines chuffed under the load. She said a prayer of thanks that they were leaving. When they were away from the dock she looked again at the surfman. He stood fixed in place, watching the craft lumber off. But he was no longer paying attention to her. He was waving to a woman at the rail, and she saw her blow a kiss to him. The small gesture was immense in its meaning, she could tell. It made her feel sad at the loss of her surfman, her first, only, and probably last, love. When it vanishes, love leaves you weakened. There is less than half of you left. She could remember the words from one of the ancient texts, "With you, we are not afraid, even in the enemy's land. Without you, we are afraid, even to go home."

CHAPTER 36

The Orphan Train

Both women watched anxiously as the boat transported them up the Delaware Bay. Their concern increased as they moved into the channel, turned northwest, and entered its widest part. The land receded, the wind came up, and each pitch and wallow of the small boat made them clutch at their benches. As they watched the earth vanish, their feet pushed and flexed against the deck, seeking a substitute for it. They looked at the others on board, off toward the horizon, up at the smoke swirling around the stack. There was no comfort to be had anywhere, least of all from the presence of the other passengers as they too gulped, and coughed, and held onto rails and benches tightly. Each fearful face and wide eye staring about made things worse. They drained each other. Elizabeth held her bag between her ankles to keep it from spilling or sliding away from her. Inside her coat she let her fingers stroke the steel barrel of her pistol. Inert, as helpless as it was deadly, the pistol was a talisman against the memory of her captivity aboard *Hathor*.

The travelers drowned in this suffering, enduring it for a while, and then thankfully, edges of land reappeared and began to close in on them from both sides. Every inch brought a small measure of relief. Visible to the east were the marshes on the New Jersey side of the bay where small rivers and points of low land poked out into the shallow water. Everyone felt safer as the waterway narrowed and they turned to the northeast, passing small towns, and felt comforted by the nearness of the land. They waved at people on shore and at the other river traffic, and boat bells and blasting horns were welcome sounds. Elizabeth didn't share this joy, however, and the more crowded it became the more she fidgeted and turned her head this way and that. Ellen noticed this strange behavior and wondered what awaited this woman that had her so visibly upset. The woman's furtive looks reminded Ellen of the pale and fearful faces of young Cora Trussel and Martha Rampele as the surfboat took them away from *Cassiopeia*.

Most of the passengers disembarked quickly and seemed to flee onto the safety of dry land, meeting people or heading off in a hurry to their various destinations. Ellen watched them go, thinking that none of them were doing what she was doing, surviving a harrowing time at sea, finding the person she had perhaps always loved in an imaginary way, and coming back from a wonderful trip to an exotic continent.

She remembered the other woman from the boat, the strange, panicky one, and looked at the faces in the crowds all around her. It had been her intention to talk to her, maybe accompany her on her way. Well, too late now, she was gone. The captain of the small river transport boat came ashore and asked if she needed help. "The surfman said I was to make sure you're safely on your way, Miss. To the train, he said. It's through there. You should take a taxi and they're out front of the port building. Just a few minutes to the station and watch what they charge you, you know what I mean?"

"I do. George…my friend, told me what to do. I will be sure to tell him how helpful you were."

"It's a pleasure, Miss, no trouble at all. Not for a surfman. No, they're the finest in my book. They saved a friend of mine, down the Carolina coast where the islands push way out into the ocean. It's bad there, wrecks everywhere and they go out all the time helping people. My friend says they risked everything for him, wouldn't leave him even though the boat was sinking. Blowing like the devil too. Brave is what they are, you ask me." He smiled at her, making them conspirators. "Crazy too, a little, to do what they do. Not your friend, mind you, he looks okay, but some of them must be."

"Thank you again for your concern. As I said, I'll tell my friend what you said. I'm sure he will appreciate it." She beamed her best smile at him and his take on the world of the surfmen. From what she had seen, witnessed firsthand, no one could understand what it took to do what they did unless they had been there, living through it with them. He tipped his hat and went back to his boat, pleased with himself and his brand of gallantry and charmed from speaking with this nice, attractive woman. He was sure that she liked him. Two hours later Ellen and Elizabeth climbed the steps onto the same train, its engine aimed at the top of the world, both women bound north, one for Boston, one for Nova Scotia.

They were early and both welcomed the chance to be still and settle themselves. Elizabeth was in the second car back from the tender and sat in a seat facing the rear of the train. She chewed on a strip of meat from a deer she had, by herself, killed and dressed, butchered and preserved. It was tough and salty, but satisfying. It went well with the bread she had bought from one of the vendors just outside the station. She looked forward to eating the sugary maple hard candy she had purchased as a luxury for dessert. She figured from what things had cost her so far that she would have plenty of money for travel and lodging and food. The bank in Lewes had exchanged some gold for her, giving her a large amount of currency for the small stack of coins she produced. Her baggage was on the seat next to her, warding off other travelers.

Ellen was two cars further back, on the same side of the train, and was in a seat facing front. When she got settled she put her head back against the antimacassar and closed her eyes. Only a few other people were in the car and they too seemed to relish the quiet. She drifted away from where and when she was, enjoying the drowsiness, and almost fell asleep, but an alarming noise outside the car dragged her abruptly back to a full waking alertness. She sat up and grabbed the armrest. It was the hiss and screech and clank and crash of another train rattling to a halt across the platform from hers. Smoke and steam all but obscured it and when it was fully stopped she gave it a cursory glance and settled back and, now, wide awake, bent over and wrestled her needlepoint from one of her bags. It was a mess. Until now she hadn't thought much about it, but it was as important to her as anything she owned. It was the picture of her relative's house and it was George's first love letter to her. The work of her hands had wrought much. Small tears slid along her eyelashes as she thought of his words, "It looks like you." Surrounded by a fire that wanted to consume them and a sea that wanted to drown them, he had taken time to tell her that she was beautiful. She laughed at how horrible she must really have looked—starved, wet and dirty, shivering and pale, streaked with blood and bent with pain. But he saw, he knew, that she was the one for him. There was something for everyone, she believed. But was there someone for everyone? That was a harder proposition.

Her canvas was hopelessly askew. It would take a lot of muscle and stretching to get it square again. Needlepoint was harder than it looked. Doing it required skill, patience, time, and hard work. Doing it well took vision, artistry, and a determination that bordered on obstinacy. Paintings and sculpture brought near immortality to their creators; needlepoint, and its sister tapestry, while not as lasting or revered in the art world, had their own virtues, a dimension and suppleness and utility not possible in other forms of art. Didn't tapestries endure, outlasting the kings and queens whose castle walls they adorned, all the while bringing beauty, telling stories, and stopping the wind itself from chilling those transitory beings who ruled at court? They heard secrets, watched lovers, witnessed plays of honor and perfidy. Were not fire screens, made with fine needles and colorful thread and born across the knees of ladies, displayed on stands in drawing rooms, maintaining the heritage of privileged lives and the pale cheeks of ladies in waiting. To Ellen these pieces of cloth—raiment of noble places—these fine art creations, while not smoothed pillars of marble nor vivid dashes of oil, were at least superior to poems and stories and musical scores. They were just collections of words or lines of notes. It couldn't take much to put words or dots onto paper. Anyone could do that.

Her musings about this were suddenly interrupted. A new noise approached and rose like the sound of a giant ocean wave mounting and mounting as it drew nearer and then smashing itself onto the land. Outside. It was chatter, then bump and then scream and then roar. Ellen worried with the needle in her hand, rubbing it between finger and thumb and wondering if it had left a rust mark on the canvas.

Elizabeth stuffed her unfinished meal back into a greasy piece of paper and shoved it into her bag. Her right hand pulled at the handle of her pistol and she shied away from the glass. Both women looked through the windows of their cars. On the other side of the thick pane there was a startling sight. It was all the more shocking in that it was so unusual and unexpected. It was children. From the newly arrived train there had emerged children, seemingly hundreds of them, spilling from the doors of the cars and some climbing, even falling, out of the windows. They were running and yelling. Young boys and girls covered the platform between the two trains, pushing and jumping and some of them pounding their small fists on the steel walls and glass windows of both trains. They moved like a frightened school of fish, flashing first one way, then seeing no escape, back again. They darted and moved in such fast and sudden movements that it was hard to pick out any one of them.

It took a half hour to settle the children and get them back into their cars. Neither train could proceed from the station and policemen and railway agents and conductors ran up and down the platform, into the building, and along the tracks where some of them, nimble and desperate to escape, had crawled, risking being killed by through traffic passing down the many lines that ran through the hub. Most of the ones who ran were toughs, boys who had survived on their own, or with abusive parents, and wanted no part of the program that was going to take them far away into a life they couldn't imagine. Where they were, they at least knew the game.

"It's an orphan train," the conductor said. He was standing next to Elizabeth's seat when he pronounced these words, like a lecturer who was bored with his subject, but willing to suffer through it one more time for the benefit of the lesser lights. The other passengers wanted to hear what he had to say and were gathering around her and Elizabeth was barely able to hold herself together. She calmed herself by counting to ten over and over and reasoning that it was very unlikely that anyone would recognize her or even pay her any notice in light of what was going on outside her window. Their faces were very close to hers since they had all ducked down for a better view. In addition, the tale being told was fascinating to her, in the facts themselves and because she had never heard anything like it or about it.

"It's an orphan train. Come through here all the time...has to stop to let somebody off or get freight and then this happens!"

The story the fat conductor told was one gleaned from a number of sources. It came from stories in the newspapers, words overheard on the city streets, rumors, notices tacked to telegraph poles, and pleas from clergymen, policemen, and politicians. Everybody the conductor worked with had his own version. Even after it was all over, years into the future, the truth of much of it would all be irretrievably lost. Despite the good intentions of the program organizers there was chaos in the streets of the big cities. The numbers of children involved were huge and the record keeping inadequate. There was simply no way to gather accurate information and the children themselves were unsure of their ages, origins, even their own names.

"Orphan trains are just that—trains loaded with orphans. They gather them up in New York by the thousands and ship 'em off to farmers out west. Or down south. So many of 'em on the streets they have to catch 'em and ship them off or they'd be overrun. Best thing for everybody. They're a nuisance, dirty, making proper folks sick, robbing them. Send those kids off to farms where they can learn hard work, earn their way, stead of livin' offa charity. People come here from overseas looking for work and bring a load of brats with them, they can't find work and turn them out for the rest of us to pay for. Yeah, this way's better. Course, some of 'em run away, probably steal from the people took 'em in, and come right back to the city. We see 'em hanging round the tracks, sometimes, jumpin' a freight back to New York. Some of 'ems devilish crafty."

In the middle of the century there were many children fending for themselves on the streets in New York. Some were orphans or foundlings, some had one parent, some were runaways. People called them poor, homeless, vagrants, street arabs, thieves, even "the dangerous class." Estimates of their numbers during the seventy-five-year time the orphan trains operated varied greatly, but ran into the hundreds of thousands. As immigrants flooded into America during the 1800s, their numbers grew. Finally, with shelters unable to take more of them in, children's aid and church groups initiated a program designed to move these unfortunates out of the city and into more rural places where they would be wanted and needed. The experience was dramatic. The children were simply taken from the streets, put onto trains, and sent west. They stopped at a succession of small towns where families lined the tracks waiting for a chance to select and welcome a new member. Town by town, station by station their numbers steadily decreased as they were repeatedly lined up and picked over, and if they found approval, left behind. Many of the children were inspected like livestock, and once chosen, whisked off into the wilderness of Michigan or Missouri or Kansas, or some other rural state, most often to work on farms. Some recipient families longed to have a child in their homes and loved them as their own; others just needed laborers, plain and simple. There were stories of success and failure, loving homes and ones of abuse, siblings separated, fates known only in the hearts of the ones, who, having been snatched from one bizarre way of life, were now consigned to survive yet another strange, new experience. Resettled, most of them at least had adequate food and shelter, better clothing and something many had never had before—shoes. Some even found love, though most would not have recognized it or known what to do with it. They might accept love, but would never understand the impossible concept of trust. They had to learn the ways of strangers, learn what they needed to do to fit in and earn their keep.

Historians would seek out their letters and remembrances, and attempt to recount their successes and failures. There was no way to determine the accuracy of any of the material they gathered. Two orphan train riders became governors of states. One, a legend says, was Billy the Kid.

The women were startled when their train began to move. Steam pushed the drive wheels and yelped from the whistle. The engine lurched ahead and the succession of cars yanked at each other one at a time until the whole line of them was stretched out like the bones of a spine. Soon the giant rattling chain of steel seemed to skim over the rails, clicking along, leaving some of the sound, struggling, but unable to keep up with the hurtling train behind them. What remained was a soothing accompaniment of harmonics, as if a composer had determined the proper length of the sections of tracks and to accompany it, the precise distance required between the trucks under the train cars. The lullaby played many of the riders asleep. The swaying motion enlivened Ellen's pleasurable memory of riding with George, his arms about her, fingers touching the bones of her hips, suffusing through her until she was spent in mind and body and succumbed to the need for sleep.

Elizabeth found no such comfort in the progress they were making. She thought that she and Jack were like those orphans on the platform and realized the inevitability of what she was doing. Nobody steered a train. There was no turning—like the rails themselves, which ran like fate far out ahead of her and now connected her to Boston—she could not veer away, nor could she stop. What she had to do was as strong and rigid as the steel that hummed beneath her. The train was the same as a ship; the terminals, where trains originated and where they ended, the same as the ports of call. Between these points, when you were underway, you were trapped. That there were no names scratched on doors did not lessen her fear of being imprisoned, once again being carried away by LeFrank. Trains have names: *Zephyr*, *The Challenger*, *The Boston Express*. She had not thought to look at the plate on the side of the engine. Was it *Hathor*?

CHAPTER 37

Taken

New York

He knew where to find them. Ones he could use. Strell often watched the orphan trains. From time to time he was successful, spotting just the person he needed and could make his own. On this day, five years ago, he knew he'd had a great stroke of luck. The harder he worked the luckier he got. Watch for good fortune, work while you watched, and it would come your way. There he was, that same boy he had seen some years before, operating like an old veteran on the streets of New York, stealing bread from the baker. Slyly taking and smoothly disappearing. He had now apparently been rounded up and was being bundled off to the frontier somewhere to labor on a farm and be lost to the world once more.

He concentrated on his quarry. This was that same boy, Strell was positive of it. He had grown some, sure, but there was no mistaking the face surrounding the sharp eyes that, Strell could tell, saw everything around him, be it a threat or a chance for gain. At this moment the boy was looking for his opportunity. He was an operator, functionally orphaned and abandoned. Strell knew how it worked for some of them—they let themselves get picked up and taken to one of the city's orphanages, where they got a hot meal, some clothes cleaner and less ragged than the ones they wore, and a chance to sleep indoors, warm and somewhat safe. Then, when the opportunity came, they escaped, not wanting to be sent away on the trains. There were stories that surged through the society he lived in, stories that Lamp used as data to calculate the odds and determine what was best for him. He didn't want to be a farmer out in the hinterlands; for all its terrors, he liked the city, preferring the devil he knew. He understood how to move unseen, to blend in. How could he do that in a place where there would be just a few people, and all of them watching him, assuredly the low man, the whipping boy. Here, while there were many threats, there were, literally, many avenues of escape. In the years he had done his work, watching from hidden places, back from the light, Strell had learned from the orphaned and stolen people, knew what they knew, what they felt, how they feared, and how they hated. Orphans and slaves were a brotherhood. Strell watched the boy move little by little toward the edge of the platform, waiting for a chance, perhaps, to slip away onto another train or under a car on the tracks. Graceful. Animal in his slowness. Alert, but not panicked. Instinctively moving to achieve protective coloration by making his silhouette vanish in the dark background of the dirty rail car behind him. Mix himself with the steam and sooty smoke.

This was one he would love to have.

"Hey, boy! Come here!" The Placement Agent knew the game as well as Lamp, and recognized the ones who were likely to try to slip away at the last minute. He was alert to the stepping back and drifting away. His job was to get these children off of the streets of New York and into the interior of the country where they had a chance at employment, at least some kind of home life, maybe even some future. He herded them on and off the trains, shepherding the process along. As he moved toward Lamp, Strell emerged from the shadows and intercepted him. His presence had gone unnoticed until now and it startled the man and the boy. He took the man's arm and said something to him that made him stop in his tracks. Lamp watched as they spoke sotto voce in a hurried intense conversation. They stood along side of each other, but both of the men fixed Lamp in their gazes. His breathing quickened and he took a slow step back to widen his field of vision, hoping for a broader choice of actions. Strell withdrew a leather folder from his black coat and opened it. The Agent looked at its contents, and back at the boy. Lamp thought he saw money change hands. Finally the Placement Agent nodded, turned his back on them, and returned to his duties loading the orphans onto the train. Lamp lowered his head slightly and drilled his eyes into the stranger who approached him. He thought about what had just happened, if he had been bought and sold, why the Agent was, so abruptly, no longer concerned with him. There was, he sensed, a gap in the crowd behind the strange man and off to his right, and he considered his chances of dashing through it and making his way to the inside of the station itself where there were numerous places to hide and crowds of passengers and piles of luggage to help obscure his movements. Yes, he thought he could make it. He couldn't risk looking in the direction he wanted to take, to see if the path was clear, for that would give away his intentions. Strell, seeming to read his mind, held up a hand, a caution, and in a way that Lamp understood, an invitation. The boy did not move. Strell stopped a few paces away form him and said, "My name is Strell. I've gotten you off the train. If you want off, that is. If that's the case, you have to come with me. I'll buy us something to eat and we can talk about a plan I have. It involves you. If you don't like it, you can go back to the street, on your own, like before." Strell smiled at him for the first time, "Crushing bread rolls under your arms to get your food for the day." Lamp took another step back, alarmed at the words. He shifted his eyes and saw the children boarding the train cars, then looked back at Strell, then over at the exit from the platform. He looked back and forth.

His body remained, still, on the platform. His memory searched back into his past, culling out almost everything he could think of that was relevant to this moment. What he saw in his mind was his mother's face.

A woman. His mother. She sang—he remembered the song—it was about his father who was coming on a ship from the old country, but he never came and Lamp knew nothing more of the words. They were crowded in one room, his mother and his aunt, a thin kindly woman whose husband drank himself to stupidity and inevitably, to eternity. Her children had died, one from a wasting sickness, the other from a beating by a local butcher who had caught him stealing. They found him in the street, cut and blanched, all of his blood on the outside of him. He was eight or nine, no one knew for sure. This kind of thing was too common for the police to investigate, too minor an occurrence. If you stole, you took a risk and knew what could happen.

Lamp's mother and aunt worked like dogs. They took turns holding down one job at a sewing factory in the city, one going in early, one late, breathing in the clouds of fabric dust, their hands raw and skin parched dry. The one dollar a week pay never covered the rent, even for one small room with no furniture or heat or plumbing. It had a door that would not lock and a small window without glass.

Layers of blankets substituted for beds and their few extra clothes were their covers. On the coldest nights they slept together with everything they owned piled upon them.

Then a man came. It was not his father, but one of the bosses from the sewing factory. His heavy footsteps were a warning to the three of them and they stared at the door and waited. When they scuffed to a halt outside their door, they stood close and held their breaths. He knocked once and then pushed himself into their room. There was no attempt on his part to hide his disgust with the squalor they lived in and he sneered at the walls and floor as if he could cow them into cleanliness and respectability. He was going to leave the city and was being sent to open another factory in Ohio. It was a big chance for him and he was, he claimed, going to be rich and successful. He wanted to take Lamp's mother with him as "his gal." He had been watching her in the factory and wanted her, but not so much that he would be willing to marry her. She was to sleep in his bed at night and train the new girls by day. He made that clear. She agreed to go at once, standing there in their meager place, saying the words in front of them. Her words shocked her sister and she held her nephew close. "But you must marry me and take my sister and son with us," she insisted. Lamp remembered her words, the way she stood up to him. But he also heard the man say, "Someone else's trash? I won't carry someone else's trash. And I don't want her in my bed, she's too skinny."

His mother began crying, her hands covering her face, and she led the man out of the room and down the steps. He didn't look back.

A week later she was gone. She didn't return from work at the usual time and her sister ran to the factory, but returned a short time later. She told the boy what happened, for it was a story everyone there already knew, and one he would hear soon enough on the streets. The boss had yelled at her on the factory floor, in front of them all, told her that if she didn't go with him, she and her sister would both lose their jobs and that he would have Lamp picked up by a policeman he knew and have the boy sent away. The noisy factory was still and the women paused to watch and to see what the woman would do. Everyone knew he could do it. He had money for bribes, and there were a hundred women waiting outside every day, ready to take any job that they could find.

Lamp had a father that never came to them and a mother that was gone. Left without saying goodbye.

He and his aunt tried hard, but couldn't keep the room. On the street she could not last. There was no food or shelter and she didn't want to try to live as her nephew was learning to live. She refused to steal and couldn't become a whore or even a beggar, for the life had gone out of her. Lamp somehow knew that she had died, even though it just happened that one day he realized it had been a while since he had seen her. She was just gone. She knew the places where he stayed at night—the stable, the alcove of a bank, the abandoned drainage pipe near the docks—but she no longer stopped there. Sometimes she did and Lamp realized it was as much to get some money or food from him as it was to see if he was okay, or dead, or alive. That was okay with him and each time he saw her he asked if she knew anything about his mother or father. Her answer was always the same empty word, no. It occurred to him, when he thought about it later, that the last time she came to see him she kissed him and held him with all the strength her thin and bony arms and shriveled chest allowed. She even cried a little, although that was not all that unusual. Her suicide, he understood, was one of self-neglect. She just stopped living. After that he drifted around New York, plying his new trade, even working at a job here and there, running messages or packages, known for being trustworthy by some of the medium-level criminals in the neighborhoods. From careful listening he picked up the argot of the street in several of the languages spoken in the city. He learned when to be bold, smart, safe. He knew what it was to be useful.

He also learned how to make a quick judgment. He figured things out. He looked at Strell. This could be good, or it could be more of the same misery that made up much of his life. Maybe he'd get a good meal out of it. He never had enough to eat. He could stall until the train was gone, that was sure. He could bolt when they got off the platform and into the crowded concourse. It was something different, this character in the black outfit saying he had a plan for Lamp. Knowing about him stealing bread. If he had been watching Lamp, he could have turned him in to the cops or done worse already. Lamp looked Strell in the eye, "You lead."

Strell laughed out loud and walked ahead. After a moment the boy followed, neither of them knowing that in five years time Chien would brutally murder him.

CHAPTER 38

Ariadne

Delaware Coast, December 20

Jack pushed to the front of the group of surfmen. He grabbed the line that held the breeches buoy. No one resisted him or said a thing.

Early light had brought the ship into view. The giant whaler was full of tried-out whale blubber, her hull low in the water and her deck piled high with the barrels of oil that would not fit in the hold. It was foundering, its main mast snapped in two and toppled into the forward mast, and the sail and rigging ripped and tangled. Some of the kegs were crushed and leaking and the deck was slippery with spilled oil. A storm out in the Atlantic had beaten the ship severely before sending her toward shore and scraping her with disdain along the sands just off the coast. Ezra didn't even consider using the surfboat. They probably wouldn't have been able to get it through the rip current, and if they had, would not have been strong enough as a unit to row it into the onslaught of water coming at the land. Ship and land exchanged signals.

While Edward Chase, the biggest of the men, used his powerful arms to dig a pit to anchor one end of the rescue line to the beach, George and Jonas Hope talked with Ezra about the positioning of the Lyle gun. Chase, smiling all the while, sang through his deep puffing and hard breathing, immune to the cold air pumping into his lungs. "Drill ye tarriers, drill. Drill ye tarriers, drill. Well it's work all day for the sugar in your tay, down behind the railway, well drill ye tarriers, drill...and blast...and fire...and drill."

Calvin Massey and Thomas Steele knew the ship was in trouble, and worried whether they could get the crew off in time, but still had to look at each other and smile at Chase. There was no point in their jumping into the pit to help him—he worked like a machine, never slowing or tiring. They all knew that men could die today, their men, or the sailors on the ship, or both. Still, all they'd get from trying to jump in and help with the digging was probably a shower of sand in their eyes or a shovel smashing into an arm or leg. Chase was strictly a one-man operation when it came to digging. Instead they moved on to the next step and dragged out the anchor boards. These were long, wide planks positioned against each other into the form of a cross. When the hole was several feet deep they would place the boards flat on the bottom, attach a line to them at their junction, and fill the pit with sand, making a base that would be almost impossible to pull up. If all went well, a heavy rope would soon connect the two groups of men, one end fast to the ship, the other holding onto the boards buried on land. Jack and Mark Tulley worked together silently. They laid out the lines, precisely positioned to the side and in front of the small cannon. Ezra had calculated that they would need four ounces of black powder to get the two- to three-hundred-yard range they needed, and while George loaded the charge, Ezra trained his glass on the deck of the ship. The faking box that would help the line play out was beside them on the sand and he idly bumped the side of his boot against it. "Ready?" Ezra called to the crew in a loud, strong voice, his word a question and a command, all the while continuing to stare at the vessel. The men answered in turn that they were waiting for his word and were prepared to do as he ordered. Kimball looked out at the ship, checked the angle of the Lyle gun, and nodded, "Ready, captain."

Jack handed the end of the shot line to him and stepped back over the array of ropes that spread out on the sand. He fastened it to the seventeen-pound steel cylinder and loaded it into the barrel of the Lyle gun.

The men looked around the area, checked each other's eyes, then out to sea.

"Fire in the hole!"

The men held their ears and waited.

Even over the crash of surf and the screaming wind, the retort was a sharp boom that whumped the air so hard that the men standing closest could feel the blow. Blue smoke gusts leaped around them. The smell was sharp and pleasant. One of the men coughed.

Gunn called down, "It's on!," even as though the line still played out. The men's eyes followed the steel slug as it reached up into the sky and then fell toward the whitecaps. The ship had tossed so abruptly that it barely passed over the far rail near the prow. Ezra peered into his glass, hoping it would hold and not slip into the water. It was close. If it missed the ship they would have to retrieve it and begin again. It didn't look as if they would have that much time. At least one of the officers on board knew what to do and he ran to grab the rope, yelling to some of his men to help him secure the line while most of his shipmates watched, clutching ropes and the ship's rails, motionless and dumbfounded. Gunn cried out again, "He has the board, he has the board!" With his better view of the wreck he could see the mate reading the instructions written on the tally board that was attached to the line, one side in French, the reverse in English.

The words read, "Make the tail of this block fast to the lower mast well up. If the masts are gone, then to the best place you can find. Cast off the shot line. See that rope in the block runs free and show signal to the shore."

The man shouted to his crew and roused them to action. They rushed to take the line, drag it aft, and secure it to a rail and then to begin to pull out the shot line, the whip line, and finally, the heavy hawser rope from the shore. Stock's men ran along the beach and fed the stout rope into the water and positioned it over a crotch of wood to lift the rope up off the sand so that they could fasten the breeches buoy and attempt to transport the men from ship to shore. Once the hawser was fastened, the apparatus worked with pulleys to ferry the buoy out and the men back. For years Ezra had insisted that instead of sending the buoy out empty on its first trip, he go out in the chair and board the ship and help with the rescue from there. This was not standard procedure, but Ezra contended that it made for a much quicker transition of the equipment out and back and saved lives. Jack's father had taken over for Ezra when he had gotten older and then, when he died, it was George Kimball who had continued the tradition.

Up until this moment.

Jack shouldered his way to the front of the group of men, stood ready, and the men hoisted him into the seat. George helped them.

No one resisted or said a thing. But it registered in their minds. It had been eleven days since Elizabeth left and he had not returned to his cabin in all that time.

Instead, they waited for a confirmation from Gunn that the men on board had fastened the line to the rear mast and had the crew prepared. He waved a quick semaphore message to the men; they could not have heard him over the loud howling of the wind. The men on the boat were all at the rail, waving and beckoning for the surfmen to hurry. With a yank on the ropes Jack was borne into the air, his legs dangling and his body swinging from side to side. Stock ran up to the edge of the boiling surf and called out, "Jack, Jack! Take no chances, Jack, do what you're trained to do, no more. You hear me, Jack?" The young man looked down, his face set, brows down over his eyes, and nodded. Spray filled the air and water and foam poured over Ezra's boots where they sank into the cold brown sand. The crew of surfmen pulled in unison, moving him through the air with a steady rhythm. In no time he was out over the raging water, and without a backward glance he pitched from side to side, swinging and bucking toward the struggling ship. Waves licked up at him and at times the ship plunged down, the rope went slack, and his boots skimmed their tops. It was hard work and the men strained to pull him out. When he got to the ship the captain ran up to him and told him their situation. Jack understood. The ship, the *Ariadne*, was returning to Nantucket from a four-year voyage. She was bulging with the fruits of their labors, carrying barrels and barrels of oil, tons of it. Thousands of pounds of whalebone added to her mass. The crew, exhausted by the long years of work and decimated by accident, near starvation, and desertion in the Pacific islands, stood to share in a fortune in pay. Each man's lay, or portion, would have been more than they could earn anywhere else with years of work. Her loss was a lance buried in the hearts of the men, twisting in them as they endured her inevitable death throes on this cursed coast, only a few days from their homes. Since the beginning of the foul weather, two days earlier, the men had muttered against the captain, as if he could have predicted the sudden storm or really had any way of avoiding it. Indeed, the captain had been prudent in his sailing, following the main sea lane up the coast, safely offshore, careful with the sail and watching the sky and sea. His log entries were mostly filled with hope, "Fair wind today. Cold air and gray sea."

If he made a mistake it was to think the clouds the lookout called out were showing him a squall, blowing itself out, far off to the east and no threat to them. But it was not a squall, it was a huge storm, with high winds blowing constantly and lashing rain. When it veered into their path there was no time to get the sails furled or change course. The men secured the ship as best they could, held on, and rode it out. The wind came at them fast and raindrops hit the sheets like bullets. Then the main mast snapped like a dried twig and plummeting down with it came the fate of the ship and the hopes of the men. Once it had been a great oak in the forest, made by God, tying heaven to earth. Then it was fashioned by man and used to touch sky and sea. Finally, it had done all the work it could do and gave up its ghost. *Ariadne* endured the rough treatment for two days. In the forecastle the crewmen whispered in despair. Aft, the captain and second mate, the only officers left aboard, sat in silence in the captain's cabin. Bit by bit she broke down.

Jack told the *Ariadne*'s captain to wait and went to the starboard side of the ship to be certain the line was tied properly. It was fastened securely behind a smashed whaleboat that had been flattened on the deck by the fallen mast. When he gave the rope a final pull, just to be sure, he heard the men shouting and turned in time to see one of them trying to climb into the breeches buoy while two others dragged him back. He kicked at them, driving his heel into the face of the taller of the two men and giving him a bloody nose. The red streamed down over his mouth and onto his coat, giving him a strange inhuman look. Yet he continued to pull at the other man. The captain stood by, calling to them, but helpless to stop them. The men felt the hull giving way to the repeated pounding of the surging water that lifted her up and threw her down onto the hard bottom. They knew the arithmetic of being saved and each of them wanted to be one of the first to leave the wrecked ship. It looked more and more like only half of them might make it.

Jack called to the captain. He didn't look up, but only hung his head and waited to see what would happen. The captain knew the men blamed him; he had already decided he would be last to leave the ship and would have, truly in his mind could have, no say in what happened. He had lost his command to the storm.

"Stop!" Jack screamed the word over and over until the men were all looking at him. "No one will leave this ship until I give the signal to shore to pull you out. So listen to me. I'll decide who goes first and who follows after that." The man with the bleeding nose held out his fist and called out, "And who is first, surfman?"

Jack had already made the decision before the melee had begun. It was the youngest man, a boy who looked to be about sixteen, and had probably shipped out at the age of eleven or twelve. He was the youngest and the lightest. Jack planned to go by size and age the rest of the way, until the oldest man—the captain as it turned out—left just before Jack did.

"Him. He goes first. Now clear a way for him and help him into the chair." The men looked at the quarterdeck where the young man stood, apart from the others. The boy was terrified. His eyes darted from the chair to Jack, but avoided the crew where a rising tide of muttering began again.

"The hell he does! He never did half the work we did, just a runt off the docks we took along. He goes last if the ship's still here. That's what I say." The other men grumbled and looked at each other. "You'll not stop me, ya' bastard!" The man moved toward Jack, his fists held ready out in front of him, the blood still dripping from his nose. Jack bent over and hoisted a harpoon from the rubble of the broken whaleboat. He found its balance point and gripped it so that it rested on his shoulder. He spread his feet apart. He gave the man one warning, waving him toward the bow of the ship. The man kept coming.

Old Gunn watched the spectacle from the tower of the station. Ezra kept looking up at him, holding up his hands for an explanation. Gunn signaled that they were not making any effort to get into the chair, but seemed to be discussing something, as far as he could tell. He knew something was wrong aboard the ship. Then he watched in disbelief as Jack bent his body back and then lunged forward, hurling a harpoon into the center of a man on the deck. The man went down onto his back, the wooden shaft of the missile standing straight up into the air. The other men on the ship were motionless. Jack walked over to the sailor, pulled the long iron end of the spear from his chest, and called out to the others, "Help the lad into the chair. Be quick about it." One man lifted the boy up by himself and yanked his legs through the holes. Jack walked to the rail and signaled the surfmen to pull the boy to land. The other men moved back and looked expectantly at him and he pointed to them in turn so they would know who was next. "If we do this right, we'll all live to tell about it."

They watched silently as the surfmen pulled them one by one to land. It went faster than any of them had expected. When it came time for the injured man to go, Jack tied a rope tightly around his arms and shoulders. "This will slow the bleeding." The man looked down at the harpoon on the deck, and back at Jack, but said nothing. His head lolled to one side on the way in and he hung limply over the water. Despite the pounding the ship was taking, he realized, as did the others, that they would all probably make it to safety. When only Jack and the captain remained and they stood watching the empty buoy coming toward them over the waves, Jack asked if there was anything on board that he should take. This brought the man out of his daze and he said, "Yes, some papers. And there is some gold. Can you help me carry it? It's heavy and we can divide it between us." His face brightened, "I can give it out to the men. It belongs to the owners, but I'm going to distribute it out to them. All of them equally. And a portion for you. What do you think of that?"

Jack shrugged, "It's your business. And I have no need of your gold." He turned his head from side to side, considered the wreckage around him and the promise of an endless succession of days like this that crouched in the branches of time that waited for him, minutes, days, years ahead. To himself, "I have my own worries." Alone on the slippery deck, broken boards and dreams strewn about him, Jack waited for his turn on the breeches buoy. His gaze went to the north, but the spray and mist along the coast kept him from seeing what was that way.

The captain heard his words, even the last utterance, but didn't understand them. He too had the burden of an unsettled mind, and, like Jack, was convinced that there would never be any help for him. He climbed into the breeches buoy to leave his ship for the final time. He had spent over four years on that tiny wooden island, rarely ever stepping onto the land and when he did, only for a few hours at a time. He didn't look back.

Gunn never took his eyes away from his long spyglass and was bewildered by what he saw. "God," he said, "watch over young Jack, there, I pray you, and help him choose rightly. Some devil has got him and he is pulled along the wrong path. Soon he'll go away, I know it, and I won't be with him to watch over him. Please, God. Amen."

When *Ariadne* pitched over and came apart the next day, all of the oil and baleen she had been carrying was lost. A blasting cold front threw itself down onto the coastal region and hard land breezes kept the contents of the ship from moving ashore. There was nothing to see; it was as if the ship was never there and nothing had happened.

A day after the ship disappeared all of her crew were gone. The wounded man had been badly injured and was very weak, but he insisted on leaving the surf station with the others.

Ezra wrote about the incident in his personal log. He didn't know what to think, but was afraid for Jack Light. Afraid of what he had become. Was it because of what happened when the ship *Hathor* had come aground, or the butchery he had seen on *Cassiopeia*? He didn't know.

CHAPTER 39

Patience

Newport News

Billy was fidgeting. Armistead was going over their postings, looking at the open cases they were working on and giving out assignments to the men. Most of the patrolmen did the same things every day and were just enjoying the warmth inside the station house and having a second cup of tea. Billy had one thing on his mind and that was seeing Joan when he finished work. They were going to go see a show at the music hall. Neither of them had ever been to a show and she was as excited as he was nervous. He hoped there weren't things there he would have to do or buy that would cost a lot of money. He was carrying most of what he owned with him and that alone made him uneasy. There were plenty of thieves in Newport News; he could attest to that. The city was changing quickly and growth brought more than new buildings. New roads fled the town in all directions and dirt and dust and noise and crime rolled along them. The transition also brought people, some spilled over the sides of ships just arrived from Europe, others timidly escaping the larger cities along the coast, and youths from the farms to the west who wanted to experience more of the world than fields full of crops and the smell of manure. They plowed the dirt, planted the seeds, tended what grew, and then cut it down to sell or store. And did the same the next year, and the next. Tomato vines became shackles around their ankles and corn stalks the iron bars of a jail cell. Most of the newcomers had a romanticized idea of what urban life would be like. Old country citizens visualized a new world with streets paved with gold. Magazine and calendar pictures showed only the modern and the glamorous. Few found what they expected.

When Armistead called his name, Billy jumped. Only the two of them remained in the office. "I want you to take this packet to Peterson, the stone maker by the docks. Make sure it gets into his hands. Personally. And give him my thanks and my regards. You know the place I mean?"

Billy clutched the envelope holding the paperwork for Lamp's gravestone. "Sure, I've been by there. Has the address, here on the top, so I'll find it okay."

The older man looked at the papers as if unwilling to give them up. "Wait, Billy, let me see them again." He opened the envelope, carefully removing the tissue of papers as he shuffled over to his desk. Billy waited as he sat down slowly and looked at each sheet, scanning it methodically and placing each with care on top of the other. He handled them as if they were things of great value, rather than the ordinary tools of commerce, to be put to their purpose, filed, and forgotten. "Before you go out, take a look at these documents. It's the order and drawing and invoice for the grave marker for that lad we found with his throat slit. Out on the west side. Lamp. You remember, where James Kensel was the man who ran the burials?"

His interest piqued, Billy no longer thought of Joan or fretted over the evening ahead, but instead lined up the questions in his mind. Why him? Why now? What was his boss thinking? What could he expect Billy to find? This was the part of his job he loved most. He felt like a warrior. It was a competition. Discover what the criminal had hidden. Or missed. Beat him at his game. Learn from your estimate of the motive for the act, mull over the means used, value hearsay, embrace hunches.

Billy had seen the dead boy, if only for a moment, been to the cemetery with Armistead, overheard a few comments, but really had not worked on the case, and had in fact forgotten it. Armistead had taught him that documents, if wrought properly, told complete stories, like novels, with beginnings, middles, and endings. At the top they proclaimed what they were. Invoice. Work order. Receipt. Last Will and Testament. Certificate of Marriage. They had dates to tell when they were created, instructions, and terms, and details, and signatures. They told what belonged to whom. If correct and complete and respected by the forum where they were presented, they were as powerful as a cannon or sword or troop of soldiers. They compelled men to act and society to show its respect. Read every word. Be sure things made sense. Is this figure what that item should cost? Would that man leave his money to that person? Who witnessed this? Could this signature be forged? How could this have been done when that person was out of the area? Can I compare it to a similar document, one that I know is authentic? Etc. Etc. He did as he had been trained to do—examine each page, each word, the transactions involved, hold the pages up to the light, get the sense of all of the papers together. He saw nothing that seemed unusual. Billy looked at the pages again, and then read it all again, this time starting on the last page and moving toward the first. Still he saw nothing.

"Nothing there? I was betting myself that you'd come up empty handed." Billy was afraid he had overlooked a discrepancy in the file and that Armistead was about to show him something obvious. "Ah, well, thank you anyway. I just wanted to be sure. You can go on now. Take the papers to Mr. Peterson." There was still a noticeable reluctance in his voice and in the way he held his head as he spoke the words.

"What is this about, Daniel? Is there more to what we saw?"

He listened carefully to the details of Lamp's death and the burial, and the appearance of the stone and the word, "*hathor*" written on his hand. Armistead's efforts to learn its meaning from various people in the community were fruitless. One of the teachers at the nearby primary school said it sounded like mythology, but no one had a book like that to refer to. Hearing this was unsettling to Billy. Somehow there was for him, too, a familiarity with the word, as if it were in his mind but was being obscured by other things that would not be pushed aside. He did know the word, somehow, but couldn't get a clear view of it and knew the nervous frustration of knowing something but not knowing it. "Patience." It was another of his mentor's admonitions, oft repeated, understood and agreed to, but hard to practice nonetheless. He decided to put it all out of his mind for now and try again to wrestle his memory to the surface later in the day.

There is nothing like hard evidence, and nothing in the city was harder than the granite stone that stood over Lamp. He didn't expect anything to come of it, but the cemetery was not far out of his way and he had no trouble locating the grave. Billy looked at the stone, felt it, observed it from all angles. It said what it said, no more, no less. More informative was James Kensel, who had noticed the visitor and come to inquire about his business in order to help Armistead.

When they introduced each other he was keen to elaborate on the irony of it all to Billy. "Here I was, ready, you might say, to be the one to solve the mystery. Thinking you knew what happened to the young man. And all along it was only you. The deputy. Your chief is quite baffled by it all, and I don't say as I can blame him. Think of all that money for an orphan that no one even knows. I'll wager no one will ever visit here, unless it's one of you, officially that is. People will look at it as a curiosity, standing up all by itself as it does, but they won't come to visit the poor lad below. 'All alone.' 'All alone.' It was all he had to say to me. 'All alone.'"

Billy started, "What did you say? 'All alone'? What do you mean he said that?"

"It wasn't that really, I mean not in those exact words, but similar like. The idea is the same after all, no matter how you say it exactly, whatever phrase you use. You could say, 'Nobody but me,' and it would amount to the same thing. Don't you agree? The idea is not all that complicated, after all."

"Tell me what you're talking about!" Billy leaned toward the cemetery keeper and bored his eyes into him, hoping to nail him down and find out what on earth he was babbling about.

"It's just that…"

"It's just that…nothing! Tell me what you mean by 'all he had to say.'"

Kensel's eyes went wide for a minute and he leaned back and straightened his coat. "Let me think a minute, get it right for you since you seem to act like it is so important."

Billy scowled at him in order to help him "get it right."

"It said, 'I alone.'"

He remembered his need for patience. "What said?"

"His tattoo."

The deputy let out a long exasperated breath, but Kensel didn't seem to take offense. It was in his experience most common for other people to do just that—sometimes more than once—when they had conversations with him. He never knew why.

"Where was the tattoo?"

"On his arm."

"Which arm?"

"Hmm. Left. Yes, left. He was right handed, I could feel the muscles in his forearm. Did it himself, I'm sure. I see 'em on the sailors when they bring 'em in for me to box up. The ones that don't die at sea, like a lot of 'em. Ocean's a competitor of mine, in a way. Well, there's business enough for us all, I say, since everybody's a customer, sooner or later. This one was not like most, though. This tattoo was strange, 'I alone.' That's what it said."

"You're sure?"

"Oh yes, I'm sure. And the other word, '*hathor*', was on his left hand, so he was right handed, no doubt about it."

"And nothing else?"

"Yes, under that it said, 'N Y,' capital letters, no punctuation, just that, those two things. And before you ask, there was nothing else. No other tattoos or marks or anything. Some scars, in odd places, like he got cut in fights, holding up his arms to defend himself. And a broken bone or two. I didn't check that carefully, no reason to really, but those things I did see. Had a tough coming up, he did, that's for sure. Probably got beat by his father. Lot of poor lads do. The way they make tattoos is they get a common old pin or a knifepoint and put ink or soot or something black on it and jab themselves over and over. None of them are too well done, though this wasn't bad. Took his time, probably. Most of them regret doing it later. Always seems like a good idea at the time, know what I mean?"

Kensel listened to another long exhale.

Billy led the man through a painstaking review and verification of everything he had done from the first time he had been delivered the body up until the present moment. He made him repeat everything and made sure the story was consistent from telling to telling. Before he finished he had used all of that day's patience and had borrowed some from tomorrow.

When he returned to the constable's station late in the day, Billy found that Daniel had already left for home. If he had had time, he would have gone to him there just to let him know what he found out about Lamp. As it was, he had just enough time to return to his room, change his coat, and rush to the theater, arriving minutes before Joan's smiles lit up the night. She ran up to him and grabbed his arm and beamed her happiness into his eyes. Up the steps, into the lobby, through the theater doors, and down the aisle they went, both looking everywhere at once. Joan walked on her toes, the better to take it all in, and barely sat in her seat with all the twisting and craning of her neck she did, right up until they dimmed the lights and the orchestra began a swirling introductory musical piece. Then the curtains parted where the shivering spotlight promised what was to come, and admitted her into heaven. She smiled, cried, sang along, and gasped with fear and delight as the songs and lyrics drew her and the actors along dangerous paths, into love's ecstasy, past fragrant flowers, and by the mouths of darkened caves. None of the women on the small stage had talent that even approached that of Jane Barr, who at this same hour sang to her devotees in Boston, but to Joan they were all angels brought down from the clouds to bring her their grace. For her the night was perfect and Billy, aside from a couple of small bruises her uncontrolled gripping left on his hands and forearms, enjoyed it as much as she did. It was something they talked about many times during their long years of marriage. She was still very excited even as they arrived at her rooming house.

"Oh Billy, let's sit on that bench down the lane. For a little while. I don't want to go in just yet. I'll never sleep, I know it. What happens in that theater! It happens over and over. Every night. And there's others. Theaters all over the town. I want to go to a big city. New York. Think of it, Billy, all those stories. I want to see them all. Thank you, Billy, thank you."

She put her head on his shoulder and squeezed him tight. He had his arms about her, not wanting the night to end either. He kissed her and stroked her cheek and she told him how much she loved being with him and hoped they could stay together. They were two happy people, wondering a little about their futures, but content to hold off the serious part of what they were doing to each other for a while longer. They laughed. She told him about some of the antics of her customers and he described some of the best and worst of his. In some cases they were dealing with the same things. He rambled on and told the story of his day with Lamp and Peterson and Kensel, the mystery of it all made permanent with a monument of stone. An expensive one at that. He tried to convey to her how uncharacteristic was Armistead's zeal in the whole thing. Yes, it was an interesting mystery, an unusual set of circumstances, the brutal waste of a young, apparently innocent, life. And yes, the man was earnest about his calling. But there were worse things to deal with, ones more likely to be solved. She reminded him that the man with one ear had never been caught.

"Yes, and more every day."

"Why don't you just board the ship and find out what the captain and crew know about it? Surely they might know something."

"What ship?"

"The one you just said, '*Hathor*', wasn't it?"

"*Hathor* is a ship? How do you know that?"

"One of her crew came in a while back. Around the time the boy was killed, I believe. He'd been in before…maybe several months ago…I'm not sure, but I have seen him at least one other time. Probably more. I remember telling you about all the silly names for ships and all the bragging the sailors do." She pretended to scold him, "Not paying attention, were you, looking at all the other girls, I bet!"

For a moment he was not really there. He was adding up what he had learned this day and thinking that he would get up early, go into work and look at the records of the case and try to put an idea together for Daniel before he came in.

"Billy!"

"I'm here, love." He didn't realize he had said the word, but she did and she snuggled tight against him, smiling more than she had done at any time in her life. Even counting the night's theater production.

CHAPTER 40

The Replacement

Boston

LeFrank had been watching her. Twice, while waiting outside Jane's dressing room, he had talked to her. This one was different, more self-possessed. Graceful. Salete would verify all of her qualifications: that she had no family to miss her, little connection to anyone here who might interfere, a willingness, despite her apparent innocence, to venture out.

It didn't matter to LeFrank that she was more or less beautiful than the others. They were all lovely young women, only in different ways. It would be interesting to find one he could stay with for an extended period of time, someone who would satisfy, excite, but be more agreeable. Jane was wild and exotic in her ways, but she had too much anger and impatience in her, and the more frequent her outbursts became the less he thought it was worth it to keep her. He was not going to spend years with someone who was split in two, high one moment, impossible the next. There had been times when she had seemed perfect for him and what he wanted, but that was before recent events had changed things. No matter, her fate was already decided. Once she was gone only Salete and Chien would know how he had become sole owner of the shipping company. He could deal with them if need be. As he considered the matter, the more it seemed to him that he would have to. It would be amusing to order Chien to rid the world of Salete. He could do it, not face to face of course, but by slipping in to kill the man in his sleep, or waiting in some dark passageway for the chance to slide his precious knife blade between his enemy's ribs and into his heart. That would make the little man happy. Settle scores in his mind. When he had control of the fleet he hoped to build he would not require someone like Salete as much as he did now. He'd find a man qualified to run a business, to conduct the routine management of the companies, much as old Harrison had done with him, but not exactly. He smiled to himself, thinking that he wouldn't make that mistake. He'd find someone good, but limited in his ambition. Richard Hazen was a perfect candidate. He'd been very successful in his operation of the ship *Robin*, and wanted to command the *Hathor*. The man loved ships and he was smart and competent.

Old man Harrison had run out of steam. He was an old boat, outdated and wallowing along with the current while newer, faster craft left him astern. Boilers raging or mighty sails full over sleek and revolutionary hull designs, his competitors had raced past him without his noticing. It had all gotten too fast for the old man. Back then he had been content to forget about growth, let the business continue as it had done, without fresh ideas, or modernization. His only interest in it had become its ability to produce revenue.

In Boston LeFrank lived well, and he spread around a fair amount of Harrison's money, ostensibly for the good of the business, but in reality for his own benefit. Every official who shared in the largesse would remember that it was he, LeFrank, not Harrison, not a company, who had been the benefactor and it would be LeFrank who would profit from it later, should the need ever arise. LeFrank knew that reliance on others, however, never guaranteed security; he had large cash reserves hidden in two houses he owned in the Caribbean, and in several banks. No one knew about that. Harrison didn't even know what was going on in his own company. He was happy as long as there was enough money for him to live the way he always had. His complacency and the ease of operating the business with LeFrank to do the dirty work was understandable. His struggles were over. Most of the time during the last years before he died he spent meeting with shippers and working on various trade councils and institutional boards, old man stuff, safe in clubs and drawing rooms, with all the comforts. He hardly ever even saw his growing daughter.

He thought more about the actress. Laura Olsen. That was the one. He had that feeling, to go along with his calculations. He'd put Salete onto her today, get him to prepare the way for her to become the one. Jane might have to go suddenly, depending on all of the other factors involved. One of his competitors, Commack Shipping and Trading, had already had two of their ships catch fire, both laden with freight and ready to depart, and all this just when the company's finances were suffering from failures in other ventures, a ship lost at sea and one pillaged by pirates. LeFrank had gone to the owner's offices immediately and offered his help, a loan, the lease of one of his own vessels, his moral support and understanding. All was appreciated, but politely refused. LeFrank laughed as he rode in his carriage away from the docks and the smoldering remains of the boats. Salete was good at what he did, no question. Pick a target, deal a deathblow. If he made progress like this, LeFrank might have to move his schedule up a little. Yes, Jane had spoiled things for herself, just as Elizabeth had. Stupid women. Not content to play the role they were chosen for.

There were other, related matters to attend to. He wrote to Father Barry, telling him that he should be available in case he was needed. At this point the man was as much an employee of LeFrank's as were Salete and Chien. Barry would welcome the letter. Letters meant cash, more than he ever imagined was available for something that required little effort, and the smallest possible unit of the priesthood's supposed specialty, discretion. If he could keep the secrets of the confessional—the furtive embarrassed fumbling words of his parishioners—he could surely keep the details of his own dealings from ever seeing the light of day.

LeFrank also dispatched a letter to O'Neill, wanting to prepare him for what he was about to do. The good thing about the man was that you didn't have to spell things out, just have him standing by, and keeping his contacts handy and ready for any documents he needed to have certified or marked with official seals. They would correspond more frequently with each other as the time approached for LeFrank to act. As was his usual practice, O'Neill would make his preparations, pay for things in advance, and would confirm it all to LeFrank by the fastest post.

CHAPTER 41

Revelation

Delaware Coast, February 28

Ezra had Jack walk with him down to the south station to meet with Vickers. He thought the time alone with him might prompt Jack to talk about himself, and was disappointed when that did not transpire. He did seem more like his old self as the days passed, but most of the men thought it somehow forced. Nevertheless, they all had resumed their normal duties and work rotation, and the birth of Calvin Massey's new baby boy and the changed circumstances of George Kimball were the most discussed topics of news among the surfmen. They had enjoyed a long string of uneventful days, which they all welcomed.

"Your dad used to talk about running a station. Did you know that?"

"No, I don't recall his saying that."

"We never got serious about it. Probably because we all thought it would be George as the next in line. And he liked that cabin of yours…never wanted to work anyplace but here. Wouldn't move to get a better job, this was the only station close enough. Was your mother had a lot of say in it I expect. She loved being there in the woods. I don't think she ever even stayed in the guest house like the other wives…always stuck to that cabin."

Jack nodded his agreement. "We all did."

"When Tom died the district captain of the Lifesaving Service and I met and made a new plan for the station, in case I retired, or died beforehand. Or old Will. You know he's too old to really do the job any more. But he loves it and they don't have a replacement as of now, so he'll stay on. The new order was George first and then you, taking your father's place in line. Did you know that?"

"It never crossed my mind," Jack answered truthfully. He realized that Tom Light would have been very proud to have his son be considered for a leadership position in the USLSS. The pain in him accumulated; this one did not crowd out the others, but added to them. He felt sorry that his father had not lived to see this moment, but was ashamed of how he was handling his life now. It was selfish to dwell on his loss of Elizabeth, gone three months now, but he couldn't make it stop. It was robbing him of sleep and he couldn't escape the dull ache in his stomach.

"It stands that way in our planning, right now, today. But that may change. All of this might change, in fact. There's still quite a bit of talk about federal legislation that would change the service. It's all disorganized now, station to station, state by state. They put it under one roof and I don't know about personnel, how it would work. Most keepers think it'll be better, with more equipment and the like, but some won't want a lot of interference from the government. I think there'll be better times. We'll have better stations and gear and the Cutter ships will clamp down on the pirates and smugglers and more ships will be able to take the safer routes offshore. Less for us to do and better tools to do it with. What I mean is that we're not sure what George is going to do. George himself doesn't know. He's never gone back to see his family, he'll surely marry Ellen when she arrives here, he may even find some way to become involved with Captain Marshall. In his work. Whatever happens there is a good chance he won't be around for much longer. That means that I will likely take him off of the list of men I want to consider for promotion. Than means that you, Jack, will be the next man in line to succeed me."

They slowed and Ezra looked into Jack's eyes.

"Something that could happen tomorrow. Or today."

This did get the young man's attention. He stopped walking and Ezra moved alongside the water and they faced each other on the sloped bank of sand. The wind had abated and was now a low susurrus that allowed them to hear their words distinctly. He looked away for a moment, then peered into the older man's eyes, opened his mouth to speak, but then failed to do so. He was tempted to tell him everything, get it all off of his mind, but he thought doing so would signal the end of this life, one he had loved and one that he felt suited him perfectly. Ezra Stock was often hard on the men. He could be very stern, rigid in his adherence to the rules, and Jack had seen more than one man disciplined severely and seen him, without hesitation, discharge surfmen who were not following his leadership to the letter. They all recognized the reasons for this, with the dangers integral to their work and the necessity for teamwork and trust. To tell his story now he would have to confess to uncounted violations of the service regulations, not to mention to the unforgivable and complete betrayal of the personal trust they had all placed in him. It became obvious to him that he couldn't do it. Perhaps some day. Doing so would result in his expulsion from the service, a disgrace to himself and to his father's memory, and would not make Elizabeth appear at his side or take away his longing. It would only make his life worse than it was.

He said simply, "You can rely on me, Captain." The words felt bitter in his throat and in his soul.

Ezra took no joy in the answer, for it was not really an answer, but only a reply, and he trudged on toward the meeting with Vickers. In winter, activity in the station centered around the wood stove. Despite the heat it threw at them, it still took a while until the visitors felt warm enough to shrug out of their heavy coats. This time it was Ezra who was honored with the preferred seat closest to the fire. He and Jack repeatedly spread their hands out over the hot iron plate on its top. Vickers, unable to wait until all the tea was drunk and pleasantries exchanged, started right in, "I remember the day, some years back, when I was out on patrol on a day just like today. Had to do something I never thought I'd do—referee a fight. Not just any fight, mind, but a big one, as big as could be now that I think on it. A championship fight. Right there on the beach. It was cold and I was wrapped up tight, like a baby in its mother's arms, like you two were just a minute ago. 'Cept it was much colder than today, of course."

One of his men, smiling from the inward looking circle they formed, echoed his words, "Of course."

"Well, you might be asking yourselves who these titans were, having a disagreement right there on the beach. So, your curiosity bein' what I know it to be, I guess I'll have to answer you straight off. Without delay. But first, I have to say I was myself very surprised at the argument they were having. Mostly because one would think it was something they'da settled long ago. They were both as old as anything could be, were both from the beginning of things, you'd have to say." He paused, turning his head around to study the expectant faces, and stretched the moment to its utmost.

"You won't believe this, but the principals in this battle were, now hold onto your hats cause I'm not kidding, it happened just as I say it did, but they were none other than the two things we recon with every day. It was the wind and the sun. Of course."

Old Will Vickers started in on his tale. Ezra stole a quick glance at Jack, who was staring out the side window toward the north, looking as if he weren't even there with them. He knew then that there was not to be a captain's posting for Jack, not anytime soon, and from the despair he saw, probably never. He resolved to begin his search anew when they got back to the station this afternoon. Maybe Edward Chase would be the next keeper, or Matthew Hastings, who was posted here with Vickers.

Vickers asked if he had ever told them about the man who was the first man to eat a lobster. Jack's eyes wandered around the room and saw from the look on his face that Matthew Hastings knew this one by heart. He inclined his head toward the boat room and Jack gladly followed him out. Matthew took a chair by the wall and leaned his head back against the cabinet where the cork life vests were stowed. Jack dragged one over next to him and they sat in silence. The surfboat rested a few paces from them, waiting. Jack had his head back and his eyes closed. They had their own thoughts and kept them to themselves, only interrupted in them now and then by more laughing from the men listening to Vickers go on with his story.

"Tired?"

"I guess. Was on duty in the tower 'til four this morning and then Ezra got me up early to come down here. A little under the weather maybe."

"You look tired."

Jack's shoulders slumped as he relaxed a little and he and Hastings talked some as they usually did when they got together. Both were ready for spring and some hunting and fishing and swimming. Warmer days. They exchanged news about the two crews.

"What did you think of that huckster?"

"Who?"

"Little dirty guy, came here last November or so, asking about everybody. Even talked about you…thought you knew him. Figured he'd come from your station."

"I don't…who?"

"He was one of those sutlers from the army forts, he said. Traveling around selling supplies, but he had mostly junk if you ask me. Funny guy, had a thick accent. Real Yankee from way up in New England somewhere. Asked about people washing up on shore…wanted to know where we lived, asked about the Service. He was talking about you I'm sure. Said you found a seal on the beach. Same thing you told me about."

Jack jumped up. It startled the normally calm Hastings. He watched Jack, whose whole being seemed transported away from the two of them, intense, motionless, absent. Jack punched his right fist into his left palm and his eyes sought something in the room, but did not find it. Suddenly Jack became very quiet in his words and deliberate in his movements. He sat down and pulled his chair close to his friend. "Matthew, this is important. It's something I'd like you to keep to yourself, for now. I need you to do this for me. Can you start over and tell me everything you can about this. Every detail."

With his organized thinking and typical economy of words, Matthew Hastings told Jack the whole story. He fielded the barrage of questions that came at him, directly and completely. Many of them concentrated on the appearance and speech of the man. Jack had never heard him speak English, only French. When they were finished, Jack thanked him. That he did not pry into Jack's intense interest and passion over this strange affair was Jack's assurance that Matthew would not tell anyone about the exchange. He only answered questions, did not ask them, although many came to his mind. They sat together in silence until Ezra and Will had exchanged the patrol checks and finished their business and the social side of their visit.

Jack now knew precisely what he was going to do.

CHAPTER 42

Chien

Boston, Massachusetts

His regular rounds included twice-daily passes through the alley. From its intersection with an angled side street he could look up Second Street and observe the front and near side of the grand house. The neighborhood was heavily wooded and he could lean against a flat place on the trunk of a huge old white pine and watch the house from the shadows. When he stood there he felt the same charge within his blood that he did just before he entered a place to rob it, or after his knife found the center of someone and waited there for him to savor that moment, before withdrawing it slowly, wiping it off. His hands gripped each other in front of his heaving chest and he swallowed painfully. It happened every time he went there to watch and wait.

Most of the time he was doing as ordered, gleaning information from the conversations he heard in the taverns and along the docks and surrounding warehouses and streets. Those he reported promptly to LeFrank, who was impatient to assemble all the facts and rumors he could gather, and constantly demanded more of him, anger evident in his speech and manner. Chien regarded the man with more than his usual caution, noticing in him a tenseness he had never seen before. LeFrank was like a rope pulled too tight. He kept moving, it being inadvisable to face LeFrank with weak excuses that he had nothing new to report. He was being paid, after all, to sit around and drink in the inns, buy a few rounds, and trade lies with his various acquaintances from the waterfront. What interested the man most were stories the sailors told each other about the business of other shippers...who was taking on men...when the owners had visits from bankers and other officials…arguments overheard…tempers on display. No matter the pressure from above, he found time every day to make at least a couple of visits to the Harrison's house so as to not miss Elizabeth when she arrived. As he was certain she would. Where else could she go? She would have to come there to see what had happened after she left, maybe hoping to find that old hag Whitehall still there. He laughed. Her "Nana." Didn't even know it when they dumped the old woman's body overboard right outside of her cabin, as soon as *Hathor* hit blue water. Chien strongly believed her arrival would take place sometime soon now, and then he would have her and all her wealth to go with her. She meant more to him than the money. His eyes glowed every time he pictured it, his fingers coiling around the beads in his pocket.

Some days he even spied on Salete, hoping to find something to report to LeFrank about him. Once he had Elizabeth, the two of them would have to go away. For a while. He would like to eliminate Salete before he went. As a practical matter and for the joy of doing it. See the look on his face when he felt death slice into him and looked up to see that it was Chien who had delivered him. His face the last Salete would see and the message that he had the girl for his own the last words Salete would ever hear. Then when the time was right he would have to find some way to rid Boston of one of its prominent citizens. He'd figure out how to do that later. And the whole time he was doing that he would be enjoying the pleasures of young Elizabeth. He wasn't like LeFrank, always needing the novelty of working his way through a succession of nymphs to own and occupy and discard; there was only one for him, one he had watched for years as she grew and was transformed. She would be enough for him and learn that he was enough for her.

He hoped she would come soon. He wanted to be there when she first appeared, to take control of her before she could take any action against LeFrank. He knew the man could change his plans in an instant and call Chien to board the ship and go. It had happened many times before, and as he thought about it he realized it was the way it usually went. He never had much warning when LeFrank decided to go into action. Something was happening alright. He had seen that with his own eyes. He thought about the night when he'd followed Salete along the wharf to an old boathouse. With his dark clothes and slow movements, his disappearance into the boathouse was like a minor flaw in a pattern, not substantial enough to be real. He stared at the spot to be sure of what he had seen. It was an odd destination for him in the middle of the night and Chien was curious. After a brief meeting with two men, Salete strolled casually away and headed up the hill toward the center of the city. His silhouette blocked some of the sparkling lights of civilization as he moved away. He did not look back. Chien followed the progress of the other two men, who each rowed a small boat out of the boathouse and into the harbor. He kept their dancing lanterns in view for a quarter hour and lost sight of them when they went further out into the water and disappeared behind the bow of a large sailing ship riding low in the darkness. He ran along the edge of the wharf, from shadow to shadow, anxious to see if he could locate the small boats. They had disappeared. He slipped behind a storage shed at the water's edge and waited.

Two brands arced into the night. Following each of the orange balls of fire was a hellish flicking tail. Then two more flew up over the side of another ship. Four more laced the sky and then it was dark and Chien heard only the silence. When he realized what had happened he moved quickly back down the way he had come, past blind, mute warehouses, tripping over the cobbles in his haste to be away from the area and from suspicion. He found a safe spot to watch from behind a row of pilings where he could remain unseen. For several minutes nothing happened, but then there was a flare up, first on the closest ship, then on the one beyond it. It became brighter and brighter and soon the flames were alive and spreading; popping with the tar and wood it consumed, it raced like a glutton through its meal. Men on deck watch on nearby ships rang their ship's bells in panic. They raced around chasing sparks and throwing buckets of water here and there onto their wooden ships. By the time he was up the hill from the seaport, the fire was a raging convulsing demon. Unstoppable. It lit the night and from that light he could see the large painted words running in block letters across the bricks at the top of the nearest warehouse: Commack Shipping and Trading.

The two rowboats, empty and light, were pushed by the waves toward the bulkhead at the water's edge. They bumped and scraped against the barnacles. They slapped the water and splashed. Chien saw them and wondered where the men had gone. Then he saw them, dark forms leaping from barge to barge, using a preplanned route away from the firestorm they had created. He understood now, watching all of this, that those barges had been positioned in advance to help the men avoid capture. They would not normally be tied end to end in the harbor, but rather be side by side, ready for loading. Someone had aligned them, letting them drift with the current until they were near enough for the two arsonists to get to them. Running was a lot faster than rowing and in minutes they were far away from danger and suspicion. While he contemplated this, the ringing of high-pitched bells intruded on the scene, calling his attention to the west. Descending the hill was the first of several fire brigade wagons. It raced toward the docks, but was suddenly brought up short and skidded over the pavers, pitching sideways and with a screeching burst of noise, overturning. Horses screamed and fell and men flew from their seats. A second team of horses smashed over the wreckage of the first and one horse lurched off with one leg broken and hanging at a terrible angle to the bleeding mass above it. It pulled at its harness and tried to drag the shattered wagon behind it. Another animal landed on a fallen fireman, twisting the man's spine and killing him instantly. Someone had tipped and broken several barrels of oil, turning the single path to the docks into an invisible, slick, sticky, impassable trap. There were other approaches to the long row of wharves, but they were far from the site of the dying vessels. When help arrived from that direction the firemen ignored the flaming ships and assisted the men in newly formed bucket brigades by hosing down other boats in the area to prevent them from catching fire.

"Salete." He said it aloud as he nodded in agreement with himself. Acknowledged in his mind a grudging admiration. He wondered if Salete would pay the men who had done this, or kill them. Probably kill them to guarantee that the story was never told. He would be furious if he knew that Chien had seen it all. LeFrank would learn of it, had surely ordered it, but was insulated by Salete from any connection to it or knowledge of the details. Commack Shipping and Trading had been singled out by LeFrank for some reason. Chien tried to think of a way he could use the knowledge to his benefit, but nothing came to mind. Still, he'd remember it, just in case…

How did this all fit into LeFrank's plans this time? Chien couldn't imagine what was going on, but resolved to be careful of what he did. LeFrank had embarked on this action the moment Chien had assured him that the girl was no longer a problem. That was what worried him most. Chien could never have that madman find out that he knew she still lived. Not until he had everything in place to remove him. He withdrew slowly and used great care not to be seen. Men were rushing everywhere now, but all eyes were trained on the carnage where the injured firemen slid through the oil and blood, no longer paying any attention to the growing fires that had brought them there, but were only trying to rescue their own.

CHAPTER 43

The City

New York. December 10

Straight ahead of her was a wide doorway leading out of the train station and opening onto a broad avenue. She heard the screech and clanking of cars being added to her train, but she ignored it; she was listening to the noise of the streets. The layover was scheduled for an hour and she carried her bag with her and walked into the cold city. Dirty snow was piled along the side of the road and heavy cart, horse, and foot traffic swelled along through ice and mud. She walked with it, south, toward the most crowded part of Manhattan. Thousands of people swarmed around her, but no one saw her. An hour later she was still walking, hypnotized by the sight of it all and letting the force of the place bear down on her and lodge itself inside her shell. Unwittingly she searched for a reason not to continue on when the train left for points north. Ellen Brahe slept on and off while the train was in the station and barely noticed when it left. Elizabeth too was unaware of its smoke and bluster as, without her, it labored its way inevitably onward to its terminal in Boston.

A few days after leaving Delaware and Jack Light, she moved with her few belongings into a small boarding house just south of the center of Manhattan. The first several days she was there wandered in joyous anonymity, imagining she was free, looking into store windows and watching ladies and gentlemen of means parade down the aisles of churches, and dawdle in museum galleries, studying them as they lounged at their tables in fashionable restaurants, devouring precious hours along with their savory meals. She preferred the look and comfort of the clothes she wore, pioneer clothes, she thought of them as she studied the wisps of her image in shop windows, but spent some of her money on a couple of more current outfits. She didn't really want to fit in, but also could not risk standing out. Clothes told who was who. Ridiculous in the bustles that followed them around like little servants or suffering breathlessly in their wasp-waist dresses, the appearance of the most stylish women had the greatest effect on her. Had she looked this foolish during the years of her living in her home in Boston? Dressed a la mode.

She thought of Jack, as she seemed to do much of the time since leaving him, of how he looked at her face, her hair, how he seemed to smile as he studied the delicate turns of her ears. Her heart pounded when she leaned close to him to hear what he was saying when they hunted together and were concealed and had to remain quiet. There were many times, too, when she had seen him look her up and down, his gaze sending questions to his mind as his wide eyes lingered here and there upon her.

If she returned to her home and could somehow eliminate LeFrank and his men from her life, what would she do? Would she go on as before, find another companion if it were true that Nana was gone? Eventually marry some Boston blue blood? More than ever that thought was untenable. What other path would be open to her? She could teach, be a tutor like Nana, work as a nurse, help at a church. No matter what she did she wondered if somehow she could also spend her time trying to locate the women who had been abducted as she had been. Sometimes on her walks she recited their names in her mind and looked at the faces of the prostitutes who lurked everywhere in this merciless chaos of a city, thinking she could be seeing one of them and not know it. Of course she understood now that the women who had been in that cabin before her had likely been sent far away, maybe even to other countries. It had almost happened to her. She could not believe she could ever be like these sad women, brazen and unashamed, exposing themselves, leering at men, even calling out to men walking arm in arm with wives, sweethearts, sisters, mothers. It surprised her, too, that there were so many of them. How could this be? Some so old, others so unbelievably young? Some of them boys. It was all impossible.

At times her body sang to her about children, the ones unborn, waiting inside her, wanting desperately to be. They deserved their time in the world, their souls informed with flesh, able to strive and suffer, their chance to know logic and emotion. And more than anything else, their chance to create the ones that would wait inside them for the same thing. It was the children of the sour, boiling stew of New York that had the gravest effect on her. They were ragged, filthy, and often barefoot; they darted from behind things, and peered from dark warrens of temporary, tenuous safety, eyes squinting with terror or in cautious calculation. They trembled with the fear of others, and from the half-frozen manure and urine and mud that oozed up between their blackened toes and hitched rides on the torn cuffs of their pants or the hems of their filthy dresses.

Elizabeth also felt sorrow for the plight of the animals. There were far more animals evident in New York than there were in the wilds around Jack's home. Horses were everywhere. She was shocked at the sight of them. Many were thin and sick looking. No small number of them were dead, left lying where they had fallen. Some, deflated and skeletal, had been there since they were worked to death in the summer's heat; others were sprawling in the gutters, whole, bloated, frozen solid, no longer useful or beautiful or a friend to someone, but now just obstacles to the unseeing and uncaring who were aggravated at having to pick their way around them. Packs of dogs worried them some. The free ranging herds of pigs that bullied everyone in their paths ignored the fallen horses, being more interested in fresher fare. Pigeons and cats and fleas and rats and blackbirds in huge numbers also made the city home and their presence felt. If all of this was part of the landscape of her hometown, she had never noticed it. They kept several horses in a stable behind her house for their carriages, and some cats had plotted successfully to be allowed to live inside from time to time, but while she did have one favorite cat that followed her around the house for several years, she had not paid animals much mind.

One day she strayed further to the south in her explorations than she had gone before and entered Five Points, the city's worst slum. By degrees the area she passed through became more and more pitiful and squalid, and more dangerous. Disease, murder, and neglect killed people here in great number. Even the police were not safe. She walked by the building where years ago Lamp had lived with his mother and aunt, now a burned out shell but still infested with the most forlorn of mankind, hiding among the jumble of collapsed and charred timbers that had crashed onto the bottom floor, but happy to at least have a partial roof to fend off the snow and freezing rain. Some of the people she passed had known Lamp, and they were, somehow, still alive, while he had been killed, away from this horror, during the days she had stayed at Jack's cabin. Lamp—killed by Chien. She did not know him, or even that he ever existed, but if she had, she would have wondered how she had escaped Chien's knife when someone like Lamp had not. The lad had survived this place of degradation and suffering, been a thief, a beggar, a terrified child, but wound up willingly using his abilities as one of Strell's underlings. That, not this place, had gotten him killed.

Five Points was overwhelming. Even in the cold there were people out everywhere. There was no place for them to go. The smells that poured out of the buildings and up from the street were sickening to her and she gagged at some of the things she saw. She thought how much worse it must be in the hot summer. Disoriented by its assault on her senses, she walked further into the place before turning back uptown to escape it. Before she was out of the inner circle of this city's hell, she became the target of a gang of boys who were throwing stones at a dog they had cornered in a nearby doorway, slowly and painfully killing it. Their leader saw her and started making crude remarks, calling on her to give them some money, or pay up with her body. She fled, walking quickly away. They ran after her. One of the youngest boys looked back at the dog, hoping to find it there later if he could find nothing else to eat that day. She was glad of her time in the woods with Jack, and scouted ahead for a route to take to escape the young savages who pursued her. She ran west, guided by the dusty yellow ball that hid in the sky behind clumps of smoke and clouds. As she recalled there was a market there, ahead of her, and she plunged into the middle of it, weaving through the haphazard rows of stalls and wagons and people, using the layout of it to act like a sieve, and letting the merchants do her work for her. They yelled at the boys, hit them, and effectively broke up the gang. Many of the boys split off or lagged behind and soon there were only two of them who pursued her. When she looked back and saw this she searched for a dark, narrow alley and, finding one, slowed down and made sure they saw her enter it. She ran to the end and waited for them in a deep shadow.

When they picked her form out of the dimness they looked at each other and smiled. They swaggered up to her, young teens who were their own law, telling her what they were going to do to her, how they always wanted to see what a rich one was like. "Prolly no better 'n Maggie!" the leader said. His words drew a snort and laughter from the other boy. "She smells better!" They laughed some more as they approached. Elizabeth stared at them. She was silent, still as a statue.

The two were wary.

"What're ya, deaf an' dumb?" They moved closer.

"Run. If you want to grow up to be men."

"From you, cunny, me run from you?"

"I won't say it again."

"Good, I hate to hear a bitch scream when I'm about my business."

There was just enough light for them to notice the pistol in her hand. It only took a second for the younger boy to turn and run stumbling out of the alley.

"Take off your shoes and pants."

"Rip yours off is what I'm gonna do."

She aimed the gun at his foot. "He needs them. The other boy. The smart one. I'm going to give them to him. Or to someone. Take them off or I will take them off your body myself. When you're dead."

He began to cry when she aimed the gun at his head.

"You're a crazy one. We's only having fun. Go on, I w-w-won't bother you no more." His words shook as they choked out of his twitching lips.

She cocked the gun. Its unmistakable steel clack echoed off the blackened walls.

When she took a step toward him he looked over his shoulder at the entrance of the alley and bent over, fumbled with shaking hands at the mismatched laces of his shoes. He pulled off his pants and stood in rage and shame in his filthy underwear. It looked as if it had never been washed and smelled abominably. His trembling legs were colorless and skinny and scabbed. She made him bundle his things into a packet and leave a lace hanging out for her to hold it. She would not touch them.

"Lie down there, on the stones, where you were going to make me do, so you can see what it's like. Go on...on your back."

He could tell from her tone and the way she looked at him that she wanted to kill him. For threatening her, wanting to rape her in front of the others and brag about it. Rob her, hurt her, take what was hers to give and no one else's. She still had that pure precious part of herself and she would do anything she could to keep it hers.

There were sins in other parts of her soul, but not there. She had been angry, felt hatred, planned murder, lied. She wanted to hurt this beast of a person lying in the urine-soaked and stinking trash in the corner of the alley, but knew it would accomplish nothing, but only further damage her poor heart. She didn't want any of this—to hate, threaten, fight—wanted only for LeFrank, Salete, Chien, all of them, all of it to go away. Revenge was not in her, but she knew there were certain things, unpleasant, repugnant to her nature, that she must be prepared to do.

"Stay where you are until it's dark. I'll watch, to see you do. Then you can crawl back into your hole. Remember this day. Remember me." She growled these words at him and waved the gun; he flinched back from its muzzle and sobbed aloud.

He didn't know what to make of this last, and she didn't know why she said it. Had she been warning him to mend his ways, find a better path through life or be killed and damned? She thought no more of it as she hurried out of the slum. She tossed the bundle of clothes to a woman with a small child begging on the street. Normally she saved her money and, having nothing but time, walked everywhere, but on this day she rode the omnibus up Broadway, squandering some precious pennies, escaping as quickly as she could, the image of herself, trapped in slavery in some far off hell.

As she the weeks passed she realized that this was not the place for her. What life it had was mostly just humans breeding offspring named disease, neglect, hatred, despair. In the evenings Elizabeth counted her money, wondering how long she could make it last. She had deceived herself, thinking she liked New York, maybe she could stay there, earn a living somehow, exchange fate for fate. It was a false impression, her idea of this city. She thought its character was something she could embrace, not knowing that its faint attraction was simply that it was not Boston. Indeed, any other place could have played this same trick on her. New York just happened to be where she was and it was able to call the loudest.

CHAPTER 44

LeFrank

Boston, Massachusetts

LeFrank's plans moved apace.

Hathor rose and fell faintly beneath him, breathing in and out at the whim of the cold water in the harbor. All the seas of the earth moved in concert with him and his ship.

O'Neill had sent a positive response to his letters and promised to line up the buyers and sellers needed to make LeFrank's most important trip to Newport News a profitable one. Strell had assured O'Neill that he would be there when needed, his mien in the strong ink-pen strokes that bore into the writing paper as threatening as his bearing in person, but his explicit willingness to pay large sums for the woman and other goods was more than enough to conquer O'Neill's awful fear of him. There are always factors in the market that one would wish to avoid, O'Neill reasoned, but when they were unavoidable, they were to be reckoned with, and those who brought them about, gouged for profit. Press him and you paid. Everything had to be worth the trouble and the danger. Sometimes the price was not the price. Sometimes it was a penalty. He stood to make a fortune off of these two demented men if he could continue to fulfill their strange wishes and keep them as clients. But why pay outrageous prices for a woman? What woman was worth the risk? How could Strell resell this rich girl? "White slavery" it was called, now that the war between north and south was over. O'Neill laughed at that thought. Anyone who thought there weren't just as many Africans crossing the water in ships as before was just dreaming.

Jane Barr waited for LeFrank to give her the final date for their wedding. Most of the time patiently. He had convinced her that she would enjoy impersonating Elizabeth Harrison, "marrying" him so that he could assume control of all of her property and considerable wealth, and then traveling to New York where, he assured her, he had made arrangements for her to launch her career in an important starring role. No more vaudeville dramas, no more playing to people who didn't count. Her reward for doing this would come a short time later, after a respectable wait, when he would marry her a second time, this time for real, marry a famous Jane Barr in an extravagant wedding in the city with all the best people in attendance. Everyone would know who she was. She would have the Boston homes, the New York apartment, the fame she craved. Concerning herself with the "behind the scenes" aspect of LeFrank's plans was beneath her. He never told her what had happened to his ward—some stupid girl that Jane, despite never having seen her, both envied and looked down upon—how he would certify her death, or anything else about what would have to happen. As did most people, she cared only about herself, what would happen to her.

LeFrank moved carefully, methodically, from step to step, putting things in place and in play. His time line had spurs and branches, alternate courses, places to idle, straightaways to allow him to accelerate when necessary, and escape routes at regular intervals. What he was going to do was simple: take Jane to O'Neill, pass her off as Elizabeth, trade her for the papers from local officials that would prove Elizabeth's death and burial in Newport News, and return to Boston to begin in earnest his takeover of the shipping companies he had targeted. O'Neill would sell Jane Barr to this pirate who scared him so much for an extravagant amount of money. That didn't bother LeFrank, who understood the economics of it better than did O'Neill. O'Neill would make one sale, albeit a large one, while LeFrank would forfeit one asset for many, and the ones he gained would produce income for as long as he owned them. Jane Barr was a depreciating asset any way he looked at it. The slow pace of the legalities involved being what they were, the actual transfer of the assets to him would take some time, but because of the preparations he was making in advance, the sellers would be ready and the banks willing to advance him whatever funds he needed. Salete's various acts of sabotage, large and small, had created sufficient turmoil in their day-to-day operations that some of these competitors had grown weary of battling misfortune, and had become more open to negotiations. LeFrank plied the bankers with favors, arranging special parties for the most powerful of them, discrete affairs where all private comforts were available. With the luck of his own making, Harrison and the other companies would become his, one after another. Playing by the rules was just plain stupid and the men who claimed they did were liars anyway. They made exceptions, hid things, skirted the laws. He remembered how he got his way when he ran slave ships—he cracked his whip. He missed the feel of the leather coils in his hand, but for the moment the bankers and attorneys and politicians he courted were all more powerful than he was. No whips allowed in their offices.

O'Neill had assured LeFrank in his letter that Jane would never be seen in the country again and that the "death and burial" were as good as done. He had written proudly that he staked his reputation on it. LeFrank actually laughed when he read that section of the letter. Reputation. The man had credentials, a history he had better conceal if he loved his liberty, but hardly a reputation.

He made sure his ships were prepared, that Salete and Chien did their parts, that no details were overlooked. LeFrank and O'Neill would soon confirm to each other their full readiness by way of vague business letters, and LeFrank would then make the biggest move of his life. This was a long way from his early days working aboard a slaver, cracking his whip, being the arbiter of life and death.

Salete had made a personal visit to Father Barry, left an unusually large "donation" for the priest's favorite cause, and instructed him in the precise way he was to handle the ceremony, this time to include a true and legal certificate of the marriage, for, as he pointedly explained to the pliant priest, the sake of realism. He stressed that the paper be ready, with the names and date to be inserted by Salete when the wedding took place, so that LeFrank could take it with him immediately afterward. Only LeFrank knew for sure, but Salete suspected that Jane Barr would become Elizabeth Harrison, then the late Elizabeth Harrison, and that Laura Olsen would then assume the role and duties of the mysteriously missing Jane Barr. So many members of the cast and crew would be happy to see Barr gone that no one would bother to ask where and why. The traveling theater companies and visiting troupes would also like it better, no longer having to contend with a firmly entrenched and cruel and demanding resident prima donna.

LeFrank climbed the steps to the quarterdeck and let the men see him. It was something he did at a different time each day to keep them alert and ready. He looked them in the eye, one by one. To him these men were scum, shallow and lazy and untrustworthy, and he knew how to balance the pressure he put on them with the rewards he gave them, meting out small portions of each in order to keep them in line. He enjoyed the contradiction of knowing how valuable they were, however, men who were good for nothing else but occupying a prison cell. Valuable only to someone like LeFrank, who could herd them along, use them up, and cast them aside when they couldn't or wouldn't do what he commanded. The devil knew there were always more of them at the ready.

CHAPTER 45

Confession

Delaware Coast, March 5

He neared the end of his tale. "I don't know how this came to be. At first it was just that the girl—Elizabeth—was so forceful. She was afraid for her life, and I did what she asked me to do. She begged me. She told me if I told anyone about her, she'd be killed. That it was all up to me, wet, cold, lying on the beach with her grabbing my face and crying and begging. I was going to get her killed! It crossed my mind that she might be some sort of criminal, or she was crazy. It all happened so fast. But I was right to believe her. She is some kind of a lady, rich I think, a lady with manners and education. She knows languages and music and history." He shook his head and laughed to himself, "It didn't look like she had ever been outdoors, though, if you know what I mean...a big city person."

The man nodded back at Jack; he understood. All of it.

"Then there was no way out for me. Everything I did made things worse. After a while, I have to confess, I was glad for what I'd done, wanted to be with her all the time. Like nothing else I ever wanted. It's not that what I did was all bad...I believe I saved her life. By myself. I know I did. You saw those men. She wouldn't trust our captain. Thought he'd be just like that shipmaster, wouldn't even consider what I said to her about Ezra. Or tried to tell her. But she begged and begged...I know what I did was wrong, but...I don't know...

"The terrible thing about it was lying to all of you. And then, later, worse still was knowing she was going to leave and I'd never see her again. When Matthew told me about that man, I knew I was still in it. It wasn't over. I can't let them find her again. When she left she said there were things she had to do. Wouldn't tell me what. But

I bet it has to do with them. That's why she wanted to take a gun with her." Jack shoved his hands deeper into the pockets of his storm coat. "My mother's gun." He looked up, "She'd gotten good with guns.

"I almost welcome it, the chance to find her and be around her again. I don't know what I'm going to do, but I'm going to have to leave. It'll be the end of things here for me, and I had to tell someone. I've felt sick in my body all this time. When I found out Ezra sent men out in the boat and searching along the shore for her, when all the while she was with me, I almost told him then."

It had not been a surprise to either of them that Jack had gone straight to Old Gunn. It was as if there was no George or Ezra or any of the others.

"You knew something was wrong that night, didn't you? And when you came out to my place?"

Gunn smiled.

"The three of you talked about me, right?"

His crinkled old eyes said that they did.

Jack had told him every bit of it, from seeing her in the water to this moment. Even the bed boarding. It had been a week since Matthew had told him about Chien and Jack had prepared to leave, but it had taken a few days to force himself to tell Old Gunn. He felt better for it, but was still afraid. The preacher had listened to the whole story without interrupting once. It took Jack a long time to tell it. He allowed Jack to think about what he had done, telling him about the girl, about going to find her. Jack was surprised that Gunn made no comment about anything that had happened. There was no scolding, no judgment. It was as if none of that mattered. "How are you going to go about it…finding her?"

"I know the name of the ship, *Hathor*, and I know it's probably from up north somewhere. Matthew said the man had an accent. Like New Englanders talk. If I can find that ship, I'll have a chance to find out about the men on it. Check all the big ports. The sailors who come by here say there's thousands of ships, but it wasn't a pirate, so it'll be registered somewhere. The captain, those two with him, all spoke French, so that's something too. I thought I'd check with the Cutter Service offices, see if they can help me. Other than that, I don't have much to go on."

Old Gunn spoke earnestly, "You gave her a lot of money. She went knowing she was in danger, so she'll be careful. Jack, no one goes to all that trouble just to get a girl to sell to slavers, so she has something they want. She must know what it is and she'll probably get someone there, where she lives, to help her. You have to go. It's your duty to go. Even if you didn't have feelings for her. I will make it all right with Ezra, the Service, the men. You're smart and you can take care of yourself. Take your surfman check with you, show it and you'll get treated right. Take your own guns; these men are dangerous."

The old man was taking some of the weight off of him. He was relieved, not having to carry it all himself. He was also surprised at what he was hearing; not the sermon he was prepared to suffer through. And thought he deserved. It was practical advice, good advice, reinforcing some of his own ideas, giving validity to plans that were until now murky and awash in doubts. But then Gunn looked toward the sky and got that look on his face and Jack thought he was going to be taught a lesson from the good book after all. Instead, he heard some kind words, helpful words, ones he would say himself over and over in the days ahead. "Say this to yourself, Jack, 'Honor my family, my friends, my gift of life from God.' It will tell you what to do at every turn. You won't need God to answer you. This prayer answers itself."

They stood up and shrugged at the stiffness they felt.

"Thank you for everything you've done for me. God bless you."

"My blessing, Jack, is that God gave me this time to listen to you and help you as best I can. I'm not worried about this. You'll do the right thing. I know it, plain as day."

"I'm going now. I already have most of my things from the station."

"I'll take care of it…telling Ezra, the men, your things. Check on the cabin from time to time, so it's there for you, and maybe her too, when you come back. I'd like to meet her." He pursed his lips as if envisioning meeting her, and smiled at the thought.

As he walked away from the surf station, Jack could hear Edward Chase trying to play his new fiddle. He wasn't too good at it.

CHAPTER 46

The Cemetery

Newport News, Virginia

"Go straight there and come right back here to me when you're finished. Understand?"

Jimmy Craft clutched the package in front of him, looked at it, and shook his head up and down in a way that did not satisfy O'Neill at all. Nothing in his manner could ever have been said to inspire confidence in anyone. "Go straight there and come right back here. Don't go anywhere else! Make sure you see the man in charge, not some worker...find the boss, and leave the papers with him. Put them in his hands and that's all. Don't talk to him or do anything else. If anybody asks you anything, tell them you're only the messenger and you don't know. Come right back here, to the ship. Remember, I can turn you in to that constable any time. He would love to throw you in the pit for good."

O'Neill knew he could keep bumblers like Craft on his payroll with an occasional handout of money and regular reminders of his ability to turn them in. To him stupid meant cheap. He gave Craft a couple of coins and promised two more when he returned. The jaunty little sailor dropped them, scrambled across the deck to retrieve them, gave a salute, which O'Neill spurned, and walked down the gangplank to join the flow of men moving alongside the congregation of ships that crammed the harbor.

O'Neill owned a prime spot along Water Street, in the center of the harbor, and since the ship rarely left port, it was more of an office than anything else. It was close to the customs house, convenient for him since he went there regularly to deliver bribes and oil the works when he needed a dispensation from the rules for his business.

Newport News was busy again, with the weather breaking favorably from time to time. Bright new sails billowed out daily all around the large harbor, and horns and bells and thumping engines alerted the world of commerce and told it to get ready. There were frequent arrivals and departures, lighters scooting back and forth, and the stevedores loaded and unloaded these ships as quickly as possible. Every man wanted to make money when he could. It was the maritime version of making hay while the sun shone. Shining white ship skeletons stood in the shipyards and waited for the builders to lay on their planks, caulk them tight, and fit them out, debutantes eager to see the world. Nearby, weary, rotting, fouled, and other experienced craft, brought in for careening, lay on their sides. Landlords and tavern owners, merchants and wives and girlfriends, all wanted what was owed and overdue.

This was a time of great anticipation for O'Neill. LeFrank's recent letters confirmed the plans the men had made in their discussions during his last visit. There would be an increase in the volume of business O'Neill could expect, or so LeFrank had promised, if all went well this time. LeFrank had intimated that he would soon control many ships, and that, if he made it all work, would mean increased wealth and an elevated status for O'Neill.

By sending Craft off to deliver the order and the advance payment, O'Neill completed another of the arrangements he had assured LeFrank would be made prior to *Hathor*'s arrival. He hoped the ship would make better headway this time. Strell had sent word that he would be in the area well in advance of the scheduled delivery date. He wanted O'Neill's guarantees that the girl would be there. His message was clear and most threatening on that point and O'Neill worried about what he would do if another of LeFrank's girls threw herself overboard. He assumed the man would be more careful this time. Cargoes were eaten by rats, stolen by the crew, spoiled by mold, sank with ships, and were lost in storms—that was part of the shipping business—but transporting one frightened girl, that was easy as pie. He was betting that LeFrank would come through this time, especially since he had ordered those documents. After today, if Craft did his job, that would be all taken care of.

Jimmy Craft knew the way by heart. The alley was so narrow that the sun never fell on the rough stones that led the way. The old pavers seemed to recognize his feet and exchange with them some secret sign that he was on the right track. They were gray-green in the darkness, slick and worn, with disease thriving happily in their damp, private crevices. Soon he saw the familiar sign, a warped board bearing the sadly ironic proclamation that this was "The Golden Inn." He took a seat at an empty table, dropped O'Neill's packet of papers on its damp blackened wood, and slapped the coins down next to it just as old Betty came up.

"Ale, Jimmy?"

"That's all the greeting I get, me, your best customer?"

"Ooh, get your hands offa me, you little bugger!"

He patted her behind once more and she grabbed his ear and twisted. His head tilted and he came off of his bench as he tried to escape the sharp pain. She brought her face close to his. "I tol' you again and again, you won't never see it, or touch it, or get it, so leave it alone. A woman like me is not for the likes a you. I got too much to offer."

She slammed the mug on the table in front of him, sloshing watery foam in all directions. The gray, chipped vessel was the first of several to sail his way. He drank steadily until it was past noon and he recalled his errand and determined that he had better make his delivery, and do whatever else he was supposed to do after that. Something that involved two coins. He couldn't quite remember, but that didn't bother him. He was used to being a little lost now and then.

It was a slow day at the cemetery and James Kensel welcomed the sound of the knock on his door.

"As I always say," he pronounced the words aloud to himself, "sooner or later they all need me. There's no getting around it." He opened the door with a satisfied smile and was nonplussed at what he saw. "Drunk and disorderly" were the words that first came to mind. "How can I be of assistance?"

"Here." The package moved into the space between them. Kensel took it.

"What's this?"

Craft giggled. "Prolly somebody's death warrant."

Kensel frowned his confusion.

Craft was at a loss as to what to do and stood there with his mouth hanging open. When he wavered and seemed to Kensel to be about to fall, the cemetery keeper took him by the arm and led him inside. Craft sank into the closest chair with a thud.

"Ha ya got a little drink for a thirsty fellow?"

Kensel considered. "Some tea, I think."

Craft's eyes closed immediately and, as he was nodding off, Kensel thought it safe to leave him be and hurry into the kitchen and put some water to heat on the stove. He took the package with him and inspected its contents while the tea was brewing. The papers were damp and emitted a scent disagreeable even to Kensel, who, in his work, was regularly assaulted by unpleasant smells. There was an order for services in the envelope, along with a draft to be used to pay for them. It was an unusually large amount for an interment. And no names. For the deceased or for the payer. Like with that boy Lamp, Kensel mused. He had no name, no cadaver, nothing. What were people thinking? The thing was a reservation. There was plenty of room here, acres of it, no need to save a space. There was no war, no plague, only the usual sickness and death. But all that was spread out, almost as if it were scheduled by some divine force or other, and the demand on Kensel matched, quite evenly, his capacity to satisfy it. More or less. At the moment he was time and coffins ahead. But it always worked out. Eventually.

It was a struggle of patience and pleading, but finally he got some tea and bread into the small, dirty man who had lodged himself in the front room of his house. Kensel was patient; spare time was something he had in abundance. Indeed, his balance of minutes and hours grew with interest now that his wife had died and he spent so much time alone.

"Who is the deceased?"

"Dunno."

"Where is this coffin I am being paid to bury?"

Craft wondered aloud to himself, "So that's what it is. Old Clint has it figured out. On the ship. He's a mean man, Cap'n Clint, but he's sharp alright.

"Here?"

"What?"

"Is the deceased, what you just said, on a ship here in Newport News?"

"I don't think it's got here yet." He threw his head back and laughed at the idea. "If it was, I'd a had the box in the bundle too. Put it on the bench next to me at the Golden Inn. Open it up and get the corpse a drink! Sittin' up and us having a conversation. Could drink me under the table." He bent in laughter at this, face red and no sound coming out of his mouth. Kensel couldn't imagine what on earth the man was going on about.

He didn't notice how little this amused Kensel. "No, soon, though, boat'll be here soon."

Alarmed at this pronouncement, Kensel waited for the man to sit up and regain at least the appearance of control.

"How do you know there is a dead person on the ship? Were you notified by the owners? Why do you say it will be a woman?" When only shrugs and more laughter answered his question, Kensel asked him, "Who sent you? Who gave you the papers to bring here? Who's 'Clint'?"

"O'Neill. The boss. Don't you know him…everybody knows him…I know him. Ha ha…I know him."

Saying O'Neill's name made him remember what he was supposed to be doing, and abruptly Craft struggled to his feet and made for the door. Very few of his visitors left the man speechless, but Kensel was too busy thinking to say any more to this unusual character and he figured that there was little to gain from questioning him further in any case. It was late afternoon when the drunken little man tottered off, his steps wavering, his mind, as usual, just capable of managing his feet and not much more.

Only after he was gone did Kensel realize that he had not asked where this man O'Neill lived. He went outside and ran down the walk, looking for him, but Craft had disappeared, leaving the gate open, but no sign of where he had gone. He was walking back toward his front entrance when his shoulders twitched with the feeling that something was not quite right in his tiny universe. He paused. Whatever it was was still there, and he began to make his way toward the highest point of the property in order to put the uneasy feeling he had to rest.

When Kensel came upon him the man was like a statue, the large gravestone that had concealed him from view transferring its placid granite nature from the place where his hand touched it, along his arm and into the rest of his body. He was a large man, bent down onto one knee, his fingers deep into the cuts that spelled Lamp's name in the rock. His hat was pulled down low and his collar up high. It was so quiet that Kensel wondered if the man were breathing. It was at this point that Kensel would normally have backed slowly away, his respect for others and their anguish accompanying him in quiet retreat. Instead, he simply stood there, a dozen feet away, behind the kneeling man and slightly to his right. Plenty of time. He was far too curious about the whole affair to let this mysterious stranger leave without speaking to him. He did not have to wait long, for the man said in a pleasant voice, "Mr. Kensel, I am glad to have the occasion to meet you." With that he stood and turned gracefully and offered his hand. Kensel took it and looked up in wonder at him. He nodded absently and apologized for interrupting him, wondering how he was known to this man and what to make of it all. Before he could speak further the visitor said, "I was a patron to the young man lying there and I feel his loss was partly my fault. Your care here is gratifying to me." He looked around at the stone, across the lawn, as if appreciating its beauty.

"Thank you, but I must ask, sir, who you are and how you know him—Lamp—and how he came to such an unfortunate end. Even I, who didn't know him or anything about him, was saddened to see him brought to me in such a state. Usually a family member tells me what happened, but in this case there was nothing. And then the stone was delivered and the firm that brought it, well, they too knew nothing." Kensel looked up from the stone, "Are you a relative of his?"

"I am the one who paid for it all. As I said, he was like a ward of mine," he answered obliquely.

"Strell." His man came out from behind the trees at the back of the cemetery and, seeing Kensel too late, realized his mistake. "Sir," he said as if correcting himself. Strell inclined his head, forgiving the error. "I'm coming. Wait." His man took a step back and held his place next to the large old oak at the edge of the expanse of grass. It was very dark between the trees that loomed behind him. At least, Kensel thought, now I have a name. Strell. Never heard the name before.

"We, too, know little about what happened. Were there personal effects...anything in his clothes?"

Kensel saw no problem with telling Strell the little he knew. After all, this surely was the man who paid for everything; he knew his name, about the money that was sent. He even nodded when Kensel talked about the stone. His sorrow seemed genuine. He gave him the whole account as he knew it, even that there was quite a bit of interest from the constable, a man named Armistead, who had, it seemed, no idea of why the boy was killed or who did it.

"The boy had a tattoo."

"Yes, I knew about that. Got it when he was very young."

"Something Armistead was interested in, or his deputy was, the writing on his hand. It was just a word, '*hathor*,' just that." Kensel spelled it out, letter by letter, and Strell felt each symbol scorch an imprint into his mind. "Don't know what it means, maybe someone's name."

Strell inclined his head, his eyes drifting to the side, not seeing anything as he thought of the message Lamp had died for. Been murdered for. "*Hathor.*" He began to move away, "Thank you, Mr. Kensel, for your care and your help. I will stop by when I can, to visit my young friend. Perhaps I will see you again."

All Kensel got out was, "Certainly. I...." But in a moment, as Kensel looked at the gray stone, Strell, and his man, had vanished. The trees took them in and hid them.

CHAPTER 47

North

Philadelphia

There was, Jack would soon learn, no sign of the sailing ship *Hathor* in the port of Philadelphia. His impression of the city bore little resemblance to the pictures Jack had seen in magazines. A big city could not be described in words or with flat black-and-white images; it had to be heard and smelled, the perpetual motion of its inhabitants brushed up against. That much was clear to him as he walked toward the Cutter Service office by the river. He was overwhelmed by the throngs of people, outfits and tongues and behaviors overlapping in a way that was disconcerting to him. He hadn't thought there were this many people in the whole country. To his way of thinking, the town of Lewes was crowded.

He kept one hand in his pocket to hold onto his money, heeding the same advice he had given Elizabeth before she left. His pistol was ready in the front of his heavy coat and he kept his pack close to his side. He realized it had been three months since he had seen her. He missed her and feared for her. How could a woman survive, alone, in a city like this? Vickers and Stock had been to similar places on the far side of the world, and told of beggars too many for even the gutters to accommodate, even in the smallest, most remote villages, jostles of souls where every sunrise lit the newly dead lying in the streets.

Medicine in those places was a potion made of magic and superstition; spears and arrows were government; the station of the people whose momentary joining led to your birth determined how you would be dragged through the years to your death. These were places where suffering and death were ruling partners. Most children died. Most people had little to eat. Thirty was old. People were owned. There was no way out.

At the office of the Cutter Service near the docks, Jack found Jefferson Edghill, the man in the port responsible for collecting the federal government's due from those engaged in the maritime trade. He looked up as Jack came into the office.

"Yes, young man?"

"Good afternoon, sir. My name is Jack Light and I am a member of the Service, a surfman that is, and I came here hoping you might be able to provide me with some information."

"A soldier then."

Jack shook hands with Edghill, wondering why he was being called a soldier.

"Sir?"

"Every service has its soldiers. They are the service. They fight the fights and win or lose what the service has as its mission. You are the Service, young man. There is nothing without you and your fellow surfmen. If you don't save the people on those ships, then a battle in the war is lost. Too many battles lost and the war is over. I see from your face that you don't quite see what I'm getting at. Come, sit with me in my office and I'll tell you. You, surfman, you of all people...it's something you should know." Edghill was a tall man, as large and powerful in the shoulders and chest as Jack, wearing a dark blue suit and a full black beard, which he had trimmed carefully.

Edghill waved his arm around the room. "The men who work in offices like this are at war also, one you probably don't know about. It's a war of money and egos and ambition. There are people in our government who want to control the services... Lighthouse, Cutter, your Lifesaving Service, Navy, Treasury Department... realign, perhaps is a better word for it. The officials in the Capitol all want to have their own way. Even ahead of what's good for the nation. Do you follow me, young man?"

Jack didn't know what to say, and hesitated. When Vickers and Stock had their long hushed conversations about the Service and money and equipment, this must be what they worried over. The surfmen never gave it much thought. They were workers, and at their level things like this were rarely discussed unless it meant more pay or better gear.

"I never gave it much thought, sir." As he said this he recalled Ezra's words—that he had been in line to become a station keeper—

and realized how much he didn't know about what went on in that part of the job. Even so, the old man was telling Jack, in choosing him ahead of some of the others, that he had the ability to do the job. No chance of that now, he thought, seeing in his mind's eye the look on the old man's face. Edghill went on, not noticing the clouds of feelings that darkened Jack's face and, for a moment, left his eyes unfocused.

"Thankfully, many of us do. We fight to keep the services as they are, but to get a central authority over them and to get more government budget money to make them more effective. It's a war on several fronts, with states, bureaucrats, senators, cabinet secretaries, and military leaders all wanting different things." Edghill went on in detail about the importance of the Lifesaving Service.

Jack had never considered the financial aspect of this. Even with the limited volume of ship traffic he saw in his small role in things, he understood at once that the money involved would be considerable. One look at the Philadelphia waterfront confirmed what he had been told about the thousands of ships plying the waters off the coast of the United States. There were a dozen or more major ports on the East Coast alone, and who knew about the Pacific, or how many vessels traveled the sea lanes to foreign nations at any one time. He knew duties were paid on goods moving in and out of ports, and he knew that certain items were taxed and others interdicted. He supposed that most of the people who avoided these payments did so because the goods they had were stolen or forbidden for some reason. The English, French, Spanish, and Dutch—all of them were forever fighting out their disputes over land and sea, seeking advantage, banning certain goods, moving cargo for gain. The fights over whaling and fishing grounds alone were long and bloody. Some countries sent warships out to escort their fishing vessels. Everyone who was in the service or worked aboard a ship knew the history of that.

Jack, for all his preoccupation with Elizabeth and the constant physical pain he felt, was still, underneath it all, the same person he had always been. He was curious as much as he was anything. It was, he thought, a smile almost escaping him, one of the things the two of them had in common. One of the things he loved about her. He was hearing every word, even as he thought of her. He interrupted Edghill's delivery, "What did you say about the women being abducted? How does that happen? Who are they? What happens to them?"

"It's one of the most troubling things, the slavery problem. Not the same as the war we have just had, no, not the same at all. Horrible as all slavery is, that was institutionalized, out in the open. This, if you can believe it, in some ways is even worse. At least some of the plantation slaves were treated passably well. That is not the case with the ones I'm talking about. Women are taken, mostly Indians and Negroes from the islands to the south...but some from this country as well...and, most of them, made to work in brothels. Until the pox kills them, or they are beaten to death, or killed when they are found to be with child. Or, it is sickening to say, until they get a little bit older and are of no use. Then they just kill them outright. People pay a lot for them, these women. More if they are young and beautiful. Now I hear these slavers, cursed dogs, are taking young girls from the cities along the coast. Most of them come here from Europe, looking for a new life. Don't get it, as you can tell from looking out my window right here in this great city. Get more of what they left. With the death and disease, many of them wind up alone here, unable to speak English, unable to make a living. They're easy targets. Some others are from the Midwest, thinking it's glamorous or exciting to live in the big city. They want to marry rich men, be important. Even children, boys and girls, are made into slaves this way. There's no skill to taking someone away from these lives. They go readily. Someone makes them a promise and off they go. And then find it's too late. I can say for a certainty that someone was taken away from this city today. Probably a number of people."

Jack remembered LeFrank, storming up and down the beach, looking for his property. Elizabeth. Property.

"I didn't know any of this. I appreciate your telling me. What I came to ask is if you can help me with information about a ship. Where it's registered...who owns it..."

"The ship?"

"*Hathor*. That's all I know. It's important to me to find it. A personal matter. One I'd like to have kept private." Jack leaned forward hopefully.

"Comes to this port?"

"I don't know. She's a very large merchant ship, although in a way she's like a warship. Foreign made, I'd say, not like the ones from the shipbuilders here. Very different looking. Travels the East Coast though."

"If that's the case, she's probably put in here. This is the busiest port of call in the nation." Edghill knew New York was bigger, having recently surpassed Philadelphia in the volume of its trade, but he had some city pride and wanted to brag a little, stretch the truth. They walked side by side down a vast row of docks and entered a government building, the stars and stripes outside snapping for their attention. "Here we are. Let's see what we can find out inside."

He led Jack to a row of shelves permanently bent under loads of ledgers. Since no one in the room could recall a ship named *Hathor*, they had to plow through the volumes themselves, running their fingertips down page edges and over rows and rows of entries. They were working backward from the latest entries. With both of them scanning the logs they went through them quickly. Jack saw the name; his whole body had been flexed with tension as he hunched over the pages. He relaxed a little. *Hathor* had been in Philadelphia two years ago. Edghill showed him how to reference the entry in another book and less than an hour after they had come to the office, Jack knew what he needed to know. Harrison Ship Lines. Boston, Massachusetts. Guillaume LeFrank.

He thanked Edghill and in parting the men assured each other that they would continue to fight on their respective battlefronts, for the good of the service. Jack put his head down and started back toward the center of the city and the train station.

"Jack?"

He ignored the call, knowing it was not for him.

"Surfman!"

Jack stopped and turned. At first he couldn't tell who had called, the motion of the crowds confusing him further. Then he saw the man's uniform, a waving arm upraised. Plain, no insignia, but a uniform nevertheless. There was no mistaking it. "Hello." The other man came up to him and shook his hand, "I thought it was you...the storm coat gave you away...what're you doing here? It's Jack, right?"

"Right. You've a good memory. "

"It's not just that. George Kimball talked about you a bit when he was aboard, telling Captain Marshall about things at the station. That you were a good man—like a son to him. All of us on board *Mercury* heard a lot of that. I'm Arthur Durant."

Jack was embarrassed by the words, especially since he had abandoned his post, so to speak. He decided not to explain anything about what he was doing. "Where's the *Mercury*?" He looked at the man, and tried to remember his face.

"She's there, beyond the long warehouse."

"Is the captain aboard?"

"Sure. Got time for a look? Captain'd like to see you."

Which way, Jack wondered, was the ship headed? If she was bound for Boston, could he go along, and did that make sense? He had to admit it, it was probably too late to escape the town by train anymore today, so he might as well go visit with Marshall.

"Sure. I'd like to see the ship and the captain and crew again."

Marshall welcomed him like a long lost son. They talked mostly about George Kimball and what had happened at the station in the intervening months. He and Kimball had written to each other, but Marshall did not know about the woman Ellen Brahe. The mail had trouble finding sea captains, especially ones like Marshall, who liked to spend most of his time out of sight of land. He was clearly overjoyed to hear the news. Marshall prevailed upon him to stay aboard the ship and they enjoyed a good meal and a long pleasant evening with some of the men. Sailors and surfmen were people from a great variety of backgrounds, with experience of the exotic and unbelievable. In their conversations they roamed the world, navigated shoals and storms and islands and continents, sailed close to rocky coasts, and made landfall on many topics. Jack got into an empty rack and slept well.

The only place in the city where the sun seemed to have any importance to anyone was the waterfront and Jack and all of the crewmen were up before it was, and ready to go. He had learned the night before that the ship was leaving on a short southbound run, visiting ports in Maryland and Virginia with a cargo of furniture and machine parts and various other manufactured goods. Jack told Marshall that he was on leave, visiting a friend up north, in Boston. He did not elaborate and the captain said he was sorry they weren't going that way, as he would liked to have had Jack's company for a few days more.

The visit with these men had lifted his spirits and he was glad to be going through the streets more or less alone since it was very early and Philadelphia still slept. One of the first trains to leave the station that morning was bound for Boston and he bought a ticket and sat in the cavernous terminal and waited. He wondered why anyone would build such a large room for so few people. Even if every bench was occupied, the place made no sense to him. He could barely see the ceiling.

CHAPTER 48

The Investigation

Newport News

The day after Billy and Joan went to the theater Billy arrived early at the police station and waited impatiently for Armistead. He stoked the fire and lit the lanterns and sat down to write out a detailed account of his visit with Kensel and the conversation he had had, only hours before, with Joan. Armistead arrived on time and was alert immediately, seeing the office at the ready and the expectant look on Billy's face. As Billy had predicted to himself, the old man was very excited to learn this new information; he questioned Billy as thoroughly as Billy had questioned Kensel, repeating the process until he was confident he had the whole story, as far as it went. Following this grilling he read and re-read the file and had Billy do the same.

"I'll wager that this ship, *Hathor*, is no longer in Newport News. Give me odds on that?"

"My betting against you is not what I want to do, if you don't mind, sir."

At Billy's unusually droll remark, a smile crossed Armistead's face. "Let me think on this for a while, Billy, and we'll talk about it some more later. Can you see Joan this morning?"

"Uh, sure, Daniel. What for?"

"I want you to go over what she said, in the cold light of day," he smiled and raised his brows, "and be sure of the story. You might have gotten something wrong last night. Other things on your mind and such. Give it a second look. See if she has any other recollections of this ship or crew."

Billy took off, glad of this particular assignment, and Armistead went directly to the waterfront. They returned later that morning, both empty handed, for Joan had nothing more to add, and as suspected, there was no ship named *Hathor* in the port.

And then he had a visitor.

"Mr. Kensel."

"Good to see you remember me, sir, after all this time."

"You are a memorable person, Mr. Kensel."

"Well, nice of you to say so, constable. The lad. Lamp. Seems there's some more to his story."

"I'm sure."

"Your man told you about the tattoo?"

"He did. Told me all about his visit with you and how helpful you have been. I appreciate it. What else have you learned, Mr. Kensel?"

Kensel told his story. He described his feeling that someone was there, in the cemetery, and then gave an account of his meeting with Strell.

"What did this man Strell look like?"

Kensel's answer satisfied the constable. "You know this man, Strell?"

Armistead nodded thoughtfully, "We have crossed paths before. I'm afraid, Mr. Kensel, I can't say more than that." Armistead pictured his old adversary. "But I do know him. You've been a great help and I thank you for coming to see me to tell me about it." He rose from his desk to escort the man from his office and had almost ushered him to the door when he casually mentioned his first visitor of the day, Jimmy Craft. "What made this meeting with Strell so surprising was that it followed right on that of a very unusual man with another strange request. Put me in mind of the whole business with Lamp, anonymous orders and such. All very mysterious." He began telling his story and Armistead was only half listening until Kensel said, "Works for someone named O'Neill, first name of Clint. If I hadn't been outside watching him go off, I wouldn't have seen Strell at all."

"O'Neill, eh, now we're getting somewhere," Armistead said under his breath as the smile broke out on his face.

Armistead made a pot of tea and his visitor happy by spending the next hour with him. This was compelling. Strell and O'Neill. *Hathor*. Lamp.

Later that day he assigned two of his men to watch the *Luluwa* and concentrate on the activities of Captain O'Neill. They were to stay on this duty until told otherwise. The men went about their regular patrols, but made visits to the area where his ship was moored. Billy spelled them from time to time, as did Armistead himself. Something was going on, the constable knew, when Strell and O'Neill were involved in the same thing. He knew there was some connection with them and that Lamp's murder played some part in it. O'Neill had long been associated with the criminal element in the city, but had never been caught doing anything wrong.

He bet himself that this time he was going to find out what it was all about.

CHAPTER 49

Elizabeth

New York

The final stage of healing is boredom, and boredom is a symptom of need. Elizabeth realized this as she sat in her room reading and re-reading the same passage from her book. It was raining outside, the depths of winter were past, and she looked down at the page and couldn't remember anything about it. She closed the book, unmindful of her place, knowing that she would never finish it. She could no longer stay here. She had a need. To go. To resume living. During the recent days she had counted her money, dividing out the funds by the days, to determine how long she could go on as she had. Even if she sold some of the gems that remained, now sewn into her new clothes, there was an ultimate limit to the time she could spend living this way. Now it was arithmetic telling her what she must do.

Through the months she had passed the time in New York, her mind and body moved from one diversion to another. Even with the empty, joyless Christmas she had spent alone and living through the misery of the worst of the winter months, she had been able, much of the time, to keep her mind off of the sad reality of her life. Despite this she had not garnered any happy memories. Nothing would stick. Days passed when she did not say a word. Once she went for a week without doing so. During that time, as she sat reading in a café, she choked slightly on her tea, the sound startled her and her throat was sore and raspy.

She figured that since LeFrank had sent Chien to look for her, he'd be watching the house, but couldn't think of a way to learn what had happened other than by going there. Maybe LeFrank was looking for her in Delaware still. There was no way he could have learned of her stay in New York. She'd been safe here at least.

She packed her things. There was a little more to her baggage this time since she had bought some new clothes, but she'd need them in Boston just as she had here. Hers might all be gone from her home. She realized that she didn't care if they were or not. They weren't clothes, really, they were costumes, outfits one wore when playing a role: lady of the house, maid of honor, opera patron, dancing partner, someone to be seen at church, a vision entering a charity ball. She preferred the clothes that had belonged to Jack's mother. As she folded these plainer, simpler dresses, the long straight skirts and blouses, old and worn; as she traced her fingertips over the thin spots and pulls and slubs; as she let her skin love these clothes, she realized that she had not really recovered during the time she spent in New York, but had, more than anything, just become accustomed to what her existence was now.

The landlady was sad to hear that she was leaving, and amazed when Elizabeth paid her for the following week, "Sorry to leave you on short notice. You have a lovely place and I have enjoyed your kindnesses. Thank you." No one had ever paid her for the lack of notice and few had ever thanked her. More than a few left owing her. She understood that what Elizabeth was really thanking her for was her acceptance; she hadn't pried into her past or gossiped about her. It was, to each of them, as if they were the only two normal human beings in the whole city. The only ones civilized.

Her bags were more than she wanted to carry on the long walk to the station so she rode a hired carriage uptown. The coach driver pulled her bags from the roof of his rig, dropped them carelessly on the cobblestones, and without a word or backward glance, climbed onto his seat and was off. The station was nearly empty and she stopped and looked over her shoulder, seeing the doors that she had walked through months before, when she had taken refuge in the city. She had known even then, deep inside of her, that it was only a delay.

"One way to Boston," the ticket agent said as he stamped the paper and pushed it under the bars that protected him and the railway's money from the public. The grid of small thick brass rods said that everyone on earth, everyone outside of his small cubicle wanted to rob him. Elizabeth thought of him as her jailer, sending her to her place. He was on the outside, free, and she was locked into a place in her life that held her fast, subject to the will of others. As the train bumped along to the north she watched the New York slide by her window, detached from it, viewing it as if it were some far off land, or a failed experiment that no one had bothered to dismantle. It was already too late for that since the sprawling and rising conglomeration of streets and buildings had taken on a life of its own. It could never be undone. Then the miles intervened and her awareness of the city faded away like the afternoon light in winter.

A week earlier Jack had been carried along this same path with the rails telling him where he could go, limiting him as to what he could see. As he watched the city pass he suspected that he had been correct in his assumption that New York was just like Philadelphia, only worse. On the day that his train clattered through the heart of New York City, Jack had passed within a mile of Elizabeth as she wandered along a broad avenue swollen with people, sad and alone, their thoughts crossing.

Two of the city's street urchins counted the cars as they clattered by, throwing rocks at some of them, feeling the swirl of the air as the cars passed close to them, smelling the black smoke. Grit joined the other stains and smears on their faces and tattered clothes. When the caboose went by they scrambled up over the cinders of the rail bed and touched the tracks to see if they were hot. The bigger boy swatted at the other's head and taunted him, "Told ya they wasn't hot. You owe me a penny." The small boy ran off crying.

CHAPTER 50

Jane Barr

Boston

"Do they have to be here?" Chien and Salete sat next to the fire, drinking wine, smoking cigars, and pointedly ignoring her.

She stared at LeFrank and asked him the same question again.

"Sit down, Jane."

"What's this all about, that you had to have me come here all of a sudden?" She stretched her arms out to her sides and raised her hands, palms up, to shoulder height. "I should be living here or at the other house already, for that matter. Not have to run all over the place every time you decide you need me." She caught her breath, "Is it time, finally, to go on with your plan, your secret plan that you won't explain to me? Tell me it is!"

"This is to remind you to be ready."

"I've been ready for almost a year. Ever since you started with all your big promises."

LeFrank examined the ends of a fresh blunt cigar. He struck a match and watched carefully as its fire flared into existence. "Lucifers." He stroked his thumb and finger across each other and the shaft of the match rotated. The flame spurted out to the sides. "What an excellent name for something, don't you agree, Jane? One little stick of pine, some sulfur…scratch it gently and it has as much power as the devil himself. With one of these I could burn away everything in the world until there was nothing left but me. But Lucifer can't do anything without me." He lit his cigar and laughed at his own joke.

She looked away, expressing her opinion of his nonsense with a slow turn of her head and a faint simpering sigh.

"By being ready, I mean completely ready. We could leave at any time now. Without notice." She heard his words and saw the smoke shapes they made as he said them.

She showed her lack of concern for his warning, as if it meant nothing to her. He would, after all, have to wait for her. She was the one with the talent. Chien, however, was intensely interested. He turned away from the fire, leaned toward LeFrank, his head up, wanting to hear his exact words. He worried that LeFrank would sail before he could locate Elizabeth, and take possession of her.

LeFrank stared into her eyes. "Pay attention. You'll be limited in what you can take. Starting tomorrow I want you to begin to remove most of your things from the theater. A little at a time. Not all of it. Leave some of your clothes and make-up, things that you don't care about. Pack the things you must have in a steamer trunk—one trunk only—and have it ready to go. You can have a carry bag also."

"If you think I'm going to leave all my things, you're crazy. All those clothes! You have a whole ship to carry my trunks. Don't tell me what I can and cannot have with me."

"It's not about room, Jane, it's about time. We may not have time to handle a lot of excess baggage."

"Nothing I own is 'baggage,' LeFrank!"

"You will do as I say."

"Then, Guillaume, you're going to buy me a new full wardrobe—with matching jewelry—when I get to New York. Carte blanche. I won't go otherwise."

LeFrank stared straight into her eyes. "It's what I intended all along, Jane."

Salete and Chien exchanged looks, showing each other the barest of smiles. Enemies though they were, held in common was their appreciation of LeFrank's abilities. Additionally, neither of them could bear being around Jane Barr.

"Salete will take you back now."

All three of them were unhappy with LeFrank's command. Chien spoke up, more vehemently than he wanted to, "I'm going back that way."

LeFrank shrugged. Chien made quickly for the door and she followed, reluctantly. She liked him even less than she did Salete. Sneaky little man. Always looking at her. Filthy in his ways and his looks. At least, she consoled herself, this would all be over soon.

Chien had one thing in mind—finding Elizabeth. Tonight he had a perfect opportunity to do something he wanted to do for a long time. When he'd left Jane Barr at her house he went immediately to the dock where *Hathor* was berthed. He walked in shadows and crept around the pallets of freight piled on the pavers by the water. He thought his luck was holding until he saw the sailor on watch walk slowly along the rail on the starboard side. "Damn his eyes," he cursed to himself. "Usually the lazy bastards are sleeping, but tonight I have to come across one who's actually awake, not only that, but walking around." He watched the man go forward and took his chance. When the sound of the man's steps faded Chien went below decks to the captain's quarters. When he scraped the match to light a candle it sounded like thunder to his ears and he waved at the smoke as if the pungent sulfur smell could be noticed by the man on deck. He crept around the cabin like a rat in a pantry, sniffing and intruding.

In spite of his caution he snagged the sleeve of his jacket on the feathery edge of a quill standing upright on LeFrank's desk. It had been left, vertical and ready, in an inkpot, which tipped and spilled before Chien could catch it. It flashed through his mind that LeFrank, who usually thought of everything, might have left it as a trap. He quickly pulled a piece of paper from a nearby pile and blotted the ink. He wiped the ink smear on the wooden surface with his hands and rubbed them on the front of his coat.

At each place he checked he felt anticipation and disappointment. Maybe LeFrank had it with him. Or Salete. The fifteen minutes he had been there seemed like hours. Then, above him, he thought he heard voices. He raced to the cabin door and noticed, slung over a hook on its back, one of LeFrank's heavy coats. With sure hands he ransacked the pockets and found what he had been looking for: the key to Elizabeth Harrison's house. It was what they used the night they had abducted her. Was probably, he realized, in that pocket the whole time since. Chien stuffed the key into his pocket and went on deck and headed straight for the rail. "You, stop!" It was Salete's voice, loud and commanding.

Chien gripped the rail to steady himself. "What do you want?"

"What are you doing aboard? You're were supposed to take her home, not here."

"I did. Just had to stop here for something." The answer sounded lame to both of them.

"What?"

Chien put his hands in his pockets. The key, the crumpled paper, and several of the beads from Elizabeth's broken necklace were on his left side, his pistol in the other. Drawing it and waving it back and forth so that it pointed now and again at Salete gave Chien a welcome distraction. "I needed this."

Salete ignored the gun, pointing instead at Chien's hands. "What's all over your hands?"

"Just oil. I had to clean it." Chien loved to provoke Salete and had recovered enough to add, "I used it recently...and I might need it again...soon."

Salete called after him, "I'll be sure to tell the captain I saw you, with dirty hands, on board the ship tonight." The words sent a chill through him, but Chien didn't look back.

CHAPTER 51

Inquiries

Boston

"Morrison!"

"Yes, sir?"

"Come in, come in. Pull the door closed."

"Sir?"

"Have you completed your review of the contracts for Mr. Bricknell?"

"I have, sir."

"Then I suggest you get them. The gentleman is waiting."

Morrison gave a quick respectful nod to Graham Bricknell. He relaxed placidly in the leather armchair opposite a wide and ornate desk behind which sat Morrison's exasperated and impatient employer, Donald Burns. He shot Burns a nervous glance and hurried out of the office. Burns was aggravated that he didn't close the door fully.

"I may be going to bring you some additional business, Donald."

"Oh?" Burns gave a restrained, but hopeful reply.

"Yes. There is to be a consolidation of some type among the shipping lines. Two or three—perhaps even more, it's rumored—of the old companies may be bought up by Harrison. The companies that are vulnerable right now are looking to Harrison for a buyout, and things have been moving along for Harrison, things in their favor, until recently. Some inquiries have been made about Harrison Lines, or more specifically, about the man who runs it. A man named Guillaume LeFrank. It's something official. Only a few people know about this, but I have it from a strong source that some investigation is underway. All of the companies have had accidents, canceled contracts, problems with loans, that sort of thing. Harrison has not, but if does go through, I'll be sure to see that your firm handles them. Should be a tidy package of business for you."

Burns squinted and licked his lips, logging all of this in his memory.

Outside his office Morrison did the same. If the investigation into the doings of this Mr. LeFrank and Harrison Ship Lines was highly confidential, then that gentleman was the one person who, it would stand to reason, would be most grateful to know of it. How much gratitude would result from this knowledge was the only question. Morrison was a poor law clerk, struggling to keep the wolf from the door. He smiled to himself. Late that afternoon Morrison walked onto the deck of the *Hathor*. Several rough and intimidating men questioned him and made him wait there, shivering in the growing cold. The wind off the water made it more bitter and it had a distinct, yet unidentifiable stench that combined with the slow pitch of the ship made him feel a deep nausea. He tried to focus on something that was not moving or swaying, but in relation to all about him, everything was.

"This way, then." The harsh words barked out and he was saved from the embarrassment of being sick in front of the various deckhands that smirked at him as they worked nearby. When he arrived at the cabin door LeFrank told him to come in. He stood behind a chart table and looked up at his visitor. "I understand you have an urgent message for me."

"You are Mr. LeFrank?"

"Correct."

"My name is Morrison."

LeFrank stared at him and did not move.

Morrison gathered his courage and said what he had prepared to say. He thought he had figured out a way to couch his desire for a reward in subtle but unmistakable terms.

"I have information that will be very valuable to you."

LeFrank stared.

Morrison had an uneasy feeling. He looked around the spacious cabin, noted the furnishings, wondered what besides darkness lay beyond the door, standing partially opened, that was off to his right.

"It could save you a fortune and protect certain investments you are about to make."

LeFrank's expression did not change, "How did you come by this knowledge?"

Morrison told him where he worked and that he had overheard a discussion between Donald Burns and Graham Bricknell.

"And you want to sell me this information?"

Morrison was flustered, "There are very serious concerns involved."

"Mr. Morrison. You have come here determined to betray a confidence. I have no concerns since I have done nothing wrong. You, on the other hand have committed a crime, several in fact. You are in effect blackmailing me. You have been very foolish in doing so in front of my witness who is waiting in the next room to hear the rest of your story. I suggest that you tell me all of it, right now, leaving nothing out. Your reward is that if I am satisfied with what you have to say, I will not go to your employer, nor to the Boston Bar commission, nor to Mr. Bricknell, nor to your family, nor to parties to any transactions I may or may not be contemplating. You have one chance. Use it now and use it wisely."

Morrison glanced toward the darkened doorway. The nausea he had felt on the deck rose from his gut and engorged his throat. Barely able to keep back his tears, he choked through the tale he had come to tell. LeFrank never moved or took his eyes off of him.

"Go home, Mr. Morrison. I will verify what you have said. If anyone is attempting to damage my reputation, I will deal with them in the proper way, after telling them that it was you who gave me this information."

Morrison fled. He tripped over a coil of rope and fell on the deck, jumped to his feet, ran down the gangway, and kept running until he was unable to go on.

Salete emerged from behind the cabin door, smiling.

"Wait for him outside that law office tomorrow night. Tell him the things we need him to find out from Burns' files. I'll leave a list for you. Give him one day to bring it to me, in person."

When he was alone LeFrank made a list of the names of people who could be responsible for this rumor, or if it were true, this action someone had taken against him. Since it came from Bricknell's "strong source," he had the feeling that there was something to it. Bricknell was a serious person, a local kingmaker who had inside knowledge, and he would not repeat idle talk. LeFrank would need him in the future, so the quick elimination of this rumor had additional implications. He put down O'Neill's name along with that of Salete, Chien, his first mate aboard the *Hathor*, Jane Barr, Father Barry, some of the bankers, the lawyers and brokers he had been working with, people from the various agencies and authorities. For a moment he thought of Richard Hazen, his most trusted captain, but he was sure it was not him. He considered briefly, but then rejected, any idea that this could in some way involve Elizabeth Harrison. "Goddam her," he thought, "even dead she won't go away."

LeFrank had been aboard many boats in his time. Every one of them leaked, some of them so badly that it took only one day out at sea to convince the men aboard that they had to turn back. But leaks on ships were one thing; a leak of confidential information about his business was another. Perhaps it wasn't a leak at all. Salete had been acting strange lately. He was possessed with everything about Chien, for one thing. For another, he may have been careless in the way he had created problems for the other shipping companies. It was getting harder and harder to put his confidence in him and LeFrank decided that maybe he would have to go. His practice was to eliminate liabilities. Quickly, permanently, and without regret.

CHAPTER 52

End of the Line

Boston

It took a long time to travel from Philadelphia to Boston and Jack was tired and stiff from the journey. Being tired and stiff from a long day of training at Ezra's hands was much different from feeling that way from boredom, the stress of foreshadowing and expectation, and doing nothing. After surfman training, or even after a rescue, the soreness, unlike this, had a pleasure to it.

Boston was unlike the cities he had left behind. It was somewhat aged, more concentrated, less powerful and imposing. It did not have New York's towering muscle-bound feel. The streets were more turning and crooked, the cobbles bumpier. There were not as many people about, the city a third as populous as New York. Even though spring was traveling up the East Coast, it had not yet reached this, America's northernmost large city. He arrived late in the day and got a room in a private home that looked clean and had a sign outside advertising favorable rates, thinking it best to start early the next day, rested and with a clear head.

The first day, spent on foot, was exhausting, and he returned to his room, disheartened and filled with doubt, and fell on his bed and slept like a dead man. The next morning he set out again, with his hopes renewed and a pledge to himself that he would not give up. His fortune changed on the second try and he learned the location of the Harrison Lines office from an ancient-looking man walking along the docks. The fellow looked to be an old seaman, weathered and a little ragged, and not likely to be involved with LeFrank. He was poorly dressed with a faded jacket and patched trousers. "It's along there a ways, son. Keep walking, you'll trip on it." The man shook a twisted finger in Jack's face. "But mark me, don't sail on none of the Harrison ships. Sign on one of the others if you want to live a long life and see your children. Have ya' seen him, the ship's master? Get a look at him 'fore ya' sign. Morning to ye, shipmate...morning. Remember me, Elijah...remember what I say."

Jack considered the man's warning. Elizabeth had told him, not in so many words, that she had been abducted. Now this old man was prophesying his death. Kidnapping and death. That day on the beach in Delaware his service mates had all mumbled about the ship, saying LeFrank and his men were smuggling or selling slaves. None of them had missed seeing the guns they carried. Whatever went on at Harrison Lines was dangerous, that was for sure.

Despite the old man's warnings Jack continued on his way. Jack knew the ship immediately. The sun, now almost directly overhead, lit her up and he could study her and appreciate her lines, and her mast and sail arrangement. He found a safe place to observe what was happening. He pulled his cap down and rested his head back against a crate, and, peering under the brim, watched and listened. He didn't have long to wait. There at the rail in the waist of the ship stood Salete. He looked clean, handsome and sleek, efficient. Salete was besieged by ship's mates, crewmen, laborers, shipwrights, coopers, suppliers, carpenters, vendors, clients, and port officials. One after another they came. Few got a long audience with him; most got a terse command, a fast signature on a document, a nod of the head, a cold reception, or an outright rejection. Jack sensed that something was about to happen. *Hathor*'s departure seemed imminent and it scared him that he would probably have to act soon.

He needed information about the company. He saw a young man carry a load of grain down the gangway of another ship and deposit it on a growing pile of grain sacks. The man looked around and then, sure that no one was watching, crept up an alley and into a tavern. Jack followed and took a seat next to the table where the man waited for service. After he saw the man down his second mug of ale with alarming speed, Jack struck up a conversation with him and then bought a round to keep him talking. Jack said he wanted to go to sea and asked about various employers, naming several he had seen on the waterfront. Vincent was his name and Vincent had a lot to say. Fortunately the man knew something about Harrison. "Hard people on those ships. I hear tell. Stay away from them. Sail with me—tell the cap'n I sent you in—I'll get a reward maybe, 'n we can come right back here and spend it. There's plenty a women here at night. Have some real fun on the cap'n."

Jack nodded, "Sounds good to me. Let me get you another, for your trouble." Vincent held up his mug to attract the barmaid.

"What is it you said about Harrison?"

"There's a captain, Lee Frang or somethin' like that, who treats the men bad. Beats 'em, kills 'em, leaves 'em on an island by theyselves. They say he has a whip, carries it on deck and cracks it on the men's backs. I woddna' stood for that. Not me."

"Does he own the company?"

"Naw, some woman. Rich bitch, ya know?" He laughed at his own wit.

It took all of Jack's strength of will to keep from hitting the man in the face. He knew it was Elizabeth the man was talking about. Instead he prodded the man, "A woman owner, eh, that's strange. How did she come to own the company?"

"Same as they gets anything, trick a man—you know how they do—maybe marry him, or just be the man's daughter. That's who owns it, Harrison's daughter. Old man died, another rich old bastard who never saw to it that the workers got the gold, no, only him." Vincent drank deep, his lament consecrating the drink. "No gold for me, nope, no gold…"

"Is this Harrison woman married to LeFrank?"

"Don't think so. He has lots of women come and stay with him. Don't think someone like her would stand for that. They say she lives atop Second Street, uptown somewhere. Probably has a hundred rooms and a hundred servants. Have so much money they can burn it in the fireplace just to keep warm. Don't do nothin' for us poor ones, know what I mean?" Vincent thought rich people just kept their money, never spent it, burned it up just to keep lesser men from ever seeing it. Just to spite them. A few minutes later Vincent had his head down on his folded arms and was mumbling himself to sleep and drooling on the table. Jack looked around him, slid off of his bench, and walked out into the afternoon light.

He asked several people for directions and eventually learned the location of the house, and one man told him it was abandoned, no one home. He decided the best place to observe Elizabeth's house was from under an old pine tree that was one of a group growing at the corner of a nearby alley. He could see the front and side of the house. In the days that followed he traveled back and forth from his lodgings to the house, looking for her.

CHAPTER 53

The Pistol

When Elizabeth alighted from the train in Boston she felt a tightness in her chest. She shook herself and shivered. A blast of steam from the locomotive startled her and passengers fussed their children and companions away from the snorting iron monster. The city of her birth was now a place alien to her, although she had spent all but six months of her twenty years in its confines. As was her habit, she looked around her and evaluated the people on the station platform for signs of possible threats. All she saw was travelers, railroad employees, and families and friends meeting each other.

Adjacent to the station there was a railroad hotel and the weight of her two bags, as much as anything else, helped her decide to go there to take a room before she decided what to do next. It had the advantage of being some miles from her house and, since its clientele were travelers, it was a place where she would not encounter anyone who might recognize her. She ate a little of her food, smoothed her skirt, brushed her hair. Although it was late in the day she couldn't wait to have a look at her house. She took a hired carriage to a small square several blocks south of her home and one street over. She walked a spiral of lanes and alleys until she drew just close enough—two blocks away on a side street—to see her home. It was quiet and dark. Lonely. She went no closer, fearing that LeFrank might have the place watched.

That night she thought of Nana. She remembered the time when Nana showed her a house key hanging on a nail in their stable at the rear of the property. For an emergency. She was glad she remembered the key—up to this point never realizing that she could have trouble entering her own home. In the morning she got up, washed her face and body as well as she could using the pitcher and basin in her room, and dressed. She took the pistol from under her pillow, examined it, and tucked it into the holster pocket she had sewn into the waist of her dress. It was concealed just below her waist, close to her left side so she could easily reach across and get it with her right hand. Its weight and the feel of the barrel pressing against her thigh were reassuring to her.

She decided to wait until late morning to go abroad. By that time most people would already be at work or be busy doing their shopping.

Chien spent his morning looking for information along the docks. He stopped to shoot the breeze with some of his cronies, sifted through their talk, but learned nothing of interest. Since his visit from the unfortunate Mr. Morrison, LeFrank had been riding Chien hard, insisting that he do whatever he had to do in order to discover anything that was being said about him. The threats to Chien were no longer implied ones. He was grilled at length whenever he came before his captain. The little man was forced to cover more ground every day and had, therefore, less time to go to Elizabeth's house to watch for her. *Hathor* was almost fully loaded and might sail any day. The fear of missing the woman grew, becoming stronger than his worrying about LeFrank. It was time to use the key, for which he had risked so much, to enter the house, see for himself if anyone had been there. Even better, he could wait inside, away from the elements, for his precious Elizabeth to come to him.

Jack, not having seen any sign of Elizabeth during his repeated visits to her home, decided to visit the customs house at the port, in the same way he had during his visit with Edghill in Philadelphia. He went inside, looked at notices posted on boards outside the various offices, listened to what was said, but didn't hear anything helpful and couldn't think of an excuse to justify asking about Harrison Lines, Elizabeth, or LeFrank. To arouse suspicion was to invite trouble. It was a busy place and he lingered as long as he could, moving among the clerks and messengers and lawyers and officials, but finally gave up and left.

Elizabeth was circumspect in her approach, and in the late afternoon, let herself into the barn at the back of her lot. It was empty—the horses, carriage, tack, feed, all had been taken away. The key was long and heavy and the bronze was dirty and pitted. Spiders had found it a handy place to anchor their spinning. She clutched it tightly as she peered through the cracks in the side of the barn, watching until she was sure she was alone, scanning the front, rear, and side lawns. A labyrinth of mature boxwoods stood formally in the side yard, as if waiting for a ceremony to begin. She took a deep breath and walked a straight line across the brown grass and up to the door to the kitchen. She had to work the key a little to make it open the door. She closed the door behind her, took two steps inside, and waited. It was cold as a tomb. There had obviously been no fires, no heat, no one there for a long time. The stale air she breathed confirmed it. Dust lay thick on the shelf tops and furniture, and the floors creaked and cracked like gunshots under her careful steps along the main hallway and into the front parlor. Her piano, case shut and keyboard covered, waited in silence. Her harp, a costly instrument that she had just been learning to play before she was taken, sat bent and lonely in a corner. Elizabeth was drawn by a strong force to go to Nana's room. She felt compelled to go there first. She stopped on the landing and looked down the hall at the door to her room, hesitated, but then climbed the next flight of stairs. She looked into the door of Nana's room. It was a terrible disappointment. Things were as she remembered them—neat, the bed made, everything in its place. All of Nana's things were gone. Some macabre fixation made Elizabeth examine the rugs, the floorboards, pull the covers down on the bed. There were no marks on the floor, but she saw immediately that the mattress on the bed was new. She pushed on it with her fists and knew it had never been used. Tears came to her eyes and she pressed her lips together and felt her face fold in on itself. She could see in her mind's eye Salete standing in her room that night, smiling, holding up his knife, teasing her, threatening to do what he had already done. Murdering someone in their sleep, and being proud of it. Slaughter another living person. How could someone do that? How much blood was on him? For a long time she had wanted to return to her own room. That wish now seemed to have lost its power over her. She knew what she would find there—nothing. It too would have been robbed, stripped of its history and of her existence. Without her possessions it will be, she realized, as if she never was. She descended the wide staircase to her floor, walked carelessly along, pausing here and there to look at and remember a painting on the wall or into the rooms she passed.

Her door was standing open and she entered slowly and took it all in. The picture she had moved the night she was taken was gone, as were the gloves and handkerchief she had thrown onto the floor.

All of the photographs of her, Nana, and LeFrank, she realized, were gone. She walked around her bed, crossed the room to her dresser, and pulled out the top drawer. It held nothing. She stared down at it, feeling as empty as it was. She knew she could search the entire house and that she would find nothing to help her. Coming to her house, the one thing she could think of to do, was a dead end. She was sad and disappointed and frustrated.

The door to her room slammed shut with a noise like an explosion.

Elizabeth's shoulders jerked up and fear tore a lightning bolt through her body. She raised her head and in the mirror over her dresser she saw him standing there.

Jack felt comfortable. He had gotten used to the waiting, become familiar with his surroundings, and with a good warm meal inside him, he was content and patient. Sometimes, standing in the tower, or patrolling the beach at night he experienced the same feeling. It was sweet, solitary, and listless, a sense of being alone in the universe, doing only one thing, and that an easy one, so that you could free up everything in you and go up a plane. Exist a different way. The old sailors said they knew it from swaying up in the crosstrees, watching for pirates, warships, squalls, or whales. They said they had ideas go through them that were like visions. You held on, they said, just enough to keep your sanity and your grip on the mast. Let go and you would go mad or fall to your death, no longer what you were before you ascended into the sky, but now only a bloody mass on the deck. One second filled with visions, the next smashed to hell. He now felt that same lightness as the afternoon was plunging away over the horizon and into the darkness. Tiny flames would soon be set to dancing atop candles and on lamp wicks in the nearby homes.

Elizabeth watched him smile at her stunned reflection and she turned around slowly and faced Chien. "So you've come home to me after all. I knew you would." He lowered the gun he had been pointing at her and took a step closer. She knew she couldn't get her pistol out of her pocket quickly enough and stalled him until she had the chance, hoping there would be one. "How did you know I'd be here? Did LeFrank tell you to wait for me?"

"LeFrank thinks you're dead." Chien smiled at her confused look. "I'm the only one who knows," he said proudly. "I found the beads, ya' see. I knew. Been comin' here waitin' for you. But I told them all that you were dead. No one gonna' know you came back to me. Been watchin' and waitin'. Heard you comin' in and waited behind your door. Ha ha." Chien dug in his pocket and held out his hand, poking at the beads, scratched and dull, rolling them on his palm with the muzzle of his gun. All she could think of at that moment was that she would never see Jack again, and that he would never know what had happened to her. As he slipped the handful of beads back into his pocket Elizabeth thought of an opening and took a chance. "I can see you're smarter than the other two. Now that you've got me, tell me what this is all about." She said, her voice an appeal to his sympathy, "Please."

Her play to his vanity worked and Chien told her everything about LeFrank. He wanted to show off for her. He explained it all in detail. The girls, Jane Barr, Father Barry presiding at faked weddings, O'Neill playing his part, Nana's death, the smuggling, sabotaging his competitors so he could buy them cheaply, Salete's role in it all. He was anxious to show how smart he was, "LeFrank don't know it but I seen his false decks and bulkheads. He got secret places on his boat that keeps the revenuers off him. He can get into any port, even get inspected. That is if he don't just bribe the customs man. Yeah, I know and he don't think I know."

She steeled herself as she took it in, doing her best to show no reaction, even to the final pronouncement that Nana was dead. She believed it now—he had no reason to lie about that when he was being so free with everything else.

"He wants the company…Harrison…and figured marrying you would do it easy. When you showed him you wanted no part of him he jus' decided to do it his way. How he does most things." Chien smirked at this, "Think he likes it sometimes when he can be cruel about it, make it hard on someone. Had it in for you, that's for sure." He told her about all the people LeFrank has bribed, how he has things fixed. She realized she had been correct in her thinking that she would have a hard time finding someone in authority whom she could trust to side with her against LeFrank. The list of people who, for a price, turned a blind eye to what LeFrank did was truly remarkable. "LeFrank was gonna sell ya to some strange man— Strell—probably you would a' wound up a whore. That's a story in itself, that man Strell, worse than LeFrank they say, but you don't have to worry about him now. So, you can see I'm the one that saved you. From LeFrank. From Strell. And so now you owe me for that."

As an afterthought Chien boasted, "LeFrank has someone gonna' give him a marriage certificate and a death certificate showing you his wife and then gone, but don't you worry, he'll get somebody else to fill your shoes—and then your coffin. That's what's going on now. Old *Hathor*, she'll be sailing soon, an' there'll be someone on board to pass for you. Someone to take your place. That's what I think."

"Who's the girl?"

"Don't know. Who cares?" He laughed at this and it angered her.

"What about the other girls? Do you know who bought them or where they went?"

"Don't know. O'Neill knows, he sold 'em all, less he kept some for himself." He raised his gun level with her heart and then lowered it again. He licked his lips, "Like I say, you owe me." He took a step closer, then another, coming around the end of the bed. "I been watching you since you was a little girl. Seen you getting bigger, going from girl to woman. Waiting for this day." The thought was revolting to her. This on top of everything else made her sick. It was all she could do to refrain from screaming and attacking him.

She was aware of the gun in his hand, now held pointed at the floor, loose but ready, but not for the moment aimed at her. Even so, he could have it up before she could pull hers from her pocket. She kept her place as he approached. Both of them were breathing hard. Grotesque and unrestrained, he suddenly reached out with his left hand, grabbed at her breasts and pushed her hard in the chest, making her fall back across the bed. At once he climbed on top of her and pinned her down. He held her wrists over her head and dug with his knees between her legs. She didn't struggle, but only turned her head away from him as he tried to kiss her. He released his hold on her arms and she could feel the hash-marks on the hammer of his pistol scratching her neck as he brought his hands down onto the collar of her dress and started ripping it open. She could tell he was too strong for her to fight off and as he grunted and drooled kisses on the base of her neck she slipped her hands down between their bodies and tried to draw her pistol from its place. It had slipped between her legs and would not come out of the tangle he had made of her dress and then he felt her hands between them, and raised himself up to see what she was doing. He looked down and saw the grip of the gun exposed and clutched in her hand. She could feel that he had let go of his gun and was pushing his hands down between them. When he clawed at her and tried to grab her wrist she jerked her arm back with all her strength and pulled the trigger.

Jack heard the muffled pop of the pistol and saw a flash of light in the window of Elizabeth's room. It was almost the color of the sunset. He bolted from his place under the trees and ran down the alley toward the house. When he was still a hundred yards away he saw a small man, hunched over, run out of the front door and limp down the street toward the center of town. Jack decided not to follow him and ran into the house. He leaped up the steps, looking for the room at the side of the house where he had seen the flash of light. He stopped, looking around him, and then he heard her sobbing. He ran into her room and saw Elizabeth, curled up on the floor, her dress a bloody knot, ripped down its front and bunched all the way up between her legs. She was crying hysterically and pressing her hands to the scalded place low on her body.

He knelt beside her and took her in his arms, "Elizabeth, it's me, Jack...the surfman."

He asked her if she were hurt, but she just kept saying his name over and over through racking tears. "Jack...how...what are you? What Jack...oh thank God, Jack..." Slowly, he placed his fingertips on her arms and legs, probing along her body. He inspected her skin carefully in the dim and failing light. He pulled her skirt down over her legs and closed the collar of her dress. It was then he felt the pistol, his mother's pistol, in her pocket. It was hot. He looked closely and saw that she had shot it through her dress, leaving a black hole and charred streaks and dark blood on the fabric. He lifted her up and laid her down on her bed and knelt beside it, his face close to hers. He straightened her dress on her and smoothed her hair and told her everything was alright, that she was safe with him. He pulled the gun from her pocket and placed it beside her on the bed. Gradually her trembling slowed and she asked him to help her up. He held onto her hands and asked, "Are you hurt?"

"No."

"Are you sure?" He bent down to look at her.

She let go of his hands and put her arms around him. He held her in his arms and kissed the scar on her forehead. She raised her face to his and they kissed each other as both of them had wanted to do for a long time.

Thinking they might still be in danger Jack glanced again around the room and asked her what had happened. She kept her tight hold on him and spoke with her face pressed to his jacket. "The man, LeFrank, worked for my father and had a small share in the business. Somehow when my father died he became my…uh…uh, guardian. I'm sure he did it illegally. He wanted to marry me and become owner of the whole company."

"Harrison?"

She nodded, and told him that Chien had been watching for her and attacked her and that she'd shot him. Jack let go of her and walked around the room. He looked out the windows. The streets were empty and quiet. "I saw him running out the front door…when I came up…I heard the shot. Where was he shot?"

"In his," she looked down at the stain on her dress, thought about it. "In his torso. His stomach or leg maybe." Elizabeth shivered, wiped her nose on her sleeve, blew softly on the burn on her hand.

"He was bent over. I saw him go down the street grabbing his stomach." Jack thought a minute. "Probably not in his leg." Jack searched the area and found a bullet hole across the room from the foot of the bed. It had gone through Chien, or part of him, and lodged itself in the wall. Plaster chips were scattered on the floor.

"Are you okay to go? We should get out of here."

Jack looked around the room. Then he saw it: Chien's gun. It was on the bed where he left it. Her revolver was beside it. He nodded to it and she said, "His." Jack went to the bedside and picked them up. He checked the loads, whirling the steel, snapped the cylinder shut and put Chien's gun in his pants pocket and gave her the one that had belonged to his mother. He removed his heavy jacket. "Here, put this on. Cover your dress. Do you know if there's someplace we can go? I have a room in town, but I can't take you there."

She hugged him again and stepped back, "Yes, come on."

They shut up the house quickly and ran along the front walk. Even in the growing darkness Jack could see the trail of blood left by Chien; it looked like he was badly wounded.

CHAPTER 54

Chien

Chien was terrified. He went, as quickly as he could, to his last secret hidey-hole, the one he kept for an emergency. From the street it looked like a small shop, decrepit and long out of business. All there was to the single-story building was the battered and peeling storefront, windows papered over inside and the blind drawn down on the front door. With a voice diminished by countless morning suns the letters on the sign atop the door said "Grocery." In front were the remains of two green painted wooden shelves, once proudly flanking the entrance and offering the promise of fresh produce, now collapsed and rotting in puddles of trash. The pain in his gut intensified as he squeezed between the rusted bars of the gate that blocked the only access to the rear of the building. Few grown men could fit through them and he had never seen anyone, not even the street urchins who ran wild in the city, near the old store. Once through the gate he hurried down the narrow channel between buildings where old broken bricks grabbed at him and seemed to close in on him until finally he turned the corner at the rear of the store. He leaned against the brick wall and wheezed as he caught his breath. He was afraid, more than he had ever been in his life: being shot, losing the girl, being chased and harried by a rough, diseased-looking dog that licked his blood when he fell on the cobbles, and followed him until he kicked it over and over again. He had the sense that if he fell down and could not get up, the beast would have eaten him. Pulling his hands away from his abdomen he was shocked to see that the blood kept seeping from his wound. The red wetness was a mirror in the dark, collecting stray light from the sky. "Christ, I'm done now," he cursed. There had been surprisingly little pain, only a stinging and burning, but he almost fainted as he stretched his hands up to get the key from the top of the doorframe. He was convinced he was tearing himself in two. The corroded metal leaf rasped open with a mournful sound. When he closed the door it was almost totally dark inside. Only a blade-thin impression of gray was visible and the dank air made it seem darker. He fished a match from his trousers pocket and struck it on the wall, shuffling along until he found the candle he always left near the entrance.

As much as he wanted to drink away the pain and elude all thought in sleep, Chien knew that such a course might be fatal, so he set about the task of examining the place where he had been shot, stopping the bleeding, and bandaging himself. Removing his jacket was excruciating. He pulled his pants down to his knees and raised his shirt, holding the hem up under his chin. He moved the candle close and looked down in fear. The bullet had entered his body just to the right side of his navel, ripped its way along his waistline, and exited cleanly about nine inches away, almost directly at his side. He was grateful for the little roll of fat around his middle, for it had taken most of the blast. He was bleeding in two places, but very little on the side where the small caliber bullet had left his body. The flesh was bruised black and burned and puckered in front, up on his chest and down to his groin. It was from the entry wound that the blood still flowed. The black powder had, ironically, left bits of white particles on him, the saltpeter and sulfur and heat and flash wrecking a large area of his skin. He looked around the tiny back room. There was a full bottle of whiskey, candles and lanterns, the bed he used when he hid there. Nothing had been disturbed since his last visit. He bit hard into the bunched up sleeve of his jacket and poured the whiskey over the hole in his stomach. It was impossible not to scream. His heart screamed along with his voice. Sweat streamed down his face and body. He used his shirt as a compression bandage, and when he ceased shuddering from the pain of the alcohol on the burn, he poured some onto the exit wound. It mixed with the dark, seeping blood and ran down his side. For a long time after that he sat, naked, hunched over and crying. The slightest movement was hell. It took him two hours to tear long strips of cloth from his dirty shirt and wrap himself tightly with them.

He labored himself up onto the bed and drank half of the remaining cheap whiskey in a long chugging draught. His eyes watered and he barely managed not to throw up. He wiped his runny nose on the back of his hand, coughed violently, and bit on his knuckle to hold off the sensation. Curled up on his left side, with his right elbow pressed against the hole in his side and his left hand over his stomach, he tried to sleep. With a pounding head, the sharp stinging of the burned flesh and a nauseating dizziness, he laid in fear and frustration, awake throughout the endless night. He watched the candle, dwindling like the measure of his hopes, until it drowned itself out on its own and left him in darkness.

The sun had set outside and his demons emerged from the blackness and came at him, rank after rank of them, each with a new torture. They gnawed at his flesh and ripped at every nerve in his body. Thoughts and questions rampaged through his mind. The girl would be gone now and he would never find her. What would she do? Get some lawyer or detective, maybe a private detective to help her? Dumb bitch, she probably wouldn't think of that. All that studying, what good was it? Didn't do her no good, nor the old woman neither. His mind raced. Over and over he thought of how close he had been, feeling her under him. I had her. I had her. God damn it, why didn't I think of her protecting herself? Now the whole thing was to get back to LeFrank, act like nothing was wrong. How am I going to do that, I can hardly walk? He'll look at me and know. Or Salete, the bastard. Shit, he'll see it, tell LeFrank. The key, oh, God, he forgot about the key. LeFrank already knows if he's missed the key. He'll go to the house, see the blood…and the girl, she's lost, the girl, that's for sure. Lost. That's what I am…lost. His intense shivering finally stopped his wild imaginings and then he could think of nothing other than the dryness in his mouth, how cold he was, the pain in the center of him.

CHAPTER 55

Reunion

She waited nervously for Jack to return. Jack had left her in the carriage and run into the rooming house to get his few belongings. Now that he'd come for her and they had said what they said to each other, she couldn't bear for them to be apart. He finally appeared, walking quickly toward the carriage. He climbed up to the driver's seat, gave him an extra few coins, and jumped down to join Elizabeth inside. "I gave him money for his speed now and for his silence in the future. We don't want anyone to know where we're going. In fact, we should get out a few blocks from the station, and walk to your hotel."

"We shouldn't be seen together," she fretted. "I'm on the third floor in the last room on the right. Number fifty-two."

"Are you sure they have rooms available?"

"Yes. I don't think it's more than half full. People come and go all the time—it follows the train schedule." At the hotel Jack waited while she went inside.

A short time later he came to her room. He knocked softly. She answered the sound, and he said his name. She closed and locked the door behind him as he walked into the room and put a small parcel by his coat where she had laid it over the back of a chair. He smiled at her. "All I've thought about these months gone by was being with you again."

She told him it was the same with her and went into his arms. After a long calming of their breath and bodies, he let their lips part. He thought for a minute, idly smoothing her brow, feeling the luxury of her. "We need to tell our stories. I couldn't stop worrying if you were safe and then I found out you were in great danger and I had to come find you." He inclined his head, "I brought some food from my pack." She started from the beginning. "I told you that LeFrank was my father's partner. He's also a slave trader and smuggler…other crimes…I don't know. I don't want to think about the things he's probably done. He has everybody bribed to keep himself out of trouble. He wanted me to marry him so he could become owner of the shipping line and then buy up some others. She started crying. "He took girls from the area, told them he was marrying them…he has some priest he pays to have fake weddings…and then he sells them. Sells them! Like he was going to do to me! I was to be sold. Make me a prostitute!" It took a few minutes before she could go on. He remembered how LeFrank had acted on the beach the day after she jumped from the ship. He was in a fury over a lost sale of property. A rage fumed up inside Jack and he pressed his left hand with his right fist. He had to consciously relax his arms and shoulders. She choked out the names of the girls who had been on *Hathor*. "I'd seen the names earlier, memorized them, and I thought about them just before I jumped from the boat and you pulled me in from the water. I can't forget them." She told him about Nana, how she was taken the night they abducted her, and that Nana had been killed, her body dumped into the sea; how Chien had tried to take her that night as well. She told him about his fight with Salete, all the things she wouldn't tell him when they were together in his cabin. "I felt I'd done you a great wrong, making you lie, robbing you of a part of your life, and in spite of my feelings I couldn't stay with you. You'd been so generous and trusting and I felt selfish and dishonest. It was hard, but I hid my desire for you."

"I understand, Elizabeth. I knew you felt something for me. That you were trying to keep me from being caught up in your troubles. I couldn't imagine there was anything like this."

"One day when you were back at the station I saw him…Chien…looking into your cabin. Looking for me. He rode a horse, started in my direction. I had him in my sights and told myself that if he came close enough to see me, I'd shoot him. He turned away and so I never knew what I would have done." She took his hand and stared at it, and held it hard. "Tonight when he assaulted me…like he was some beast…I just did it. Like an instinct. I've spent my whole life learning…and that included reading about greed and violence and lust. I knew those things existed. That time, though, with my finger on the trigger and him, a monster clawing at me, that was not the same as just knowing about it. Reading a book. Not the same at all."

She shook her head vehemently, "But this isn't what I want! I'm not like this! I never wanted to shoot someone, even someone like him. I just want it all to go away. But it won't, it can't. I find myself now, even after all this, hoping that he won't die from the gunshot. I don't want to have it on my soul that I killed someone."

Jack was very serious and he looked her in the eyes, "The way he was running, I don't think he could have been hurt that bad."

She told him about the girls. She said she wanted to try to find them, no matter how this all turned out. Jack watched her, waiting for her to go on. "Before he attacked me, Chien told me all about LeFrank's plans. There's another woman who LeFrank's going to use to take my place. She's going to impersonate me in another one of his faked weddings and then I suppose he'll kill her and put her in a coffin with my name on it. We have to stop LeFrank from taking another woman."

They ate the remainder of the food and watched the fire. He told her everything that had happened to him and how Matthew Hastings had also seen Chien. Elizabeth got up and went over to the bed and slipped off her shoes. "Come over here with me, Jack." She got into the bed and pulled the covers over her. He pulled off his boots and got in next to her. She arranged the blanket evenly over them. They lay on their sides, facing each other, and she closed her eyes and he ran his fingertips across her lips and down her neck. He could tell by the attitude of her shoulders and the look on her face that she had relaxed.

They talked some more, filling in details of their trips north, and before long the day got the best of them, their eyes closed, and they drifted down to sleep as the fire fell and the candles and lamps in the room quietly went out.

CHAPTER 56

Morning

They were close together. Elizabeth seemed to have burrowed into him during the night. Jack stayed very still, listening to her breathing and feeling the soft swell of her body as it rose and fell. Her breathing took his breath away. Her face was against his neck and her hair, mussed and curly, tickled his nose. He put out his lower lip and puffed air up against it, but without success, and after it tumbled back a few times he gave up trying. The whistles and the hoarse steam panting of the engines outside the hotel seemed loud to him, but neither those sounds nor the low insistent clunks of the train's couplings roused her. Jack tried to move his arm, but his movements woke her.

After a while they fell asleep again, drowsing for an hour until the sun invaded their privacy and they both rose. They examined each other from opposite sides of the bed.

"Our clothes look like we slept in them," she laughed. Jack's shirttails were out and he was missing a sock.

"I'll go to my room and change. Then we can get some breakfast. Downstairs okay?"

"Yes, I'll meet you there in a few minutes.

Jack thought, as he walked down the hallway to his room, that there could never be another year in his life like this one, not if he lived to be a hundred.

The serving girl in the hotel dining room was surprised at how much they ordered and how much they ate. They talked little over the eggs, the rashers of bacon, and the rolls and butter and jam. They had pooled their money and had found that they had a large sum between them. When their plates were cleared they sat back in their chairs and Elizabeth poured cups of tea from the pot the waitress had just placed between them on the thick white tablecloth. She looked over the rim of the cup at him as she drank; he peered into the brown liquid. Jack lifted his cup level with his eyes and peered at the steam running up into the air above it. "This reminds me of the mist that comes in from the ocean sometimes. It obscures everything, even yourself: you look down and can't make out your own boots. Everything's hidden by it. It's an endless cloud that could vanish in a second or stay for days."

She cut some butter from the plate on the table and rubbed a thin sheen onto her hands with care, favoring the red and raw place on the backs of her fingers left by the back blast from the shooting. Jack reached for her hand and looked at it carefully. They sat and talked, too full from breakfast to want to get up from the table.

Chien never felt more alone. He was going to die alone. He knew it. Some hours earlier, he couldn't tell how many, he was terrified that a dog was going to feast on what was left of him. Through the night he saw it again and again, diseased and wasted, fur matted and body scarred, licking his blood, his eyes white and wild, yearning for more of it, all of it. Now he could hear the thing, he was sure of it, scratching the outside of his door. It had followed his trail of blood, smelling the death on him, instinct telling the dog to watch for the weak one from the herd, cull it out from the others, run it down until it died. Or maybe it was just rats. Same thing for him, in any case, one slavering mouth or many.

Once more, clinging inexplicably to his miserable life, desperate to save it despite its horrid prospects, Chien struggled with all his might to raise himself up and swing around so that he was sitting on the bed. His mind reeled with the pain. Long low moans crawled up his throat and pushed past his lips. All he wanted to do was look at himself, see if he was losing more blood, do something to try to stay alive. He stood, swaying and stumbling until he could make it to the wall. He held his pants up with one hand and, like a blind man, used the other to steady himself along the wall until he got to the door of a short hallway that led to the front of the old store. The front room was bright, at least compared with the back of the place. Pale, sickly light filtered through the old craft paper that had been pasted onto the inside of the glass and forced him to squint his eyes almost closed. Nails were driven by the sunlight into the nerves of his head.

He had to see what he looked like. Letting his pants go so that they bagged down around his knees, he stood near a window, held up his torn and bloody shirt, pulled down on the bandages, and looked at his reflection. He could make out the swelling and the discoloration, the burn marks and the continued oozing, but worse was the look in his own eyes as they came back at him from the pallor of his face in the glass. Nothing had ever terrified him like this vision of himself. All he could do now was lie down and wait. To live or to die, he did not know which. He began to cry and walked slowly under the burden of his deep dejection away from the dim light, into the darkness at the back of the store. Cold claimed his body.

CHAPTER 57

Harrison Lines

Satisfied, with the full meal and hot tea inside of them, Jack and Elizabeth returned to their rooms and put on warm clothes. They met outside and went toward the waterfront.

"It's gone!" Elizabeth cried out. At first Jack didn't know what she was talking about, but then he saw it. The empty berth. *Hathor* had sailed. From the top of the hill they could see rows of ships, a tumble of warehouses and sheds, and many of the shipping company offices. There was no trace of her in the harbor either. Early in the morning Jack had talked to Elizabeth about ways to approach the ship, find out what they could, make inquiries to see if they could find an ally, locate someone in a position of authority who could help them. She had resisted strenuously, pleading with Jack to be careful in this. She had been through this in her mind countless times, at his cabin, in New York, here in Boston. What Chien had told her only reinforced it. LeFrank's reach was far greater than she'd suspected. She trusted no one in the city, regardless of how upright and reliable they might appear to be.

Together they reasoned that with the ship gone there was much less danger to the two of them along the waterfront. Now all that was left for them was to go there, walk among the workmen, listen in the taverns, and make a casual visit to the customs office. People shouted in the markets and gossip and rumors were free to anyone who would listen. Perhaps knowing her destination would help them decide what to do. They descended the hill at a slow pace. It was overcast and breezy and the people they passed had their heads down and many had a hand raised to hold their caps in place. Jack's identity was unknown to anyone in the city now that *Hathor* had departed. Elizabeth's too, in that her appearance was changed.

No one knew them, save Chien. If he lived.

Elizabeth was haunted as much by what she had done to Chien as by what he had told her. Now it seemed likely that the ship had sailed with a young woman aboard who would be a scapegoat for her, die in her stead, and be buried in her grave. All of this seemed impossible to her, except for the hope, now admittedly a diminished hope, that she could stop all of this, rescue this one girl, remove LeFrank from her life, and find the innocents who had been taken before her. Every day that trail grew colder. She knew how they felt, because after only a short time held captive she had felt the same. It was what made her jump from the ship that cold October night.

Jack watched the people passing by. "We'll have to get into the Harrison office."

"How can we do that?" But then her eyes shone brightly and she said, "We'll have to break in when it's closed. When no one is around."

"Don't they have a watchman?"

She moved her head to the left and right, her eyes cast down, as if to find an answer in the air before her. "I don't know. We'll have to walk around and see for ourselves."

They observed the place from all four sides. Many people came and went throughout the day and couriers entered the front door bringing bundles of papers, most containing bills of lading, invoices, contracts, and routine business documents and correspondence. More traffic came to the warehouse doors at the rear where a steady stream of goods were either shipped or received. When it was late in the afternoon they left the area to eat and make their plans.

Almost twilight. One watchman went by, but it would be a while before he returned on his circuit. There was nobody else around. Jack used his knife to force a lock on a private entrance door on the side of the building. He'd jam it shut when they left, hoping that since it wasn't a main door it might be a while before anyone noticed the damage. It was at once obvious that there would be nothing of interest to them in the ground floor office. They mounted the long stairway to the second floor, both glancing around at the furnishings, Persian carpets, model ships, and photographs. LeFrank had numerous pictures ornately framed and arranged in groups on the walls of the large waiting area outside his office. She remembered that it had been her father's and it occurred to her that everything there was now hers. Elizabeth tried to fix the time of her last visit to the building in her mind, but could only attest to the fact that it had been years ago, probably just before her father's death. The light inside the building was fading, but Elizabeth took the time to point out to Jack that while the rich and politically connected were among those pictured, there was no evidence of her father. Only his name remained, and it was being sullied by a successor whose aim was, surely, to remove it altogether. For his benefit, and to bolster her position that there was no one to trust, she named the men in the photographs, explained their positions of influence, and pointed out that since there were many she did not recognize, she could not risk exposing herself to one of his allies.

All at once they both felt like they were being watched. They turned around and saw LeFrank, standing before them, big as life, and looking directly into their eyes. They were shocked into silence. Both of them stared at the huge oil painting of LeFrank that dominated the opposite wall, the man life sized, wearing black, one leg forward, his right hand on the hilt of a sword hanging down his left side. A whip lay coiled like a snake on a bench in the background. The artist had captured his face by halves: one brow raised above the other; an ear cocked, the other hidden in his hair; the two parts of his smile—smirk and scorn. Jack bored his eyes into the image, as if to stare it down. Elizabeth turned away and did not look back.

They walked into LeFrank's office and waited, listening to the building itself, straining to hear any unusual sound from the streets that surrounded it. Jack moved first, breaking the grip the place had on them, rounding the wide desk that commanded the room, and pulled the drawers open, one at a time, closing them slowly in turn, and looking up in amazement at Elizabeth. "They're all empty." He looked up, noting that outside the office, directly across from the desk, LeFrank was still staring at him. When at his desk, Jack realized, the man must watch himself.

She came quickly to his side. "What?" She opened a few of the drawers, having to see for herself that this was true. They froze as they heard shouting from the front of the building. What sounded like banging on the front door left them staring at each other, wondering what to do. Jack went to the window and looked down between the curtains. "There's a man there…he's the one banging on the door. He's looking in the windows. Should we just wait for him to go away?"

He saw that Elizabeth wasn't listening. She had partially opened a closet door and was looking at the large safe recessed into the wall inside. "It's all in here. Everything that could help us is on the ship or in this safe. We'll get nothing here." She looked down. "All for nothing."

The banging continued. It became harder and faster. The man's muffled words came through the heavy wood.

She whispered to him, "Go down and answer the door. Tell the man you're LeFrank's assistant and see what he wants. That'll get him out of here before he attracts too much attention and then we can leave too…before that watchman comes by again." He nodded and removed his jacket and walked downstairs.

He took a deep breath, opened the door slowly, and held onto the handle to help calm himself. He leaned around the narrow opening. "What is it? The office is closed." The desperate-looking man craned his neck to try to see inside and then swallowed before managing to say, "Is he here…did he go with the ship…did he say anything about me? I know it's late, I'm late, but I have what he wanted and more. Is he here?"

"Mr. LeFrank is not here. I handle his business when he's away." Jack tried to sound like the officious clerks he had seen at the local exchange offices, and appear to be disinterested, "Exactly what is your business?"

The man held out a large package. The paper wrapper was wrinkled from his frantic clutching at it and he shoved it into Jack's hands as if he feared it were about to explode in his own. "He told you about me, didn't he, me, Morrison, that I'd have what he wanted. I have it all. I'm sure he'll be satisfied now…leave me alone."

"Oh, yes, Morrison, he did say…"

Morrison's look of relief vanished quickly, "He went with the ship…Salete…didn't he? Gone, right?" He jerked around to look behind him, and then both ways along the deserted street. "Don't say anything about me to him, will you? Please."

Morrison took a step back, perspiration coursing down his temples, tried to smooth his wrinkled shirt and pulled at his coat.

"Please tell Mr. LeFrank that I can't get any more. I know I'm late but they watch you. They'll catch me, sure thing. It's lucky I got what I did. It's all there. What he wanted." In a final plea Morrison reached out and held Jack's arm and begged, "Please tell him that…there's no more I can do…and Salete…" He sobbed, "Don't send him to my home any more, or to the firm…I can't do it…he comes and he…please tell him."

With that the man stumbled down the front steps and ran into the darkness.

They cleared a table in a windowless storeroom between the offices and the warehouse and brought in candles and lamps and closed the door. It didn't take long for them to realize that Morrison had brought them a treasure chest of information. In his precise lawyerly way he had summarized what LeFrank was doing and gave warnings and advice about companies that could be bought cheaply and ones that should not be considered. He had financial account information, with profit and loss figures, debt analyses, lists of assets, and trend lines that showed the rise or decline in the business of many of the firms LeFrank wanted to buy. One scribbled sheet gave the name of a rival law firm that rumor said was investigating Harrison as part of the due diligence being done prior to the sale. There, too, was dirty laundry, things Morrison had heard from partners of his law practice that could be used to threaten a seller into making a quick and easy sale.

Neither of them had any sense of business or accounting, but it was clear what was happening: LeFrank was stalking businesses in the area with an eye to buying them when they were weak and at a disadvantage. Both knew also that these columns of numbers, taken together with the events of the last year, constituted a mathematical proof. They proved that LeFrank wanted, no, must have, the life of Elizabeth Harrison. She would have to die in order for him to possess all of this. For the time being, from what Chien had told her, LeFrank thought she was dead. "You cannot stay dead," she said to herself. She realized, however, that she could not resurrect Elizabeth Harrison until after she had dealt with her murderer. Only then could she try to undo whatever immoral and illegal harm LeFrank had caused in her family name.

They looked over the material for a few more minutes in silence and decided that it could be of great help to them in the future and that they surely didn't want LeFrank to have it.

After a final circuit of the offices to be sure they had left no trace of their visit, they passed through the storeroom and entered the warehouse. As Jack closed the door they both stopped abruptly and stared. Right in front of them, looking at them in the semi-darkness, was a large schedule board. Written down its left side were the names of the ships of Harrison Lines. Across the top were columns with headings showing dates, cargo categories, shippers' names, and under the last heading on the right they saw chalked in, the list of destinations. Ports of call. Halfway down the list they saw *Hathor*, and to the right, her destination. They knew what they were going to do next. Both of them stopped reading when they saw the name *Hathor*. Had they looked at the last row on the list they would have seen the entry for another Harrison Lines ship, the *Robin*, a smaller, faster vessel that had left the day before *Hathor*, also bound for Newport News, Virginia. Captain Richard Hazen, commanding.

CHAPTER 58

Mercury

David Marshall watched from the quarterdeck of the Mercury as the first mate stood on a ratline and shouted instructions to the crewmen aloft. His whole body swung out from the shrouds with only the smooth sea below him as he ordered them to take in some sail. As their bare feet gripped the ropes they called down from the yards, "Aye, mister." From his vantage point on the deck Marshall saw the familiar sight—men moving like spiders in the web of the rigging, each man dancing over the lines on four limbs as if he had six. The wires and cordage appeared to be thin dark threads painted on the powder blue sky. Pleasure could be had from every act, Marshall reflected as he watched his men follow the commands, their satisfaction gained from performing the tasks quickly and well, and his as he observed their willingness and their proficiency. Today a great pleasure awaited him. He was taking the ship south with her holds filled with non-perishable cargo, and since he was well ahead of schedule, he had altered course visit his friend George Kimball.

From his place in the surf station tower Calvin Massey could see three sailing ships between the shore and edge of the sky. He squinted into the spyglass and steadied himself, elbows on the window ledge. The wind, fresh and tangy, ruffled his hair. He called down to his buddy, Thomas Steele. "Guess how many ships are out there under my command, Tom?"

"None now, and none never will be!"

"Well, we'll see about that. I'll have a frigate and 100 men under me and you'll be my fart catcher, following right behind me as I walk the deck, giving orders. You'll shine my boots and fetch my meals and you'll, you'll...say, look...look...come here Tom, look at this!"

Though they were fast friends and never ceased in their mutual teasing and taunting, sometimes Massey's incessant jabbering stuck

Steele in his gizzard, "Sure, Calvin, sure. My 'captain' calls and I must obey."

"No, I mean you to see this."

Steele rolled his eyes, a satisfying gesture though none was there to see him do it, rose reluctantly from his bunk, put down the sock he had been darning and climbed up the steps to stand beside his friend. Massey pointed his finger a few degrees north of east and handed the glass over. "Look at the two ships closest to shore. Tell me what you see."

Steele carefully checked the three ships. The boat away at the horizon was just a white smudge on a blue sky, a minute imperfection in the outline of the planet. The other two vessels were much closer in, and their hull shapes, sail pattern, and rigging could be discerned, even if their flags and names could not. Though fairly far away it was clear to the men that both of these fine ships were seaworthy, with clean hulls, new sails, and knowing sailing masters. They moved like different fluids, sliding over the salt water.

"What'd you call me up here to see? Ships under your 'command'?"

"That proves it. I'll be the captain and you'll be the mate. Can't ya' see? I wonder that Ezra keeps you on. It's not just two ships, Tom. Look again, look at them. No joke, now Tom, no joke."

Steele raised the long glass to his left eye and closed his right. "One's on a southward heading and the other's on a tack, coming this way. Mm. I see the long blue banner. Think it's the Mercury?"

"Yep. I'll bet you we're about to have visitors. George'll be happy. But look at the other one. Remind you of anything? Remember last year, what Old Gunn called the devil ship, *Hathor*? I think it's the one. Not making the same mistake as last time, sailing too close to shore."

For the moment there was no joking or teasing from either of the two friends. Steele's demeanor told Massey that he had been right, it was *Hathor* out there cleaving the waves, off on some dark mission. They wanted no part of her or her captain and crew. A ship like that in trouble, well, maybe, they whispered to each other, maybe that was a time you didn't have to go out. We did once. Maybe once was all they got. But that was all bravado. They knew better. They'd go.

When *Mercury* was closer to the station Massey called out below for the men to find Stock and Kimball so that they could welcome their guests ashore.

Marshall and LeFrank looked at each other through their telescopes. They could clearly see each other's faces. Both swung their glasses around, looking alternately toward the surf station and back at each other. Marshall touched the brim of his hat in a respectful salute, a gesture to which LeFrank responded with a look of contempt. *Hathor* and Mercury moved at right angles to each other, Mercury west and *Hathor* south, the hypotenuse of distance between them lengthening slowly.

As *Hathor*, heavy with her cargo of doom, plunged on toward Newport News, Mercury was brought smoothly up to an anchorage by the skill of her crew. Many of the men came ashore. Just before sundown the sailors rowed back to their ship. Prevailed upon by his friend, Marshall agreed to remain at the surf station for the night. Ellen invited them to the guest house for dinner and they spent the early evening in her pleasant company. George was happy to see that she and David had taken to each other.

Ellen knew when one thing had reached its end and another was ready to begin, so she excused herself and the men said goodnight. Back in the barracks, Kimball, Gunn, Marshall and Stock sat at the small table in the kitchen and talked through tobacco smoke, over tea, and under lamplight. They talked about politics, the Service rumors, caught up on news, and as usual wound up talking about their men. "I see young Master Light has not yet returned." Marshall's casual remark caught the three men by surprise. He gave them a questioning look. "I saw him…in Philadelphia." Gunn and Kimball said nothing, deferring instead to Ezra. "How was that, that you saw him?"

"Arthur Durant, one of my men, met him walking along the docks. Recognized him. He had finished his business there and was leaving, in fact. He came to the ship and stayed the night with us. Seemed bewildered by the big city." Marshall laughed, "Likes it less than I do."

Ezra prompted in an offhand way, "Did he say what he was doing?"

"Gone to see a friend is what he said. In Boston." Marshall yawned, and rubbed his face. "We were sailing south or I would have taken him aboard. He seemed interested in what we did, where we went. Maybe I'll lure him away from land one of these days, Ezra, take away one of your best men! George won't come with me, maybe Jack will. Or, you, Mr. Gunn!"

The three men smiled politely at Marshall's joking, but behind their masks they were all thinking about Jack, and their promise to his father to care for him if anything ever happened. Ezra was bitterly disappointed with himself, thinking he had failed at this all-important task. Old Gunn was glad Jack was alright and making progress, since apparently he had found out where the girl lived. Kimball wanted to leave at once for Boston to see if he could help.

Kimball and his friend walked on the beach the next morning, and George told the story of his boarding the Cassiopeia, filling in the details that Jack had omitted when he met Marshall in Philadelphia. He said he planned to marry Ellen Brahe once some things were settled at the station. Marshall was very happy for his friend and accepted the offer to stand up with him on his wedding day. It was for David Marshall the most poignant expression of forgiveness he could have received, one only to be exceeded in the years to come when a Kimball son would be named for him.

Later that day, when the tide was high, Kimball said goodbye and lowered himself over the side of Mercury, ready to return to shore. Kimball stood in the bow of the surfboat and looked up at his friend, who leaned on the rail of the ship. Marshall waved his hand as the two boats were separated by the current and reminded George of his offer, "Don't get married until I come back."

"Where are you bound?"

"South, to Charleston, then back this way, and finally to home in Baltimore."

"Will you be able to stop on your way past?"

"We will if time permits. We do have one port of call in Virginia."

Kimball waved and called out as the surfboat moved off, "Where in Virginia?"

"Newport News."

CHAPTER 59

Anna Ulter

Boston

"Marbury." Elizabeth was excited. "I know that name. Chien said the girls were from a theater, here in town. I didn't connect it when he said it. The girls…maybe LeFrank got them from there." Elizabeth paused and looked to the side. "How about the newspaper?" Her face brightened at her own idea. "They have reviews of the shows. You could go there too and ask to see back issues, or maybe talk to the writers." Jack considered this as she began to pace around their room, thinking out loud. "I can give you a list of dates, along with the names."

They made their plans. It delayed their trip to Newport News by at least a day, but she insisted on it. She argued that some knowledge of the women, anything, might help them when they got there. His questions at the Marbury Theater went largely unanswered. Some of the stagehands thought they might have recognized a couple of the names, but weren't sure. Jack quickly learned that many of these men were transients as well. He was sure that he saw recognition in the faces of a few as he said the names of the missing girls, flickers of emotion that told him there was a connection between the casts of these performances and some of the lost girls. One young man's face betrayed him when Jack said Anna Ulter's name. He was slender and looked underfed and his clothes were more worn than those of the other men. Jack pulled the man aside and offered him money for any information he might have. Though embarrassed, the man grabbed at the coins, described her, and said that one day a long time ago she failed to show up for a performance, and he never saw her again. He remembered her because she was one of the few who had been kind to him. "When I find her, I'll tell her about you." The lad mumbled his thanks and gripped the money in his hands as he walked away.

Elizabeth packed their things and went to the train station to arrange for their travel south. She took her time and bought some food to eat on the train, and considered where to spend the night on the way to Virginia. There was no telling how long it would take Jack to talk to people at the theater and at the newspaper.

At the hotel that evening they went over their day's activities. A cynical and worn out old staff critic had regaled Jack about how pathetic the talent was in Boston, which he called "the backwater" of the art world. He was shabby and gruff with a shock of wild gray hair that fell this way and that when he talked. "My talent is as wasted here at this newspaper as the one or two decent people they get in there at the theater." He knew some of the girls by name, described Anna as a beauty, but quickly added that she was someone who should stick to dance, and forget about singing. "Carry, range, projection, pitch, ugh!" His vehemence on this point fascinated Jack. Jack couldn't tell if the man's concern for Anna's career choice was for art or for the artist, but his involvement was passionate. And he was, as the surfmen described Captain Vickers, "windy." Language was his tool and his product, and he clearly was not reluctant to go on at length on this subject. Although most of the analysis was comprised of a rave review of his own talents as writer and critic, he did know the theater and arts scene and it was no surprise to him when these women went missing. "Usually it was because they got what they were really after—a man with money—and that was that. Gone, and not a bow or curtsy as they left the stage. Others are vain or stupid enough to think that they will be 'the one,' notice I said 'one,' who will glory in the top billing and shine in the spotlight, but how can one of a hundred girls not notice the other ninety-nine standing next to them?" He gave himself a hard two-handed face rub and went on, louder than before. "Art is dead. Few can produce it and fewer appreciate it. People in this country have no education, that's the problem. An' it's getting worse all the time. Go along the docks, watch them pour off the boats, all criminals and illiterates and their bastard children. We have more than enough of all that already. People so stupid they can't spell their own names, from countries no one ever heard of or cares about. Do we need them? What good are they? Just wait ten or twenty years, by the turn of the century I'd say, and you won't have one man in a thousand that'll be able to read and write. Who'll buy the papers then, I'm asking you?"

"You were right, Elizabeth, LeFrank's name came up at the theater and at the paper. He's well known there, has a box at the Marbury, usually has a woman with him. Girls disappear from there all the time. The newspaper man said they run off with men with money." He told her everything he'd seen or heard. "There's something else. A prominent woman named Jane Barr has just disappeared. She, by all accounts, is a rising star, destined to go to New York. Everyone knows of her connection to LeFrank, but some say he has another woman now to sport around, so I don't know if it means anything. It caused a big commotion when she didn't show up for a performance yesterday and the police are looking for her. The other woman missed the show too."

Elizabeth pictured her imprisoned in that cabin aboard *Hathor*. She added her name to the list of women she hoped to help. Jane Barr. Where was she and what was happening to her? She could still be alive and Elizabeth was determined to find her.

She showed Jack the travel schedule she'd worked out and they hoped they could get to Newport News before the ship did. They had no idea how long it would take and what surprises awaited them there. Once more, they realized, they would have to wait until they arrived to decide what to do.

CHAPTER 60

Hathor

"What was that awful crying I heard last night?"

"I heard nothing."

"But, LeFrank, you did. You stirred in your sleep and even said something. About a bar, I think you said."

"Maybe a sandbar. We have to take care we don't run aground. There is much to attend to aboard a ship." He swung his legs over the edge of the bed and took a few steps to the bowl and pitcher that were mounted upon a satinwood console. A low rail surrounded the bowl to keep it from sliding side to side with the yaw of the ship. He gripped the yellow-brown wood and steadied himself as *Hathor* rolled side to side up and over the massive swells that crossed her beam, paraphrasing the Appalachian foothills that rose from the plains to her west. He spread his legs and rocked naturally with the ship, splashed water on a towel and wiped his face, all the while watching himself in appreciation, eye to eye in the mirror in front of him.

"There was a noise, I'm sure of it. Like a howl, but carrying, like something musical. It was somehow familiar, like I knew that sound from somewhere."

Laura Olsen sat up in bed and brushed the hair away from her face with both her hands. In reply to her graceful movements the sleeves of her satin gown slid down to reveal her beautiful white arms.

He dressed and spoke carefully. Directly. "I don't think it's a good idea for you to wander around the ship. In fact, I forbid it. It's dirty and dangerous and you should not go around the men. They're not like you and me, Laura, they are rough and violent, and can't be trusted. I don't want you near them. Don't look at them or talk to them."

Before pulling on his boots he examined them closely, making sure they had been shined properly, that the soles were clean as well.

He sought his image in the glossy blackness of the toes, to no avail. "I'll look in on you before long."

Disappointed for a moment, she plopped back onto the feather bed, and then settled into it, enjoying the luxury of the cabin, and still thrilled that LeFrank had chosen her. She could put up with the minor annoyances of being told what to do, and his moods as well, especially when she considered how he had showered gifts on her and given her a large allowance and had her escorted everywhere she went. No one in her family would believe the richness of her surroundings, the furnishings, the clothes, the meals she ate, and LeFrank's devotion to her. It was treatment she couldn't have imagined. When she heard him lock the cabin door she knew he did it for her protection. After all, they were going to be married. This was an adventure and she was going to enjoy it, no matter what. Later, they could settle into a more traditional life, with home and hearth and maybe even children. He had talked about these things when they first met, and hinted about them again the night she was brought aboard the ship.

On the quarterdeck Salete stood like a statue and drilled his eyes into the east. Chien, as he had for several days, dominated Salete's thoughts. He hoped he was dead, thought it must be so, but he'd have no rest until he was sure of it. Chien would not have risked LeFrank's wrath by ignoring his summons. From what Salete had learned in his furious casting about for him, Chien simply had vanished. He must be dead. He had abruptly stopped making reports to LeFrank about the rumors and news he picked up, and his failure to show up for the mock wedding and then for their departure, despite messages left for him in the usual places, had left LeFrank in a foul mood. LeFrank's heart pumped cold, bad blood, and Salete could see that same blood in the captain's eyes as he turned to look at him.

"See to it that there is no more of what we heard last night."

"It's already done." Salete thought of how he had bound and gagged Jane Barr during the night and relished the acts he contemplated as he gave LeFrank this assurance.

With an accusing look at the sky, and at each of the men on duty, LeFrank made a circuit of the deck, letting the men see him, making every one of them meet his eyes, and then went below to the captain's mess for breakfast.

Salete thought about the "marriage" of Elizabeth Harrison and LeFrank. As previously arranged, Chien's absence aside, all went off as if it was a real sacrament of matrimony, from the first "Dearly beloved" to the "Amen." They left the country church with the signed documentation that LeFrank had insisted be delivered to him after the ceremony. A final and key part of the plan was completed the next day when LeFrank and Barr, dressed again in suit and wedding gown respectively, had their portraits made by LeFrank's photographer. Jane's impersonation of Elizabeth, makeup and hair and even manner, was flawless. She studied Elizabeth's picture, jealous that LeFrank carried it with him, but bent on getting the role right. In a few days the photographer delivered the prints to the counterfeit bridegroom. No one who saw them would doubt that the lady in the white dress was in fact Elizabeth Harrison and that she had willingly married Guillaume LeFrank. Jane had been returned to her home and told to be ready for a departure that would take place within a few days. She was elated, knowing that her time had come, and that she'd soon be the talk of Manhattan, America, the world. Virtuoso performances onstage and off, talent and scandal, soulful acting and heartless behavior, she would stir up the perfectly combustible mixture and people would worship at her feet.

Oiled against rust and sound, the heavy bolt that held the door tight slid to the side. Salete opened the door slightly and moved around it. Jane Barr was on her back, her legs in the air, just as he had left her the night before, when she called out in the darkness. Not knowing what to do, the sailor on watch came to Salete's cabin and roused him. He immediately gathered up some ropes and rags and went to her cabin to quiet her and she screamed at him and struck him in the face. He smiled at this and smashed the palm of his hand into the side of her head, dropping her to the floor. His hand moved so quickly and struck so hard that she didn't see it or understand what had happened to her. He climbed onto her as she lay there and sat high on her chest with his knees on her shoulders. She gasped as he placed one hand on her breast and with the other slid the point of his knife along her cheek, stopping it just below her right eye.

"You're not as pretty as you think, Jane, but even what there is can be taken away from you. You don't know what's happening to you, do you? I'll tell you." He pressed the point into the soft skin just below her eyelid and her body stiffened enough to tell Salete she would not move, no matter what he was about to say. Real tears made a rare appearance around her pleading eyes. One tear spilled from her and ran the length of the blade. Salete hesitated, watching it cling with all its might to the keen silvery edge. It cleaved to the steel until it became too weighty and let go, landing on her lips. Salete watched her take it into her mouth with a quick touch of her tongue. "You're finished with LeFrank. He's going to sell you or kill you, I don't know which." It didn't seem to matter to Salete. "Death would be better. Cause, if he sells you, it'll be to a slaver, and you'll be the same whore you've always been, only now anyone with a little money will have you. It won't take much. That means, Jane, where you're going, every filthy sailor and jack and toothless drunk will be lining up, stinking and diseased, night after night, until one of 'em kills you or leaves you with something horrible like a child or the plague. 'Poxy Jane,' that's what they'll call you. You can't imagine the sickness you'll have, and the dirt you'll live in. And then you'll die anyway. Ugly, Jane, that's how you'll look, ugly. You'll not get much older, Jane Barr."

"But LeFrank. I have to see him. Tell him I..." Salete's laughter stopped her words and chilled her worse than anything he had yet said or done. She began to shake beneath him.

"Now, Jane, you're going to stand up and sit on that chair and stay still. If you don't, I will let the crew have you. Right now." Holding his knife straight out he rose in an easy motion and stepped back from her. Terrible reason trumped her pride and temper and she nodded. Her face was twisted and disfigured with anguish.

He let her stand up and brought a chair to the middle of the cabin and made her sit on it. He tied her ankles to the front legs, her hands behind the ladder back of the chair, and placed a coil of rope around her body. He stood behind her and yanked her head back suddenly and stuffed a dirty rag into it. She gagged and thrashed, but could not dislodge it and he tied a long strip of cloth around her mouth to hold it in. Her hair was pulled into the knot at the back of her neck. In panic she thought about damage to her voice. She struggled and tried to thrust her body about but couldn't work her way free. She couldn't move and could barely breathe. Salete told her to stay still. She went into a rage and strained even harder at her bonds. He stood in front of her, laughed at the murder in her eyes and kicked her with the heel of his boot as hard as he could in the middle of her chest. The chair crashed over backwards and her head cracked hard onto the deck.

That was how she had spent the night.

Her eyes widened that next morning as she saw Salete and the men who entered behind him. They stared at her, rudely but silently, and removed what little furniture there had been in the room. Only the chair remained. Her trunk, bags, and all of her possessions were taken away. She had nothing but the nightgown that was bunched around her. Then they carried in more rope and something else that almost made her faint: four long spikes and a large mallet. She struggled and screamed in her throat, but little sound escaped her. Her actions were weak and futile against their strength and lust as they used her roughly, and when the men finished and left the cabin she was on her back, spread eagled on the deck, tied at ankle and wrist to the nails and looking up at Salete.

"LeFrank told me to do this," he lied, "for disturbing him and the young girl who sleeps with him in his cabin. I must admit, this time he's found a real beauty as his companion. This one, he says, he'll marry for real. Something he never intended for you." With his middle finger he stroked the hilt of his knife where it stood out from its sheath. "Make more trouble and I'll tie you up on deck, with no clothes, and turn the men loose on you. One sound, Jane. One sound."

The door was shut and the bolt pushed home. She laid in the gloom and her mouth contorted and she grimaced as she lost control of herself and felt her insides pour out of her. The pitching of the ship made the filth run up around her and the horrid smell of her own ordure and a limitless terror made her fear she would vomit. The gag that was jammed into her mouth had been dry, but now she salivated with nausea. She realized she could die as a result of this, choke and suffocate here where she lay, and she pulled at the ropes to create the distraction that the pain brought. Her fear compelled her to torture herself continuously. She pulled and pulled with all her strength, trying to rip open the skin around her wrists and ankles and, once started, she could not stop. She snorted wildly to blow the mucus out of her head and her eyes started and bulged with every lunging movement of her body.

Several days before, when Salete came to her home to get her in the middle of the night and brought her aboard the ship, he told her that she should stay below, be quiet, wait until they were far out to sea, convincing her that it was part of LeFrank's plan for her to finally get what he had promised. Her calling out had brought this on, but she knew this imprisonment had been his plan all along: LeFrank had used her, and would discard her. She desperately wanted to live, but couldn't think of any way to escape. "If only I could talk to him, touch him," she said to herself, "I could make him love me again."

Above and behind her there was a heavy metal screen bolted to the window frame. She strained her head and neck back and arched her body up to look at it. Through the mesh there straggled a sullen gray morning light. An occasional wave smacked against the new pane of glass. Even if she could break her bonds, the door was locked and that way out was blocked by the steel barrier. Salete had seen to it that no one else could escape from that cabin. She was the last woman that would make her final passage there, but she would never get a chance to add her name to that of the others.

CHAPTER 61

The Ambassador

Newport News

From his hotel window Strell's man could see the *Luluwa* and glimpse the main channel into the Newport News Harbor. The ship was staid and swollen and had rested by the dock for so long that algae clung to her sides in thick green clumps and moss festooned her mooring lines. O'Neill had calculated, with accuracy, that he could amass more treasure and live far more safely and comfortably alongside land. So his once sleek and beautiful ship had grown old and fat, her body as sedentary as her owner's. What had been his vehicle had become his office, and was now his houseboat. In contrast, the Ambassador had maintained its appearance and was in good repair. The hotel was the right age— sturdily built, slightly weathered like the waterfront around it, but still charming and comfortable. Strell and his man had taken three adjoining second-floor rooms, the one between theirs accessible from both sides, and left empty. They had arrived well in advance of the announced docking of the ship that would deliver the cargo Strell burned to possess. He'd stared at the picture of Elizabeth Harrison for a long time and now he was about to get her. Both men believed that this time O'Neill would have allowed for the vagaries of the weather and given himself some leeway, and that, therefore, the exchange of money and "goods" could occur soon. In the days since their arrival, Strell's man had made regular circuits of the area, memorizing the layout of the port, the locations of the various authority offices, the police and Cutter Service headquarters, anything that could interfere with what they had to do. Knowing which direction trouble was likely to come from was a determining factor in their contingency plans, be they pursuing or pursued, both of which were possible outcomes of this endeavor. He had even stolen a key to the rear service door of the hotel, one which was kept locked by night. Getting in or out quickly and unnoticed might improve their chances of success.

He held the curtain back, beckoned to Strell, and pointed to the man moving slowly along the cobbles in front of the building.

"Armistead." Strell said the word as if it were a curse.

"He's onto something, and it has to do with *Luluwa*. Must be. This is the third time I've seen him walk past it." It didn't seem possible that the man was aware of the business that they had with O'Neill, so it may have had something to do with another of O'Neill's dealings or some unrelated crime in the same area. Strell ventured, "Can it have to do with Lamp?" They discussed it but neither of them could see how it could have any relation to the young man's death. Armistead had visited the waterfront the day of Lamp's murder, but after all this time it was unlikely that he would even remember it.

Armistead stared up at the buildings and let his eyes consider for a moment the Ambassador Hotel, thinking how nice it looked and how orderly and reserved were its patrons as they arrived and departed by the front door. Its brass plates and handles flashed like the flanks of fishes in the water as the dark wood leaves swung open and closed. Those people were the other half. He hoped it was as much as half. On a day like today, when the weather and the behavior were calm, it seemed as if the world was a good place, a happy place, a place to be. Maybe, he thought, things will be better from now on, maybe there's nothing to this business with O'Neill, he can forget about Lamp and *Hathor* and whatever else it's all about and put his troubles and worries behind him. He could fade into retirement and forget it all. Although he felt positive about it, he still figured it was ten to one. Against. Math trumped emotion. Always did.

Strell watched Armistead settle in, observing everything around him. He remembered his old adversary and how obstinate and dogged he could be. Whatever it took, he was not going to let Armistead get in his way.

Elizabeth looked down at Jack. His head rested in her lap and he slept soundly. They had gotten a private compartment and hoped to sleep on the train, but while she could rest, Jack had been unable to relax and was alert to every sound outside their door and agitated at each of the many stops the train made. Luggage banged down the corridors and people talked loudly as they caromed along the narrow passageways getting on and off at a sad parade of small rural stations. From what could be seen from their car window, it was hard to believe anyone lived near or could even find these unlikely looking little platforms that poked up from the soil like reefs in a sea of grass. Jack had been awake for almost twenty-four hours and finally had fallen off in exhaustion. She gently stroked his forehead and whispered some of her favorite songs to him and thought about how different they were, yet, as things turned out, how much the same. She felt hollow. Maybe it was living without a home, constantly moving, being hunted. Maybe it was just fear. People longed for the future, but the present and past kept them from it. She was trapped in today and tomorrow and the next day and the next—until there was an ending to her horrible story. She would find her purpose, she said to herself, when the other things were cleared away. It would be her life with Jack. She looked closely at him and thought about children.

Morning invaded the car and she felt the temperature begin to change as the sun cleared the horizon. She unbuttoned the top of her shirt and fluffed it out to let the warm air away from her chest. It didn't disturb Jack's sleep, but she felt how hot his face had become and thought how good it would feel to bathe. The train jumped from rail to rail as if it was happy to run the last few miles to its home and the engine shot hot sparks into the air as it pulled them southward. In less than an hour they would be in Newport News where once again they'd have to get their bearings and figure out what to do. First they'd have to find a place to stay and then the priority would be a bath, a change of clothes, a meal, and some rest. She watched the trees race by her window. Trying to pick one from the rest was hypnotic.

During the night the train had passed the latitude position where the Harrison ship *Robin* beat south against the weather. As had *Hathor*, her sister ship had made good time in the early stage of its voyage, but now had been slowed and the sea fought her with its overpowering weapons of wind and wave. Elizabeth's ships were coming to meet her.

It was early morning when Strell and his man left the Ambassador Hotel. They walked casually toward the central boulevard where a host of shops were clustered in readiness for the day's business.

Sidewalk signs had been put out, "open" placards dangled in windows, and smocks and aprons were donned in expectation. The range and variety of offerings attracted ladies and servants looking for bargains, and businessmen who lunched and bought tobacco and had their hair cut, faces shaved, and shoes shined.

The two men chose a small café and took a table by the window and ordered bread and jam and coffee. "Are we ready?"

"Here's the sketch I made of the area." He took a large folded sheet of paper from his jacket and spread it out for Strell to see. "O'Neill comes on deck and always looks toward the far end of the east dock, by the grain warehouses. The deck watch also uses a glass to scan in that direction every quarter hour. He's expecting someone and I'll bet it's the ship we're waiting for. Or maybe a signal. Or it's the meeting place."

Strell considered this, pulled the map closer and studied it, "Should we move the ship?"

Strell's man ran his finger along the drawing, "I think we can get clear and be underway in time to prevent anyone from escaping us if we need to. The men have their orders and there's no leave. She's swinging easy at anchor and we have a launch manned and ready, so we can get out to her fast. None of the ships I've seen can outrun us or outgun us. Let's stay where we are." He looked at the people in the street, briskly moving along on their way to work, heard the neigh of horses pulling wagons and carriages, and asked Strell, "Nothing else from O'Neill?"

"Nothing." Strell's eyes caught on a spot on the tabletop. It was a dark mark in the otherwise perfectly straight grain of the maple. He wondered what made it grow that way. "The time is now. He'll sell us the girl and we can go ahead with the rest of our plan. It could all happen today." Strell sensed movement just outside the window and his eyes latched onto a stylish young woman being helped down from her carriage by a liveried footman. He studied her face intently. "It has been a long time, my friend, but in a day or two at most, we'll see this to its end. We'll have the girl. No more waiting." They considered this silently and Strell added, "You'll watch today?"

His man nodded. "Everything else is in place."

"I'll see you in an hour."

When they finished their meal Strell left and his man struck out for the harbor. When he was a short distance from the café he saw the young woman Strell had been watching earlier. She was walking toward him very slowly, looking with scant interest into a few of the shop windows and returning to her waiting carriage. Nothing had been good enough, he surmised, for she carried no packages, nor did shopkeepers trail her with armloads of purchases. No wonder Strell had stared at her, he thought, the woman is beautiful, graceful, composed. They were close to each other and he continued to watch her, but she didn't seem to notice him. He paused for a moment and watched her pass by and then turned to continue on his way.

And immediately stopped.

A second young woman approached. She had been hidden by the first, but now eclipsed her entirely. It was one of the most remarkable things he had ever seen. She was striking. Not beautiful—in fact somewhat bedraggled—simultaneously proud and humble, tired looking, but remarkable nevertheless. For all that clearly highborn.

It was the woman from the photograph. Elizabeth Harrison. The one they had been waiting for.

"Sweet Jesus," he breathed to himself. "Where is Strell?" A flood of questions poured into his mind like the massive storm waves that washed seamen overboard. Why is she here already? Who's that man with her? He's a companion, not her captor. What's O'Neill doing? Has he been lying to them? Neither Strell nor his man fully trusted O'Neill. All the time he'd spent in preparation was wasted. Minutes ago he had assured Strell that everything was in place. At least, salvaging the situation in his mind, they maintained some advantage, because no one could know that he had seen her. He would have to keep it that way.

Despite the change in her appearance, he knew he was not mistaken about the woman and hesitated, briefly, rooted where he stood with indecision. Then, awkwardly, he looked up at a store sign, feigned confusion, and acted as if he were looking for an address in the area. From this pose he was able to take several critical looks at the young woman, directly and in reflections in the shop windows. The glass bent her form into waves. She came closer and closer. He shrugged into his invisibility mode, became the average man, the nonentity. Relax the body, make the face a blank, become small, bland, unimportant. He had done this many times. It proved successful for the woman never looked at him as she approached. He reminded himself that she was not alone. A young man was by her side, and he did make it a point to inspect Strell's man, but he too was satisfied that this was just another bystander, not a threat, nothing to worry about. He dismissed him with a glance and looked for trouble elsewhere. Strell's man searched the avenue feverishly in hopes that Strell might still be nearby, but there was no sign of him. More people were moving about the commercial area and the street was filling with wagons and carriages and men on horseback. It was city morning loud, and alive with movement. There was nothing for it but to follow them. He removed his black cap, jammed it into his coat pocket, and replaced it with a light gray one, which had been tucked into his belt. It was a minor change in appearance, one that always worked, to help him track them without being noticed or remembered.

It seemed that they were going his way for they turned after a few blocks and angled toward the waterfront. He crossed the street behind them and hurried down the opposite side until he was in front of them and could follow them in that manner. Despite his rapid heartbeat he soon regained his composure and began to observe the two young people and think about what was going on. They carried bags, like travelers. They wore heavy clothing and may have come from the north or west, where it was colder. They looked exhausted and were probably going to meet someone or find a place to stay. From their halting movements and the way they looked around, he was sure that they were unfamiliar with the area. He had his suspicions confirmed when they began making stops before a succession of hotels, the Finley, the Barnes, the McCabe, and others, each time lingering outside, looking things over, discussing whether to try this one or that one. He began to worry when they turned down Water Street, where he risked being seen by Armistead or his men. They slowed, taking more time at each place and making him suspect they wanted to be near the harbor. Or near ships. Maybe a particular ship. Still he could see no sign of Strell.

Armistead and his men were not in sight and only one man walked *Luluwa*'s deck, the loony one they called Jimmy. He'd heard O'Neill yell his name several times during his surveillance of the ship. He smiled when they paused at the front door of the Ambassador. For some reason it was not to their liking, however, and he couldn't decide if this was good or bad. Their taking a room there would have been at least interesting, and beyond ironic. Strell would not believe she had come to him. In the middle of the next block they made their choice and from the way they were moving he thought it might have as much to do with their fatigue as anything else. They may simply have been unable to go any farther. It was the Good Hope, a venerable, yet modest old establishment that caught their fancy. It stood alone, with an alley on one side and an unoccupied store on the other. He waited in morning shadows, checking his pocket watch intermittently to gauge how much time it should take for them to check in and go to their room or rooms. After fifteen minutes had passed, he went into the lobby and looked around quickly, registered the layout in his mind and went back outside and quickly up the street to the Ambassador.

Strell was punctual. Exactly one hour had passed and they arrived at the lobby entrance at the same time. Within minutes of their meeting Strell had heard a concise account of what had happened and was probing for answers to this mystery. This was not what O'Neill told them or what they expected. In every previous purchase things were handled in the same way: O'Neill signaled them that things were ready, they met or exchanged messages, they traveled to a warehouse and made the trades agreed upon. This young couple had wandered right past the *Luluwa*, obviously unaware of what it was and what was supposed to happen there.

Both men circled the Good Hope Hotel, checked sight lines to and from the building and settled on a place farther along the street where they could watch the front door while they talked. They would have to forget Armistead and O'Neill for the time being and watch the hotel, without being seen themselves.

When Jack and Elizabeth settled into their room, registered as man and wife, they changed and refreshed themselves and Jack stretched out on the bed and dozed. He still seemed feverish to Elizabeth and three hours after they checked in she decided to let him rest while she got something for them to eat. They'd passed a small market a block from the port and she wanted to go there quickly and get back while he was still asleep. She left a brief note and gathered her purse, put on a light coat, and left the hotel. As she crossed the alley at the end of the building a man stepped onto the pavement in front of her. Her impression was of someone dark, looming toward her, and she stopped abruptly and looked, not up at his face, but at what he held in his hand. It was one of the pictures of her that LeFrank had insisted she have taken. Her chest heaved and she felt faint, terrified by her own image. His words were a death sentence, "My name is Strell." This was the criminal Chien had told her about. She could barely breathe and what he was saying was impossible to believe, and she stepped away from him so that she could run back to her hotel. But her way was blocked by another man who grabbed her arms and took her purse, where her pistol lay useless, and together, with practiced efficiency, they took her into the alley.

When Billy showed up for his shift at the docks all was quiet. He recognized the usual workers and sailors, ships bobbed in the port, vendors called out from their stalls, and gulls skirmished over fallen scraps of food. He slouched against pilings, shuffled along the bulkheads and stopped in a couple of taverns, but saw nothing unusual. Back at the pilings by the *Luluwa*, he watched the day drain away to the west and looked at his watch again. Afternoon. Strell's man noted his presence as he waited outside the Ambassador, watching for any change on or around O'Neill's ship. He too looked at his watch. His instincts always told him when something had gone on long enough. Strell had been in the center room with the woman for over two hours. He decided to go back upstairs. Strell was coming down the steps as he entered the building and the two men took chairs across the lobby from the main desk, and described for each other what was going on inside their rooms and outside of the hotel.

"We have to go get the man. I have the key to their room." His man understood.

"The woman?"

Strell answered flatly, "She's not going anywhere."

They entered the Good Hope separately and met at the top of the broad old staircase and crept along the hallway until they came to the room the two people had taken. The floorboards in the hallways seemed to explode under their boots, but no one seemed to notice. Strell pulled the door tight against the jamb and turned the key slowly, released the knob and they let themselves in. Jack was asleep and didn't wake up until he felt the barrel of a pistol pressed hard against his chest. When he opened his eyes he saw the two men and then focused on the gun itself. It was his mother's, the one Elizabeth had been carrying. It was late afternoon when Jack was taken away. Strell's man removed everything from the room and with money he had gotten from Elizabeth, paid their bill.

CHAPTER 62

The Signal

Before the going down of the sun, Captain Richard Hazen brought the Harrison Lines Ship *Robin* to rest near the east end dock. He ordered the anchor dropped and the sails reefed but the ship otherwise made ready to depart at a moment's notice. The watch was doubled. "Load the bow and stern chaser guns and have a man ready at each one," he told the first officer. "Have the keys to the weapons lockers with you at all times." Hazen went ashore, told the men in the longboat to wait for him, climbed up the ladder to the wharf, and disappeared from their view. He went west along the water's edge, looking at the ships tied there, stopping to read each one of them, the land their binding, all chapters in the same book. Maritime history, to Hazen, was world history. He wished he could have sailed on every type of ship that ever was at sea, learned how she handled, known the world at the time she was built and was alive. So earnest was his examination of each of the boats that he was surprised when he looked up and saw that the next one in line was O'Neill's boat, the *Luluwa*, the one he had come to see.

Hazen's first thought was that she was, regrettably, no longer beautiful. She was shabby. If he owned or commanded such a ship, she would be something to behold. It was too late for that now; past the point where she could be saved, she would only degenerate, wrinkled and drooping in her dotage until she would have to be towed away and scuttled. Even now he could hear her pull at her mooring lines as if longing to escape that fate, and the great ropes holding her fast rubbed and creaked out loud with painful noises that made his skin crawl. Above his head her rigging stretched and groaned. There was no signal flag on her lines and only one man walked the deck, looking out occasionally and then only in a desultory manner.

Hazen walked up a slight rise near the end of the long wharf and took a small collapsible telescope from his jacket pocket. He carefully scanned the port, looking for Cutter Service ships, local patrol boats, naval vessels, anything unusual. A few ships were underway and the late sun lit their billowing sails with a brilliant battle between orange and red. He put the glass down and watched. Even without its help he could see men scampering up the ropes, sheets full of air, hulls leaning, men's minds parting sky and water. To him this scene was one of beauty beyond measure. When he was rowed back out to the *Robin* the world was in darkness.

Small beacons of light delineated the Atlantic shoreline. They popped into view and vanished in blinks of the eye. On and off they went, dashing behind buildings, dancing among trees. As they disappeared astern, to the south their replacements sparkled at the men navigating the ship. The ocean was smooth and the sky was so black it looked blue. LeFrank and Salete watched from the starboard rail and felt the ship mount and ride the long languid swells as *Hathor* approached Newport News. The seaweed and jetsam that littered the coastal waters slid by them, rubbing quietly and unseen along *Hathor*'s sides. "We need her cleaned up and put into that dress. O'Neill has to believe she'll pass for this buyer of his." It bothered LeFrank that he could not think of a reason why a slave trader would want a particular person, but in exchange for her he'd get proof of the Harrison girl's death and burial from O'Neill and that was good enough for him. Together, the marriage certificate and the record of her subsequent demise were worth a fortune. He would have the means to do whatever he wanted to do. Salete gripped the rail, brooding and silent, and LeFrank wondered again what was on his mind. It was no longer a great matter of concern to LeFrank, however, for he had made up his mind about Salete during the voyage from Boston. Harrison had escaped from his ship. Chien was missing and surely gone. Salete would have to pay. He had not accounted for Chien, and from Morrison's pitiful attempt to bribe him about an inquiry into his dealings, LeFrank suspected that Salete had left a loose end somewhere and that their sabotage operation had been traced back to him. He'd had to spend some extra money to put a halt to the police investigation. Salete was paid to eliminate problems, not initiate them.

LeFrank was not sure how or when he'd take care of this, but Salete no longer had his trust and his days were numbered.

LeFrank went to join Laura Olsen in his stateroom, and Salete went astern to the cabin where Jane Barr was being held. He closed and locked the door behind him and brought a lantern near to her face. "Jane. I'm going to take off your gag. You'll be quiet, won't you?"

She moved her head vehemently. It would be a relief just to have a chance to close her mouth and move her jaw. Twice a day Salete had brought her food and drink, and each time he let her get up and clean herself and stand and walk around the cabin. LeFrank called it taking care of the inventory. They couldn't have her look like a sickly mess when they got to the port. Buyers wanted "fresh goods, healthy stock." She suspected this much. But this was something new. He had never come to her in the night. During this voyage time had lost its firmness. It had become elastic, undependable, in league with the enemy. She guessed that it was nine or ten o'clock. What, she wondered, was going to happen. He removed the cords that held her wrists and ankles and helped her up. She spit out the gag and grabbed the water he brought and for a moment there was nothing but the feel and taste of it in her mind. She poured it onto the chafed circles on her arms and legs and there was pleasure in the cool stinging. Some of the pain dripped away with the water, down her hands and feet and flowed away across the deck where her blood, and his, and Elizabeth's, mingled in a sordid union that stained the boards and made *Hathor* darker. Until now the only thing in her life that mattered was physical pleasure, rich and varied, frequent and perverse. Now as simple a thing as a moment's release from pain was miraculous in its effect on her. It was a thing to learn for someone so self-absorbed.

She peered through the screen and saw the lights on the shore. They were very close to land. She closed her eyes to make them go away and a sliver of inspiration came into her mind. What followed was all instinct. With a slow turn and with obvious purpose she walked up to Salete and took him with her eyes. He stared back. Using all of her training and all of her strength she controlled her lips and her eyes and with slow and halting movements she began to take off her gown. She lowered it over her shoulders, over her breasts, pulled her arms from the sleeves with lithe and artful movements, and stopped, holding the folds of the garment with one hand just below her waist and caressing herself with the other. With barely perceptible movements of her lips and eyes she signaled him. She waited. She knew from his eyes that she was having an effect on him and she lowered her voice and lisped softly into his ear, "Don't let him do this to me, Salete. We can stop all of this and I can make you rich. You'll have me, and no one knows what I know about pleasure. I would owe you. Everything. And I would pay. Gladly. I can see that you want this. I think that you always have. Please." She took his hand and placed it on her body. Pulled him against her and kissed him. "He'll do the same thing to you sooner or later. You know it. I've heard him say as much," she told him honestly. "Nothing matters to LeFrank, only himself. But we can matter to each other, trust each other. I get back to my career and you can live any way you want on the money I make. I promise you."

Salete could not resist her.

Later that evening he left her cabin. He restored to her a chair and her dresser, her mirror and bed and everything she said she needed to bathe and fix her makeup and comb her hair. She was brought one dress, the one Elizabeth had worn in the photograph. Jane studied the picture he left with her. In the morning she would make herself look exactly like Elizabeth Harrison. She had ribbons, earrings, the dress, everything that appeared in the photograph but a plain and simple bead necklace. For a moment she wondered about Elizabeth, the woman who lived in the grand house and had all that money. Why would she have such modest clothes and jewelry? Buttoned up to the neck, nothing of her to be seen by other men and women. What was the point of having all that money if she couldn't at least make herself look like a woman? But she wasn't worried about a missing necklace or unattractive clothes. With her ability to command the attention of men, no one would notice that.

While she slept the sun announced its coming in a glowing arc of light and *Hathor* slipped under it, up the James River and into the harbor. LeFrank was on deck watching his men row out ahead of her, towing her slowly into position at the east end. He made a quick scan of the area, saw the *Robin* waiting where she was supposed to be, and ordered the mate to hoist a signal flag. It was a rectangular red flag with a prominent yellow cross, the semaphore for R, agreed upon in the letters exchanged by LeFrank and O'Neill. Hazen would see it too. They were ready. Even Jimmy Craft was able to understand what this meant and he went below to awaken O'Neill and collect the coins he had been promised. He'd been forced to remain on the deck for three days, around the clock, in hopes of seeing this signal, and it had seemed like a lot of work—cold, wet work—but no one else ever hired him for anything and now he had the promise of a day in a tavern to warm him up.

CHAPTER 63

The Meeting

Jack and Elizabeth overheard everything that was said. Strell and his man stood by the window in their center room at the Ambassador Hotel and discussed and agreed upon what they were going to do. They saw O'Neill's signal flag run up a line a short time earlier and it took Strell's man only a few minutes to locate a second ship flying the same ensign. For a short time no one but Jimmy walked the decks on board *Luluwa*, but then O'Neill emerged with a sheaf of papers under his arm and a nervous air about him. He looked both ways along the quay and took off at a brisk pace toward the east end of the port. Billy saw him approach and turned his face away so that O'Neill wouldn't notice him, but the man, mind reeling with angst and stomach churning with fear, paid no attention to him. Billy wasn't sure what to do, whether or not to go get Armistead, follow O'Neill, or stay at his post.

Strell and his man came out of the hotel quickly and ran along Water Street. They dodged around carts and vendor's stalls and men lugging the first loads of the day's cargo. Jack and Elizabeth could see them from the hotel room window, confused by all they had heard and seen, and asking each other what was going on. They saw Strell continue to follow O'Neill, but saw Strell's man stop suddenly and talk to Billy. They saw the deputy listening to Strell's man, and shake his head in agreement. He was extremely animated, waving his arms and pointing after O'Neill and speaking rapidly. He dashed off at a dead run toward the center of town. In minutes the men Jack and Elizabeth had been watching were lost in the growing crowd.

As soon as they felt certain that they were alone Jack and Elizabeth looked at each other and said simultaneously, "Let's get out of here."

Warehouse nineteen was a long wooden building, one of the oldest in the port. It had a twenty-foot eave height, numerous small doors along the sides, and large swinging doors at each end. Skylights that had never been washed allowed small pools of light to smear the dirt floor. Outside and nearby, a colonnade of grain storage bins flanked its walls, extra capacity for seasonal overflows, and its approaches were powdered white by the horses' shoes that crushed the spills of wheat and corn. Small tornadoes of this coarse flour jumped erratically in the cool morning breeze. Strell and his man met inside the closest of these small steel enclosures. From there they could see anyone entering warehouse nineteen through the main dockside doors. Sunlight fired in at them through the small ventilation holes that pierced the curved metal walls and hit their tanned faces and dark clothes like white buckshot. "Our men are all in place." He pulled his pistol from his coat and checked it one last time. "There'll be others with guns, Strell. O'Neill's men and this slaver who's supposed to be bringing the girl. Him and his men for sure." Strell agreed with his friend, checked his own gun. They crouched side by side in their silo bunker and thought about what this day would mean to them. "We'll wait for one more minute, give O'Neill some time, and then go in."

Daniel Armistead was writing reports. For him, as for most of the men who had his job before him and for most of those to follow, it was drudgery. One day in an unimaginable future maybe someone would look at the records he was making and write a history of the time, or concoct a theory about behavior. Some day, God knows how, he thought, this chicken scratch of his might be important to someone. Billy burst into the station and began spouting nonsense. "Daniel!" He jumped over the low railing that separated the entrance from the office area. His coat whirled around and papers blew off of the desk. "Daniel, it's about that kid, we can go find out! We have to go now! We should bring the men. As many as we can. That's what he said." He had run all the way from the docks and had only enough breath left to say what he'd just said. He bent at the waist and began coughing, for which Daniel was grateful. While Billy was recovering he went to the door, looked around outside, and closed it.

"Billy, sit down."

"No," he choked out, "Daniel, you don't understand."

"Correct. I don't understand. Now tell me what's happened. Slowly, Billy, slowly."

Billy was a good policeman, but a bad witness. He would have made a worse newspaper reporter. It took Armistead a number of interruptions, many clarifications, some repeated questions, and all of his patience to get the young man to explain what had happened and to decide what to do as a result of what he had heard. When he did, it was quick and deliberate. Simple plans are usually the best and Armistead's was a gem with one facet.

O'Neill was surprised that the warehouse door opened and closed smoothly and quietly. He took a deep breath and stood just inside and let his vision adjust to the gloom. He walked down the center aisle of the long shed like an actor going from spotlight to spotlight. He wrinkled his nose at the rank smell of the place. Thirty feet from the entrance he stopped abruptly when he heard a noise to his right. LeFrank emerged from the darkness and stopped at the edge of the swath of light that held O'Neill. "All ready?"

O'Neill nodded. "Just like you said. And you?"

"Yes." O'Neill's shoulders relaxed a little now that he knew the girl was here. Get this over with, get square with Strell later in the day and he'd finally be able to get a good night's sleep. He looked around but didn't see her. LeFrank held out his hand, "Let me see the papers."

Surprised at his own voice, O'Neill said, "Let me see the girl." He pulled the sheaf of documents from under his arm.

LeFrank took a step closer and held out his hand. The papers rattled as they were passed to him. He looked at them carefully, and did nothing to indicate that the girl was there.

"The girl, where is she? She's here, right, LeFrank?"

"Look behind you."

O'Neill spun about and saw Salete and Jane Barr side by side at the other edge of the light. He was holding her by the arm. Close to him. Salete's knife was in his free hand dangling by his side. O'Neill stared. She was the person from the picture. Strell wouldn't be able to tell. The resemblance was good enough and she'd pass. She was standing there, unnaturally calm, and O'Neill thought she must be drugged, but in any case, breathed a huge sigh of relief. He'd signal Strell and he'd come to the warehouse and make the exchange. It had cost him less than he had expected to secure the death certificate and purchase the gravesite from that man Kensel, so he'd make a fortune for this one sale. Several other "traders" were coming to see him in the following week and if all went as scheduled, he'd have the most profitable month of his life. He'd make more this year than ever before. Soon he'd be taking a long vacation.

"She's yours. Take her."

Jane Barr looked at Salete, expecting him to act, do whatever he had planned. Shoot them all and run away with her. Stab LeFrank. Something. He had told her last night not to worry, that he would take care of her. She tried to move in front of him and get him to look at her, but he locked her arm in place and would not let her go. She gave a short cry as his fingers dug into her arm. O'Neill thought she was merely trying to escape and LeFrank paid little attention as he was tucking Elizabeth's death certificate into his coat.

"None of you move!" Strell's voice thundered at them and echoed back from the far end of the cavernous building. The shock of the sound and the sight of two men holding pistols made all four of them stand stock-still. Strell's man came forward, stepped to one side, and aimed his gun at Salete. Jane Barr became hysterical and yelled at Salete, "Is this what you mean by helping me? Is this how you..." She pulled her arm away from him, but he grabbed her and tried to hold her in front of himself as a shield. They were face to face and she struck his head with her own and kicked at his shins and feet. She didn't stop until she felt the tip of his blade dig into her side. She pushed away from him and stared at the people around her in disbelief. Didn't they know who she was?

As they struggled O'Neill yelled, "What are you doing here? Get out of here, this is private, none of your business." The last thing he wanted was for Strell and LeFrank to meet. Or learn each other's identities. He made panicked eye and head gestures to urge Strell to leave, mouthing that he would see him later.

LeFrank watched Salete and Barr, thinking he'd been correct—Salete could not be trusted. In addition, he could easily see that O'Neill knew this man and that he was probably the one who was going to buy Jane Barr. The crazy one. He took a small step away from the group, a slide of his feet, inching back toward the side door behind him. Let O'Neill fight it out with this man on his own. This was the slaver that O'Neill said was the devil himself. LeFrank thought he had seen him before, but that was unlikely. At any rate this might work out. The stranger might kill Salete for him too. Save him the trouble. He had what he needed, proof of the Harrison girl's marriage to him and evidence of her death and burial. He was sure he could safely walk away since these two men had no reason to want him involved. This pirate might want more from LeFrank in the future. LeFrank calculated that this was some disagreement between

O'Neill and the men with the guns. O'Neill said that the man was vicious and that he was afraid of him. The big one had dark clothes, a high collar, and his hat pulled low. It was not worth it to try to get a better look at him, although LeFrank wanted to know who he was. Another time maybe, he told himself. For now he would be satisfied to slip away from this whole thing. He'd just have to deal with Salete when this was over. If Salete lived through it.

As he was about to take one more step away from the light, LeFrank heard a voice in the darkness say his name.

"LeFrank."

The intonation, the timbre, the pronunciation, the finality of the utterance of his own name, it was the worst thing he had ever heard. Elizabeth Harrison. *Foutre!* God damn her. His eyes sought her in the dark.

Fear, malice, bitterness, aversion—in the moments that she watched LeFrank calmly bargaining away her life, offering up her avatar, she felt all of these things in a rush of emotion that took from her every goodness, all of the grace of her soul. For those moments she let the devil possess her. It felt wonderful to be in his embrace. But once she uttered his name she had had the truth of herself restored to her. She looked on it all dispassionately, a problem solved, a sad thing that now concerned him, not her. It was over.

Although faced with ruin, LeFrank quickly recovered and he gathered his thoughts and plotted his escape. He reached into his coat, pulled out one of his pistols, and fired it into the earth at his feet. The circle of people—Strell, his man, Salete, and Jane Barr—suddenly expanded. O'Neill, immobilized like a bulls eye in the center of the group, like the others was hunching down his shoulders and ducking his head. They looked around at each other, wondering if anyone had been hit. Strell, Jack, and Jane Barr were all screaming at LeFrank. He slid toward the door again and they all yelled for him to stand where he was. Jane wanted him to take her with him. Jack wanted to kill him with his bare hands. Strell wanted him alive; he had the woman, now he wanted her abductor. O'Neill he could take any time he wanted to. Strell's man flashed a look to see what they should do, couldn't catch Strell's eye, and kept his gun trained on Salete. He couldn't see LeFrank in his peripheral vision, but was alert for any movement. He tried to wave Jack and Elizabeth away, but couldn't tell where they were. He called to them but they didn't answer. O'Neill had squatted down in the dirt and was pleading with anyone who would listen. He might well be a target, but he was not a threat.

Strell wanted to prevent any more shooting and keep the others from harm. He wanted Elizabeth and LeFrank to live through this. "We're federal agents. Cutter Service. Our men are outside, LeFrank, and we have your ship, *Hathor*, blockaded. Surrender to me and I'll guarantee your safety away from here." Salete and Barr turned to look at Strell in astonishment and O'Neill began to sob. Strell repeated his words.

Gunfire came in answer.

LeFrank was obscured by the deep shadows near the wall of the warehouse, almost at the door. If he could stun them, confuse them, he could make them hesitate for the split second he would need to open the door and get out.

He fired three quick shots, one at Salete, one at O'Neill, and one at the point where he thought Elizabeth was standing. More than anything he wanted to kill her.

Strell fired at the fleeing silhouette as the door opened and slammed shut.

LeFrank ran around the front of the building and once away from it slowed to a quick walk west on Water Street. He leaped onto the deck of a trawler that was moored in the third slip down from the warehouse. He crossed the deck, picked up a hat and slicker that his men had left on the boat for him, and lowered himself over the far gunwale into the waiting longboat. Its crew rowed him through the water traffic toward the *Robin*.

Jack had thrown himself on top of Elizabeth. "Are you alright?"

"I'm okay, Jack." He helped her to her feet and they both brushed their clothes and looked at the others. Salete had been hit by LeFrank's shot and laid on the ground clutching his stomach. The edge of the light circle revealed his twitching legs. O'Neill was still rolled up on his side trying to hide although the shooting was over and he was the only one clearly lit by the sun. Jane Barr did not know what to think. She had been cheated, deceived, and abandoned by both men and fixed her attention on Strell in her confusion. He was giving orders to his man.

When Jack was sure Elizabeth was not injured he pulled his gun from his coat and followed LeFrank. He was the first one out of the door and he never slowed when Strell called to him to stop. The previous day, when Strell and his man had confronted Elizabeth and told her who they were and then had brought Jack to the Ambassador, the four of them had exchanged stories and came to a complete understanding about what had happened. Jack and Elizabeth told them that they knew about Lamp's death, that he had been killed by one of LeFrank's men. Chien had bragged about it to her when he assaulted her in her house in Boston. They worked together on their plans. Since O'Neill told Strell he had the girl from the photograph, they reasoned that there must be someone impersonating Elizabeth. They would go to the meeting, but not wait for later when O'Neill signaled them; they would go to witness the sale of this unknown girl. Their following Strell and his man to the warehouse had not been part of the scheme, however. Jack and Elizabeth were supposed to have waited at the Ambassador. Both of them wanted to be there, see LeFrank taken into custody, see his face when he realized that he was going to hang for what he had done. Without a word between them they knew they would find a way to witness all of this. For her it was partly because she felt she should represent all of the other women, not to mention the one who was on the ship now. For Jack it was because he wanted to be sure it was done, that she was safe, that they could live their lives without worry. And he wanted to kill LeFrank himself.

Elizabeth thought about her fatal leap from *Hathor* on that cold October night. Had she not escaped that night she would have been taken to Newport News, sold to Strell and then freed. LeFrank would have been captured, and by this time, perhaps, executed. Months ago. None of the rest of it would have happened. She never would have known there was someone like Jack Light. It was astonishing to her.

Jack ran down Water Street. At first he could see the white flour dust tracks of LeFrank's boots leading from the building. Clear, definite, and wide spaced, they showed the path of a man running in long strides. Then the stark white prints dimmed and lost their shape as they turned to dun and then vanished, but Jack was certain the last traces led toward the water. And then he spotted LeFrank looking back at him from the stern of the longboat. He was bound for a smaller sailing ship, nimble looking, with her sails being unfurled. It was the air filling the canvas that first caught his attention. The rigging was alive with sailors. Jack moved west until he saw a dingy bobbing against the bulkhead. He jumped into it and frantically pulled at the lines that had her snug against the landing stage. When the boat was freed he pushed off with one of the long oars and glanced quickly over his shoulder to line up the ship. His course set, he began to row. It had been a long time since he had taken his little skiff across the bay to his home and his muscles hurt at first. It was as if the water in the harbor was thicker than in his bay. The grips of the oars felt rough. As he strained he realized that it was more that the palms of his hands had lost some of their calluses. One of the oarlocks was out of round, "wallered out" as the old surfmen said, and he had to correct each stroke on the oar to stay on his line. He knew he was rushing and slowed his pace and tried to calm his breathing. He couldn't continue at the rate he was pulling. The wind was in his favor and he was sure he could get to the ship before it began to make any headway. He looked again. He was gaining. The little pops of the rifle shots behind him seemed far away, but the water splashing alongside the small boat was very real to him. He turned to look and saw LeFrank and several others loading their guns for another volley. He waited for the captain to make his first tack and renewed his rowing. He ran at them, pulling with all his might, while the marksmen made for the other side of the ship to get a shot at him. He heard sailors yelling to each other as the gunfire had attracted the attention of some men on nearby ships and officers were ringing bells to alert their crews to be ready in case there was danger to their ships. When the *Robin* came about again Jack thought he was safe. He turned and looked over his left shoulder, holding his hand up to shield the sun from his eyes. He must get LeFrank. There might not be another chance and he and Elizabeth could not live wondering when he might intrude on them. He was a pitiless, vengeful man and ought not be allowed to live. Jack would get aboard and deal with him. Somehow. He had to.

With crushing force that conviction and his small boat were blown to bits by a cannonball that struck its bow and sent Jack and a mist of shrapnel flying into the air. Like fresh dirt over a new grave, splinters of wood marked the place where Jack had disappeared into the dark water. There was no hunger for LeFrank's blood, nor thought nor consciousness as life slipped from him into the cold that embraced him.

LeFrank rubbed the hot barrel of the stern chaser and accepted the congratulations of his men who cheered his shooting. He hissed, "Surly little bastard. That score is settled." He searched the docks for signs of the others. "One day I'll have the rest of you." Then he turned his back on Newport News and looked ahead, already considering his plans for the future. *Robin* picked up speed and made for the Atlantic.

Armistead and Billy led their men in a sweep from the west end of Water Street toward the sound of the shooting. They boarded the *Luluwa* and secured the ship, arresting Jimmy Craft and the other men aboard. Four of their men stayed to guard the ship. When the cannon went off they climbed the shrouds and scanned the water, looking through the harbor traffic to see what had happened. Men called out from all sides, those who had seen the fighting piping out the news to those who had not. In a moment there were rumors in full flight—of attacks, fire, pirates, war, gross casualties.

Armistead led his men east. As he went he called out to ship's captains along the way and told them to send men out to find the person who had been thrown into the water. Billy stayed behind to help with the rescue, if there was to be one, or, more likely, the recovery of a body. From what Strell's man had told him earlier, numerous crimes were being committed this day and Billy knew Daniel would want him there to get all the facts—clear and organized.

The last time Strell and Armistead had been involved with the same case, Strell had taken the prisoners, put them aboard his ship and left, ignoring Armistead's claims that he had jurisdiction. Armistead never forgot a thing like that. He had no way of pursuing the ship or of charging a federal officer with any crime. But he had been denied any chance to investigate the crimes involved, restore property, serve his citizens. He had no answer to the injured parties and they blamed him for not doing his job. Armistead did not take kindly to accusations of misconduct made against him. Billy had relayed the message to Armistead that Strell was involved and that this time Strell would work with him on all phases of the case and that was why he wanted his help. For Strell it had been simple expediency. Armistead was already connected in some way, and it would be better to have his help since with Billy on the scene there was no way Strell could execute his plan without Armistead finding out about it.

After Jack ran out, Strell also left the building in pursuit of LeFrank. Inside, his man moved along the east wall and opened several doors. Gun smoke and dust filled the air, and now that they could see the old musty piles of grain they were all more aware of an alcoholic odor of decay. Elizabeth walked up to Jane Barr. She was standing over Salete, dazed, afraid. She moved to within a foot of her and they examined each other, both fascinated. Actress and understudy, icon and impersonator, what were they to each other? Jane Barr, Elizabeth saw, was a cheap imitation of her. It was only the trappings that made them seem similar. Elizabeth knew who she was, now more than at any time in her life. Much of what she had set out to do was done. There were people she and Jack could trust to do the rest. People who weren't corrupt or afraid. People who did this kind of thing and knew how. In contrast, Jane didn't know who she was, or what would happen to her. She had been a victim, taken against her will, arguably innocent of any wrongdoing. But now federal agents and the others had all heard her as much as confess that she was in league with Salete, and then in desperation switch alliances and beg LeFrank to take her with him. She thought there was no price too high for what she wanted. Now it seemed she had paid the price, but would be cheated of the prize. No one would know who she was. She would not live in a suite, but languish in a cell. Or worse. She cried. Elizabeth had the strangest temptation to hold her and comfort her, but moved back, confused by her feelings and sorrowful for this bizarre woman who, through tricks of stage magic, resembled her.

Through the open doors and windows light chased farther into the shadows and it was then that the two women noticed the coffin. It was a pine box, like the building surrounding them and they walked side by side toward it and looked at the lid. Painted in plain black letters across the light wood was Elizabeth's name, date and place of birth, and the mockery of a cross. As if LeFrank were not a godless monster. Barr cried out and Elizabeth, feeling light headed, brought her hands up to her lips. She gasped as she knelt down beside it and tried to open the lid. Fetid air enclosed her. Strell's man came to help her and saw that it was nailed shut and he pushed it, feeling its weight. "God, have they killed someone else? Salete, who is in this box?"

"You'll help me, right? I'll tell you everything you want to know if you help me! Get me a doctor. I'll die if you don't." He shuddered and gasped and looked at the blood seeping from his gut.

"Tell me and I'll get help."

"It's empty. Just sand…filled with sandbags. O'Neill's doing. LeFrank was going to sell Jane—to you as it turns out," he coughed, "and this was going to go in the ground so the records would show Harrison was dead and buried. Now help me."

Strell's man went to the door of the warehouse and called for his crew. He gave them orders and they left.

CHAPTER 64

Debris

Strell and Armistead met face to face on Water Street.

Strell was watching from shore as his ship came directly astern of *Hathor* and his men jumped onto her deck. Though they outnumbered the boarders three to one, LeFrank's men quickly surrendered. The call, "Cutter Service!" sufficed to freeze them in place. Word passed among them that they'd be released, after they were questioned. None of them would say anything unless it was to their advantage. Soon they'd find another man like LeFrank to take them on. There were plenty of them.

"Armistead."

"Strell."

"He got away."

"Who?"

"His name is LeFrank. It's a long story. I've been using O'Neill...you know him?"

Armistead, "Yes."

"He's been selling me slaves, white slaves, and I've been taking them—along with other things he smuggles in. The brass in the Cutter Service has several of us agents posing as pirates and slavers, trying to find out who's involved. They want us to get up the chain more, see who's doing it all, how they do it, find ways to stop it." Strell snorted. "I'm getting some of these people free, but what I'm really doing now is helping the service make policy. If I had my way, I'd make policy with broadsides fired from my ship, and hanging ropes." He looked at Armistead, "I've seen too many of these scum over the years and it never gets better. We should take the navy down to the islands and kill every last one of them. Sink every slave ship. And there's plenty of them still coming from Africa. English, Dutch, French, Spanish, Americans...you name it. You're not going to reform these pirates. And you won't deter them. But they want to prevent it here on our shores. It'll never work."

Strell watched his men swarm over *Hathor's* decks, herding her crew amidships and searching her carefully.

"This time things were different. LeFrank had a society girl. Showed O'Neill a picture. He gave it to me. When I told the Service people they decided that I had to get this girl. It's politics now. When they take poor people, islanders, blacks and browns, it doesn't mean that much to them. They say they care, but they don't. But when it might be a senator's daughter, or the child of a rich friend of some official, things are different. The Service needs money. They believe they can go to Congress, the Navy, I don't know how it all works, but they think if they can show that society girls are in danger, they'll get what they want. This young woman, Elizabeth Harrison, was bait. There are more of them taken now, rich girls, but we've never been able to get any of them back. She was going to be the first, make them see—the powers to be. Service people knew it would work with the Congress, just like it has before. I've had constant pressure about this. I had to get her."

Strell looked around him, back at the buildings where people buzzed like bees, in knots on the walkway, and crowded from upper-floor windows to see the commotion. "Tragedy of it all is, she had no influence. If LeFrank's plan had worked, no one would have missed her. Turns out he was the one with the influence. All bought with her money, and the sale of these girl slaves. And where did he get the influence? He bought public officials—half of Boston the girl says. Lamp died trying to stop it, the Harrison woman almost died, the surfman too, maybe." Strell picked up a rock and threw it with all his strength at a piling. It cracked off a chunk of the wood and threw up a splash of the dirty water. "You think they'll go after those Boston politicians? You know they won't."

"I still don't like what you did, Strell. You should have told me what it was all about. Back then. I would have helped."

Strell looked Armistead in the eye, a nod his only apology.

Billy's footsteps pounding up to them broke the silence. "They've got him. Jack. The surfman. A couple of sailors pulled him out of the water and they took him to a doctor up on Church Street. Where's the woman?" Strell directed Billy to the abandoned warehouse and Armistead ordered him to get Elizabeth and take her to see Jack. He and Armistead agreed that Billy should stay with them, no matter what. This wasn't over and some of LeFrank's men might still be about.

"Is he hurt?"

"I don't know what it is. He was unconscious and cut up bad. All limp and white as a ghost. One hand wrapped up, bleeding, like it was crushed...or gone. His face...was blown away...that's what they said. I couldn't see it...it was covered up. Some of the sailors ran along with him seeing as they found out he was a surfman. Said they wouldn't leave his side." Billy ran off toward the grain warehouses.

They talked about Lamp. "It was someone called Chien. One of LeFrank's thugs, some perverted little sneak thief. He attacked the woman up in Boston, bragged to her about all the things he'd done. Gotten away with. Thought he could kill LeFrank and take it all over. He was a fool and she escaped from him and shot him. He ran and they don't know if he's alive or dead. Believe me, 1 want him caught and punished as much as I want anything in this world. Lamp was like a son. His life was bad. I took him on, taught him." Strell's voice softened and he lost focus, seeing something that had vanished into time. "Smart boy. Would have been a fine man. When this is all turned over to the Service I'm going to Boston. Now that I know who he is I won't rest until I find him."

Armistead set his face, "I'd go with you if I could. Let me know when you get him. I'd like to close that file too." Armistead thought about his conversations with Kensel at the cemetery, and Peterson the stone worker.

Once it was clear to them that *Hathor* and *Luluwa* were in control of their men they went to the warehouse to take the others into custody. They found O'Neill still down on his knees, pleading, "I know nothing about this, I came into the warehouse by mistake...I don't know any of these people..." but he stopped when he saw Armistead, knowing it was useless. Salete asked Jane Barr to help him, bandage him until a doctor came. She gave him a bitter laugh and spat in his face. "I'll help you to the gallows," she shrieked. "I'll tell them all about you, you bastard. You'll hang. I spit in your face and I'll spit on your grave." Armistead volunteered his jail cells to hold them until they could organize proper charges and get direction from the Cutter Service and Armistead's superiors.

Hazen looked out at the Atlantic. It was a bright day, with fresh wind and an even sea. He was taking the *Robin* due east as fast and as far away from the Virginia coast as possible. LeFrank had not given him any other course directions and he held her steady. His head jerked around to starboard as the sailor in the cross trees called out a sighting, "Sail!" It alarmed Hazen, but for LeFrank this was merely a contingency he had anticipated and one for which he had a ready plan. All eyes went up to the lookout and followed his pointing arm until they located the approaching ship.

Her bearing was north by west, obviously bound for Newport News, and Hazen called out, "Helm, to port, ten points!"

LeFrank countermanded, "Stay, helm. Mr. Hazen, pull in sail, we'll come by her for a short visit. I want her to see us, know our name and our heading: Boston Harbor. Tell them we're carrying grain."

Hazen didn't understand what LeFrank was doing, but barked out his orders.

David Marshall saw the other ship slowing to intercept them, and looked through his glass at the deck. Both Marshall and LeFrank had the same strange sensation at the same time. Marshall felt his right hand twitch and said to himself, "Didn't I see that man several days ago? On another ship, though, a much bigger one. Stared at us but ignored our signals, ran south?"

"*Merde.*" LeFrank knew that the man had recognized him. It was the same ship and captain he had seen off the Delaware coast. He couldn't undo it, so he took Hazen aside, gave him his instructions, and went down the companionway a few steps and waited. When the ships were abreast, Hazen called out, "Harrison ship *Robin*, sir, returning to our home port, Boston. Grain and other merchandise."

Marshall looked in vain for the man he had seen before, but could see no sign of him. "*Mercury*, out of Baltimore, delivered all our goods and gone to pick up cargo in Newport News. All is well in the port?"

"Peaceful, sir. You'll find the place hospitable. There's room for your ship, and good food for your crew." LeFrank was pleased with the irony as he waited, concealed, but able to hear their words.

Mercury's men cheered. Marshall smiled, "Will you come aboard for a visit, captain?"

Hazen demurred, saying they had urgent business in Boston and must sail there straightaway.

Two very different ships, on opposite courses and divergent missions, both took back to the sea. *Robin* stayed on her course east and picked up speed. When *Mercury* was long out of sight, LeFrank's ordered Hazen to turn the ship south. LeFrank had money stored, favors owed, and influence banked in the Caribbean, and he had men to gather, and plans to make. It was time to visit some old acquaintances.

"What about *Hathor*?"

"What about her?"

Hazen spoke sharply, "You promised her to me. All along. It was my price for all of this, all these years. It's not the money, LeFrank, it's the ship I want." LeFrank said nothing. "That ship, and the sea. I have no love for these islands of yours. It's a backwater, full of pirates and killers. It's all there is in that shithole. That's not where I want a home port."

LeFrank let him blow off steam. He was thinking of the gold he had hidden on *Robin*—courtesy of Harrison Lines. He'd have plenty of money to do what he wanted to do.

Hazen was insistent, "I want *Hathor*."

LeFrank studied the man, "Then we'll have to get her back."

CHAPTER 65

Jack Light

"Sister, where is he?" Elizabeth paced back and forth in the lobby of the hospital. Billy was behind her looking around and trying to catch his breath.

"You mean the young man, your husband?"

Elizabeth didn't correct her, "Yes, where is he? I have to see him."

"The doctors are going to take him into the surgery. It's his hand. It's...how should I say, damaged, hurt badly...they say they'll have to amputate it."

"No! No!" she cried. "You have to stop them. Where is he? Take me to him, please!"

Her screams echoed back and forth in the cavernous hallways.

"This way, Miss. Please, quiet, quiet...the others."

The two women ran into the ward where Jack was being treated. The nun's full white habit flew out behind her like billowing canvas sails. Elizabeth ran to the bed and knelt down beside it. Tears poured from her as she looked at Jack's face. His face was laced with cuts and large splinters from the devastated boat were still embedded in one side of his head. His cheek was torn and his eye was swollen like a great egg, purple and bloody. She lifted the towel that covered his hand and gasped.

"Oh God, his hand..."

"Miss," the doctor replaced the towel, "it's lost. You must wait outside and let us treat him. He's lost a lot of blood and we have to do what we can for him."

"What are you going to do?"

"The cuts can wait. They're bad and they'll leave scars, many of them will, and we can't help him with that. His eye, too, we can't treat. Only clean it up. I have no idea if he will be able to see."

He swallowed and ducked his head down to look at the floor, then up at her, "Or even if it's…if it's still there. There was a blast of things that hit him. We don't know. We have to remove his hand, that much is sure…just above the wrist."

"No. You can't do it. I won't let you."

"Miss, who are you? Are you his wife?"

Without hesitation, "Yes. I'm his wife. And I forbid you to do this. I speak for him and I know he wouldn't agree to it."

"We can bind it off. But three of his fingers are missing. Gone. He'll have his thumb and forefinger, that's all, some of the palm, if the remaining tissue doesn't get infected. Things like this often do. This will, I know it will. There's dirt in it and he was in the harbor water. Gangrene is a terrible thing, Mrs.?"

"Light, Mrs. Jack Light."

"If you insist on this, I'll do as you say, but all the risk is yours. With an infection he'll lose more than just his hand…maybe even his life. Even if he has part of a hand, he probably won't be able to use it for anything. It will just be something that causes him pain. Amputation is the best way, the safest way."

He stood there with his hands out in front of him as if this gesture would convince her.

Elizabeth was only half listening to the man. She was picturing Jack, shooting, fishing, writing, hammering and sawing. He was right handed, and this was his left hand. "Please take him now. Do as I'm asking and leave his hand. Save him, doctor, I beg of you," she wailed, as the nurse shushed her softly and gently pulled her away.

Later that night Armistead and Strell came to the hospital to relieve Billy and to bring some food to Elizabeth. They told her about LeFrank's escape, and the impoundment of *Hathor*, her company's ship. Her ship. Strell had sent his men after the *Robin*, but they had to delay their departure for hours while blockading *Hathor*, and they couldn't find any sign of the fleeing ship. His man did, however, signal another ship, called the *Mercury*, as it approached the port. *Mercury*'s captain, a man named Marshall, met the *Robin* hours before, and verified that her course was north and that her destination was Boston. She was surprised to hear this news. Elizabeth wondered what LeFrank planned to do. Damage her company, she guessed. Loot it probably. Just to spite her. She still felt she had no one in Boston she could trust, but was tempted to accept Strell's offer to contact the Cutter Service men there for help. They too might be under LeFrank's control, but at least they could not harm her.

"All I can think of is Jack. The rest is too much. I'm staying here until I know how he is. They won't let me in to see him and now the other patients are sleeping, so I have to wait." She wept into her handkerchief and turned away from the men.

Strell said, "I'll stay with her. She knows me a little from yesterday." Strell's tone betrayed the irony of that. He had been the most recent person to abduct her. He knew from her attitude, however, that she did trust him and felt unafraid around him. My man will be along and between us we'll watch over her."

Armistead agreed, "I'll get Billy to post some men around the hospital as well. Too many of those devils got away for my liking. I'll be here early in the morning."

In the middle of the night a young nun roused Strell and Elizabeth and took them to see Jack. He was awake, but delirious, the drugs and the ordeal altering his understanding of things. He mumbled but Elizabeth could comprehend none of what he said. The others left her. Alone, utterly sad for him and for herself, she cried at the hurt he had suffered and kissed the right side of his face, which had not been hit, but which was swollen and red. Errant streams of antiseptic had stained his skin yellow and orange. Most of his face and his swollen eye were concealed by bandages. His ravaged left hand was encased in layers of gauze and immobilized against his chest. It lay there like a small pillow, waiting for someone to return it to its place in a cupboard. His right was strapped to the side of the bed so he wouldn't pull at his face or hand in his sleep. She spent the rest of the night wrapped in a blanket, curled up on the floor beside his bed. It made her think of their first nights together in his cabin.

CHAPTER 66

The Alliance

Within hours after he had gone abroad in the city of Newport News, David Marshall heard stories about the ruckus of the previous day. In his log Marshall had made an entry about the merchant ship *Robin*, just a few lines, brief and forgettable. Now that he had new information about the police action involving her, he reviewed that meeting in his mind. His interest piqued, he made some inquiries and eventually found out about a policeman named Armistead and a Cutter Service man named Strell. Through persistent questioning he learned that they were at a nearby hospital and he found them there at mid-morning.

"Gentlemen, David Marshall, captain of the merchant ship *Mercury*, at your service."

Armistead answered for both of them, "It was you that saw the ship called the *Robin?*"

"Yes, sir, that is correct. I regret I did not know that it was in flight from you, or I would have done my best to detain her." Marshall looked from one face to the other.

"Our thanks."

"There is more, however, and that is why I sought you out. When I first looked at the ship, she was traveling east, full on with sail, and bound to pass well north of us. Then she turned. When we met I invited her captain to come aboard. He refused, saying he had urgent business and was bound for Boston. If there was such a hurry, why did her master bring her up to us. There was no reason for it. One other thing, just a coincidence I'm sure, but several days ago I saw a large ship heading south along the coast. Well north of here. Through my glass I saw her captain. That same man, I'll swear, was on the *Robin*. He was talking to the captain, saw him plain as day, but when we passed alongside he was nowhere to be seen."

"You are not mistaken, sir. His name is LeFrank and the ship you saw is called *Hathor*. She's here in the, harbor near the east end. A beauty. Take a look, you'll recognize her," Strell informed Marshall, who wondered what Strell would think of *Mercury*. Strell interrupted his thoughts, "Foreign made I believe. He abandoned her and escaped on the *Robin*. *Hathor* is impounded. LeFrank is a slave trader and is a wanted man. You were right to come tell us. But we already knew."

Marshall turned to go, "Well, good luck to you men."

They bade him goodbye.

Marshall strode off, but remembering that they were in a hospital, stopped and asked, "Were your men hurt in the fighting?"

"No. They're okay. A young lad is hurt. We're with him and the woman he was protecting. She was one of the people LeFrank abducted. Boy is badly injured. Lost his hand. It's a shame, he's a surfman."

Marshall came back to where they stood. He thought of George Kimball, but the man said the person hurt was someone young.

"I have close friends in the Lifesaving Service. What's his name?"

"Jack Light. From a station in Delaware." Marshall felt a twinge in his right hand.

"Listen to me. I know this lad, all the men at his station. Tell me what's happened."

When Jack awoke a short time later, his eye fixed on the face of David Marshall standing at the foot of his bed. He mumbled, "Cap'n Marshall, what are you…" Then he felt Elizabeth's hand squeezing his. "Jack, oh Jack. We're safe, it's over Jack." He turned his head and looked at her and smiled a painful grimace with half of his face. It was a battered and freakish visage that looked at her, and he beheld a worn and exhausted face twisted with sorrow and bathed in tears. Still, he and Elizabeth saw more happiness than pain in each other's expressions. He tried to move.

"Shh, Jack. Lie easy for a minute and let me tell you what's happened."

She told him what she knew, from the time he left the warehouse until that moment. Jack looked back at Marshall, and said his name, and Marshall took over for her and gave his account of how he had happened to be there.

"Jack, I have to tell you something." Eyes wide, she glanced quickly at the men surrounding the sickbed. Armistead, Strell, and Marshall withdrew. She held his right hand up close to her face and pressed it to her cheek. "You're going to be okay. The doctor said a little time yet but okay. But Jack, your hand was hurt. Badly hurt." She pulled her chair closer and leaned over and soothed his lips with hers. "You have to know, Jack, that much of your hand was so shattered that they could only save a little of it. They won't know until they take off the bandages and clean it again how well it will heal. And your eye, Jack, they just don't know. It's swollen shut and the doctor wants to let it go down on its own. There is worry about infection in your hand, but they'll keep it clean and do what they can to stop that. Jack, your eye...they don't even know if...if it's even there." Tears poured from both of hers.

He strained his neck up and stared down at the mass of bandages on his left hand, took a breath and stifled a deep sob. For a few seconds his right eye crushed tightly on itself and then he swallowed and looked at her. A long breath escaped from his chest. There followed an almost imperceptible nod that said he was okay and would prevail over whatever obstacles he faced.

"Soon we'll go home to my house and we'll have time to rest. There are good doctors in the city and you can get the best treatment. Or we'll go wherever we have to. These Cutter men will help us."

From his dry throat rasped the question, "The doctors here...are they civilized?"

She cried and laughed and said yes they were. After all, they lived in the city.

Elizabeth rested her head beside Jack and he slumped back into the pillow and after a while both of them slept. The three men left the room and made a triangle of chairs in the hallway and began to talk about what had happened to these people and to devise a plan to help them and protect them. The girl, they agreed, must be made to go and get some rest. They would insist that she go to the room at the Ambassador Hotel where someone would watch over her. Armistead volunteered Billy, and Marshall said he would assign Arthur Durant, one of his crewmen who had befriended Jack, to assist also. Armistead said his wife Harriet would visit with Elizabeth and offer her a woman's comfort. With all of the people under their command the three men would assure that at no time would either of the young people be alone or unguarded. It would take several more days, they reasoned, to conclude matters with the prisoners, the cargo, and the ship. That time coincided with Jack's predicted stay in the hospital. Marshall said he would write to his friends at the surfboat station in Delaware that Jack was with him and that he was okay.

When Armistead left to resume his sorting of prisoners and the untangling of charges, Marshall and Strell remained by Jack's room and posed the question to each other about what should happen next. Marshall gave Strell a brief history of his involvement with George Kimball, and through him, Jack and the other surfmen. As always, he held nothing back, his lifelong program of atonement, even with a stranger, extending to the confession of his weakness in the face of danger. So sympathetic was Strell to the account he heard that, for the first time in his life, Strell confided his own story. He told Marshall what he and his man had witnessed aboard the *Christian Frederick*, of the slavery and brutality they had seen during the Civil War, how they vowed as young men to fight against it. Only Strell and his man knew of this. No one else. As he listened Marshall was struck again by the power afforded to a man, just any man, by virtue of his placement in charge of a ship at sea, no matter how arbitrary the appointment nor how unsuitable the candidate. Few men, he reflected, can resist the temptations such control offers forth, its exercise ungoverned and its possession perceived as a divine right. That power is a wanton woman, mammon, an irresistible drug to the ego. In the moments of silence that said amen to the two stories, both of them were aware of how similar their lives had been, what impact the actions of strangers can have, what price must be paid when one asserts ownership over his convictions. Strell told the story of the crewmen taken from the *Christian Frederick* and given to the slave ship's captain, but still did not realize that the man he saw with the whip that day was LeFrank.

As evening came nearer they concocted a plan that would solve several problems: with crewmen from each of their ships they could navigate *Hathor* back to Boston. *Mercury*, *Hathor*, and Strell's ship, *Harrier*, would travel north together. All three ships would be a little short handed, but *Harrier* and *Mercury* had seasoned crewmen and officers and they would stay close together the entire voyage. This way they would transport Jack and Elizabeth to her home, give him time to rest and heal during those days at sea, return *Hathor* to her home port, and they could watch for LeFrank along the way. Maybe they would arrive in time to bracket *Robin* in when they got to the Boston Harbor. That ship too had been stolen from Elizabeth and capturing it would also serve to deprive LeFrank of an easy means of escape.

It was something that sickened all of them, LeFrank's outsmarting and eluding them, and they wanted a second chance at him.

CHAPTER 67

The Name of the Ship

Jack's left eye was as deep a red as the sea was blue. They were in the Gulf Stream, bottlenose dolphins rode in the bow wave of the ship, and sapphire slabs of ocean edged in foam trailed out like the plates of the earth behind them. *Harrier*, armed and ready, could be seen to the north and east of *Hathor*, and *Mercury* lay astern, a couple of points to the west. Each day in the hospital Jack had suffered through the ongoing work of the doctors who pricked his skin and pried out bits of wood from his face and neck and scalp. Without his bandages he looked like a monster. Suddenly, on the third day, he began to eat like one. It was a turning point and then he was up and about, eternally hungry, limping down the halls with Elizabeth at his side, talking about what they had been through and about the future. He did not complain about the constant pain, itching skin, burning cuts nor the deep aches in his arm and hand and neck. The cannonball had struck the boat, not him, but he felt as though it was the other way around.

Nourishing his body as well as his spirits, the sea air accelerated his recovery and he regained a sense of himself. There was no sensation in his hand, but it showed no infection and to their great relief his eye was intact, if still too clouded for him to see well with it. First thing each day he tested it by standing by the mainmast and covering his eyes, one at a time, and looking at the anchor chain. His vision was blurred, and the chain looked like a braid of rust brown hair, but the eye was improving a little at a time.

When they both felt up to it she took Jack below to *Hathor's* main deck and into the room where she had been held, showed the window—now screened off—from which she had leaped into his life, and the door of the closet where the names of the girls remained afloat, like bottled messages vainly sent out, tumbling hopelessly around the world. Had the girls been realistic they would have understood that the door was likely to become a tombstone for a mass grave. Strell had copied the markings on it carefully, and neither he nor his man could speak as they stared at it. It flew in the face of all they had worked for and proved to them that they had failed. She barely knew this enigmatic man Strell, but it was the look on his face that gave Elizabeth her idea.

She kept it to herself for a few days, mulling it over and refining it, and then talked to Jack about it. He was surprised. Most of the time he spent trying to get better, regaining his strength and staying active. He had taken to pulling on the lines with his right arm, helping as best he could with the constant adjustment of the sails. During the day, his sight returning gradually, he took the helm, thereby relieving some of the men from that duty. There was little rest for those aboard *Hathor*, for as able as they were, they were still a mixed crew, Strell's and Marshall's best, but men not used to each other or to the huge ship and her towering sails. "Every horse rides different," Arthur Durant said to Jack as he stood watch by the wheel. Marshall had assigned him to stay by Jack at all times, an order he gladly received, and discharged as though his personal honor was at stake. He surreptitiously watched the compass to be sure they stayed on course, and made suggestions to Jack when *Hathor* needed to come about. Jack was not a sailor after all, and *Hathor* was not a one thousand pound surfboat. She was a thousand tons, stretched out over more than two hundred feet. Durant thought he was doing fairly well with one arm, one eye, and no experience.

Elizabeth waited for a calm day. She had Arthur Durant signal her request and in reply Strell and Marshall were transported from *Harrier* and *Mercury* to meet with her aboard *Hathor*. Settled in what once had been LeFrank's cabin, she told the men what she and Jack had been thinking. "When this first happened to me, back in October, I made a pledge to myself. About the women who suffered aboard this ship, my ship—the ones we know from their pleas written on that cabinet door. I vowed that if I survived, I would do what I could to find them, bring them back. Or if they were dead or couldn't be found, I'd try to locate their families and get word to them." She held her head up and looked from one man to the other, "I am going to keep that vow."

They waited, knowing there would be more that she had to say.

"I can't sail a ship, nor can I shoot a cannon. Already I suffer from thinking of the violence I have done. Or at least wanted to do. There can be no more of it done by my hand. I don't mind telling you that I don't think I want to spend my life at sea." Elizabeth leaned forward in her chair, "But you can do these things and from your words and deeds, and from what my heart tells me about you, I believe this is something you both would like to do. With my help, and for me, and for the women. I know you'd like to do it for yourselves." She reviewed the encouraging things about her plan: she was sure she would have the money; they had ships and crews available; they had Strell's contacts in the service for intelligence; they had Barr, Salete, and O'Neill's statements. Potentially there were records on *Hathor*, on other Harrison ships, maybe at LeFrank's home. Armistead said there were many documents aboard *Luluwa*, and Chien said LeFrank hid things in his office and on his ships. They could find them now that they knew they were there.

Her judgment proved to be sound; both men believed as she did and both were ready for change. Much depended on how this would be accomplished and the freedom and resources they would have. They stated this plainly. Strell had his superiors in the US Revenue Cutter Service to answer to, and Marshall had business partners whose only thought was return on investment. They didn't want more of the same. It was something she had anticipated and with Jack's help something she had prepared for. As a surfman he met nearly as many sea captains as they did. He had listened and learned, recognized their motivation and drive. He knew Ezra Stock and Will Vickers. He remembered all the things Old Gunn had said, but uppermost in his mind as he sat at the table with them was what he had learned from George Kimball. He and Marshall had made choices that had had grave consequences. Unknown to him was the fact that Strell had done the same. It was simple, he told Elizabeth, they'll want the tools and they'll want independence.

They were up late.

Strell and Marshall wanted to find LeFrank, the women, and others involved in the slave trade. Both were reluctant to lose their ships. *Mercury* and *Harrier* were home and neither wanted to give them up. Elizabeth offered them a solution. She would buy *Mercury* from Marshall's partners and he could keep her. *Harrier* was government property and so, would not be for sale. For giving her up she offered Strell *Hathor*. They needed her size, speed, and firepower to go where they might need to go. Both men agreed.

They also agreed that the name *Hathor* must be stricken from her hull and that she be christened anew. The two captains suggested the family name, Harrison, or a name like Vengeance or Protector to match her title to her mission. Jack said the ship should be named Elizabeth. She decided the name.

The name of the ship was the *Anna Ulter*.

CHAPTER 68

The Trap

East of Nantucket they signaled good luck to each other and ran parallel to the curved forearm of Cape Cod. During the night they turned again, and the Atlantic changed from blue ocean to green. Early the next morning *Mercury* entered the Boston Harbor and took a berth a fifty yards from the Harrison Lines office. Marshall immediately sent twelve of his best men ashore with instructions to spread out along the waterfront to search for the ship *Robin*. When they reported back that the ship had not returned to Boston they were ordered to cover the waterfront from end to end and mention to anyone who'd listen that at their last port they talked to sailors from the ship *Hathor* and that she was due in Boston any day." Marshall had his first mate casually mention this same story to several vendors, the harbormaster, and at the exchange offices.

Harrier was on station at the narrow entrance to the harbor, alert to ships entering or exiting the busy port. Strell had his men concealed, but on alert. If LeFrank planned to visit Boston, he would have no reason to pay any attention to the ship, and it would be easy to surprise him and bottle him up in the port. His man had sailed in aboard *Mercury* and by now was working with Cutter Service agents ashore. Strell didn't like the arrangement, him waiting out here away from the action, but it was a good plan they had and he made do. He never left the rail, peering through his glass, and keeping after his mates to make sure the men were vigilant. The morning was bright and clear. Strell's eyes fastened on *Hathor* as the ship sailed slowly past *Harrier* and into Boston Harbor. Like a reigning monarch.

Word of her arrival spread through the area and a number of people readied themselves. Any appearance by *Hathor* and LeFrank widened eyes, quickened breathing, and kindled expectations for not a few of Boston's citizens. Because of LeFrank's pending purchases of several of Harrison's rivals, there was much tongue wagging and speculation about what might soon transpire. Some people went to the Harrison office to wait for a chance to meet with LeFrank there. Others gathered about the gangplank and waited to see what would happen.

Chien pushed his way to the front of that group and looked apprehensively at the few hands working on the deck. He didn't recognize any of them. This was not unusual for LeFrank went through crewmen like a child eating peanuts. He was relieved that there was no sigh of Salete. Chien had to get LeFrank alone and convince him that he'd seen Salete sabotaging ships, and that the police saw him and shot at him thinking he had done the dirty work. He had rehearsed it, "LeFrank, look at my wounds. I hid for days on an old barge. I was unconscious and near died. I hid to protect you, God's truth." The second part of his plan was even harder. Burning in his hand like a hot coal was the key to Elizabeth Harrison's house, the one he had stolen from LeFrank's jacket. Somehow he had to get it back into LeFrank's pocket without him noticing. He had no idea how he would do it—he'd just watch for an opportunity and take a chance.

A man challenged him as soon as he came aboard, "Off the ship!" Chien held his hands out and said, "I got word for the captain, he'll want to see me." "Who are you?" the man said belligerently.

"Chien."

"Aye. LeFrank said you might come groveling. Go along or I'll change my mind and tell him you never showed up." Chien glanced around quickly and tried to control his terror as he made his way down to LeFrank's cabin. The door was slightly ajar and through it he could see the man's back, hunched over a chart table. He recognized LeFrank's coat and boots. "Cap'n?"

"Mm," a throat cleared.

Chien gathered his courage and went in, closing the door against Salete following him. He rehearsed his speech quickly one last time. Then the door clicked shut and the figure before him swung his body around violently and Chien's shocked face looked at Jack Light, the surfman, wearing LeFrank's clothes. The key rang out as it dropped from his hand and hit the deck. He grabbed at his pockets, but stopped abruptly when he felt two pistol barrels being jammed hard against both sides of his head. Wild eyed, he stared about the cabin and looked for escape. When the surfman came close to disarm him, Chien looked over his shoulder and saw her, seated against the bulkhead and watching him calmly. Elizabeth Harrison.

Chien sobbed. "Miss, thank the stars you're okay. I never meant you no harm, Miss, that's the truth. You near killed me, miss. That was enough. Let me go. Please. Aw, Jesus, please. I only did what LeFrank said, never no more." He babbled on, but she never moved, never wavered in her stare at him and it unnerved him when he realized that there would be no mercy shown to him. There was no resistance when he was led away by two of Strell's men, and thrown, bound hand and foot, into an empty hold.

A number of other petitioners and petty officials came aboard, looking for their usual payoffs, and were given the same welcome. They kept coming, in their greed the men in line never noticing that people went on the ship, but that none came off. Elizabeth questioned them. Some were easily tricked into saying that she could not be Elizabeth Harrison, since she was dead. Some even had documents with them addressed to LeFrank, graciously bringing incriminating evidence with them to their own arrests. Some had money to pay for items that they supposed had been smuggled into the port aboard the ship, and wanted to arrange for delivery. Many were detained, held for the Cutter agents that Strell's man had positioned around *Hathor* and the Harrison buildings.

It was a good plan the four of them had made. They had cast a wide net and it was filling with fish. *Harrier* cruised into the harbor later that morning as scheduled and Strell sent his men ashore to help as well. That there was no interference from the local police attested to the fact that they too were on the take and could not be trusted. Strell didn't even bother to consult with them about his activities. His man assured him that he did not suspect any of the local Revenue Cutter Service personnel.

Strell spent an hour with Chien in the hold of the ship before handing what little was left of him over to the Revenue Agents.

Strell arranged for cooperation from the federal authorities in the city and in a swift blow a number of bankers, lawyers, and port, city, and state officials were either taken into custody or given notice that they were being investigated and must remain in the area. Theirs was an easy task since the first person they arrested gave them information about a number of others and each subsequent interrogation yielded more names, and soon a list of persons and a chart of their relationships took form. The package Jack and

Elizabeth had gotten from Morrison contained much of the same information and, like an independent experiment, proved their results. The sun set that day on the clamoring voices of people unused to being caught on the wrong side of things. These men committed executive crime. They were almost never charged with offenses and rarely ever prosecuted; police captains, district attorneys, prosecuting attorneys, judges—these were their friends, relatives, club members. One did not do in one's fellows. Unless there was no choice. That was now the situation and they all knew it. Elizabeth made it clear that she would pursue all of them until she had removed every threat to her safety and to her future. Late that night despair hovered in drawing rooms, lights burned in the private offices of law firms, there were several clandestine departures, and a suicide. The tree of corruption had been chopped down and it would be a while before, inevitably, suckers sprang from the decaying roots and poked up through the dirt.

Within a fortnight Jack and Elizabeth had settled many of her affairs. They were married, with Strell and his man, and Marshall, and Arthur Durant as witnesses. Elizabeth was unattended and the minister's wife stood with her and acted as matron of honor. They lived in a small but expensive hotel in the city and worked every day in the Harrison Lines offices. It did not take long for them to learn who had been loyal old time associates of her father's and who were aware of LeFrank's activities. They cleaned house and took on some new people recommended by her father's old employees. They moved back into her house once it had been cleaned and refurbished. They changed banks, lawyers, and accountants. She learned that there was a considerable amount of money held in trust for her and that the company was free of debt and operated at a profit. The buildings and fleet of ships alone were worth a fortune. She was wealthier than she had imagined.

In the following month, Strell and Marshall became her partners. They celebrated and then they plotted. Both men set about the task of investigating the circumstances of the abduction of the missing women. Jack took them to the theater critic at the newspaper and Salete and Chien both informed on the priest who officiated at the mock weddings. Father Barry stared at them in wonder and pretended not to know anything. He was intimidated by Strell, but held his ground. They knew he was lying, but could do nothing but consider that avenue a dead end. Little in the way of fresh evidence was forthcoming at the theater. Their records were poor and their memories poorer. They corresponded with Armistead and began to focus on O'Neill's role in the sale of the women. *Mercury* and the *Anna*, as they now called *Hathor*, sailed separately for Newport News. The *Robin*, like *Mithras*, the ship that had attacked the *Cassiopeia*, was added to the Cutter Service and Navy watch lists.

With the departure of the two ships some calm, for the first time, came into their lives. Elizabeth sat with Jack in her music room, playing favorite songs. She told stories about Nana and the things she had learned from her. They spent hours in places in the city where pleasant memories of earlier visits still dwelled in her. However Boston was no longer home to her; it held too many reminders of things that made her sad. It was a place she wanted to leave, never to return. He too was not happy with the idea of living in Boston. First of all it was a big city; second, he told her, it was bleak and cold; and third, it was far from his home and friends. Besides, he pointed out, the people talked funny. They decided to move the company, and their home, to Baltimore. It had an excellent port, was close to his property in Delaware, and it was the place that both Marshall and Strell called home.

The decision removed a great deal of worry from her mind. It was exciting to know what the future would hold for the two of them and Elizabeth loved Jack for how he had dedicated himself to what she wanted. He took on the leadership role of her rescue effort, wanting what would make her happy, and knowing what she had endured, feeling a similar passion for their cause. Searching for those girls filled the gap in his life now that he could no longer be a surfman. Elizabeth had escaped from her cage, eluded her pursuers, and with her wits and will sprung a trap of her own. Now it was time to go after the ones who had gotten away. LeFrank was still out there and Jack was determined to get him. In the future the cause and the hunt would almost consume him.

CHAPTER 69

September

Newport News

It took Armistead a while to separate Harriet and Kensel. As it always did, Kensel and his Retti were thick as thieves. He knew about thieves. Armistead watched them talk about her cooking, his praise for it outmatching her denials. He finally extricated his guest from the kitchen and led him toward the parlor. It is not often that a man makes a good friend late in life, and each of them, of necessity solitary men in their professional lives, welcomed the camaraderie of their late starting but growing friendship. Armistead walked around the room, looking at various gewgaws and knickknacks as if he never noticed them before and was wondering how it was possible they were here; Kensel settled himself with a sigh of contentment onto the couch.

"What happened that day was remarkable. I've told you some of it. Forgive me if I repeat myself, but I've gotten more letters and reports from Elizabeth and Strell. Well, here it is: My jail cells were full at first. There was some rearranging to do that I did not anticipate. In an error of judgment I put the two women together—Jane Barr and Laura Olsen—thinking that that made sense. It would have been improper to put them in with the men. That lot. Jane Barr, willingly acting as a replacement for the Harrison woman, did not like it when she met her own replacement. Pulling hair, pulling off her clothes, and biting and yelling like murder, she went right after her. Just about met her match with the Olsen girl, who had some muscle from growing up on a farm. Billy tugged and pulled, finally had to smack them with his nightstick to get them to stop fighting. Stunned the Olsen girl, but broke Barr's arm. How she screamed. She was a singer, you know. Lungs like a blacksmith's bellows. There was lots of cheering from the men in their cells during the tussle, unseemly things as you might imagine. This LeFrank, as cold and vicious as any man alive, had just abandoned both of them, but all they did was shout at each other, 'He loved me, he never loved you.' If there was ever a cursing contest, I'd bet every penny I had on Jane Barr. I've had some barmaids and prostitutes and rough women in my jail over the years and none of them were near as ornery as those two.

"Later, I'm told, the Olsen girl was released by the Cutter agents and she went back to her home in the Midwest, going to go back to farming with her family. She got off lucky, the way it turned out for her."

Kensel, a talker himself, was also a good listener and enjoyed Armistead's oral history of the last eleven months. Kensel was enthralled by the story; his participation in it, after all, had been crucial—all the way to the end—since he would have been receiving and burying the pine box with Elizabeth's name on the lid and sacks of sand inside. Had she been dead, as LeFrank believed her to be, and as all official documents would then attest, Kensel's burial of that box would have put the stamp of approval on all the corruption in Boston. It was good he'd reported his suspicions to Armistead. By doing the right thing he had kept the narrative open. He felt proud. He even allowed himself to say he felt smug. That was okay if you were right about something, he mused, as he justified the private employment of that term to describe himself.

The federal courts, Armistead explained, leveled a slew of charges against Clint O'Neill and Jimmy Craft, and neither would have an unobstructed view of the stars overhead for the remainder of their lives. O'Neill avoided the death penalty because he agreed to provide information to the authorities about LeFrank and the rest of his "customers."

"They should hang him for buying and selling those slaves. It's a horrible thing he did. Horrible."

Armistead broke down the doors of three warehouses full of stolen or interdicted goods, and found cash, weapons, jewelry, gold, and most valuable of all, O'Neill's records. "You should have seen it, James, buildings full of stolen cargo. We'll be thumbing through his books for a long time trying to find the rightful owners. The Commonwealth of Virginia and the government agencies in Washington will fight over this for some time, I imagine. The United States of America will win that battle, of course. Odds are a hundred to one."

Kensel sat forward on the couch, stretched his legs, and tugged at the knees of his trousers. "LeFrank, did you ever see him?"

"No. Not that day, for sure. He was on the other ship, the *Robin*, when I got to the docks. Another time, I can't say. He came here to deal with O'Neill before. On his ship, *Hathor*. We'll look through the records, see what we can find. Salete said he always bribed port authority officials to 'overlook' his visits. Could have been here before and there's no record of it."

"Damned shame he got away. After all that, him practically surrounded and his ship lost."

"Mmm. Strell was furious that he got away. We spent hours working together after that day. You're around him and he looks like he's calm and in control, but inside he's tight as a wound up spring. At the end of the day, most days that is, I come home and forget things. Spend my evenings with Retti, family and friends, enjoy my time. I have the criminals all day, I don't want them coming home with me. Like your 'clients' in a way, James, it's sure they'll be there tomorrow. Not Strell, though. He thinks about those things constantly."

Armistead rubbed his hands together to warm them over the fire, turned around to warm his back, and then took a seat opposite Kensel.

"Strell's man told me it goes back a long time. They shipped out together when they were little more than kids. See the world, you know. Like a lot of young men. But what they saw was its brutal side, the treacherous way some men use others, the people who act like animals. There was one time, his man didn't tell me everything about it, but I got enough from him to know that the two of them saw something terrible on their ship, something they had never thought could happen. Men traded for money, right in front of them. Not slaves, crewmen from their own ship, men they knew. It scarred them, especially Strell. Then they fought for the Union Army, wanting to help free the slaves. His man said once they came upon a plantation where the owner, rather than free the ones he owned, had killed them all. Butchered them like cattle. It was a big place, prosperous, but it'd been looted and part burned. Nothing was left but all these unburied bodies. He said it was worse than battle. In the Cutter Service, Strell worked as a spy, did what he was told, but I got the idea he'd rather been at sea, him and his man, running down slavers and blasting them to hell right where he found them. His man said there's almost as much slave trading as ever, it's just moved to different places. And it's more whites being taken. Children, young women. Still a lot from Africa too." Armistead shifted noisily in his seat and the two men went inside themselves for a minute, each tossing about his own thoughts.

"Traded ambition for a cause."

"What?" Kensel asked.

"Strell. Started out with ideas, plans, his best friend by his side, the world before him. It didn't get him far. He saw another set of things, all bigger than what he had imagined. It bowled him over. He thought he was going to shape events, but events shaped him. He was doing what I do. Only he had to pose as a criminal, and spend his time with people like O'Neill and LeFrank. He hated it, I can tell. Now it's all politics, wanting the Harrison woman to testify to what happened to her, the others she found out about, help the service in its case for more money and men and ships. Hope it all does some good."

Kensel made a prediction, "I expect it will."

"You know, James, we're pretty removed from all the big troubles in the world. Most of the time. I like it that way. I hope the whole bunch of them goes away and leaves us alone. We have enough of our own problems right here on land."

CHAPTER 70

38.63 North, 75.08 West

The Delaware Shore

Things were familiar, yet irrevocably different. He pulled at the oars. It felt good. The skin of his right hand was soft, but his arm was still strong, and he gripped the old wooden shaft tightly. His left wrist was bound to the other oar with a wide leather strap he had devised to help him do his work. He could adjust its size on his wrist and tie it to anything he wanted to hold or lift or pull. His left forefinger and thumb curled around and met with enough force to direct the rowing motion, but little more. Jack's middle, ring, and small fingers were gone, along with some of his palm and much of the feeling, but aside from the recurring dull aches, he was getting used to having it that way. He was no longer surprised at his scarred face when he saw his reflection and his eyes were fine. Everything at his cabin was in good order. Old Gunn, true to his word, had looked after things. He had removed the foodstuffs and aired the place out, cleaned up around the area, and even his small skiff had been dragged away from the water and turned over to keep the inside dry. In the middle of the bay he drifted for a while and enjoyed the view. There was a lot more of heaven showing here than in the cities where he had been. He thought about rowing Elizabeth across this same stretch of water. It seemed like a hundred years ago.

When he got to the eastern shore of the bay he began to feel nervous. He'd written to and received from the men at the surf station many letters during the past few months. Everything pointed to the fact that the men missed him and wished him well and that they all wanted to see him. Still, now that he was this close he was apprehensive. He knew he would be greeted warmly. It was not that, it was that he no longer belonged. He was no longer a surfman. He never would be again. Old timers like Vickers and Stock had plenty of time to get used to the idea of leaving, retiring, turning to something new. No longer did he occupy a cabin in the forest and work as part of a group of men on a small strip of beach; Jack's world now was the whole world. With Elizabeth his new life was perfect. They had purpose, means, and each other. He had been a man who lived by the strength of his arms, his instinct, his knowledge of the woods and the sea. Now he helped manage a seagoing venture that had the potential to become an empire. All of it was good. All of it was exciting. All of it was done with Elizabeth by his side. But all of it had happened too fast. He had been wrenched, thrust, compelled—forced forward so violently as to be barely able to marshal a clear thought or draw in a full breath. It still had an air of unreality to it.

Hints of autumn surrounded him. The cries of the birds were different, some beach grasses were browning and, drier now, swishing new sounds in the wind, and he could smell the pines as they readied themselves for a winter rest, slowing down and shedding golden needles and thorny cones.

He came through the wooded strip that bordered the bay and climbed the dunes. At the top he could see the station tower and the ocean beyond.

When he came around the side of the surf station and onto the beach he saw Ezra Stock and Old Gunn watching the water, their backs to him. He called out their names as he approached and the two men came up and shook his hand and gave him fatherly hugs.

"This is a sight for these old, tired eyes, Jack. We knew you were coming but didn't know just when you'd arrive. The men are out," he pointed to the surfboat, plowing through the waves, "but they'll be in soon." Gunn beamed a smile at Jack and they stood three in a line and watched the men go through their exercises. Then the surfboat flipped and all the men went into the water. Jack laughed to himself…thinking again that cold-water dunks in the fall was one of the few things he didn't like about being a surfman. Compare a few chills and a little shivering to what he had lived through in the last year. He laughed again. He admired the way the men righted the surfboat and pulled each other in and immediately took to securing their gear and following the orders of the boat leader, who he saw was George Kimball. All three men shifted their shoulders and hips this way and that as they watched the men climb over the sides of the surfboat, helping out with body English from shore. Out of habit Jack looked up at the tower and saw Jonas Hope quietly scanning the horizon for signs of trouble. Hope noticed the men in the surfboat waving to shore and looked down and saw Jack. He gave Jack a salute and a broad smile and went back to his watching.

Dinner with the men was catharsis. They welcomed him, laughed, chided him, told him about a number of rescues they had been involved with along the shore, and gave him news about friends and families. Though they all had read the accounts, they stayed up late, insisting that Jack tell his story. That in itself was an experience for Jack. He remembered Marshall and Kimball telling about their early lives and as he spoke, he saw all of what had happened to him in a different light. It was because he was saying it all at once, and because of who he was with. He was in the company of his brothers. Aside from a few questions, they were silent while he spoke. Even Steele and Massey listened with awe. Jack noticed that the men's eyes were wide and their mouths at times hung open. Some shook their heads and looked at one another as he told certain parts of the story, and a long musical whistle escaped from the lips of Edward Chase when Jack was through.

"All of us are glad to see you, Jack," Ezra said. He was letting the men know they should rest. A call to duty could come at any time and everything is worse, he reminded them further, at two o'clock in the morning. "We'll have more time tomorrow. Jack's going to spend a couple of days with us."

They all went upstairs and Jack saw that his bunk was as he had left it. It was funny sleeping alone, in a small bed, without Elizabeth curling up with him. The light, the snores, the scrunching springs, and rough blankets were familiar yet different. He was like a man, gone away for many years, who returns to his boyhood home and looks at things he knew as a little child. In his room he sees a few toys, a tattered book, a tiny cap his mother knitted for him. He sees glimpses of the past, recalls bits of scenes played out in this home, but cannot make anything from the slices of days and hours he spent there. He regrets it, but now that he is a man, understands it. Echoes of some of Gunn's sermons came to mind, "Now that I am a man, I have put away the things of a child."

Jack spent the next morning talking to the men as they went about their routine. In the afternoon he walked with George Kimball down to the next station to visit with the men there and to have a chance to talk to Captain Vickers and his friend Matthew Hastings. This time, as he went through his story for the men gathered around him, he emphasized to them that it was Matthew who told him about the sutler—who he found out later was the one called Chien—who was looking for him and Elizabeth. The moment he learned this was the time he knew he had to try to find her.

Before he left Vickers told him about a ship that had so many sails that it could fly. He and George laughed about it on their way back up the beach. "Where does he get those stories?" George answered, "I don't know. I think he makes most of them up as he goes along."

Out of habit they both scanned the horizon and periodically looked behind them as they walked along by the surf.

"Tell me about Ellen, George."

"What there is to tell is that we'll be coming to Baltimore to visit you. On our way to Nova Scotia, to visit her family. She wanted to be married near her home and I think it's a good idea. She'll be living here with me and won't see them much. Maybe you can give me some advice on married life, since you beat me to it," he joked.

"The secret is very simple: it's the woman you marry."

"Then I'm sure I won't have any problems."

Jack didn't tell Kimball about an element of the plan that he and Elizabeth had made. It had been David Marshall's idea and they wanted Marshall to be the one to tell his old friend about it. During the conversations that led up to the final agreement among them, they came to the conclusion that they would not stop when they had done all they could for the women who had been taken by LeFrank, nor forsake their pursuit of the man himself. Learning anything at all was a long shot, but they would go on as long as they had leads and hope. Then they would stay together and take on a mission of exploration, trade, and intervention. This meant longer voyages, new markets, and the continued effort to stop the slave trade wherever they encountered it. Marshall and Strell both wanted to see more of the world and they believed they could bring Harrison new opportunities for profit.

What Jack did not tell Kimball was that they wanted him to be a part of their company. They envisioned capturing the *Robin* for him, but if that did not happen, Elizabeth promised that she would give him another ship from her fleet. Or, if he preferred, he could sail with Marshall aboard *Mercury*.

All of them would have more independence, greater incomes, the chance to do what they wanted to do. Jack wondered, after all that Kimball had been through in his life, what his answer would be. He figured it would have a lot to do with the wishes of one Ellen Brahe.

Jack was scheduled to leave early the next morning. That night he ate with Ezra, George, and Old Gunn. He told them that he and Elizabeth wanted to spend much of the year at his cabin, once they had reorganized the company and concluded her affairs in Boston. Jack would not be a stranger in the future. They were interested to learn that she had agreed to provide written statements for the Service to use in testimony before Congress and would appear there herself, if it would help.

When everyone else had gone to bed, Jack and Old Gunn sat next to the stove and talked about Jack's father and mother and what the past had brought and the future might bring. Gunn looked at him and said, "Let me see your hand."

Jack placed his left hand in the wrinkled old palm that was stretched out before him. Gunn examined it and looked at Jack, "You're lucky, Jack. You have something no other man has."

Jack took back his misshapen hand and held it up before him. He raised his eyebrows.

"You have a hand that can reach into places and grasp what other men cannot."

He wasn't sure, but he thought he understood what was being said.

"Let me put it this way, Jack. Three wise men met at the ceremony where every year they tasted the new wine. The first man said, 'The wine is bitter.' The second man drank and said, 'It is sour.' The third man drank and said wisely, 'The wine is fresh.'"

Dawn was a long, orange streak on the horizon. Jack started along the beach. He was sad to leave, but anxious to see Elizabeth. He took a last look toward the station. What he saw was one man, standing in the tower, looking out to sea. The surfman.